Alaska Wolff Pack

Margaret Wolff

PO Box 221974 Anchorage, Alaska 99522-1974
books@publicationconsultants.com—www.publicationconsultants.com

ISBN 978-1-59433-154-1
eBook ISBN 978-1-59433-214-2

Library of Congress Catalog Card Number: 2010934305

Manufactured in the United States of America.

DEDICATION

I dedicate this book to the heroes and heroines contained within these pages. A more remarkable and wonderful group of people do not exist!

ACKNOWLEDGMENTS

I am grateful to my brother, Jim Lawrence, who salvaged and placed all the pictures. Also to my daughter, Shianne and her husband Jason Minekime, who can spell and who helped me through conflicts with the computer. My thanks to my family and friends who encouraged me, and to, Evan Swensen my publisher, for making this dream come true!

CONTENTS

Dedication 5

Acknowledgments 7

Invitation 11

Cast of Characters 13

Chapter 1 ....ON MY OWN 17

Chapter 2 ..... ANOTHER TURN 25

Chapter 3 .... MR. AND MRS. BOB 31

Chapter 4 ..... NORTH TO ALASKA 37

Chapter 5 ..... CAMPING WITH MOM AND DAD 43

Chapter 6 ..... HIGH WATER 49

Chapter 7 ..... TOO MANY MISHAPS 55

Chapter 8 ..... ONLY ONE MINUTE NEEDED 61

Chapter 9 ..... BOUNDARYITS.................................... 67

Chapter 10 ... ALONG CAME FLINT 73

Chapter 11 ... HOME 81

Chapter 12 ... AINT GOT RED HAIR FOR NOTHING 87

Chapter 13 ... GET UP!.. 93

Chapter 14 .... NOT IF BUT WHEN & HOW MANY FLOODS. 99

Chapter 15 ... IT ALL HAPPENED IN 1976 105

Chapter 16 ... OOPS! 111

Chapter 17 ... LIFE IN A CHICKEN HOUSE 119

Chapter 18 ... THREE FIGHTS IN THREE DAYS 125

Chapter 19 ... A NEW LITTLE GAL 131

Chapter 20 ... WHERE IS TIMBER? 139

Chapter 21 ... GOLD, JOHN, GOLD! 147

Chapter 22 ... DOG GONE! 153

Chapter 23 ... BOUNDARY WOLFFS 159

Chapter 24 ... COME OUT OF THE CABIN 165

Chapter 25 .. OVER THREE BEARS 171

Chapter 26 ... DOUBLE WHAMMIE 177

Chapter 27 ..... BUMPS, CUTS, BRUISES, AND PUNCTURE 183

Chapter 28 ... ON THE MOUNTAIN TOP 189

Chapter 29 ... FIRE, TOIL, AND VANDALISM 195

Chapter 30 ... RUN AWAY 203

Chapter 31 ... NOT MY BOBBY! 211

Chapter 32 .. BURIED IN THE SNOW 217

Chapter 33 ... SHOT! 225

Chapter 34 ... FATAL FALL 233

Chapter 30 ... TRAUMATISED 239

Chapter 36 ... LONG TREK 247

Chapter 37 ... NO CAR AND $10,000 OWED! 253

Chapter 38 .. A LAP FULL OF MOOSE 261

Chapter 39 ... PLEASE HANG ON! 269

Chapter 40 .. 131 YEARS WITH NO PAROLE 275

Chapter 41 .. THAT BRINGS US TO NOW 283

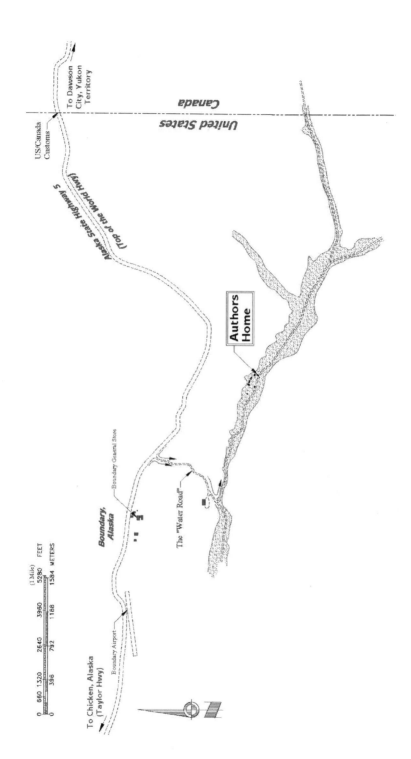

To Dawson City, Yukon Territory

US/Canada Customs

Canada
United States

Alaska State Highway 5
(Top of the World Hwy)

Authors Home

Boundary General Store

Boundary, Alaska

The "Water Road"

0 660 1320 2640 3960 5280 (1 Mile) FEET
0 396 792 1168 1584 METERS

To Chicken, Alaska (Taylor Hwy)

Boundary Airport

INVITATION

It is my pleasure to invite you to visit us to get your book personally au-
tographed. During summer, if you're in the area, follow the map to see the
country, the old cabin (designated a historical monument), and our mine.
This is a mining road (not a highway) so you must use caution, especially if
in a car with low clearance. If it isn't summer, you can find me listed in the
North Pole and Fairbanks telephone books.

Our old cabin, now designated a historical monument. photo by Sam Dick

Cast of Characters
HEROS AND HEROINES

FAMILY

Robert (Bob Bobby) Wolff ....My husband, my life.

Margaret Lawrence Wolff .... Just me.

Flint Wolff ....Our son.

His ex-wife, Sherry, and his last girl friend Daphne. Daphne's brother Timmy and her sister Heidi.

Timber Wolff ....Our son.

His wife, Tracie, and their children Bruce, Tasha, and Flint.

Shianne Wolff Minekime..Our daughter.

Her husband, Jason, and children, Megan, Morgan, Stephanie, and Dustin.

Harold and Elinor Lawrence ....My mother and father.

Jim Lawrence .... My brother.

His wife, Betty, and their children, Bill, Patti, Lou Ann, and Nancy. Patti's husband, Rob, and their children, Carolyn and Becky.

FRIENDS

Ken ....A man I was once engaged to.

Joanne .... A friend in San Jose.

Marilyn ....A girl who was once engaged to Bob.

Carolyn .... A friend from San Jose and her husband, Joe.

Norma .... A fellow teacher and friend in Fairbanks.

Ron, Tom, and Betty....................Neighbors on Blueberry Street.

Sammy .... Former boy friend of my mothers.

Swede and his wife, Thelma, Thelma's daughter, Margaret, and her husband, Tommy, and their daughters, Kathleen and Susie .... Dear friends for life.

Julie .... Fellow teacher and friend.

Squeaky .... Neighbor and friend.

Bob Cooper .... Bush pilot and friend.

Action Jackson .... Owner of Boundary Lodge.

Norma II .... Boundary cook and her daughter Carol Ann.

John and Kathrine .... Friends and mining partner.

Ron Warbelow .... Bush pilot.

Terry and his wife, Joan, and their daughter Jamie .... Friends.

Dan .... Sheet rocker and friend.

Claude .... Owner of a barge.

Riley and his wife, Ina .... Residents of the old village of Shageluk.

Dale and his wife, Martha .... Residents of the old village of Shageluk.

Jeanie .... Nurse in Shageluk who later became a priest.

Jim, his wife, Kathrine, and their sons Jim and Shawn, and their daughter. .... Total population of Iditarod.

Barbara .... A fellow teacher and friend.

John .... Postmaster at Flat. His wife Bertha.

Ernie .... Trapper in Flat.

Doug .... A neighbor's son who stayed with us.

Ski and his wife, Coleen .... Mined on our claims.

Hoss and his wife, Jan .... Mined on our claims.

David .... Bob's nephew who came up to stay with us.

Poker Creek Bill .... Our next creek neighbor.

The Sander's family .... Leased his claims and sang at the lodge.

Ken II .... A man who visited and stayed to hand mine.

Crazy Larry and his wife, Joyce ...... Troublesome neighbor's near Boundary.

Grader , (Hygrade) .... A warlock staying at Boundary.

Kaylee .... A miner's daughter, Flint's first girl friend.

Grady .... Kaylee's brother who stayed with us for a couple of years.

Norm and Lloyd ... Two men who mined with us and became family.

Glen .... Updated the Boundary air strip and mined with Flint.

Sam and her husband, Jeff, and daughters, Amy and Carrie Good friends.

Snuffy ....Neighbor at Boundary who stayed with us regularly.

Gizila ....Flint's girl friend from Brazil. Her daughter Annalua.

Bob Y and his wife, Carol....................................Neighboring miners.

Tony...Shianne's ex-husband.

Charley and Phillip ....Timber's close friends from Taco Bell.

Bob and his wife, Lynda............Our cherished friends in North Pole.

Dr. Ellenbogen ....Chief Brain Surgeon, Morgan's doctor.

Whitney Morgan's close friend and mother, Devin who often stay with us.

Ken Foy............ Close friend who mined with Flint and now with us.

PETS

Stupid, (Stupe) .... Our first Siberian husky.

Boots.. Black lab that we took care of.

Ellmer ....Tri colored collie.

Susitna (Sissy I) ....Grey and white Siberian husky.

Jekiak {meaning devil} ....Black wolf/husky/German Sheppard mix.

Sissy II ....Grey and white Siberian Husky.

Sambo (Booger) ...Black husky –wolf mix. Born of Stupe and Puppy.

Stormy ....Black Siberian husky. Born of Stupe and Sissy II.

Stray .... Mixed breed that joined us in Alakanuk.

Gunsmoke ....Black and white cat.

Sassy .... A dog we took care of.

Sissy III ....Grey and white Siberian husky.

Smokey, (Big Guy) and Kisses........ Huskies born of Stormy and Sissy III.

Scamper (Little guy) ....Kisses' unexpected puppy.

Tasha ....Large McKinsey River husky belonging to Flint.

Bobby ....Black Siamese Manx cat with a bobbed tail.

Sugar ....Black blued eyed husky mix belonging to Flint.

Little Girl .... Timber's golden Mckinsey River Husky.

Sissy IV .... Timber's brown Pit bull.

Tiki and her sister Midget .... Tiny golden dogs.

Sheeba ....Jason's sweet Rottweiler.

Cookie ....Shianne's costly birthday present, a pug puppy.

Chapter 1
ON MY OWN
1963—1964

Margaret Lawrence, San Luis Obispo 1956

Writing the story of my Alaskan Wolffs is the one thing that I most want to accomplish with what's left of my life. They are too remarkable to just disappear from memory. I only hope that I can find the right words to tell their stories.

As I look back forty-five years ago, when I first met my Bobby; it was a different person who walked alone into a church in San Jose, California where a group of single young adults were having breakfast. The girl that I was before Bob, although twenty-five, was naive, totally lacking in self confidence, and fearful of doing new things and of meeting new people. Yet I had left the shelter of family, friends, and an eight year engagement; to move into a new apartment, in a new city, with a new job; to attend a breakfast where I didn't know anyone. I was terrified! As I stepped into the noisy room, above the chatter and clatter of forks on plates, from deep in throat; Bob burped "Hello Honey! Sit by me." Everyone laughed and I did just as he suggested. I didn't know at the time that I would spend most of my life, at his side, in Alaska; through fires, floods, and plane crash; often without a dime in our pockets. We never even neared monetary wealth; but we lived as we wanted, and life with Bob was never dull!

How do I describe my Bob? There was no one like him, yet it's hard for me to put my finger on just what made him so special. Tall, dark, and handsome he was not; but rather of medium height and build, blond, and with normal looks. There was nothing striking about him, until he moved or spoke; then the attraction was strong and virile. Once struck, one would never recover or be able to forget him. Where ever he went, in what ever group of people; he was always unintentionally the center of all activity. He had never been to college, yet he could hold his own and surpass people with their PHD's. He would receive laughter by saying and doing things that only brought anger when said or done by anyone else. He frequently had people holding their sides or falling out of their chairs in laughter. Thirty one years with him did not diminish his ability to make me laugh. He was always true to himself, never allowing anyone to change him; and he was intimidated by no one. He was fiercely protective, always helping anyone lost or in trouble; and it was this trait that brought him to me. The trait was passed on to our children and eventually it cost him his life and that of our first born son.

It was October 1963 and I had just moved to San Jose from San Luis Obispo, California. There I had graduated from California Polytechnic College; and had for two years, taught a class of wonderfully special children with varied mental, physical, and emotional challenges. I had been engaged to a man throughout my senior year of high school, through four years of college, and had waited three years while he was in the army, stationed in Germany. Just weeks before he was expected to return, June 1963; I received word that he had married someone else. Since he was my first real boy friend, I thought that I was crushed for life. I literally slept through June, July, and August; but revived myself enough in September to take a train trip to the Grand Canyon and to buy myself a brand new car.

I had wanted a baby blue car, but instead found a cream colored ford falcon with blue interior. I was dumbfounded and unprepared; when the salesman asked me how I was going to pay for it. What was he asking?

I managed to squeak out a tiny, "With money?"

His answer put me at ease, "Umm, yes, err a...How do you intend to finance it?"

That was easy, I dug my $2,000 savings from my purse; and it was enough, back then, to make it all mine.

In October, I pocketed my fear of rejection enough to face a new life all alone in San Jose. I started work and training as a psychiatric technician at Agnews State Hospital, about twenty some miles away from San Jose. When I attended church one Sunday, they told me about a group of Single Young Adults, SYADS, who gathered for breakfast before church each Sunday. I was shy and afraid; but I was in the—do new things in spite of fear mode—and thus attended anyway. Besides the Sunday morning breakfasts; they played volley ball on Thursday evenings, had parties, progressive dinners, and went to the beach, plays, concerts, and such. To my surprise, as I attended the different activities; I made friends and began to go out with several guys. Bob was not included; he already had a long list of girl friends and a longer list of would be girl friends.

So my life was turning out to be quite pleasant after all, not the bleak lonely one that I had feared. I found my work at the hospital challenging, rewarding, and mostly fun. The first ward that I worked in was with mental patients who were also physically ill. Here I was reviewing procedures that I had learned in the six months of nurses training that I had had, before I decided to go into teaching. There were several other wards, separate for men and women, and two maximum security wards in which I also worked. Each of us trainees had several patients who we worked with and we kept records of their treatments, progress, etc.

One of my patients would not allow anyone to touch her. She would usually do what ever I asked of her; but if she was reluctant all I had to do was make like I was going to touch her and off she would scurry. Oddly enough, she did occasionally touch others. If one had their back turned toward her; she would run up to them, goose them, then bend down and touch the floor.

One morning I was listening while a doctor was discussing one of my patients with the head nurse. When she saw an opportunity, my little friend acted with speed. She quickly nailed him in the rear, and was down on the floor by the time he turned around. I was standing behind him and the look he gave me mirrored his shock at what he thought that I had done. I was horrified and couldn't say a word! Instead, I turned and ran. I never did talk to or even look at that doctor again. I don't know if he ever found out that it wasn't me who had goosed him; for whenever I saw him coming my way, I would dart in another direction.

All the patients were interesting and I enjoyed the time I spent with them. They all gradually told me their stories and about the griefs that they felt had brought them to the hospital. Sometimes it would come out later that it wasn't the grief that had caused their breakdowns but instead it was feelings of guilt. Once they talked about the guilt, they often seemed to improve immensely. I never spoke of right or wrong, agreed or disagreed, or made any suggestions about what they should or should not do. Rather I just listened, understood, cared, and let them draw their own conclusions.

One supervisor told us that in our conversations with patients we could never tell them anything about ourselves. We were told to answer personal inquiries with, "How will it help you to know this?" I never followed this instruction, it seemed rude and nonconductive to conversation. I never saw eye to eye with this instructor and I noticeably did things in my own way. My attitude and stubbornness often caused clashes between us. On our last clash, she asked me to wash some curtains. Many things were washed in the laundry and when I asked if the curtains should be taken there her answer stopped me in my tracks.

"Miss Lawrence, go into the bathroom. Fill the bathtub with water and soap. Put the curtains into the tub. Slosh them up and down. Put …"

I didn't say a word but I suspect that I had smoke coming out of my nose and ears. She took one look at me and turned and walked away. She never talked to me again and that suited me just fine. I washed the curtains.

Most of the workers in the hospital were great, but occasionally a bully would seek a position that put him or her in control of others. One such person was standing in the doorway of the sunroom, pushing the patients as they stepped through the door. When one of the women stumbled and turned on her in anger; she slammed the door closed.

Her face was red and alarmed and she yelled at me, "You should have come to my assistance!"

My answer was not what she wanted to hear. "Any assistance from me would have been given to her. There's no need to shove the patients around like that!" I thought that she might report me; but apparently she thought better of it for I heard no more about it.

I was dating a John, Jack, Pete, Bruce, and I went out with a guy named Lee. He was good looking and seemed nice at first, but it only took me one date to realize that I didn't want to see him again. Unfortunately he didn't think that I should have any choice in the matter, and he was determined that we should be married. I quit going to SYAD's because whenever I looked his way he was staring at me with a moony expression; and he muscled in if I tried to talk to anyone else. I began to find gifts and love letters in my mailbox; and sometimes, when I drove home, I'd find him waiting at my front door. Then I'd make a U turn and go somewhere else for a while.

One of my dates found it disconcerting when we returned to his car and found DEATH written in big black letters across his windshield.

After Lee threatened to kidnap me, I called the police; but they said that they couldn't do anything until after he did something illegal. So I turned out the lights and locked the door whenever he came around. When at home, I always had to listen for anyone coming up the steps, and then check to see who it was. If it was him, I'd have to sit silently in the dark and ignore the doorbell, knocks, pounding, and calls; until I could be sure that he had gone. I also borrowed a pistol from my brother in case he should break in.

I had stopped dating and all the precautions that I had to take at home were making my life pretty dismal. I was really getting disgusted about becoming a prisoner in my own home when Joanne, from SYAD's; called to ask me if I wanted to attend a party at her apartment. I asked her if she had invited Lee and when she apologetically answered "no;" I told her that I'd come if I could get out of the house and away. Lee had made everyone think that we were a couple.

Bob had just returned from hitchhiking to the Mardi gras in New Orleans; and Joann told him about the trouble I'd been having. The next Thursday, wanting to see Bob, I went back to volleyball again. Much to my chagrin, Lee was there and it made me shutter to even look at him. I managed to get on the team opposite from him at volleyball, so that he couldn't touch me; but then whenever I had to look in his direction I found him staring at me. My discomfort and efforts to avoid him did not go unnoticed by Bob; so when we all went out for coffee afterward; Bob beckoned me to an empty chair between him and his friend Milt. Since Lee couldn't sit by me, he stormed around the restaurant glaring at everyone. Finally he turned on Milt, demanding that he fight him. If Milt had had dentures, I'm sure that he would have dropped his teeth. His mouth fell open in astonishment, "Huh?" While I was wishing that I could drop through the floor, out of sight; Bob told Lee to sit down and stop making a fool out of himself. Then he wanted to fight Bob and was told to go out and wait.

After finishing his coffee, Bob left to meet him. I never knew what Bob said or did; but later that night I got a call from Lee. He told me that he wasn't going to bother me anymore; and that if I should meet him on the street or anywhere else, that I should pretend that I didn't know him. I happily agreed and did just that on the one time that I saw him down town with another girl. Some time later, I got a call from the police telling me that he had stepped over the line; and had sent out brochures about the services that some poor girl would render if called. They had gone to his apartment and found a lot of women's underwear; and they wanted to know if I wanted to claim any of it. I assured them that I had never been there and that none of it was mine. The good news is that I never heard from or about him again.

Soon after, Bruce, one of my friends, asked me to give a Valentine party at my apartment; with him buying the food and things. I agreed and it was a nice party, especially since Bob came to it. When the party ended, everyone thanked Bruce and I and left. That is everyone except for Bob and Bruce. The three of us cleaned up and waited and waited until finally Bruce reluctantly left. Bob stayed and my life changed forever. God, how I loved that man! Falling for him was like being shot from an airplane. His touch or even a word or glance, kept me reeling throughout the years.

He liked me, I think a lot; but mostly he just felt protective toward me. I was such a mess, so timid and vulnerable; always afraid that I would not be liked. Anyway, for what ever reason; I joined the ranks of his girl friends and we began to go out. On our first date he took me to a restaurant with wooden menus; and afterward I floated home with his arm around me. Soon after, we went on a skiing trip with some friends. That night Bob made me my first drink ever, a very potent screw driver. It was good and I gulped it down. When I was asked how I felt, I tried to emphasize my "Great!" by twirling around; and I fell into the closet.

Most of the group was accomplished skiers, but it was Bob's and my first time out. When I held on to the rope to pull me up the mountain, unthinkingly; I had my skis pointed outward. I was pulled up with my skis going in different directions, until I thought that I would split in half. With difficulty, I managed to straighten my skis just in time to avoid there becoming two of me. Once up on the top, Bob sped down the mountain, tumbling several times. He popped up and off so quickly, that he was still the first one to the bottom. I had been shown how to slow down by snow plowing; and I cautiously snow plowed all the way down. I was last, reaching the bottom much much later than everyone else.

Bob and I went places with our families, SYADS, and friends. Joanne had been his friend for a long time. She was not and had never been his girl friend; but typically of him, he befriended her because, like me, she needed befriending. She was attractive and nice in her own strange way; but she just seemed to rub people the wrong way. She had no boy friend, and only went for guys who would have nothing to do with her.

Bob attended SYADS mainly because of the volley ball. He was a one man team, never encroaching on other players; but he was there to save the point if anyone missed. After the game when two guys left to get a ladder to take down the net; Bob ran up the wall and had the net untied and down by the time they returned.

Bob continued to date his other girls; so I determinedly went on dating as well. During the three years that my ex-fiancé had been gone in the army; I had refused to so much as have coffee with another guy. I had made up my mind that, never again, would I wait, and be at anyone's disposal. We had no commitment, but that didn't stop me from feeling badly; when on Easter, at a beach party with SYADS; Bob went walking with Marilyn. I wasn't the only girl at the campfire that night, watching in dismay as they walked away; or the only one waiting anxiously for their return. I went home that night and drank a whole bottle of vodka in grape juice and dyed my hair black. It didn't help! I only got sick and the next day I washed out the rinse.

Bob was going out with Marilyn more and more and with the rest of us less and less. Then late one night, he came to my apartment after a date with her; and said that he and Marilyn had just gotten engaged. I was saddened, but not surprised; as I had never expected anything permanent. Bob sat on a chair and held me on his lap for the rest of the night. The next morning, we went our separate ways. Bob's roommate, Ron, called and asked me out and I accepted, but he stood me up. I found out much later, that Bob had told him that he'd break his neck if he took me anyplace.

Chapter 2
ANOTHER TURN
1964

Bob and I Concord California 1965

Needless to say, I found it painful to see Bob and Marilyn together; so once again, I stopped going to SYADS. I did continue to go out, adding Jim and another Jack to the guys I dated. I had to be at work by 6:00 am and it was over thirty miles to work. I was going out most nights until well after midnight; and with the lack of sleep, I began to fall asleep while driving. I was a sleep walker; and I believe that is why I was able to stay on the road, turn with the turns, stop at red lights, and avoid hitting cars and people. I never did get into any trouble while driving; but I didn't stick to my intended course, and I often woke up not knowing where I was. Once I followed the car ahead of me all the way up a winding road that dead ended at their house. The family got out of their car and stood in their front yard; watching me as, wearing the bright red face of embarrassment, I pulled forward and backed, over and over, to get turned around. I left without giving them any explanation.

One night, after going out to dinner, I suggested to my date Jim that we visit my brother Jim and family in Concord. After a pleasant visit, while driving home; I fell asleep. I dreamed that my least favorite supervisor from work was waiting beside the road for me to pick her up. My statement, "I'm going to drive right on by and leave her standing there," brought an inquiry from Jim. I woke up just as he was asking me, "Who? What?" I thought that it might make

25

him nervous for me to admit that I had been dreaming; so I attempted to make up a story to add an element of sense to my comment. I fell back to sleep almost immediately and drove past the turn off for San Jose, waking up on the road to Santa Cruz. Then I had to make up another explanation of why we needed to turn off the high way and get back on, going in the opposite direction. I don't know if my explanations were very convincing, as I didn't have the occasion to drive him anywhere again. After that night, he did all the driving.

I had become friends with Joanne and she kept me informed about what Bob and Marilyn and others at SYADS were doing. When school got out in June; Marilyn, who was also a teacher, went back to Kansas to see her folks. Shortly afterward, Bob left to join her there. Joanne had been out of work for a long time; and she was about to be kicked out of her apartment. I moved into a two bed room unit so that Joanne could move in with me. I was earning considerably less at the hospital than I had been as a teacher. Now with extra money needed for rent, food, and things; I was always broke. To remedy this condition, I would start by hocking my television, then my stereo, and finally my sewing machine. It was a mean cycle, for each month it took most of my paycheck to get my things out of hock. Then having unmet needs, I was forced to rehock them all. I became a frequent sight going to and from the hock shop, with the attendant from a near by parking lot carrying my things for me.

When grocery shopping became pretty much just a memory, Joanne got hungry. I was going out to dinner often enough to keep me from suffering, but that was not so for Joanne. One night at SYADS, a guy mentioned that he had a big roast of beef. Joanne suggested that he bring it to our apartment; promising that we would supply the rest of the dinner. The problem was that we had no food and no money with which to buy any. When he arrived we put the roast in the oven to bake, and then we played cards until it was done cooking. Not wanting to admit our poverty and that we were welching on the deal; I put the roast on the table along with several empty serving dishes. We sat down at the table with him looking confused. After we passed the roast beef and each had a serving; I offered him one of the empty bowls. "Would you like some mashed potatoes?" It was difficult not to laugh at the expression on his face as he looked at the bowl and then at me. He sort of jerked the serving spoon in the direction of his plate; and quickly passed the bowl to Joanne. He ate his meat in silence; while Joanne and I chattered as we passed, served, and pretended to eat the invisible food. He made no comment about the food or lack of it, declined our imaginary desert, and left. Like the raven says, he came back "never more."

I used to have a beautiful black Persian cat who was devoted to me. Joanne never forgave me after I fed the cat our last can of tuna fish. Neither did she forgive my cat for eating it. After that, when I got home from work each afternoon; I noticed that the cat would come out from under my bed to claim her place on my lap. Whenever Joanne came our way, the cat would dive under a chair or back under the bed. She had never been afraid of anyone else; and since I was away so much of the time, I thought it best to give her to my sister-in-law, Betty. Betty had always wanted the cat and with the gentle treatment that she received in her new home, she was once again happy. I did miss her though. At night she purred me to sleep, curled up next to me under the blanket. She also liked to sit on my lap in the bath and play with the bubbles. I forgot this once and closed the bathroom door. After my bath, as I was drying myself; I clutched the towel in fear; as the door knob began to turn back and forth. After what seemed like ages, the door finally opened and in walked my indignant cat. I never forgot to let her in with me again.

At home in San Luis Obispo since my cat had been outside most of the time, she had never had to use kitty litter. This was not the case in the city, as it was too dangerous to let her go out. The first time she used it in the apartment; she scattered sand all over the bathroom floor and watched as I swept it up. Then after, she still scattered sand all over; but now she took a long time to sweep it all up into a neat pile with her paw.

My mother came for a visit and she did not take to Joanne at all. She insisted that, while I was at work; Joanne took whatever she wanted from my room, and that she pretended to be me when talking on the telephone. Before going home, Mom bought lots of groceries and left money for whatever I needed. With this financial help, I was able to save enough money to buy a small motor cycle. This was lots of fun and I could ride it amazingly well. I could make it move forward, stop, turn, and keep it upright most of the time. It was only in the heavy San Jose traffic, when cars failed to give me my own lane and they got too close, that I became dangerously wobbly. Given plenty of time, if there was a stop way way up ahead; I could slow and safely come to a stop. It was only when I had to stop suddenly that I forgot where the breaks were. Dragging my feet and yelling "Whoa" didn't help!

My days and nights were busy. Although I had had to work both Thanksgiving and Christmas (doing my first post mortem care at 6:00 A.M. Christmas morning); I had been given a holiday on the 4th of July. On this beautiful Independence Day, my life took another turn. It started with me enjoying a picnic with friends; and then rushing home to go to the board walk in Santa Cruz with John. Best of all, late that night, Bob called. He was back in town and no longer engaged! I didn't know at the time that he had told friends that breaking his engagement was the reason for his trip.

I saw Bob at volleyball the next night and afterward, although we were still dating others; it was not nearly as much as before, and we were together the greater part of every week. We went places with Joanne and other friends, hung out at the apartment: swimming, T.V., cards, etc. and we attended most of the SYAD activities, usually going and leaving together.

One night Bob said that he had promised to take another girl to a SYAD party; and I told him that that was Okay with me. I was determined not to go alone, I had no date, and I wasn't about to call anyone. Instead, I called an escort service and hired a date. Bob and his friend did not show up at the party after all; and everyone kept asking me who my date was, how did we meet, and where was Bob? I never did tell.

After a SYAD dinner in November, Bob took another girl out for coffee. On the way home, after noticing that his car was still parked in front of the restaurant; I decided to take a drive. I drove along the coast line, all by myself, for the rest of the night. The next morning, Bob was waiting at the apartment, apparently worrying and wondering where I had been.

The guys who I was dating were really nice and I liked them a lot. John was a college professor, he'd raced through school to attend college at thirteen and he had his PHD at twenty. He loved to argue, was good at it, and his arguments used to make a lot of people angry. His attempts to draw me into a heated dispute only struck me funny, and the harder he tried to anger me the more I laughed. Jim also taught in college. He was tall, quiet, and sweet. Both Jacks were especially attractive and fun to be with. The only real problem with all of them was that none of them were Bob. I was more at ease with Bob, right from the start, than I ever was with anyone else, including the man I'd been engaged to for so long.

Bob was a sheet rocker by trade. When I went on a job with him; it was difficult for me to focus my eyes on him, he moved so quickly. Being with Bob, where ever we were, what ever we were doing; was like being with no one else. Walking home from a movie, he would sometimes play leap frog with the parking meters. Climbing out of my car, home from work one evening; Bob swooped me up in his arms and ran upstairs with me; romantically proclaiming, "The shit eating buzzards are out!" At a fancy restaurant once, we were stopped at the door. "Sir, you need a tie to be served in here." Bob handed him a twenty and plucked the bow tie from his collar. "I just bought yours." The waiter started to object, but the manager stepped in, "Right this way, Sir."

One day Bob caught me riding my scooter with no helmet or shoes; in just shorts and a tank top. Bob took my keys away from me, saying that he would give them to the new owner when I sold it. Nothing I said or did changed his mind or got me my keys back. So, given no choice; it was sold and my motorcycling days were over.

In September Joanne got a job and moved back into her own apartment. In October after completing my year of training as a psychiatric technician; I accepted a position teaching in a school for children with special needs. Now, with expenses going down and my salary going up I was able to get off of the not so merry hocking-go-round.

On my birthday, I hired a wagon, horse, and hay; and planned a dinner and hay ride. I invited only men, telling them to bring their own girls. Bob and a date for Joanne were not given the same opportunity, they were stuck with us. It was a little awkward at first, when Joanne's date thought that he had been invited to be with me. We had dinner first, sang old songs on the hay ride, then came back to the apartment for cake. Marilyn was Milt's date and while she was examining an ugly troll doll in my apartment; Joanne told her to ask me the doll's name. I was too embarrassed to tell her that I had named the doll Roberta after Bob. From the look on her face, when I refused to tell her; I'm pretty sure that she thought that I had named the doll Marilyn.

Bob and I had planned to spend Thanksgiving in Northern California, where my parents were fishing. First Bob's car broke down and then, in my car, on my way to work on the day before Thanksgiving; the steering wheel came unattached to the steering column. These mishaps quickly put a halt to our plans. I refused to show up unexpected and uninvited for dinner with Bob's family; so, annoyed with me, Bob took a nap instead of going without me. Once again, no food, no money! However, now I had a small wooden well in my apartment. It was designed as a planter but I had water in it instead, and I encouraged visitors to make wishes. I promised them that the bigger the coin, the better chance of fulfillment. It had long ago been robbed of most of its riches but I found that it still contained thirteen pennies, just enough to buy the smallest hamburger at a nearby stand. While Bob napped, I went to the stand and as I counted the pennies in the clerk's hand, she made only one comment. "Ooo, they're wet!" With little bites, Bob and I feasted on that small 13 cent hamburger. It was the least lavish of all our Thanksgiving dinners; but it was cozy and it somewhat lessoned the stomach rumblings.

With December came all the decorating, shopping, gift wrapping, parties, and all the seasonal activities with my children at school. Age had not diminished all the excitement and fun that the holidays held for me; and now sharing them with Bob had me swimming in the clouds by day and swinging from the moon at night.

On one weekend I went home to San Luis Obispo to be with my parents. We were dining with friends, when Bob, after trying to reach me at home, called their house. His call sent me crashing through the ceiling, to sail amidst the stars; Bob had asked me to marry him! I didn't think that it could be for real, and it didn't seem any more believable after returning to San Jose; when Bob didn't even mention the call. I didn't bring up the subject either and so I just assumed that we weren't engaged after all. It was disappointing to say the least; but no matter what, under any circumstances, I just had to be with Bob for however long it lasted.

On Christmas Eve we visited Bob's mother and step father; and we spent Christmas with my parents, my brother Jim, my sister-in-law Betty, and their four children. It was a wonderful day with fabulous company, delicious food, and many gifts for everyone. The only gifts that I remember now, are Bob's gifts to me. He bought a black stuffed poodle with big blue eyes and long eye lashes, from the window display at I Magden's in San Francisco; and my first bottle of Toujours Moi, the perfume that I have worn ever since.

On New Years Eve we went to a dinner dance. I wore a black low-cut cocktail dress, a red silk rose that had previously adorned one of Bob's gifts to me, and my Toujours Moi. After eating we left instead of staying for the dance. I saw the New Year in, sitting alone in the car; while Bob was in a hall, gambling. Early New Years Day, Bob came out with empty pockets and the suggestion that we should drive to Lake Tahoe and get married! At a service station we used my gas card to get fuel, a cartoon of cigarettes for Bob, and enough cash to get across a couple of tow bridges between us and the chapel.

On the way to Nevada, the car broke down and we got it repaired, again on my gas card. By then 1965 was many hours on its way and Bob began to get sleepy; so I took over the driving while he slept. Later, when I got sleepy; for the first time ever, instead of sleep driving, as I had done so many times before; I felt like I just had to pull over and sleep too. After our naps, Bob was barely back on the high way when we went around a turn to find a blockade across the road. While we had been sleeping, a car had sped past us, gone around the turn, hit a patch of ice, and had flown off of a cliff. The high way had been dry and I had been going 70 miles per hour. If I had hit that ice in my sleep, we wouldn't have stood a chance. I was a California girl with zero experience on ice. It's too bad that there wasn't someone watching out for the people in the other car too!

Once in Lake Tahoe, we were able to get some cash on credit; but alas the gambling tables got it all. Broke again, we drove to Reno, called my parents, and slept in the car. On the evening of Sunday January 3, 1965; money arrived from my parents, and we found a little wedding chapel. Bob had on jeans, I was still wearing the black cocktail dress; and there was no music, flowers, or pictures. There was a minister and a witness however, and I became Mrs. Bob! It was the first and last marriage for us both.

Chapter 3
MR. and MRS. BOB
1965

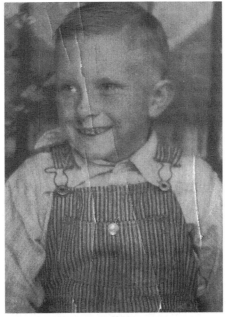

Bob Wolff, Texas 1941

I don't know how to explain the magnitude of being Mrs. Bob, but it was enormous! He led me from girlhood to womanhood and from naivety (more like idiocy) to something, I don't know just what. Even Bob couldn't lead me to sophistication but that's okay. He took me to a place where I can be just me, for better or for worse. I don't have to wear a paper bag over my head, as I once wanted to; I don't have to hide in a dark corner; and I don't shutter at the sound of my name anymore. I had a new name, I could be a new person, and if people didn't like me, it was becoming something that I could handle. Bob led me on the path to losing my fear of rejection and to becoming brave enough to offer others the open hand of friendship, instead of the guarded fist of caution. I now know that it's entirely unlikely for my hand to get slapped, but even if it got smashed to pieces, the cost of protecting it is far too high.

I will always be grateful to Bob for giving me my life, our children, and for giving me myself.

If you knew her you would have to agree that the strange person that I was, before Bob, was incredibly dumb. I marvel at her stupidity. As a young girl I was smug when people told me that I look like my father. I knew what they apparently did not, that I had come from my mother rather than my dad. I thought that there was something in the marriage ceremony that enabled wives to become mothers and that it had nothing to do with fathers.

I was in junior high school when I stopped in a small grocery store to pick up something for my lunch. There were no other customers that early in the morning and the store keeper grabbed me and drug me into the storage room, where the freezers were kept. Still being totally in the dark about sex; I thought that he was going to cut me up, package and freeze me, and that I would eventually end up in the meat department to be sold. This thought was not appealing and I fought, escaped, and ran back into the main part of the store. He chased me around the counter a few times until I was finally able to duck out of the front door.

My best friend was the only one who I told about the incident and I never went back. Later, when it came out that he had been bothering other girls; I had to testify in court. I was bewildered when his lawyer asked me to describe what I had been wearing and if I had worn panties. (Of course I wore underwear and what did that have to do with anything?) When he asked if I liked it, I was dumb founded. (Who in the world would want to be cut up into pieces?)

By my early twenties, after having been engaged for several years, I knew about the male role in reproduction. However there were still several gaps in my knowledge about the subject. I was staying in a boarding house in San Francisco while taking graduate classes at San Francisco State College. I was confused when one of the girls asked if I would sleep with her. I asked her what the problem was; after all we each had our own rooms and beds. She told me that I would never know what love was until I had made love to a woman. I thought that she must be insane and declined.

I was even more backward about the daily human function of elimination. I would never talk about using the bathroom and I would go to great lengths to avoid letting anyone see me go into a restroom. I guess I thought that if no one ever saw me they wouldn't know that I did such things.

When I first started dating my ex-fiancé, Ken; we went for a drive after a dance. I was a senior in high school and Ken was in the electronic engineering department at Cal Poly. I was fortunate enough to be taken to all the dances and functions of both schools. I was just getting to know him well enough to be comfortable with his arm around me and was enjoying the ride, when I suddenly needed to use the bathroom. I told him that I wanted to go home "right now!" and he wanted to know why. There was no way that I could bring myself to give him the reason and he was not about to take me home without one. We were at a stand still until the inevitable happened, I wet his car! The shame cut through me like a chain saw and he took me home, with me in tears. I never wanted to see him again, but he said that he wasn't going to leave until I came back out to talk to him. He was never put to the test, for somehow, I managed to change clothes and make the dead man's walk out to face him. The magnitude of that dreaded task still carries a sting after fifty three years.

———

Bob and I returned to Lake Tahoe and we spent our wedding night at Harvey's Wagon Wheel. We were snow bound for one day so I was one day late getting back to work. On December 31st I had moved into a new apartment across the street from the school where I taught. I had no idea that my first night there would be with Bob, as his wife. When I called work from Lake Tahoe, to tell them that I would be late; I told them about our marriage. They gave me a surprise wedding shower on my first day back. Both of our families also knew about our marriage and we celebrated with them individually, with many separate dinners. We did not tell any of our friends for a while and we continued to play volleyball and to go to other SYAD activities. Naturally we quit dating others but that was easier for Bob since I was still getting calls from boy friends and having to make excuses for not going out with them.

Bob was a wonderful husband and I relished everything about married life. Bob gradually led me on the way to becoming a new person; but the make over was never totally completed. I still bumble and stumble and Bob still occasionally fetches me out of predicaments from afar. He always said that it was dangerous for me to think and unfortunately his sons carried on after him, interrupting my "I think..." with "I told you, you're not able to do that; so quit thinking!" Now I have a grandson who, from time to time, asks me what I've been smoking.

One evening at the apartment in San Jose I was driving home with groceries and I passed up the car port, in favor of parking on the street. There were no available parking places so I tried to go around the block to make the car port the next time around. Somehow I managed to turn the wrong way and to keep on making wrong turns; until I ended up many miles away on the other side of the city. I didn't know my way home so I had to call Bob to come get me. The grocery store was only two blocks from our apartment and Bob could never understand how I had gotten miles lost, even while driving awake.

We had been married a very short time when cramps had me folded up like a letter. Bob took me to a clinic where the doctor told me that I had a tubal pregnancy and that I needed to be admitted in the hospital. I said all right, but I didn't believe him and instead of going to admittance I told Bob that I was done and ready to go home. That night the doctor called me asking why I wasn't in the hospital. Bob told him that I didn't want to go there and that he would take me to see another doctor in the morning. He was told that he could only do so, IF, I was still alive by morning. Bob spent the whole night sitting up, watching me sleep. The next morning a different doctor told me that I had a serious infection of the ovaries. He prescribed the strongest possible antibiotic and said that I could only remain out of the hospital if I stayed in bed. Bob saw that I followed his instructions exactly.

Bob's friend Milt told him that he was becoming concerned about his intentions; whenever he drove by (day or night) Bob's car was always in front of my apartment. Bob admitted that we were married and SYADS gave us a party and made an exception so that we could still attend activities.

———

Bob had wanted to live in Alaska as far back as he could remember. He read every Alaskan book that he could get his hands on and at about the age of eleven, he struck off hitchhiking to Alaska. This attempt failed and he was sent home, but he never gave up his dream.

As a boy, Bob lived with his mother, step father, two older brothers, three older sisters, and one younger half sister. Bob was two years old and the youngest of six children when his mother left his father to go with his step father. Later his little sister joined the family.

They traveled from place to place and from job to job. Bob attended seventeen high schools and probably about twice as many elementary schools. They never stayed anywhere long enough for them to make friends, go in for sports or school activities, or to feel at home. They would find whatever shelter they could, sometimes living under a bridge or in their car. They ate whatever food they could buy or find. Once Bob dug up some green potatoes from a field and he got really sick from eating them raw.

I don't know how they kept their old car running, but somehow they managed. Whenever they got a flat tire, they would stuff it full of old clothes and keep on going until it could be fixed or replaced. Once they left one of Bob's sisters in the rest room of a service station. It wasn't until they had gone quite a ways that she was missed and they returned to pick up the crying little girl.

34

Although all of Bob's sisters and brothers were tall, Bob was small for his age. The skinny little toe-head sometimes walked miles to school or to the library, often without shoes. During the times that he owned a pair of shoes they usually didn't fit him. He had no choice in the size or design of his clothes, if he could get into them and there was more cloth than holes, they would do.

As poor as their living conditions often were, it wasn't that or even the loneliness that made their childhoods so difficult. His mother and step father, like everyone else, were good or bad in their own ways; and they lived their lives according to their beliefs. The problem was that their beliefs were very different from and adverse to societies. Their religion was all tied up with sex, and they lived both defensively and aggressively; always guarding themselves from or retaliating for the wrongs that they believed they had received from other races and religions. The younger the child was, the greater the negative impact. As one of his sisters explained, when they were little they believed what they were taught. Little by little they learned that outside of the family, the world thought very differently. She remembers how she felt when she was first struck with the knowledge that her parents were crazy.

Both of Bob's older brothers left home while Bob was still very young. Bob stuck around much longer than he wished in defense of his sisters; and because, in spite of everything, he still loved his parents. He had some ferrous fights with his step father; and he was in and out of the home since the age of eleven. They were always on the run, often leaving in the middle of the night. Bob always thought that they were running from the law and that was certainly part of the reason. Bob thinks that just before one of their hurried departures, he saw his step father kill a black man. Bob always blamed his biological father for leaving his mother to fend for herself and their six children. This belief was not totally fair; one of Bob's sisters told me that they were also running away from their father, moving whenever he discovered where they were.

Chapter 4
NORTH TO ALASKA
1965—1966

Twenty years after Bob's aborted trip to Alaska he had not given up his longing to live here. That spring I wrote to Dr. Lafferty, the North Star Borough School District's director; and I received a wire offering me a job teaching in special education in Fairbanks, Alaska. Our preparations for this long awaited trip consisted of giving up a visit with my parents in Mexico, in favor of sheet rocking jobs for Bob; and trips to San Francisco to buy our tent, sleeping bags, packs, etc. Time flew and after attending going away parties given to us from work and friends, camping trips with both of our families, packing, and cleaning; we were off at last.

We took our time on the trip, spending more than a week's time. It was our first long trip together and I might have considered it our honeymoon, but looking back I now realize that it was only the first part of a honeymoon that lasted for over 31 years. Not that these years weren't difficult at times or that we never got angry, but bumpy as they sometimes were they were overwhelmingly awesome!

So our second home was our little tent. We sought its' shelter and privacy each night after a day of driving, exploring, or fishing. Most nights we cooked our dinner over a camp fire and we just snacked during the day.

The Alaska Highway told a story of nature in the raw and beauty punctuated with so many different kinds of animals, friends both old and new. It was unpaved and much rougher then. At one point, where construction was going on, they didn't ask one if they had four wheel drive; they just hooked them up to a dozer and pulled them through the bad part. Driving through the mountains with their ragged peaks and craggy crevasses was the high light of our trip. Along with their rugged splendor they offered us our first acquaintance with many of the animals that were later to become our closest neighbors. The mountain ranges had always called to Bob, especially the Ogilvie's, the gorgeous range that was to become the northern border of our forty square mile yard.

We camped at Moncho Lake for a few days and Bob was taken out on the lake to fish. I mostly stayed at the tent watching the drama of arguing squirrels, a thirsty moose wading in the lake for his drink, and the birds searching for bits of food. The few cities that we passed through held the least interest for us with the exception of Dawson City. Here we felt like we had gone back in time as we explored the old cabins, walked the wooden sidewalks, and ate at the Flora Dora.

When we crossed the border between the Yukon Territory and Alaska, at Boundary; we paused at the welcome sign to take a picture. In one of his rare serious moments Bob stated, "I'm home at last!" I thought that he was referring to Alaska but he meant that exact part of the state. The surrounding mountains and the valleys below, that whole area shortly became our home forever. We wandered around from time to time and experienced a kaleidoscope of diverse things, but the forty mile was always home. It has been for over forty three years and it will always be my real home.

Our meandering trip north afforded many pleasant stops and side trips to Mayo, Eagle, on the Camble and Klondike Loops, among others. We made it to our destination by late June. As we neared Fairbanks, we were dazzled by the lovely sun set that faded into the bright eager sun rise. We found a place to rent and Bob checked on work, but the sheet rocking jobs were not yet ready.

Our vacation had been extended for a while so we drove to McKinley Park. Back then people were allowed to drive and camp in any part of the park that they wished. We set up camp at Wonder Lake at the base of McKinley Mountain. We walked, fished, played, interacted with and photographed the animals, and relished our spectacular surroundings. We could view all the mountains close at hand except for McKinley Mountain. The top part of this giant was lost in the clouds. Then one morning the clouds cleared way up high and only the top of the mountain showed above the clouds. It looked like a castle floating in the sky, towering above all the surrounding mountains. It was difficult to take our eyes off the sight.

While we were camping we celebrated our anniversary at six months just in case we didn't make it to a year. The months had not been at all rough and we had not been arguing, but Bob had not really expected to get married and he didn't know for how long he would take to it. We didn't know what the future would hold or how much of it we would spend together. We just knew that we were happy then and we had something to celebrate. Because of the way that Bob had been brought up; he was afraid that he would not make a good father. I wanted children desperately, but because Bob was the only man for me, I wanted to be with him for however long it lasted, under any circumstances. With a painful portion of regret on my part, we took the necessary precautions right after we got married.

Once back in Fairbanks Bob began to hang sheet rock. He was good at his job and was quickly in great demand, almost wrapping up the sheet rocking business. Over the years he sheet rocked a good part of Fairbanks; schools, the *News Miner*, the new theater, houses, the hospital, some of the medical clinics, etc. etc.; and he did houses, schools, sewage plants etc., in many of the villages.

On weekends we went for drives and camped on all the surrounding roads. The first time that we drove up the Steese Highway to Circle, a bullet came from some where and shot out the wing window of our car. Some evenings we would go out to dinner and to an occasional show. Our favorite restaurant was the Tiki Cove where we enjoyed privacy in a rickshaw table. There were no fast food restaurants but one could buy a sandwich at the Doggie Dinner. We didn't have to deliberate about which movie to watch as there was only one selection at the old Lacey Street Theater.

We met Carolyn, a girl we knew from SYADS in San Jose. She was up here with Joe, her new husband, and we began to go places with them too. When Bob suggested that we should take them fishing up the Steese Highway I exclaimed, "We'll wreck the car!" They asked me what I meant and if I thought that we shouldn't go, but I didn't have any answers. I didn't know why I had said that, from where the statement had come, what I had meant, or what we should do. We went. We were having a silly but fun time until we got into some slippery mud and slid off of a cliff. No one was hurt but we had to wait until the car could be pulled up and towed back into town.

After the repair of our car we sold it, and then we were on foot. We'd walk every where we wanted to go, carrying packs when we shopped for groceries. We still walked for fun, going quite a long distance when we wanted to get out of town. Then Bob completed his work and it was time for me to start my job.

I had the first class of children with severe mental challenges in Fairbanks. Before 1965 these children either stayed at home or they were stuck in the back of a class and given play dough or something to keep them amused. I don't choose to give the name of the school because it was long ago and the principal's attitude toward my class was very different from that of today. My twelve children and I spent our days in isolation from the rest of the school.

Walking with my children to and from the bus was our only contact with other teachers and children. Even that contact was mostly silent with only the rare "Hi," a nod, or a stare. We could go outside for recess but only during the times when all other classes were inside. We cooked our lunch on a burner in the room and ate at our desks. We were not invited to the gym, music, puppet shows, the cafeteria, assemblies, etc. Later in the year the class of children with physical challenges began to go swimming on Fridays and we were actually allowed to go along! Fridays became the high light of our weeks; we had some great times, enjoyed some much needed interaction with other children, and we began to feel less shunned.

One of the twelve delightful children in my class was thirteen and considerably larger than I. He functioned at the level of a two year old child but he always attempted to be gentle with his smaller classmates. The principal did not like him and she believed that he should not be allowed in the class. Fortunately the director agreed with me so Chucky was allowed to stay. The principal's distaste was not reciprocated by Chucky, he liked the way she smelled. When she visited our classroom in the early days; Chucky would grab her, tilt her almost off of her feet, and sniff. "Teecha, what's this?" I would tell him her name as she struggled to regain her balance and freedom. Her visits became scarce and then they disappeared altogether.

I was totally captivated by my first real fall and I couldn't view enough of the season's dazzling colors. It became my favorite season, at least until winter brought the adventure of snow, ice, and cold.

I had never before lived where my world changed so drastically with the coming of each new season. I loved it then and I love it still! Bob bought me a fur parka with matching fur mittens and mukluks, and as the temperature lowered I found that I remained comfortably warm in them. Only the gentlemen teachers were allowed to wear pants in class so I wore insulated long underwear under my dresses while walking to and from school. I discovered that I could feel a cold streak on my leg whenever I got a run in my nylons. Bob walked both to and from school with me each day and soon we did so in the dark. I found the darkness, the visible cloud of cold that rushed in whenever the door was opened, and the sparkle of the snow and frozen trees, delightful.

On one of our walks out of town we ran across the kennels of one of the dog mushers. Here we discovered a litter of beautiful Siberian husky puppies. One charcoaled, masked, little fellow captured Bob's heart; and as my birthday was nearing, Bob bought him for me. Stupid, as we named him, was a gift for me and I loved him but he was always really Bob's dog. He had never been inside of a house before and when we brought him in, he stood exactly where we put him, afraid to move. For a while we had to carry him from room to room. His name came from the fact that he thought that we wanted him to stop going potty altogether. We'd take him outside and nothing would happen, regardless of how long we waited. Then back inside, when he could wait no longer and would go on the floor; he'd hang his head in shame with his tail between his legs. Months later he was in the process of performing the inevitable, when he was picked up and dumped out in the snow. After he finished and he received praise and pets, he finally got the idea.

Stupe had his own blanket and when we got it out at night he would pull and tug, move and rearrange it, until it was just so. No toddler ever loved his blanket more than Stupid loved his. It lasted throughout his puppy hood until it was eventually rearranged out of existence. When we first took Stupe to the vet for his shots we were asked his name. Our reply, "Stupid," brought a startled look from the vet. "Excuse me! How would I know his name?" Throughout the seventeen years that Stupe was with us there were several misunderstandings about just who we were calling stupid. Years later when we visited the house of one of our neighbors their little son, Termite, would call out, "Here comes Margaret, Stupid, Bob." When told about this Bob never thought that sounded very flattering to him.

We moved to a new house on Blueberry Street where pets were allowed. We got acquainted with our new neighbors, Ron, Tom, and Betty, in the duplex next door; and we began to get together with them frequently for meals and card games. Stupe enlivened our daily walks and he attempted to put an end to the play that worried him. There was to be no chasing, throwing, teasing, or wrestling; or he would become frightened and howl and get in the middle of it all.

In December Bob shot down two trees with his .30-06, one Christmas tree for school and one for home. It only took one shell for each tree, in later years he had an axe to use. After days filled with preparation and festivities at school we went out to dinner with Ron before pouring him on a plane headed for his home. Then we borrowed his car to spend Christmas day in the home of Norma, the very special lady who taught across the hall from my class. In January we celebrated our first whole year wedding anniversary by going out to dinner at the Tiki Cove. In March after Bob and I returned from a train trip to a teachers' convention in Anchorage, we discovered just how attached to us Stupe had become. On our return, he put his head in our laps and howled. For days afterward we couldn't take a step in any direction without tripping over him.

It was on that train ride to Anchorage that Bob captivated the hearts of my fellow teachers. Afterward they insisted that he come to all future school gatherings and we were showered with invitations of all kinds.

In April we took Ron out for dinner to celebrate his birthday. It was pay day, and that night Bob earned the nick name of Champagne Bob, at the cost of $600. That would be at least $6,000 at today's prices. Bob ordered a magnum of Mums champagne for this table, that table, and for the people over there. With help we drank our rent, bills, and the fiber glass canoe that we had ordered.

I had told them at school that I was only teaching for the one year since Bob and I intended to go live in the bush. With the spring thaw came the knowledge that we were not yet financially prepared to make the change. So that we could live a ways out of town, Dr. Laferty offered me the position of teaching all eight grades at Nenana Road School. We bought a used station wagon and waited for the three month visit of my parents.

Chapter 5
CAMPING WITH MOM AND DAD
1966

Harold and Elinor Lawrence

My parents arrived in Fairbank just before the last day of school. They drove and took the ferry in a one ton truck with a cab over camper and with our fiber glass canoe on top. They had lived in their camper all year fishing in Mexico during the winter and camping and fishing most of the way up to Alaska. My mother had given up her home and my dad his garden so that they could live and fish on the ocean year around. If my mother had expected a break from camping while she visited, she discovered otherwise when she arrived and saw everything in our house all boxed up ready for travel.

My mother had never enjoyed camping and she was not a fisherwoman, but she cheerfully put things in storage and made their camper their home. For a long time my dad begged Mom to go fishing with him. When she finally agreed to go; she broke his tackle box, gave up some of his fishing gear to the ocean, got tangled up in the lines and net, and got into so much trouble that she was never invited again. She said that she should have agreed to go a long time ago and have saved him all the coaxing.

It would be difficult to find two people as remarkable and as well loved as my parents. My father, Harold Tilden Lawrence, was born in 1900 in what was then called Southern Rhodesia. His parents were medical missionaries and he was the oldest of their seven children. His father was a doctor and his mother a nurse and teacher. She taught her own children at home and also taught home economics and health to the women in the village.

When my dad was fourteen he left the mission, all by himself, and moved to Chicago, Illinois where he worked and put himself through high school and college. He was the first to leave home and it was his first trip away from home. In the following years he helped each of his brothers and sisters when it was their turn to leave home to finish their schooling.

My father received his bachelor's and a couple of master's degrees and then taught, first in high school then in college. He had always loved the outdoors gardening, fishing, and hunting. He was a scientist and that helped him become such a terrific gardener and fisherman. People traveled long distances to see his garden and everyone wanted to fish with him. If any fish were to be caught it would be from his boat, he always knew where to go, how deep to fish, and what bait to use.

My dad was a man of few words, he was easy going, and he had a strange sense of humor that was missed by many people. He quietly enjoyed the humor of the pranks that he pulled on others without ever letting them in on the joke. Once he wired the seat of a student sending very light pricks of electricity to her backsides. When she squirmed he admonished her with the accusation of having ants in her pants. She left the class in confusion, never knowing what had happened. I inherited my father's temperament, his odd sense of humor, his looks, his love of mathematics, his shyness and awkwardness in large groups, and his absentmindedness. Unfortunately I didn't also inherit the keen intelligence that off set his less desirable traits. Whenever my mother or I went some place with him we had to watch closely to make sure that he wouldn't go home without us.

Once when we had just moved to a new house my dad mistakenly entered the house of our next door neighbor. When the neighbor came out of the kitchen to find a strange man sitting in her living room; he afforded her a two word explanation, "Wrong house." He came home without ever mentioning the incident. It was much later, after we had become friends that we heard the story from our neighbor.

In many ways it seems that my mother and father were exact opposites. My mother, Elinor Grace Lawrence, was very talkative, out going, easily flustered, and always getting into trouble with the things that she did and said. Her father was a Methodist minister and he had died when she was very young. Her mother worked as a secretary to support her two children and to put them both through college.

In the early twenties Mom left school after her junior year of college to go to the Smoky Mountains of Tennessee to teach. Her experiences there from the first donkey ride up the mountain, to the long weekly hike to play the old pump organ in several different settlements, to her romance with a young hillbilly, to her interactions with folks in their homes, and to her mishaps in the class room; were such that many years later the director of the mission schools burst out laughing when he heard her name mentioned.

She returned to Denver, Colorado to finish college bearing a saddened heart from leaving her Smokey Mountain boy friend and many new expressions that set her poor mother's nerves on edge. I still carry some of these sayings with me; but one of them when used on me in later years would leave me crimsoned, horrified, and wishing that I could disappear from the face of the earth. If I lingered after church talking to my friends when Mom was ready to leave, she would call out, "Margaret, stop piddling and come on!" People would stare at me and laugh, just as if I had been squatting right there on the church steps.

My mother's college boy friend, Sammy, stood six foot six inches. He was studying to be a minister and was nice but he was a little too serious for her. He didn't even see the humor and got angry when she accidentally pinned him to the side of the house while he was cranking up his old Model T Ford. One night during the summer they double dated with my father and his date, while Dad was taking some graduate classes at the University of Denver. The following winter when Mom visited a friend in Chicago, her friend talked her into calling Dad just to see if he remembered her. He did! He wasn't home at the time that she called, but as soon as he got her message he showed up at her door. They were married not too much later on the same day that she got her master's degree from Denver University.

More than ten years later after my brother and I were in school, Mom began to teach school along with my dad. Her principal said that she was like a mother hen with her feathers all ruffled and chicks peeking out from under everywhere. She managed to make progress in her class and to keep her colleagues well stocked with laughter. With good reason everyone left a very wide space where she parked, as they had had to repair the school porch once when she didn't limit herself to the parking lot.

While on play ground duty when she had left her keys inside her locked classroom, she thought that she would sneak through the window to retrieve them without anyone knowing. She was half way through when her principal came around the corner and saw her bottom half sticking out of the window. He thought that she was a student and he grabbed her, pulling her back out. They were both surprised and embarrassed.

Later at a convention for teachers, principals, and superintendents; Mom and her principal (a very large man) were doing a skit together for the final program. He stood on stage with his arms held at his back and Mom was hidden behind him, with only her arms and hands tucked under his to show in front. He was reciting the poem, "An Onion in a Petunia Patch (or maybe the other way around)," while Mom did all the motions to go along with the poem. At one point she pulled a handkerchief from his pocket and wiped his brow. She was going to replace the handkerchief but she got her directions mixed up and she tried to put it in his fly instead of in his pocket. This was not the plan! No matter how much he wiggled and squirmed, he could not get away from that relentless hand! Mom did not understand why he was being so difficult or why their colleagues were screaming in laughter. She could not see her principal's bright red, distraught face; or the tears rolling down the faces of the audience! That was the last time that she ever attempted that skit. Once before in a convention in another school district she had done the skit with a fellow teacher. That time the only mishap was that she was too vehement when she hitched up the teacher's pants, and she picked her clear up off of the floor.

When we moved to San Luis Obispo for my father to teach at California Polytechnic College, my mother began to teach in special education. I visited her class throughout college and fell so much in love with her children, that I quit nurse's school to become a special education teacher also. Later she led the way for her eldest and youngest grand daughters and a great grand daughter to do the same. This field has harvested a wealth of experiences and satisfaction that has enriched all of our lives.

———

Mom and Dad joined us at a picnic on the last day of school and we left our little house and Fairbanks early the next morning. They had the whole summer to see Alaska and we began to sow the seeds of love for the state with a trip to Valdez. There could be no better place to start this process; with all the beauty of the ocean, mountains, and water falls.

From there we drove over to McKinley Park to camp for several days. It snowed and Mom marveled at how strange it felt to be swimming in the ocean off the shores of Mexico in December, and to be camping in the snow in Alaska in June. They had their camper and we were back in our little tent. By day we explored, enjoying many encounters with moose and more distant one's with bear. In the evenings we sat around a camp fire and talked. Bob was one of the few people who my dad would really talk to; and they had many long conversations about guns, fishing, Alaska, Africa, etc. Dad was always the first at night to turn in, he never did say into what.

Bob always said that he wanted to be away from people, but his actions often indicated otherwise. When Mom and I started to wash dishes, we had to go around and gather cups from every other camp where Bob had left them after visiting. Once some tourists took his picture, thinking that he was a mountain man, he hadn't told them anything he just looked the part. His favorite activity was teasing Mom; keeping her flustered, sputtering, and stewing. Dad and I would just laugh but Stupe thought that he had to come to her defense. He howled, tried to comfort her, and held his paw up begging Bob to stop. When he wasn't on duty as Mom's protector Stupe was having a grand time camping and going on walks. Given the chance he would take off running and we would all have to look for him. Once he encountered a porcupine and he came back with many painful quills in his nose and gums. It was months after Bob had pulled them all out before he forgave the pliers and quit growling at them on sight. The good thing is that he never went near another porcupine.

We bathed in a wash tub in our tent. The first night Mom got stuck in the tub and had to call for help. This was not easily accomplished as the tent was zipped shut from the inside and she was in there pretty tightly. By the time Dad got her out; our sleeping bag, clothes, and everything else in the tent was wet. She didn't sit down in the tub again.

We left McKinley Park as it was then called; to go camping near Boundary, Dawson, Liberty Creek, Eagle, Circle City, and along the Livengood Road. We continued doing the same things, viewing a variety of scenery, and fishing on the various streams and rivers. Unlike me Dad had never been a sleep walker and when he fell asleep while driving, he went off the road. It's fortunate that he chose a field to drive onto, instead of choosing to drive off of one of the many cliffs that we passed.

At Circle, Stupe got into a fight with a mastiff inside our tent. He was barely a year old and it was his first dog fight, so the outcome may have been dismal had it continued longer. In the midst of their fight the tent came down on top of them, and when Bob got them untangled the mastiff ran off.

About mid summer we returned to Fairbanks, bought a trailer, parked it by the Chena River near the Cushman Street Bridge, and moved in. Bob went back to work sheet rocking, I took two classes at the University of Alaska, and Mom and Dad baby sat for Stupe. At the start they would walk Stupe every afternoon, but he kept begging earlier and earlier until he had them taking him twice a day, morning and afternoon.

One evening while we were all having dinner with Norma and her family, someone drove off of the Cushman Street Bridge and drowned in the Chena

River. Our canoe had been tied right where they went into the river, if only someone had been there to use it to save them!

After Bob wrapped up his work and I finished my classes, we headed back to the Forty Mile Country for Mom and Dad to begin their trip back to California. When we reached the mountains of home, near Boundary, Bob paused to shoot two caribou bulls. When Bob woke Dad, he hurried to get ready to go hunting with Bob. He was really surprised to learn that the caribou were already down and ready to be taken care of. It took most of the day to get them gutted, drug out, hung, and skinned. The next day Mom and Dad headed south, and we took our meat back to Fairbanks. We moved our trailer out to Nenana Road so that I could start teaching all eight grades in the Nenana Road School.

Chapter 6
HIGH WATER
1966—1967

Bob and I with the cats, Stupe, and Elmer Ukiah California 1967

It didn't take long for us to get settled and to meet the four families living on Nenana Road, about half way between Fairbanks and Nenana. I started out with nine children ranging between first and eighth grades. During the course of the year three more families joined us, making an additional seven children to the class attendance. At first it seemed cumbersome with all the different curriculums and I was trying to go in too many directions at once. In time however we worked things out and by helping each other, we got everything sorted out. With our school being over thirty miles away from all other schools we were pretty much on our own. I looked to Bob whenever I needed or wanted anything for school and he never let me down.

We drove into Fairbanks about once a month, shopping and getting together with friends while there. Mostly we just stayed in the area, reading, walking, and visiting with our neighbors. Swede and Thelma, the parents of Phillip one of my students, became our friends for life. Frequently Thelma's daughter Margaret, her husband Tommy, and their two daughters Kathleen and Susan; would visit from Fairbanks. Whenever they came out to visit her mom and Swede they stopped by our place and insisted that Bob and I had to join them. We had so many good times with them and throughout the years they have always been there for us.

Our little family began to grow. We agreed to take care of Boots, a black lab with (you guessed it) white feet; for Mary of McKinley View Lodge when she went outside for the winter. Whenever we returned home, no matter how short the absence, Boots would bounce up and down just like a big black ball. Then Elmer, a tri-colored collie (black, brown, and white) just moved in with us. He was named after Elmer's glue by his former owner, I don't know just why. Before we even realized that Elmer wasn't just visiting, he got into it with a porcupine. The result of the battle was that almost all of the porcupine's quills were transferred to Elmer; they were even down in his throat. There were so many, in such bad places, that we took him into the vet to have them removed. While he was recovering from the anesthesia, almost too wobbly to stand; Stupe followed him around protecting him from the neighboring dogs.

On our second anniversary we went hunting with friends. It was one of the few times that we didn't see any game, but we did find a cat frozen to the road, miles from the nearest house. She was on the brink of death but under her, kept alive, were two tiny kittens. One was long haired and black with a little white and the other was short haired and white with a little black. We thought that they were male and female but later we found out that they were brothers. Bob had no choice but to put an end to the mother's suffering, but the kittens were taken home and they became part of our family. We stopped at Parkers Patch on the way home and I went in for dinner with a kitten in each pocket.

Once home, after the kittens had been warmed up, fed, and comforted; we made a soft bed for them in our bathtub. We were anticipating a peaceful night, since they were tucked away quite some distance from our bed, but that was not to be. Stupe worried and paced and whined and pawed us with every little peep that they made. Sleep did not become available until they joined us and the dogs in bed. Later when we let them out side to play, it was Elmer who thought that it was his responsibility to watch them. They would wander a short distance away from the trailer and Elmer would herd them back with his nose. Then he would look pleadingly at the trailer, begging for me to either come get them or to come outside to watch them.

As they grew they were constantly together, playing, cuddling as they slept, washing each other, and hunting with and for each other, sharing their catch. If we called one cat they both came, if we found one cat we found them both. This closeness was interrupted when they came of age. Then for a while there were some ferocious fights between them, with some nasty scratches for us which were the consequences of separating them. Another trip to the vet for neutering and we had our loving cats back.

At the end of the school year I resigned from teaching again, since living only thirty some miles from town and on a road was not what we had planned. Bob made arrangements for us to stay at a cabin on the Yukon River, fifty some miles down river from Eagle. We sold our trailer and had sort of a garage sale minus the sale part. I put out everything that was electric and almost everything unnecessary for the bush to give away. Mary came back from outside and after many failed attempts to give Boots back to her, we finally were able to get him to stay home. Then we packed up our small car with what was left of our possessions, and the two dogs, two cats, Bob, and I squeezed in. We were off to California to visit our families and friends before moving to the bush.

Swede made the trip as far as the forty mile with us, hauling our canoe and supplies which we stored there to await our return. We hadn't even left the forty mile yet when we drove over a burn pile in the road and got a hole in our gas tank. Back in the sixties the Taylor Highway was rarely used and it was in no condition for a low to the ground car. It used to take us most of the day to drive the one hundred twenty miles from Boundary to Tok and we often would not see a single vehicle along the way. After we got off the Taylor it seemed that we rode the jacks up and down every service station trying to get the gas tank fixed. It seemed like we were jacked up as much as we were driving on the highway. I don't remember how many times we attempted to fix it, how many days it took, or how far we got; but it seemed like a lot and forever. I do remember that after it was finally fixed we made much better time.

By necessity this could not be a luxurious trip and we slept in our car beside the road. We had taken out the back seat and the back was loaded with everything excepting the kitchen sink (we'd sold that along with the trailer). The dogs and cats rode on top of the boxes with their heads brushing against the ceiling, or on our laps. When we awoke one morning it was to find people peering in the windows to see us both sleeping on the front seat of the car with the dogs and cats on top of us, just one big heap. By the time we arrived in California we were a disheveled mess, but we were welcomed into the homes of our loved ones anyway. We found that a bath, clean clothes, and a good night's sleep took care of the situation.

After the round of visits in all the many homes of family and friends and a little work for Bob with his brother-in-law Bob Stout, we camped in Pollok Pines with my parents. This is a beautiful spot for camping and we fished with my dad in the lake, picnicked, and made a day's trip over to Lake Tahoe. Here I almost got kicked out of the gambling halls, but fortunately since I lacked I.D., Mom was there to persuade them that I was thirty years old, old enough to be gambling.

While walking Stupe and Elmer on the banks of a lake, Bob asked Mom to hold their leashes for a few minutes. As soon as he was out of sight the dogs decided that Mom needed a run. She could not keep up and had to let go of their leashes. She was running after them, screaming hysterically for help; when Bob came back. He calmly gave them a call and they both came sheepishly trotting back to him, dragging their leashes behind.

It was with mixed feelings that we said good bye to my parents and California. Parting was sad but we were also eager to start our new life in the Alaskan bush. When we arrived back in Alaska we camped near Eagle on the banks of the Yukon River. It was pouring rain, it had been pouring for weeks, the river was extremely high, and our tent, everything in the tent, and we were wet, wet, wet. It was virtually impossible to start and keep a camp fire going, so we celebrated Bob's 31st birthday in the tent, wet, cold, and eating cold pork and beans from a can.

While we camped we had three visitors. The first one was a man who informed us that he had just shot and wounded a bear in the woods, right behind our tent. The second visitor was, fortunately not the wounded bear; but it was a man bearing the news that the cabin in which we had planned to live had been washed down the river. The third visitor was the Yukon River it's self which had abandoned its bed to come lapping around and in our tent. We weren't prepared to start building a cabin from scratch and we didn't have the funds to buy what we needed. So a change in plans, we went back to Fairbanks, rented a house near the dump, bought a little slant six truck, and I went back to the school district to see Dr. Lafferty. This time when he offered me a job he asked, "Are you going to resign at the end of the school year again?" I had to admit that probably I would.

We had just moved our belongings into the rented house when we had to move them back out. The Tanana River upon hearing how hospitable we were, decided to come visiting also. We had walked into the house carrying our belongings, now we waded out pushing our floating boxes (via our canoe) in front. We drove over to Hamilton Acres on the other side of town and while we were attempting to persuade some friends to leave their house, we were flooded by the Chena River. I sat in waist deep water steering our car, while Bob in the truck pushed me through town, around abandoned cars, to the hills beyond. All four of our pets, (the dogs and cats) were huddled on the little shelf by the back window of the car. My knees were shaking so much that I was splashing myself. After its muddy bath the car never ran again, but luckily for us the truck never let us down.

We camped on the hill side and Bob used the canoe to fetch people from their roof tops. There were many cars parked all around Fairbanks with scratches on their roofs from various boat motors. The friends from Hamilton Acres had gotten away from their house but Bob had to rescue their dog which had been left behind, shut inside. He had had to swim for two days with no let up above all the furniture, up close to the ceiling. He was one tired, hungry, scared, and wet pup and he was very relieved to see Bob!

We let it be known that we had several months supply of dog, cat, and people food, which we gave to people who were without. One man, who only had one small dog, wanted fifty pounds of dog food when he found out that we were giving it away. He was the only one who Bob charged for the small amount that he received. With people and their pets stopping at our camp, the cats were occasionally put on the run. They would invariably seek protection under Stupe and Elmer who quickly put a stop to the chase. The dogs began to feel like big shots and tooted their growls like horns, whenever they smelled another dog. They were in the process of making their proud threats when an Irish Wolf Hound walked around a bend in the road. Their tails and ears quickly came down and they wore the silliest most sheepish grins that one can imagine. The dog (he was almost the size of a horse) walked around them with dignity, then he left without a second glance.

Chapter 7
TOO MANY MISHAPS
1967—1968

When the water receded we moved to a little house on the Steese Highway near Fox. Bob helped people around town with the repair and the drying out of their things and houses, and I started a new year of teaching, this time at Birch School on Fort Wainwright. The school was made up of five special classes of children with mental challenges; mine was the class with the children with the most pronounced challenges.

The principal of the school was new to the state and as far as I know he left right after the school year. He said that he had stayed in his upper floor apartment during the flood, watching what was going on from his window. He did his part to fight the battle against germs by pouring detergent into the water below. He was sure that he'd saved a bunch of us from getting seriously ill.

This principal called a meeting after the first day of school. He wanted to know if we would think that he sat down on the toilet, if he politely put the toilet seat down for us ladies. I don't know about the other teachers, but seeing him either on or in front of the toilet was not a picture that I wanted. I was positive that I was not going to waste time speculating about his toilet habits!

The nicest things about our strange principal were that he left us alone to teach as we saw fit, and he gave us wonderful reports on our teaching. My only objection to him was that he could be too easily dislodged from his stand. By instinct when asked about my first evaluation I only said that it was Okay. Julie, one of the other teachers went into detail about how good hers was, BIG MISTAKE! Two teachers came to ask me if I didn't agree with them that Julie was not ready to get tenure and should not have such a good evaluation. I told them that I was kept too busy in my own class room to know what was going on in hers. I had only observed favorable things about her teaching and her relationships with the children. I had never seen any reason to doubt her qualifications. Afterward these teachers went to the principal and prevailed upon him to change Julie's evaluation and his recommendation. I literally blew up when these same teachers sympathized with my bewildered friend after she'd been informed of the changes he'd made. After we both licked our wounds and put our body parts back in place, we learned of which teachers we had to be cautious.

One of the good things about that year was all the new friends that Bob and I made. We had fun with our new neighbors on the Steese Highway and many good times with Julie and her boy friend. All the while we continued doing things with all of our old friends. We celebrated my birthday and our 3rd wedding anniversary by going out to dinner with Tommy and Margaret. We spent Thanksgiving at the homestead on Nenana Road with Swede, Thelma, Tommy, Margaret, and both sets of their children. After the most lavish dinner that we had ever had, we went snow machining. I borrowed Swede's snow machine but woe to me the throttle stuck! I have never been a very clear thinker in a pinch and all I could think to do was to hang on, yell, and try to weave in and out of the trees without crashing. Tommy raced up beside me, leaned over, and turned off the key; it was something that I should have thought to do in the first place.

Other nice things that year were all the whole school activities that I enjoyed, along with all the fun in my own classroom. There was a carnival at Halloween, a Thanksgiving lunch for the children and their families, a Christmas party with gifts for the children at Murphy Dome, and a train ride and picnic at the end of the year.

About mid winter we bought our first snow machine. Then there were many evenings and weekends spent racing around the country side, with me riding behind Bob. Once when we went over a bump I fell off. Bob was having such a good time that he didn't notice, at least that's what he said when he came back for me later.

March was a worrisome month. Bob's mother had a stroke and my father had a heart attack. They both recovered but then Elmer disappeared. Unlike Stupe he never went far unless we were with him. We walked and called all around the area, then while Bob was searching in the truck, he had an accident and the truck was totaled out. We never found Elmer but Bob was able to repair the truck and it continued to give us excellent service. Elmer had disliked one of our neighbors and this feeling was reciprocated in greater than full force, as Elmer had once squirted on his leg. We couldn't know for sure what had happened to him but we wondered. What we did know was that we all Bob, Stupe, the cats, and I, missed Elmer terribly. He was so sweet, smart, and nurturing.

Another mishap that spring was the one sided battle between our canoe and a dozer. The friend who was operating the dozer was not paying much attention while backing up, probably with too much help from a beverage. The dozer had no noticeable damages but our canoe was now a heap of fiberglass chunks. Ouch!

That summer I resigned for the third and final time. We camped in the Wrangle Mountains while we considered making a move. Lovely as the country is it just didn't seem like home, and we knew that we would need to go back to the Forty Mile to live. In the mean time we went back to Fox and Bob started sheet rocking again. Bob was paid good wages for his work and because he did it so well he was in high demand. He didn't have to go looking for jobs if there was work to be done the contractors found him. He did a lot of jobs for free or sometimes he would charge something like a round of cheese or a steak and beer dinner for sheet rocking a whole house.

Bob taught one of our neighbors how to help him hang sheet rock as he sometimes needed someone to hold up one end of the sheet rock on the ceiling, while he nailed the other end. On the first day I packed a lunch for Bob but since his helper didn't have any lunch Bob shared his. After that I started packing a lunch for him too. Soon he started stopping at the house to have breakfast before work. Next his wife began to come with him staying with me during the day. It wasn't long after that that they were both staying for dinner after work. One morning after we had been feeding them three meals a day for quite some time, they brought a can of bacon, suggesting that we try it. I thought that that was considerate and I cooked it all to have with breakfast. Right after eating he asked us to pay the two dollars and some cents that it had cost. As cheap as he was, he probably had been given the can as a gift and only shared it in order to get money for it! I wondered what they did for food on the days that he didn't work.

We sometimes went out at night with the guys Bob worked with. One evening when I was trying to persuade Bob into letting me have some goats, a friend took my side of the discussion. He said, "If you're name is Wolff, and you live in Fox, and you have cats and dogs, you need goats." Bob never understood the reasoning of that or agreed to let me have any.

On the 4th of July, Swede and Thelma grabbed us for a picnic on their way up the Steese Highway. After a good time we came home with full stomachs, Graylings that Bob had caught, and a beautiful little female Siberian husky puppy which Bob had bought in Central. We named her Susitna after the river but since she had already been called Sissy we continued to do so. We barely got her home when we realized that she was ill, REALLY ILL. We took her to the vet but she had distemper and she only got worse. I stayed home with her all the time. It began to sound as if we had a horse living in the house since her pads were so hard. Then she became blind and finally died.

Once again I could leave the house to go to town, on the jobs with Bob, and to visit friends. We missed sweet little Sissy so much that when a friend's dog had puppies we got another little female. She was a husky-German shepard-wolf mix; and all black. We named her Jakiak meaning devil. The name was certainly fitting but we ended up just calling her Puppy. She wanted to play all the time and she played rough. At night I would need to wrap my arm up in a thick bath robe and just let her naw on it and fight it all night long, otherwise there would be no sleeping for me. I used to tell her that I could hardly wait until she had a whole litter of puppies to chew on her and keep her awake. That never happened.

There was a large pond near the house we rented where a family of ducks resided. Watching them added to the enjoyment when we took the dogs and cats out for a walk. There was a windowless hole in the front door of the house where we could look out and see if anyone was coming. Although it was high the cats jumped through using the hole as their door. After hunting the cats would jump through and turn live birds loose in the house. I guess they were full and wanted the birds to be where they'd be easier to find. It was a chore to catch or shoo the birds outside to safety before the cats were ready for their meal. Sometimes we'd end up with two or three birds in the house before I could get the first one out. One of our cats once swam out into the pond and dragged a full grown duck into the house, unhurt. The duck made quite a ruckus with flapping wings, squawking beak, and flopping feet before I could get her outside to safety.

Puppy grew tall but she stayed extremely thin in spite of a ravenous appetite. When awake she was on the move forever pacing back and forth across the room. She didn't like the feel of my hands on her and would growl viciously whenever I hugged and pet her. Yet she was almost glued to my side and would never bite, regardless of how much loving I forced her to endure. She was devoted to Stupe and gentle with the cats, but I thought that we had to keep her away from other dogs. Whenever any dog came near she was ferocious! She was never allowed to fight and the dogs always turned tail and ran. Later both the dogs and I learned that if she was outside without me she was friendly and would play. If visitors familiar or not were in the house, she paid no attention whenever Bob was there. If Bob stepped out for any reason Puppy was instantly between the visitors and I, showing her teeth with a ready to pounce stance.

We sometimes left our pets at home when going out, however this did not work with Puppy. Whenever we tried to leave her she was right behind us. We chained her up and she unfastened the chain. We left her in the house and she unhooked the door. We left her in the truck and she rolled down the window. We left her locked in the house and she broke a window. She was never far behind us when we reached our destination. We finally gave up and friends learned that if we came to visit, there would be at least one four legged family member with us.

Chapter 8
ONLY ONE MINUTE NEEDED
1969—1970

In the fall, we bought a small trailer and moved it to a small camp ground, Summer Shades; where Bob did a job at the Air Defense Base at Clear. Upon the job's completion we moved back near Fox but now our little trailer was our home. We were without electricity and plumbing but with each other, our pets, and the open country around us we were happy.

In January the temperature dropped to -70 degrees and it did not get many degrees warmer for three weeks. We were not walking much and with square blocks for tires, if the truck moved at all it did so reluctantly and with a big thump. It was bad timing but that's when the fuel line leading to our furnace decided to freeze up. We were without heat! It was quite a job for Bob to get the line thawed and the fuel flowing again, and then it was difficult for him to keep it that way. While the animals and I huddled and shivered under sleeping bags, Bob was out struggling in the cold. It is so difficult to do anything even move at those temperatures, but he managed to get and keep us warm.

Bob's work had vanished for a while so we began to drive to Fox each morning for me to call and check on substituting jobs for the school district. My first day of subbing was in boys' shop in the high school. They couldn't have found a less knowledgeable teacher if they had tried. The lessons on that day consisted of the boys showing me their projects and telling me the whats, hows, and whys of them. At least, I learned something.

Coming back from calling one morning we turned into our driveway only to have a car crash into our truck. Bob had signaled the turn but the driver had not been paying attention and he had chosen that moment to try to go around us. The truck had taken us through the flood and now had been totaled out twice, but the faithful workhorse was repaired and it continued to plug on.

That spring I had a job offer to finish out the school year teaching the sixth grade in Nenana. What a time I had there! A few of the boys had been held back several grades and they were in their teens. I know that they were not unmanageable but they had no intention of being managed by the likes of me. I wish that I could say that I had been able to inspire these boys into wanting to learn but that didn't happen. The only thing that I inspired was their laughter at my attempts to teach and discipline them. At least they got a little enjoyment out of the experience; I can't say the same for myself. They weren't interested in school work and after they had received enough amusement at my expense, they'd climb out of the window and go home. They set fire to the school one night but it was caught early and didn't do too much damage. They threatened to beat up a little third grader, but we heard about it and were able to put a stop to any such doings. I won't say that there wasn't any fun that spring even at school, but all in all they were difficult months. For the first time I was not happy in and about my work.

With the summer and the end of the school year we moved back to our trailer on the Steese Highway. We still saw and did things with our neighbors and friends and now we had new neighbors Squeaky and Pat, and other new friends. Squeaky had had throat surgery and his high voice had brought about his nick name. His voice was startling coming from a very large masculine body. He would become very annoyed whenever his voice misled men into thinking that he was something that he was not. He also had the strength and the determination to put an end to any such notions. He had a huge appetite and most of the time Pat would feed him before they went out for dinner. They had lost the truck in which they had come to Alaska so now they were with out transportation and income. We sometimes gave them rides to town and Bob taught Squeaky how to hang sheetrock so that they could do jobs together.

Once when we were driving them into town I informed Pat that the restaurant we passed had just been moved to that location from across the street. Pat nodded and believed me. On the way home I exclaimed that now they had moved the restaurant back to its original location. Pat gave me a weird look, this time she didn't believe me.

Bob had gotten used to my sense of direction or lack of. When I had business in an office one day Bob asked me if I could find my way to meet him at Margaret's house. I assured him that of course I could, one could see the back of Margaret's house across the street from the office building. I would have been able to do what I had said I could, if I had gone out the right door.

How ever I went out the wrong door and once out my destination was not in view. I didn't know in which direction to go. I wandered around for what seemed like hours, through people's back yards, over one fence, I was chased by a dog, and I got tired and discouraged. Finally, I came across a familiar house and found my way. I told Margaret not to tell Bob but I ended up telling him all about it.

We got a message from the kennels at Central saying that they had heard about the loss of our Sissy last year and inviting us to pick another puppy. We did and our little Sissy II was beautiful, light grey with lots of white. She and Stupe made a striking contrast and together they produced lovely puppies that were in high demand.

Shortly after Sissy II joined the family Puppy and Stupe became the proud parents of one fat all black puppy, Sambo. Although Sissy was about two months older she and Sambo grew up together and were always very close. A single puppy was not the litter of chewing feisty pups that I had wished for in order to pay Puppy back for having kept me awake so many nights. However she did take motherhood very seriously and she was protective of and attentive to her son. She fed, washed, played with, and taught him how to do things for himself. Days before Sambo was born Puppy had holed up in one place, but she moved him to our bed immediately after his birth. She was getting him safely away from the odor which might attract other animals. Wolf like she didn't allow him to go right from nursing to eating solid food, every night during the transition she regurgitated her dinner on our bed. I thought that she was sick until I realized that this was for Sambo's benefit.

When it was decided that my parents were going to make another trip up in August, Bob arranged for his friend Bob Cooper to fly us up to his hunting camp in the Brooks Range for a fishing trip. We were having dinner with Tommy and Margaret the night of their arrival when Bob told them about the trip. Bob told Mom that there was no place to land up at the sheep camp and that we would have to parachute out. Mom panicked, protested, pleaded, fretted, and almost cried, all to no avail. Although Dad knew that Bob was teasing he went along with it. He responded to her arguments with, "Now Elinor, that's the only way we'll be able to get there."

As it turned out we never did make that trip, parachuting or otherwise. We had planned to fly up after the return of some hunters from Pennsylvania. We believe that Bob must have had a stroke or something because in his mind he was back to being a pilot in World War II. He dropped the hunters off at his camp and flew away to rejoin the fight. He landed his plane in the middle of nowhere, stripped and then he left the plane to die of exposure some distance away. Left untouched in the plane was the box containing long range patrol rations, water purification tablets, bug dope, first aid supplies, fish line and hooks, water proof matches, etc. etc. My Bob had recently given this box of survival gear to Bob as a gift. His loss was felt so greatly by so many people; he was one of a kind!

We stayed close at home that month with Mom and Dad sleeping in the trailer and Bob and I in our tent. Bob and Squeaky worked some and we fished, picked berries, and walked. We'd start out on a walk with Stupe on a leash held by Puppy. With his leash in her mouth she did an excellent job of leading him, and she would neither dash off after a rabbit nor allow Stupe to do so. As we walked along we would be joined one by one, by the cats, Sissy, and Sambo. We would first hear then see each animal as they joined us and Dad would comment, "Another country heard from."

Dad became especially fond of Sambo and he took over his care. One day my dad was enjoying sour krout with his lunch when Sambo begged for some. Dad gave him a bite and then laughed when Sambo shook his head and sputtered. He kept coming back for more and he had the same reaction to each bite. Being 1/8th instead of 1/4th wolf like his mother, made Sambo more manageable and doglike. His puppy hood seemed more intense and longer lasting than most dogs however and he grew up to have a wild grace that many found fascinating. He also grew up to be fiercely devoted to Bob.

After Mom and Dad had gone; our long haired, black with white cat disappeared, and he was never found in spite of extensive searching. That fall we had two hunting trips in the forty mile country, one in September and one in November. Bob and our friends got caribou on the November trip but it was -60 degrees which made it miserable to take care of the meat. Later that night the thermometer dropped out of sight below -70 degrees and we had to start and run the truck frequently to keep it alive. That was the coldest that it got that winter.

One night in February we let Puppy outside and for the first time she didn't come back immediately after the completion of her duties. That was also the only night that Sambo sat by the door howling. We called and called but did not find her until we were on the way for Bob to work the next morning. We found her beside the highway, dead and frozen. By the tire tracks we could tell that someone had gone off of the highway to run over her without ever having used their brakes. Bob left a shovel beside her body so that he could pry her loose after going to call in the delay to work. When we came back someone had stolen the shovel. We couldn't bury her while the ground was still frozen so we kept her in a protected spot outside to wait for spring. At feeding time it was all that I could do to keep from taking her the food that she had loved so much.

Bob continued to do a lot of sheet rocking with Squeaky and several other guys. I often went to work with them and on remodeling jobs I sometimes scrapped out and cleaned up the buildings after the guys had finished with the sheet rocking. Once I was asked if I was going to come back and clean up after the tapers but I said that I was afraid not.

One night one of the guys promised to bring home take out from Tiki Cove. He couldn't decide what to order so he ordered the menu. He brought almost a truck load of little white boxes which we all ate for breakfast, lunch, and dinner for a long time. I never was told how much it cost; the guys probably guessed that knowing would put me into shock.

Another night while the guys and I were relaxing in a bar after work, one of the supervisors had a visitor from California. They joined us at the table and each accepted several beers. The visitor let his bottles pile up in front of him and Bob told him to either drink or wear them. He just sat there without a word and the beer ended up in his shirt pocket. After that if the supervisor needed to find and talk to Bob his friend waited in the car.

I once went to meet Bob at a bar and I was delayed at the door by an over friendly service man. The bar tender informed him that I was Bob Wolff's wife and that he'd better leave me alone or Bob would wipe up the floor with him. He let me pass unbothered. It turned out that he was in the special services just as Bob had been, and the two of them ended up talking for most of the night.

In the spring Sissy and Stupe had the most beautiful litter of puppies that one could imagine. Friends came to see them and they quickly found new homes to go to. We kept Stormy, a little black puppy with white markings and face mask. Now we had the four huskies which were to be with us for many years to come.

As the time for the ice to break on the Tanana River neared, Bob left me a list of the times on which he had bet. The prize for guessing the correct time is enormous and divided between the people who choose the right day, hour, and minute. I listened over the radio as the announcer gave the exact time that the tripod moved (which automatically stopped the clock). I was stunned when I looked and saw that the exact time was on Bob's list. I was still in a daze and trying to comprehend what differences that a great deal of money would mean, when the announcer said that due to day light saving time the correct time would be one hour different. The disappointment felt like I had been pushed off of a cliff! We never bet on the Ice Classics again.

As Bob was winding up all his work we rented the Lion's hall to give a party for old and new friends, neighbors, and Bob's fellow construction workers. I had shopped and cooked for days and we had turkey, ham, roast beef, caribou pepperoni, potato, macaroni, and tossed green salads, pies, cake, and so on. There were probably around fifty people there, two of which neither we nor any of our guests knew. We certainly didn't mind them joining the party and all went well until towards the end of the party. We were down to our last bottle of whiskey and I took the whiskey from our unknown guests' table to give Swede a drink. Then the couple politely thanked us for allowing them to come and followed their thanks by squirting us all and the food with mace.

Bob got out his forty four magnum pistol and stated, "I'll give you two minutes to get out!"

The man replied, "I only need one minute!"

They left and we never saw them again. It's good that they were allowed to leave; a few of the construction workers relished a fight and would pounce on any excuse to indulge.

Chapter 9
BOUNDARYITS
1970—1971

In September we were at last in a position to go home. We bought a second snow machine, a truck load of food, and moved our trailer to Boundary. The people population at that time was seven, Action Jackson who owned Boundary Lodge, his cook Norma, her daughter Carol Ann, and John and Kathrine and their children Brenda and William. We got permission to park our trailer near the lodge but we barely knew the people, we only knew and loved the country. In 1965 we had had a sandwich prepared for us by Action Jackson himself on the day that we had first arrived in Alaska. On one of our many trips to the area Norma had served us pie at Boundary Lodge and Carol Ann had climbed on Bob's lap and had helped him eat it.

Boundary consists of one lodge located four miles on the U.S. side of the border between Alaska and the Yukon Territory. It's perched in the mountains beside an air strip and it has a spectacular view on all four sides. The high way if you want to call it that is maintained from late spring until early fall. From October through April one must fly, snow machine, or sometimes drive part way with a good four wheel drive truck. When the road is open Boundary is populated with the residents, tourists, truck drivers passing through, hunters, and gold miners on all the surrounding creeks. In the winter the population varies from one or two to several. The winter of 1970-1971 Bob and I boosted the population to nine.

Norma cooked for herself, her daughter Carol Ann (age 3), and Jackson, and when she had to she reluctantly cooked in the restaurant. She used to sit in the window saying, "Go on by, Go on by," to all the approaching cars. She had tried to convince Jackson that no one wanted home made pie and he agreed that she didn't have to bake any. He probably knew very well that home made pie was the most sought after items that they had had on the menu.

Once she answered a family's every order for dinner with, "We don't have that."

The bewildered family finally asked, "What do you have?"

She answered, "I'm not going to decide for you. Make up your own mind what you want."

I came to their rescue and told them the one thing that she had prepared. Other than being in the wrong field of business she was a wonderful, kind woman; and once she got to know someone she could become a treasured friend.

It was Norma's daughter Carol Ann's mission in life to find as much mischief as possible and to push as many of Action Jackson's and Mama's buttons as she could. She was the typical little three years old willing to try what ever she could get away with. One day she broke all the mantles in several Coleman lamps. Jackson had not prepared for this when he bought his winter's supplies. One of her favorite pass times was to lock people in the out house. She once came pounding and yelling at our door. Bob yanked the door open and told her that that was not the way that she could visit with us. After that she knocked quietly and was always welcomed warmly.

During the days and early evenings Action Jackson stayed mostly in his bar. He was known far and wide and had his picture (all decked out in his cow boy hat and two pistols), on post cards, cups, shirts, etc. He could be extremely hospitable, funny, and interesting or he could be grouchy. He could be ridiculously generous, helpful, and caring or he could be one way and penny pinching. All in all he was a great man and he earned and deserved the notoriety that he so enjoyed. Jackson tended bar each night until he had had enough to drink and got tired, and then he just walked out and went to his trailer to bed. The first time that this happened while Bob was in the bar, Bob tended bar, closed, and locked up, bringing all the cash to our trailer. The next day when Jackson complained that his cash register was empty again, Bob said he knew and brought him his money. Jackson had never known how often or of how much money he was robbed, he just knew when it was time for him to go to bed.

Bob started tending bar and I started helping Norma in the restaurant and with Carol Ann. We had not been hired we were just doing it for fun and they only needed our help while the last of the tourists and hunters were there. We both enjoyed it and met many very interesting people.

That fall the caribou traveled through the area by the thousands. The mountains came alive and looked like giant animals with the fur on their backs rippling. It was an awesome sight! Bob easily got our meat for the winter. The only difficulty was being sure that he didn't hit more than one with each shell and accidentally shoot more than our limit. We did actually end up with too many animals, but that was only because some of the other hunters killed and took only the antlers. We ate a lot of caribou that winter and gave away what we didn't eat.

Most days if it wasn't really windy or colder than -30 degrees, we'd go riding on the snow machines. The dogs loved to run with us but while the cat would go on our walks, he never tried to keep up with the snow machines. This form of pleasure came to a halt for a while after Bob was thrown forward and one knee was crammed into the coverless motor. After that the snow machine was called the meat grinder and Bob's knee was a mass of torn cartilage, tendons, flesh, and chipped bone. It should have had stitches but we settled for tape and he had to stay off of it for a very long time.

I developed a very strong urge to write and after chores were done I was lost with pen and tablet. I didn't have any real plan in mind, I just wrote and at the end of the day I would read to see what I had written. I had no idea what was going to happen next until after I had written it. I wrote two fictional manuscripts that year. They were very different from each other but they each brought me a new world of enjoyment! Like many fictional novels they were based on experiences I'd had. The first one was about a man and wife living in Alaska. The man was very much Bob but the wife was fiction. I could make her pretty and give her accomplishments that I didn't possess. The second one was about a single special education teacher who lived a very different private life than mine, but the children in her class and many of the classroom events were based on my mother's and my teaching experiences. I had dreams of getting them published but other fates awaited them.

We had an oil stove in our trailer with a drum of oil sitting out side on a wooden stand, from which the oil was piped to the furnace. One very cold night the wind was blowing so hard that it knocked the stand over, breaking the pipe. That was when we learned just what a four dog night meant. Although we had four star sleeping bags designed for -40 degree weather, the dogs were welcomed under the bags and they added a great deal of warmth.

In December Sissy had her second litter of six lively lovely pups. Ours was a very small trailer and now with two people, ten dogs, and one cat; there was no room for a Christmas tree. There was no decorating or shopping that year but there was lots of writing, healing, and merriment.

Right after the puppies were born Sissy was having a hard time going through the night without trips outside. Every morning I found a can on the floor of the kitchen with fluid in and around it. I didn't know what was going on until one day when John's dogs prevented me from letting Sissy outside. Sissy stood hee hawing at the door with her back legs almost crossed. Finally she went to the waste basket, removed an empty can with her teeth, put in on the floor, and squatted over it. How I wished that I could have gotten a picture of that!

The puppies all chose the same place to perform their little chores. Placing newspaper in that area made clean up much simpler but the cat did not approve of the arrangement. Several times each night we would be awakened to the sound of puppies yelping and running, with the cat close behind them. Then we'd hear the rattling of the newspaper as the cat dug and scratched, crumbling the newspaper into a little package for us to throw away.

One air company had the contract to bring the mail up to Boundary once a week. That winter they came in only once in seven months. While they were being paid and failing to bring the mail, Ron Warbelow was delivering our mail at no charge whenever he flew our way. He would shop, package, and deliver whatever we bush people wanted for 10 cents a lb. He put a great deal of effort, thought, time, and expense into helping us and he asked so little in return. On one of Ron's trips to Boundary he picked up the six puppies, kept them at his house, then delivered them to Swede in Fairbanks on his next trip there. That was the kind of man he was, men just don't come any greater than Ron!

On the day that Ron took the puppies, Kathrine thought that Bob and I might be saddened and lonesome. She invited us over to their house that evening, and Bob took the case of beer that had just been delivered and I made tacos. We had a great time and after that we would get together with them frequently. Their friendship became too close not to be considered family.
As Bob's knee got well, he was once again able to take over some of the daily chores. We began to shake the dice playing four-five-six and other games, to decide who would bring in the snow to melt for our water, fill the Coleman lamp, and do various other chores.

Again we were able to go out on the snow machines and Bob hunted for ptarmigan to add some variety to our diet. Stormy was nearing the age of one year and he seemed to be maturing at an awesome rate. Just one time he ran after a bird and was scolded, from then on he waited until Bob shot then he'd run to fetch the downed game for us. The dogs got so that they would look for a fallen animal every time they heard a shot. Few if any shells went without results.

As the days got longer and warmer and spring was approaching, the road crew came in and opened the highway. Leaving our trailer at Boundary, we grabbed the four legged members of our family and drove into Fairbanks. We had a camper shell and a mattress and some of our belongings in the bed of our truck. Here we and the five animals lived while we were in town.

We visited with our friends and Bob worked some. One acquaintance visited at Margaret's and Tommy's house where Bob was doing some work.

Looking around she asked, "Where's Bob?"

"He's hanging in the basement."

The look she gave me was pure horror as she let out a gasp!

I laughed as I explained that I meant that he was hanging sheet rock in the basement.

One day, while down town; we returned to our truck to find the camper door open and a man asleep on the mattress, right in the middle of all the dogs. We didn't mind him sleeping there but we were concerned about the door being left open. The dogs and cat could have gotten out and have been lost or hit in all the traffic. I guess that the dogs knew that he meant no harm and they didn't hurt him. Some years ago one of the dogs had bit someone who had reached in the truck cab in an attempt to steal.

Squeaky was among the friends we saw in town. His wife Pat had just left him for another man and he was feeling low. We had just decided to make another trip outside to visit family and we thought it best for Squeaky to go along with us. We headed out making Boundary our first stop. Bob and Squeaky took turns driving so we were on the road long hours and made a quick trip out. When both men got sleepy I suggested that they let me drive so that we could all sleep. They didn't go for that idea even when I protested that I was a good driver asleep or awake.

When we arrived at my brother Jim's house the family was surprised to be greeted by a strange man, pleading in his high voice, "Feed Me!" All of our families soon learned never to pass Squeaky a full platter of food that was intended for everybody. Half of the food ended up on his plate.

We had a wonderful time visiting with everyone and Bob and Squeaky worked enough to keep us in gas and food. We drove home by way of Idaho and the Canadian Rockies. What a spectacular trip that was with the gorgeous scenery and the animals everywhere: moose, elk, deer, antelope, mountain goats, Dall sheep, bears, etc. Back in Fairbanks we continued to live in our truck and Bob went back to work.

Chapter 10
ALONG CAME FLINT
1971—1972

During the late summer and early fall Bob was kept busy sheet rocking on both large and small jobs. We slept in the truck parked near what ever job he was doing. When we weren't visiting or going places with our friends we snacked in the truck and took the dogs and cat for walks. On one of the jobs Bob worked with Terry, a sheet rocker who had recently moved up here. The two men hit it off well and they started doing jobs together. We began to go places with him, his wife Joan, and their daughter Jamie.

In September they wanted to go hunting, so we took them up to Boundary for several days. While there we walked four miles to a cabin on Davis Creek. It was a one room cabin that had been built in 1900. It sat on a small hill over looking Davis Creek, nestled in the mountains. It had a sod roof in which grew grass, weeds, wild flowers, and a tree. It was old, tilted, rugged, and stooped; but it spelled HOME to us. We weren't going to make it there for a while yet but that's where we knew we had to move when we could. We were so enchanted with the area that on the next day Bob moved our little trailer down beside the cabin.

Two hunters and the two girls who they had met in Boundary were going for a ride when they crashed their truck. The two in the camper were more seriously hurt than the two in the cab, and the two injured parties were put to bed at the lodge. Bob and I sat up with them all night trying to keep them as comfortable as possible. This was difficult because I didn't know if they had internal injuries, so I didn't think it was safe to give them anything other than ice chips by mouth. It was arranged for a plane to fly them to town and a hospital. They were reluctant to go dressed as they weren't, so I did what I could. The girl fit into my underwear so that was easy but the guy was too big to fit into Bob's.

John came by his nick name "Big John" honestly, and he could seem intimidating at times. I went my timid way on a borrowing mission to John's and Kathrine's house. I had a difficult time finding and choking out the words to explain to John just why I needed his shorts. He said that it wasn't his habit to give up his underwear to just any gal who asked. He ended up letting me have them anyway and since he never got them back I guess that they were a gift rather than a loan.

Our cat had become ill on the trip so as soon as the patients were on the plane, we rushed to town and to the vet. We found out that he had a sort of cat leukemia and that short of a complete blood transfusion he could not be saved. The vet was not mistaken and all of our efforts failed to get him well. It was with great sadness that we buried him next to Puppy and Sissy I.

With October and cold weather Bob was still working, so we moved into a little cabin on Swede's and Thelma's homestead on Nenana Road. Bob and Terry finished up the work, but as it was so late in the year we decided to stay at the homestead for the winter. We occasionally went into town to shop and to visit friends but mostly we stayed at home. I began to feel sick, Bob took me into the doctor, and our lives took another huge turn.

The doctor laughed when he told me that I was pregnant, saying that now at last Bob and I would have to settle down with a life style like everyone else's. I told him to just watch and see that that wasn't going to happen. He did and I was right about being able to keep our same life style, it wasn't basically changed but it was enormously blessed. We'd been married for nearly seven years and I don't know just why our precautions finally failed, but it was wonderful! Surprisingly since Bob had been so adamant against having children, he was not angry or upset, just worried. I was really sick and I was unable to keep anything other than water down but I was unbelievably excited and happy. My feet never even came close to brushing the ground for ten long bumpy months.

The cost of living plus doctor bills quickly diminished what money we had. Bob was getting $17 unemployment every other week but that didn't even come close to covering expenses. Bob had a snare line for rabbits which we used for our food (actually his), and we cooked the intestines for the dogs. The spruce needle smell of the rabbits cooking kept me constantly green. I was also very tired and every evening after cooking dinner, I would go to bed by way of the table, pausing on the way only long enough to give Bob his dinner. If he wanted seconds he got them himself for I was out for the count.

Most weekends Terry, Joan, and Jamie would come out to the cabin to sled, visit, and have dinner. One day we had a rabbit thawing in the house. Joan found the sight of the dead rabbit disturbing and she asked that it be put out of sight. Later we let Sambo out to take care of his business. When he came back in he was baring a gift which he dropped in Joan's lap. She looked down to see the head of a decapitated rabbit starring back at her. She was too horrified to speak and going by the way that she looked and the sounds that she made, I was afraid that she was going to croak!

Kathrine from Boundary came to town to give birth to their third child, Buck. She stayed in a motel in town since we lived about forty miles away from the hospital. I drove into town each day while she was there to visit and to drive her to the places where she needed to go. All too soon (from my point of view), Buck arrived and they flew home so that Buck could meet and be with his dad, brother, and sister. Terry and family also moved back to California but we still had lots of wonderful friends with whom to visit.

Finally after my weight dropped down nearing 100 lbs, I got over the 24 hours a day "morning sickness". Then I could eat again, stay awake some, and I could go outside with Bob once more. Often I would go along with Bob on his snare line. He did everything with the rabbits other than cook them. Once when I was putting a rabbit into our home made cache (a large wooden box nailed in a tree with a make shift ladder leading to it), I fell backwards in fright. One of the rabbits which had been put there to freeze and to await its use had been only stunned instead of dead. When I opened the little door he jumped out at me. He hopped off into the woods and I crawled out of the snow bank, shaken up but unhurt.

Another time I opened the cabin door to get a rabbit that we had left on a shelf outside. About two feet away from my head was a great horned owl with the rabbit in claw. He looked determined and fierce and his outstretched wings seemed to span across the whole country. I had no inclination to argue the point of ownership, but he dropped the rabbit and flew off anyway.

A quiet pleasant Christmas, New Years, and 7th anniversary passed. I was so glad to be able to eat again and I made up for lost meals. My appetite was all too good now and the only thing that still made me sick was jalapeño peppers. What did I absolutely have to have? That's right jalapeño peppers, lots of them! We didn't have electricity or T.V. but our battery operated radio was always on. Back when I was so sick it seemed that they played the song *American Pie* all the time and it seemed that when playing, it went on and on forever. They continued to play it constantly after I got over the sickness and they even added on a second version. Hearing the song made me so nauseated all over again that I had to turn off the radio. After waiting I'd turn it back on and the blasted song would still be playing. I'd turn it off again wait and try once more, then they'd be playing the second *American Pie*. There was no getting away from it!

That winter Sissy had another litter of puppies and judging from their looks both Stupe and Sambo were the fathers. Sambo, who we had nicknamed Booger, was an especially doting father. He let the puppies crawl all over him and he constantly washed and played with them. This came to an end when we mistakenly started calling a solid black puppy, Little Booger. Sambo became a grouch, stopped eating and playing, and started sulking all day. He was totally dismayed! The remedy as soon as we realized what we had done was to rename this little black replica of Sambo. Then we had our rolly, polly, good natured Booger back and the puppies once again had a loving playful friend.

Like usual when we had puppies in the house we received many visits from people wanting to see and claim them. In March after the puppies had gone to their new homes, Bob and I drove to Tok and flew back up to Boundary. It took many trips on snow shoe for Bob and John to pack all the necessities down to the cabin and our trailer on Davis Creek. When this was done and the trailer was ready I walked the four miles home. For over a month we lived contentedly hauling and melting snow for water, using a Coleman lamp for light, listening to the radio (Bob had strung nearly a mile of wire up the mountain side for an antennae), and going for walks.

When the road opened Bob caught a ride to Tok to get our truck and then we walked up to where it was parked, and headed for Fairbanks. On the way we were barely out of sight of Boundary Lodge when we slid off the road and it took some time to get the truck unstuck and back on the highway. We hadn't gone far before the truck started to act up and there were many stops while Bob worked to get it started and going again. We finally reached Tok and got the truck repaired. By now it was dark and on the way into Fairbanks a lynx sprung out of the trees right in front of us. Bob could not avoid hitting it so he put it in the truck cab with us. I watched the lynx all the way in to town, hoping that it was dead not just stunned. I remembered the difficult time that Bob Cooper had once told me about. Two polar bear cubs had come untied in his plane while he was flying them down to a zoo. I wasn't anxious to find out first hand what it must have been like! However the lynx was dead and Bob skinned it out and sold the fur. Another experience of Bob Cooper's that I wouldn't have liked to share, was a charted polar bear hunt. Bob was taking a movie and the bear kept getting closer and closer. When Bob glanced over to see what was delaying the hunter, he saw that he had thrown the rifle down and was running toward the plane. Bob dropped the camera, picked up the rifle, shot the bear, and he went down almost at Bob's feet.

Once in town Bob found work, I resumed my monthly visits to the doctor, and we had fun with our friends. We stayed back in the cabin on the homestead for a while but I came into town with Bob every day while he worked. Then we bought a very tiny camp trailer and moved it to Rosie Creek Road on the outskirts of Fairbanks. I gained eighty pounds, was utilizing every tuck and pleat in my maternity smocks, and resembled an elephant without the trunk. I was becoming afraid that I would have to start wearing a circus tent as my smocks stretched tighter and tighter across my tummy.

In June I got toxemia and the doctor said that I could only eat fresh fruit and plain rice. I don't like plain rice and didn't eat any but the fruit at least was good eating. Even so it wasn't too long before I began to long for and dream about other food. I found that eating coconut made me chew the most and feel more like I had eaten a meal. I began to lose weight daily so I didn't have to go to wearing a tarp after all.

The baby's due date was July 7th and that was the day that I first went into labor. I was in labor long enough to have the pains become a couple of minutes apart and then I stopped. Later, on my July visit to my doctor, I told him about what had happened. He told me that I was mistaken, that this could not be happening. I guess that I was "mistaken" many times more for I did the same thing through out July. People began to ask me, "Are you ever going to have this Baby?" and Bob would answer, "She's not pregnant, just fat." I even began to wonder myself.

On the first of August I was actually in labor during my visit to the doctor and he sent me hurrying to the hospital. By the time he arrived at the hospital I had stopped again. Then his comment, instead of "You can't be doing this." was "Why are you doing this?" They tried inducing labor for several days but every time that I got close to delivery, I quit again. All this time my toxemia was worsening, I got eclampsia, and my blood pressure got so high that I was out of my head. I cried and cried and tried to explain how I felt but everyone would just shake their heads in disbelief.

About a week before then, I had found a peanut and had eaten it. I was filled with guilt and I was afraid that I had damaged the baby for life. Since no one seemed to be able to understand me I began to write down things. I still only got strange looks and shaking heads whenever I asked anyone to read what I had written. What was wrong with everyone? I was desperate and totally confused until much later when I read my own scribbling. What gibberish it was! Now I knew that it had been me that had been nuts all along.

On August 7th after several days of induced labor that did not result in delivery, Bob talked another doctor into examining me. He found that there was a blockage in the birth channel and he demanded that I be taken off the induced labor immediately. He said that delivery was the last thing that they wanted, that it would probably kill both the baby and I.

I was taken right down to surgery and Flint was taken caesarian. Before surgery the injection to my spinal column was not effective, and I could feel when they started to cut me. Soon I was up near the ceiling watching them desperately scurrying around me, and hearing them talk about me as if I was gone. My regular doctor who was assisting in the surgery was crying. Thirty seven years have not diminished the vividness of what I experienced at that time. Worries and problems that I didn't even know existed fell off of me like giant weights. I felt unbelievably light and free. Then I went through a tunnel and saw Bob. The next thing that I knew I was in the recovery room and Flint our skinny, ten pound, 23 inch long, red headed baby was at last here! Later when I told Bob about my experience and about seeing him, he said that he knew but he was adamant about not wanting to talk about it. I never mentioned it to him again.

After over two months of eating only fruit and one peanut I will never forget the first meal they brought me after Flint was born. It was a hamburger, potato salad, and cherry pie. I wanted it all but I knew that I couldn't eat that much all at once. So I took and relished one bite of each. Losing weight after Flint was easy and fast. What was too tight one day, fit the next day, and was too loose the next.

Since Flint was one month late in coming he was and acted like a month old baby. When Margaret gazed in at him through the nursery window he seemed to be looking back at her. She moved over to the other side and his eyes followed and focused on her in the new spot. The nurses were reluctant to turn him over to me, saying that he was the only new born who would wrap his arms around their necks.

I don't need to describe to any mother how wonderful it is when you first hold your new born baby. It was breathtaking, especially since I was nearing thirty five and I had never expected to have the experience of motherhood.

The first time that they got me out of bed to walk they could not convince me that if I removed the tight grip of my hands from across my stomach, that my insides would not come tumbling out. It took longer for me to get my head straightened around after all that I had been through than it did to recover physically. It took even longer for Bob to realize that I was back to being myself and to stop being concerned if a comment seemed a little odd.

Bob and the dogs stayed in the truck in the parking lot the whole while that I was in the hospital, both before and after Flint's birth. The nurses all knew that he was there and could be called if needed, any time day or night.

It's a good thing that Flint was so big for although I had been around many babies, I was frightened for Flint at first. His ten pounds seemed so tiny and fragile; I would have been terrified if he'd been small. On our first night home I tried to give him mouth to mouth resuscitation when he got the hiccups.

Flint was jaundiced at birth from his ten months in the womb. He had to have time under a lamp while in the hospital and after our release we had to have his blood tested every day. While we were in town Margaret gave me a baby shower. At the age of one week Flint got an early start at staring at women and of trying to get into their blouses. I guess that he thought that we should all take turns feeding him.

At the age of nine days he had a good blood test and he was good to go. We were all packed and off for home early the next morning. On the way back to Boundary when we stopped for lunch in a restaurant, a tour bus pulled up. I was eating with Flint's head on my shoulder and with his legs across my lap when a little old lady came up to me asking the age of my baby. When I told her that he was ten days old she exclaimed, "My gawd, he's half grown!"

Chapter 11
HOME
1972—1973

Bob and Flint, Davis Creek 1972

There were several stops on the way home so that we could introduce Flint to the road crew and the folks in Chicken and Boundary. We stayed in our trailer only for as long as it took to make the old cabin habitable. Once settled in the cabin it became my cherished home for life. The country was also Flint's only real home starting from the age of ten days and continuing through the thirty four and one half years of his life. He loved the country so much, later built his own cabin there, and he always intended to make it his home permanently.

In 1971 after our winter of only one regular mail delivery, I wrote a couple of letters that resulted in the Warbelows getting the mail contract. It was only right that the people who actually delivered the mail should be the ones getting paid for it. After that Warbelows Air Service brought the mail every week, rarely missing the scheduled time and then only under extreme circumstances. On Saturdays Bob and I would take Flint up to the lodge to receive and send out mail and to visit with our friends up there. Usually we'd stay and have a meal with John and Kathrine.

The rest of the week we'd stay down at the cabin getting wood cut and hauled for winter, going for walks, reading, talking, playing, and just enjoying being at home. Bob bought me a rocking chair the first I'd ever owned, and rocking and nursing Flint while listening to Bob and the radio brought no end of pleasure. The whole country was ablaze with reds, yellows, and oranges, the temperature pleasant, and we were surrounded with miles and miles of country, with only our four legged neighbors near by. With hunting season came our winter's meat and many visits from other hunters. We were really happy and anticipating a terrific winter together in the place where we most wanted to be.

September brought the shadow of concern for my father who had had another heart attack, along with a stroke. He was in a coma in the hospital and we were all praying for his recovery. Then he got pneumonia and died on October first. We drove into Fairbanks and called Mom. She said that she was going to come up to stay with us and we bought several 55 gallon drums of fuel for the trailer, another Coleman lamp, extra food, and everything needed for Mom's comfort. Once back at the cabin we got our little trailer all set up for her arrival. The road was closing so Bob took our truck back to Tok for the winter.

In November Mom flew to Fairbanks, bused to Tok, and then she flew up to Boundary with Ron Warbelow. We didn't have or use a sled with our dogs but they each had a dog pack, similar to the saddle bags used with horses. On our walks the dogs chased around exploring and playing, unless they had their packs on, then they were all business and stayed strictly to the trail. It only took a time or two of dashing off the trail with a pack, sinking to their necks in snow, and being unable to get up and out; for them to figure out that it wasn't worth it. With Flint in a pack on Bob's back and with the dogs wearing their packs, we walked up to the lodge to meet Mom's plane. After she flew in we visited at the lodge and with John and Kathrine and then we walked the four miles down to the cabin. The dogs carried Mom's luggage, the mail, and some food that we'd ordered from Tok.

What fun it was to have Mom with us and to introduce her to the attractions of our chosen home. Snow had come to stay and on moon lit nights our yard—as far as the eye could see—was aglow. The days were short, getting shorter, and since we lived in a canyon shadowed by mountains, direct sun light was gone not to return for months to come. Most nights the northern lights splayed across the sky, riveting our eyes to their multicolored splendor. Occasionally we could hear wolfs howling in the distance and our walks were enlivened by encounters with different nonhuman neighbors. The tracks in the snow told stories of chases, romps, searches for food, fights in which the loser became a meal, and of animals bedding down for the night. Our whole world was a glitter with ice and snow, yet each little stretch presented a different view of mountain, frozen creek, rocks, trees, brush, sky, and clouds. There was much choice in the direction of our walks, but every path was bombarded with so much beauty and interest, and was so different from day to day; that it would have still been fascinating if there had been only one way to walk.

There is nothing to compare to a hot cup of chocolate, next to a warm fire, after a brisk walk at -40 degrees. Bob's rabbit snare line and other outings offered Mom and I adventurous activity, and the cabin in turn supplied us with comfort and the pleasure of each other's company. Mom slept next door in the trailer but she spent her days and evenings and had all of her meals with us in the cabin. On the radio we listened to music, news, talk shows, and stories like *Lux Radio Theater*, *The Whistler*, and *The Green Hornet*. We played cribbage, read, talked by the hour, and of course held and played with Flint. Mom's other grand children my brother Jim's four, were near or in their teens. A new little grandson was just what Mom needed to help in her struggle to get back on her feet after her loss, and to learn to live without the man with whom she had shared the last 40 plus years.

How I wished that my dad could have been there to share the pleasure and to spare us the grief of his passing. All my life my dad had remarked, "You aint got red hair for nothing " when anyone, of any hair color, did something unusual. Now he had this remarkable little red headed grand son and he wasn't there to say it. How we all missed him!

Mom was there to hold Flint while I butchered and cooked the meat and kneaded and baked fresh bread. We shared the washing of the dishes and clean up. Bob kept us warm with the hauling and cutting of wood, and of course he kept us amused with his constant antics and teasing. He was so fast and unusual with his come backs that no matter how hard one tried no one could keep up or get the best of him. He could get Mom so flustered and dizzy with confusion that even Mom couldn't stop laughing. When they played cribbage Mom would end up miscounting, moving her pegs the wrong way, moving the wrong pegs, missing points, taking points that weren't there, and generally forgetting everything she knew.

One evening Mom thought that she would get back at Bob and embarrass him. She put a negligee on over her clothes and approached him as he laid reading on the bed. When Bob saw her coming he called, "Margaret, HELP!" Mom started laughing at the pretended panic in his voice and as she did so, she fell right on top of him. Then Bob started screaming, "Rape!" and Mom was laughing so hard that she couldn't get up. Through all the years their relationship was filled with laughter and tenderness, and try as she would she could never get and stay angry with him, regardless of how outrageous he became. Years later, after we had lost our Bobby, a family member got slugged when he tried to tease her in the same way that he had seen Bob do so many times before.

On Thanksgiving I stuffed a moose roast which we had with freshly baked rolls and pumpkin pie. We did not receive our Christmas orders in the mail so we found a pretty spruce tree with lots of pine cones for decoration. On Christmas Eve Ron Warbelow saw that lots of packages had just come in and he wanted to get them to us for Christmas. Although it was not a regular mail day he made a special trip to fly them in. Then John brought a whole sled load of the things that we'd ordered and our mail down to us with his snow machine. That evening we were kept busy decorating the tree and wrapping all the gifts that had come in. A special order of food came in too so we had a Christmas turkey. Flint was now four months old and sitting up and we were able to capture his delight with his new toys and the tree in the pictures that we took.

When Mom first arrived it was news to us that she was just visiting. She had no intention of living with us as we had believed. On December 26th Bob and Mom walked up to the lodge at -35 degrees with a wind that made the wind chill factor bring the temperature down to about -50 degrees. Those four miles straight up the mountain are a totally different story than the walk down hill to the cabin. She was 68 years old at the time and Action Jackson knighted her with the name, "Tough Old Tomato." He was much younger but he had not gone on any walks of any distance for many years if ever. Ron flew in to pick her up and from the cabin, I watched them fly off into the sun set.

It was and remained very cold through out January so we stayed at home all month not even walking far. It was very quiet in the cabin without Mom and we missed her. I did not become as flustered as Mom so I was not as much of a stimulant for teasing as she was. But Bob being Bob, the cabin was soon enlivened with his ridiculous antics and jokes and with Flint's and my laughter. He could do voices, and what he said, plus how he said it was a never ending source of hilarity.

At the end of January with a break in the weather Bob walked up to the lodge and got a month's worth of mail and some pictures. After that we all walked up on most Saturdays to get the mail. I put Flint under my parka and Bob tied a scarf tightly around my hips to hold him there. There he dozed and nursed, cradled all snuggly and warm. I had to be careful when taking off my coat at the lodge to be sure that I was all put back together again, to avoid exposing myself. The first time that we walked up Ron saw us from the plane as he flew in. He was quite concerned thinking, *Did they leave the baby down in the cabin alone?* When he saw me step into the lodge he wondered? *how did she get so very pregnant again so soon?* I removed my parka, took Flint out, and his mind was put at ease. While up there we would visit and have lunch with John and Kathrine; sometimes bringing the food that we would share. It was fun!

The rest of that winter we were able to get out considerably more. Flint, at six months, was pulling himself up and walking while holding on to furniture. The cabin floor was wavy from frost heaves and since it was made of a rough wood with splinters, Flint was never allowed to play or crawl on it. He did love to crawl and roll on the bed, play with the dogs, go outside, and to see other animals. There was a treeless area on the side of the mountain across from the cabin. Here the caribou liked to linger where the wolves could not jump out of the trees unseen. One day we watched as two caribou bulls fought. It was very tense for me but fortunately they did not fight to the death.

I have never lived in the Arctic Circle so I am not familiar with the long days and nights that drag on for months at a time. However we did lose direct sunlight in early November and we didn't get it back until February 1st. What a day that was, I didn't know how much I had missed the sun until we got it back. We ran outside to be in the sun light but it was almost gone by the time we got there. It only lasted for one minute that first day but it held the promise of more to come.

Although it was not totally dark, the days got really short, requiring us to light our lamp by 1:30 P.M. After hours with the hum of the lamp and the blackened windows it would seem like it was bed time by 7: oo P.M. To wash clothes we had to haul in snow, let it melt, heat the water, scrub the clothes by hand (I used a scrub brush), wring them out by hand, dump the water, and start all over again with rinse water. We had to go through much the same procedure for drinking water and for baths. The hardest part was the wringing of the clothes and I would be drenched before I was through. Another difficulty was finding hanging places in the cabin for the clothes to dry. They dripped all over the floor and cast shadows every where. If they were hung outside during winter our clothes would freeze solid and still be wet when they thawed.

In reality March is still winter but with longer days, we began to look for spring. If the nights are cold in March and April (it can still easily be -40 degrees or colder), then the days are usually sunny and warm. In winter the days and nights are only a few degrees different, but in spring there can be an eighty or more degree difference. It was difficult to stay in the cabin at all on nice spring days.

In April the road opened and after Bob got the truck from Tok, we walked up to the truck to begin another trip outside. We didn't pass a single car on the first ninety miles (the Taylor Hwy) and we stopped at Scobey's 40 Mile Road House for lunch. Flint was now eight months old and he was under the impression that the earth was populated with less that a dozen people. In the road house he couldn't stop starring at all the new people there. We ordered and when the waitress brought our food, Flint clapped his hands in delight. His ideas of the world changed a great deal on that trip. On our drive through Canada Flint picked up his first word, "aye?" One can't understand the enormous pleasure of eating out with the huge yummy selection of food, or of staying in a motel with its TV, bath, and bed; unless they, like us, had just spent a winter in a cabin without electricity, eating moose and beans, and hauling, melting, and heating snow in a tub to bathe.

As usual we had a wonderful time visiting with all of our families and friends in California. There were so many wonderful baths, T.V., terrific dinners, both in restaurants and in their homes, and places to go. We were in a whirl of trips to the beach, baths, T.V., shopping, fishing at Catfish Row, and best of all, seeing and talking to everyone. Again Bob hung some sheet rock and we did all the things we'd been day dreaming about all winter.

Flint got a very high fever and would not eat, and then shortly afterward he broke out with the red dotted rash that spells measles. It was the first time he'd ever gotten sick but he recovered quickly.

On the trip home we drove only a few miles on the Alaska Highway. First we took a logging road on which we had to wait until night (after hours for the loggers) before we could use it. Then we took the Caesar Hwy which was not officially open yet and it was almost totally untraveled. Then the Camble and the Klondike Loops brought us the rest of the way home to Davis Creek. Mom had bought a wagon for Flint while we were outside, and in it being pulled around by the dogs or us was where Flint wanted to spend most of his time. John and Kathrine had built and moved into a house near Chicken so we made a trip down to visit with them. We would have liked to have stayed home indefinitely but once again our pockets were empty and we had to go to town in search of work.

Chapter 12
AINT GOT RED HAIR FOR NOTHING
1973—1974

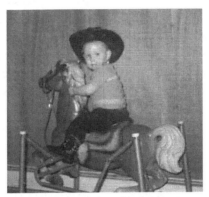

Flint at 1 year, Fairbanks 1973

Back in town Bob ran into Dan, whom he had hung sheet rock with before. They decided to work together and we moved our little camp trailer from Rosie Creek to Dan's yard on Dale Road. After a couple of jobs Bob and Dan got their contractor's license and they were bonded. There was a lot of work, they were both good sheet rockers, with good reputations, and expectations were high.

Occasionally Flint and I would go on the job with them but most often we spent these summer days at the trailer. Dan's yard ran right into the Tanana River with no beach or fence in-between. Neither one of us wanted to spend much time in the trailer so I had to have my eyes glued on Flint every second. If he moved where the trailer or anything else was in between us, I panicked until I could see him again.

While the guys worked I pulled Flint around in his wagon or we played in the yard. Flint had started walking while holding on to things at five months. Now at eleven and twelve months, he still was unwilling to try to walk on his own. He was always glad to walk while holding my hand, and sometimes he would walk holding one end of a stick while I held the other end. When he wasn't looking I would let go of my end and he and the stick would keep on going. As soon as Flint noticed that I wasn't holding the stick instead of being proud that he was walking on his own, he would get mad, sit down, and throw the stick away. Then it would be some time before I could get him to walk with a stick again.

We bought a big old river boat which I fiber glassed and painted. When I was finished we bought a motor for it and had some wonderful rides on the river in our beautiful like-new boat.

In July we went out to dinner for Bob's thirty seventh birthday. When the waitress asked for our orders Bob answered, "Surprise me." The waitress did and she made a selection that Bob enjoyed. Then while she was serving us, Flint put his hand up her skirt and snapped her garter. She glared at Bob and almost slapped him, but Flint repeated the performance and this time she could see that both of Bob's hands were on the table. She laughed, told us what she had thought, and managed to avoid Flint's hands for the rest of the meal.

We went out for a Mexican dinner on Flint's first birthday and Bob said that it was so great being a father that we should try for another child. I was more than willing and could hardly wait. Shortly after that dinner Flint viewed his first Alaska State Fair from his perch on Bob's shoulders. He was ecstatic with all that he saw, heard, felt, and ate. We continued to go to town and to visit friends and it was a very productive and pleasant summer.

In the fall work was still aplenty and going well, so we moved into Dan's basement for warmth against the approaching winter's cold. The basement was plenty warm and it made a nice home except the only windows were up high, near the ceiling. If I got a chair to stand on I could see out, but I only had a view of the ground with occasional feet or tires going by. Also Dan's dogs were kept in a room between us and the stairs leading outside. Whenever we took the dogs out to run we had to put Dan's dogs in another room while our dogs passed through. Dan had three labs and a poodle and they did not extend their hospitality to our dogs. The prospect of eight dogs fighting with Flint in my arms was overwhelming and to be avoided.

At thirteen months Flint finally decided that it was time for him to walk and he quit getting mad at me for tricking him. On my birthday Bob brought me a shrimp salad, some pajamas, and some panties. A friend, who was shopping with him, told me that when Bob had purchased my gifts he had startled the clerk. When she asked him my size he answered, "I don't know, what size do you wear?" She must have told him and apparently she was my size since the clothes fit well; but he did make her blush.

One day while in town shopping Flint had an ear ache and he wouldn't stop crying. It was extremely rare for Flint to cry for any reason and Bob's tolerance for it was low. When Bob had had as much as he could take he pulled over to the side of the street and got out. Much to his surprise I did as he had suggested and drove on home, leaving him standing there. I guess that ten years wasn't long enough for him to know me too well. He was afraid that I was angry and that I was planning to take Flint and leave him for good. He was very apologetic and relieved to find us at home when he arrived there later. By then I had discovered what ailed Flint and had been able to relieve the pain, so all was quiet.

We continued to have pleasant times visiting our friends and we discovered a new favorite restaurant to which we could take them. It was Club Tokyo and here the food was not only delicious but it was served on a low table that was partitioned off from the rest of the restaurant. We would sit on the floor while we ate, talked, teased, and laughed with our friends without other customers in sight or hearing.

We accepted an invitation for Thanksgiving dinner with friends and they also invited Terry and Joan, since they had just moved back up to Alaska. When I told Margaret about our plans she said, "NO! You always have Thanksgiving dinner with us and this year is no exception!" Fortunately our friends lived next door to them, so we ran back and forth between the two houses and ate at both places. It was hectic and we were coaxed and badgered into eating too much but the company in both places was terrific.

Again Flint enjoyed the Christmas tree and this year since for once we had electricity there were lights to put on it. Flint loved the wrapped presents so much that when it came time for him to open his, he refused. We pleaded with him, tried to show him how, and told him about the toys waiting inside; but he wasn't buying it. He wouldn't let us open them either so we had to wait until his nap. When he woke up he had fun playing with his unwrapped toys. We bought him a horse that bounced on a big spring and our little cowboy spent most of the winter in the saddle.

Bob and Dan bid and received three big jobs that were to keep them supplied in work all winter. The starting dates for the sheet rocking jobs fell nicely in line. Unfortunately one job was on time, one job was early, and one job was late. Consequently all three jobs fell at the same time, each one demanding to be done at once. The jobs had been bid at a price where Bob and Dan could make good money doing the work themselves, but they didn't allow for paying carpenters journeyman's wages. Bob and Dan could each hang 100 sheets a day, most carpenters would be lucky to be able to hang 25. The pressure on the jobs was huge and it really got to Dan, making him take off from work sometimes taking the help with him. Bob was working long hours seven days a week, leaving early every morning and not getting home until late at night. The time for visiting friends, going out, spending time together, or even shopping for groceries came to an end. I spent my days and nights with Flint and the dogs, eating canned salmon (that we'd gotten from Dad's fishing and Mom's canning), and exchanging a sentence or two with Bob in the minutes before he fell asleep. After two or three hours of sleep, he was up and off to work again.

These conditions lasted for all too long but eventually Bob got the jobs under control. It was so wonderful for Bob to be able to spend some time at home, to shop for groceries, and to occasionally be able to visit with friends again. The handsome reward for Bob's skill and all his hard work had to go toward the unexpected pay role, but at least he managed to get the work done well without going into debt or losing his reputation. Laidlaw's big bus barn, the Music and Art's Center at the University of Alaska (with all its acoustical clouds), and the Medical, Dental, and Art's Building were very costly in time, stress, and frustration, but they were done and done right!

Shortly after things at work began to ease off I became very sick. Happily it was morning sickness again. Although it lasted day and night and I quickly split company with any food that I tried to eat, the end more than made up for the means. However I did have to stop cleaning up the messes from Dan's dogs. The four dogs were shut up in the one room all day—every day and often for part of the night. When I tried to clean up that dreadful room I was forced to add to the mess. I gave up trying to keep it clean and whenever we wanted to come or go we had to carefully weave our way through, while holding our breath and noses. It was especially difficult when I had to take the time to herd their dogs into another room so that our dogs could pass through.

It helped a great deal to be able to finally get out of the basement to go shopping, for rides, and to do things with our friends. Most important was that Bob was now able to come home in the evenings and spend time with us. Bob started bringing me different kinds of treats in the hopes that I could eat them, and sometimes he'd bring me a little gift, it was for no occasion—it was just for fun.

In March we packed up, drove to Tok, then flew up to Boundary. I had not heard that one is not supposed to fly in an unpressurized airplane during certain stages of a pregnancy. Apparently our flight was not at a good time during this pregnancy. We spent the night of our arrival at the lodge and I had some very sharp pains. I did not cry out and since Bob was asleep, he did not see me double up. We had spent all the money we had buying supplies and for our charter. I did not want to let Bob know about the trouble I was having as I knew that he would insist on taking me right back in to see a doctor. I didn't know it at the time but flying again would not only have cost us money that we didn't have, but it would not have been the best thing for me to do anyway.

The next day we rode down to the cabin on a borrowed snow machine and sled. By the time I reached the cabin I was spotting steadily. Fortunately Bob made several trips up to the lodge to get our supplies and belongings. Every time that he stepped out of the door I lay down on the bed with my feet up. When he came back to the cabin I would think of something to do that required sitting with little activity. Somehow I managed to keep all this from Bob and thank God, we did not lose our Timber!

We were able to spend the spring at home together, doing all the things that we loved. Our walks and play outside were delightful, especially now with Flint to enjoy them too. There were caribou in the area, not thousands like there were in 1970, but we would see a few here and there every once in a while. A special Easter treat that spring was a close view of two young caribou calves playing and nursing.

Chapter 13
GET UP!
1974—1975

Flint and Timber, Christmas 1974

On the first of June we took a trip up the Dempster Highway, North out of Dawson City as far into the North West Territories as the unfinished highway went at that time. The country is fabulous and camping in places where we have never been is always exciting. We made the trip both because we wanted to do some exploring in the North West Territories and to check on a lodge that was for sale. With the possibility of buying the lodge in mind, we headed back to Fairbanks for Bob to work. Bob did find work but saving enough money to buy the lodge was not meant to happen.

We moved our little camp trailer back to Rosie Creek Road where we had lived while I was pregnant with Flint. Bob didn't like to live too far from town with me pregnant. Flint and I would go on the job with Bob every day. Here Flint and I would play, I would read to him, we would sing and dance, or Flint would work beside Bob using his little plastic hammer. Going "boom boom" with Daddy was one of Flint's favorite activities. What a picture they made, father and son, side by side, hammering on the walls. They were so alike, even to the tongue peeking out of the corner of each of their mouths as they hammered. Flint even tried to copy what Bob said. Bob would accidentally hit his hand while nailing and I would first hear,

"Hurt the baby's finger!" in Bob's toddler voice; then I'd hear Flint echoing him as best as he could.

On weekends and evenings there were lots of activities, visits, picnics, etc. with our friends. Right after arriving in town while on a picnic, we looked out across the river to see our river boat and motor go by with strange passengers on board. Bob called the State Troopers but he was told that they don't have a boat and that there was nothing that they could do about it. Bob's reply was that he had a rifle and there was something that he could do. That brought the police hurriedly to the scene. By the time the police arrived Bob had already persuaded the would-be boat owners to pull up on shore. They said that they had found the boat and didn't know that anyone wanted it. The police asked Bob if he had papers proving his ownership. Bob answered that of course he carries papers for everything he owns in his pocket just in case he needs to prove ownership. The patrolman did not pursue the subject and we were allowed to keep our boat.

One evening after work Bob was enjoying some beer with friends in a bar. Flint and I were with him (it's allowed in Alaska) and that was fine for a while. When Flint began to get tired and restless, as most one and a half year olds will do; I took him out to the truck in the hopes that he would sleep. He was too tired or too wound up by then and slumber was not in his agenda. Eventually I got tired of the stories, songs, and games; and his yet to arrive brother and I were getting sore from being climbed and jumped on. When I had had enough I decided to walk the approximately fifteen miles home, carrying the two boys (one inside and one out). I was more than half the way home when Bob picked us up. To say that he was angry was putting it mildly. I'm not sure whether he was angry at himself, at me, or at both of us; but there was no question about the anger.

When we arrived at our trailer it was locked. As Bob was trying to get into it he broke a window and cut the artery in his wrist. The bleeding was profuse and I didn't know how to stop it!

Our trailer was sitting at the bottom of a hill with a long, narrow, winding trail leading down to it. There was no room to turn the truck around at the bottom, so Bob always had to back up the hill for us to leave. This was not a problem for Bob; but for me to inch my way up, over turning, correcting, under turning, and correcting would take many hours. (Thirty years later when backing out of my short straight driveway, here in North Pole; Flint asked me why I didn't just back straight out. I answered truthfully that I don't have a straight back.)

I didn't have a straight back then either; and I certainly didn't have a curvy uphill back, in a truck with a camper from which one couldn't see where they were backing. Bob's blood supply wasn't such that we had hours to spare either. So with me holding a cloth tightly around his wrist, Bob backed up the hill while looking back out of the open truck door. This was working well until Bob got dizzy, passed out, and fell out of the truck. Bob was unconscious lying on the ground partly beside and partly under the truck. The cloth was gone from his wrist and a pool of blood was forming on and around him.

Flint began to scream and I sat shaking from head to toe, with my foot clamped down hard on the brakes to keep the truck from rolling over Bob. I couldn't move the truck in either direction, I couldn't reach Bob's wrist to replace the cloth on it, and I couldn't leave him laying there to bleed to death. So I sort of hung half way out of the truck with my foot still on the brake. Then I proceeded to kick Bob with the other foot and yell at him to *wake up and get up*!

I don't know what I would have done if Bob hadn't roused himself enough to climb back into the truck and finish backing up the hill. Somehow he managed and then I was able to drive him the rest of the way to the hospital. There the doctor exclaimed, "I can't stop the bleeding!" Bob's reply was, "I sure as hell hope you can!" They did stop the bleeding and stitched up his wrist. The stitches got infected and we had to go back to get some medicine. They made an error on the directions for the antibiotic, giving him twice the dose that he was supposed to have. This gave him the trots which interfered with his work. Then we had to go back a third time to get something to stop him up.

Shortly afterward we were driving home when a couple of horses ran into the road and we hit one. Actually since Bob had almost come to a stop it was more like the horse running into us. Anyway the horse belonged to Lisa Murkowski and it was no longer in good condition. Senator Frank Murkowski told us that he would pay for any damages but our truck was undaunted, being used to floods, collisions, etc. We were unhurt also so the only one who fared poorly was the horse. It was sad to bring harm to a young girl's pet!

During a lull in work we made plans to go home for a while and for Bob to sheetrock a room which John had added on to their house in Chicken. We were all loaded up for the trip, including enough sheet rock; when Tommy stopped by to tell us that Bob needed to postpone the trip long enough to bid on the sheet rock for the new Hutchinson Career Center that was being constructed. John and Kathrine were expecting us and there were no telephones in the forty mile to enable us to tell them of any change in plans.

Tommy was aghast when Bob explained why we couldn't wait. "You can't just pass up a million dollar job!"

"Oh yeah, just watch me." I'm not sure if he watched as we drove down the road; but down the road we did go, on our way home. After a nice visit in Chicken and the completion of the sheet rocking, we went back to the cabin on Davis Creek. This was the place where we could get things back in perspective and restore our sanity, this was home! The week or two that we stayed there were great, but we felt that it was necessary to return to Fairbanks and work. One of the reasons for our need to return was that the time for Timber to join our family was approaching.

Instead of going back to our tiny camp trailer on Rosie Creek Road, we found a place to rent on Chena Hot Springs Road. We had lots of room and privacy there and it was a good place to stay. There wasn't an actual drive way leading up to the cabin and the place where we turned off the road turned to mud when it rained. We were twenty some miles from town so our truck was needed to get in and out. Bob always managed to get to work when he had it, but it seemed that whenever we tried to go anywhere else, the truck either wouldn't start or it was stuck in the mud. In August we bought Flint a wind up truck for his second birthday and we showed him how to make it drive across the floor. However that was not Flint's idea of how things went. He would wind it up and block it so that it stayed in one spot as it unwound. This he did over and over, he would wind it, it would spin in one spot, and he would wind it again. We could never convince him that there was any other way to play with it. Bob and I would send it running across the room but Flint continued to make it spin only while it was stuck in one spot.

Early in September my mother flew up to be with us again. This time the date for Timber's birth had been picked and scheduled ahead of time. There was no waiting for a tenth month. There was no going in and out of labor. There was no toxemia, eclampsia, or induced labor. I could eat what I wanted and I retained my right mind (as right as it normally is anyway). I went into the hospital on September ninth and Timber was taken cesarean on the tenth. The date that the doctor picked was a little early and his lungs were not fully developed. They didn't have the ultrasounds and tests to determine how developed a fetus was at that time; at least it wasn't commonly used up here. Timber weighed slightly over six pounds and he had to go into an incubator for a short time. After we took him home he would not stay awake to breast feed and he was losing instead of gaining weight. He would wake and cry, I would pick him up to feed him, and he would immediately drop back off to sleep. At night I constantly needed to get up and down until in desperation I gave up and brought him to our bed. Then he slept and nursed throughout the night while I slept on. Only then did he finally begin to gain weight.

Bob was working and while I was in the hospital, Mom took care of Flint. That first morning when Flint woke up to find us gone, Flint was distraught. If he had thrown a temper tantrum Mom would have known how to handle it. However instead, he scooted way over in the corner of the bed, as far away from his grandmother as he could get; and then he sobbed. "Mommy gone. Daddy gone!" It broke her heart and it took a long time and a great deal of effort for her to get him to come around.

After Timber and I were at home; Mom, the boys, and I mostly stayed at the house while Bob worked. Each day Flint would put his toy tools in his wagon, give his grandmother and I a kiss, and tell us that he was going "Boom, boom." I had told Flint that the baby that I was expecting was his baby. Flint accepted this as fact and he never showed any jealousy or resentment toward his little brother. Just about all of our friends visited that September and when one woman from Chicken visited, she said that she wanted to take Timber home with her. She had been holding Timber while Flint played, but after her comment Flint stopped his play and demanded that I take Timber away from her. After that he watched her closely and he didn't want her to touch or even get near his baby!

Mom returned to her friends and volunteer work in California. The truck broke down and Bob hitch hiked to and from work while I stayed at home with the boys and the dogs. Our days were long but quiet.

I was sick on Halloween and Bob was especially late getting home that night. I went to the doctor the next day and found that I had mastitis. I had to put Timber on a bottle while I was taking an antibiotic; but I kept my milk coming with a pump. By the time Timber was allowed to have breast milk again, he had gotten used to the faster easier bottle and he refused to nurse anymore.

Tommy picked us up and took us to his house for Thanksgiving and we borrowed a car one day in December so that we could go Christmas shopping and out to dinner. We just missed letting the boys see Santa Claus. We had a real nice Christmas at home and a pleasant quiet winter.

Chapter 14
NOT IF BUT WHEN AND HOW MANY FLOODS
1975

Flint and Timber, Alakanuk 1975

We got our truck fixed late February so we were able to make a couple of trips in to town to shop. It had been a long time since the boys or I had been away from the cabin. We had spent our time playing at home while I wrote belated Christmas letters which I mailed along with pictures of the boys. In early March Bob finished up his work and we packed up in preparation for going to the lower Yukon. Here Bob had bid and received the sheet rock for three schools and sewage plants in three different villages. He never signed a written contract for these six buildings, he agreed to do the work and his word was good enough for the general contractor. Bob had expected to start this job during the winter, so when he was asked to sheet rock the Doyan Building in Fairbanks, he had to give the job to Terry. The general contractor agreed to this since Bob gave his word that if they weren't satisfied he could be called to take over. As it turned out if he had known of the delay Bob could have done most of the work himself. However Terry did a good job, the company was satisfied, and it gave Terry a good start in the sheet rocking business.

The first village that we went to was Alakanuk, near the Bering Sea at the mouth of the Yukon River. There are no roads leading to any of the villages in this area so we chartered a flight with Warbelow's Air. This time Ron's younger brother Charley was our pilot.

We rented a house next to the general store from the store's owner. The house had no furniture or appliances but it offered the shelter that we needed. There was no plumbing in the village but we had electricity, so I used an electric burner for boiling our drinking water and for cooking meals. Here we cooked, ate, lived, and slept on the floor.

There are almost no vehicles or roads in Alakanuk; the people either walk, snow machine, or travel by boat. The river played a big part in the people's lives. It was where they got their water, it was their transportation, a source of food, the livelihood of fisherman and boat builders, and up until they got their new sewage plant it was their toilet. Being so close to the river the water table was barely below the ground, so people could not dig holes for outhouse as every hole that was dug immediately filled with water. Everyone used a honey bucket and I never got used to that. I would get up before day break and sneak out to dump our honey bucket, making every effort to avoid meeting anyone. I kept it hidden out of sight and smell, unless a visitor flat out asked, "Where in the world is your honey bucket? I can't find it anywhere." Some people kept theirs in their kitchen or even used it as a chair. I also never got used to seeing people nonchalantly stole out to dump theirs, pausing to visit with their neighbors on the way.

Bob chopped two holes through the ice on the river, one for dumping and one for getting our water. More often than not when he went after water he would find evidence that someone had dumped their waste in our water hole. Then he would chop a new hole for water. In the evenings we'd take the dogs out and let them run on the ice, the rest of the time they had to be tied up outside.

Due to unseasonably cold weather there was another delay and Bob was not allowed to start his work in mid March as he was supposed to do. So as we waited we explored the area and got to know the people. People flocked to our house wanting to see the blue eyed babies. A couple of people even asked us to give them one of our boys. When we refused they argued that we should be willing to give them up as we could always have more blue eyed babies for ourselves. Even when we didn't have any adult visitors, our house was still the hang out for the village children. From the time that we got up in the morning until we chased them out so that we could go to bed, we usually had close to a dozen children. As broke as we were, buying and preparing enough food for everyone was not always an easy task.

When we had packed our things in preparation for our move, we could only bring a few things with us. So we shipped some things and we stored everything else in our truck camper. Two of our mail days turned out to be disappointing. We had been watching and waiting anxiously for the things that we had shipped. Instead we received word that the airlines had lost everything. They sent a check for twenty five cents a pound. I don't know where one can find boat motors, cameras, etc. sold by the pound; and I certainly had no way of replacing our things for that amount.

The next mail day we got a letter with a substantial towing and storage bill on our truck. Apparently the guys who had agreed to take care of our truck for us had driven and then deserted it on the streets of Fairbanks. Our check from the air lines was not enough, we didn't have any other money, and since Bob wasn't working yet we couldn't pay the bill. So the truck was auctioned off to cover the costs. There went our truck, camper, and everything that we had stored in it. This was the first of a few times that we were knocked down to owning little more than the clothes on our backs. Instead of toys the boys played with rocks and sticks and of course the visiting children. They managed to have fun anyway but the Easter box that arrived from their grandmother with new clothes, treats, and toys was welcomed with relish.

In May it warmed up enough for Bob to be allowed to at last start his work. Unfortunately the company was unable or unwilling to make an allowance for the two months delay. It wasn't long before Bob had to hire two carpenters from Fairbanks to come help him. Here we went again, the unexpected cost of their flights, room and board, and wages took most of the profit that Bob would have made if he'd been able to do all the work himself.

Now that Bob was working at the end of each day, I started chasing the village children out of the house so that the boys and I could walk to meet Bob on his way home from work. Then we'd have dinner and a couple of evening hours to ourselves before bed. The guys from Fairbanks often chose to have dinner with us but they were sleeping at the construction camp.

The buildings in Alukanuk are built on stilts as it isn't a question of whether the Yukon River will flood but only a question of when it will happen. This year break up and the flood came at the end of May. The whole village congregated on the banks of the Yukon River to watch and hear the spectacle. After the winter's stillness the river was alive with huge chunks of ice lumbering by, crashing into each other. Everything that was within the grasp of the raging river (trees, brush, an outhouse, etc) vied with the chunks of ice as they stormed by.

After the first rush of ice and debris, the river abandoned its bed and took over the country. This part of the Yukon River is too wide to see across at any time, so now it felt like we were right in the middle of an ocean with no land in sight. The dogs of course had to come inside, much to the dismay of our landlord. When we left the house it was either to swim or to catch a ride in someone's boat and once again work had to be delayed.

When the flood receded and the river tamed enough for travel, Bob's workers went to Emonic to start the job there. While Bob finished up the work in Alukanuk we hired a guy to build a boat for us. Now in the evenings we would walk over to watch its progress. At this time we acquired another member of our family. A long haired collie-husky-who knows what-mixture moved in with our dogs. We never could find anyone who would admit to owning him so now we belonged to Stupe, Sissy, Sambo, Stormy, and Stray.

Our boat got finished in time for us to buy another boat motor and use it to travel to Mountain Village. It took us all day on the river and we arrived there in the evening in pouring rain. On the banks of the river we zipped our two four star sleeping bags (two of the few possessions that we still had) together, and we all crawled in. It rained all night long and the many hours drench even penetrated the heavy duty canvas cover and the thick thick lining of the bags.

The next morning when we went to the construction camp we were soaking wet and bedraggled. We looked like we had just been fished out of the river. The cook gave us an extremely welcome hot breakfast and she offered us her unfinished house to stay in. I think that it took a week or two for our sleeping bags to dry out. At first they were so heavy that I could barely manage to drag them in and out of the house before and after rain storms.

The house was finished on the outside and while we stayed there Bob finished the inside walls, ceiling, and floor. Again we lived and slept on the floor and cooked on our little electric burner. This time we could use an outhouse. Never before had I appreciated an outhouse as much, and never again did I regret having to use one. While Bob worked the boys and I would play at the house and sometimes walk to the store. One could not drive to or from the village but there was a road in the village and a couple of cars had been brought up by barge. With Timber in arms, Flint and I would walk along the road. The first couple of times that a car passed us, Flint dived into the bushes. It was difficult to convince him that getting out of the way was adequate to keep from being run down. Fortunately we rarely had to make way for cars.

In the evenings when we weren't working on the house, we walked and occasionally visited at the construction camp. I cooked a special meal and bought what I could for Bob's 39th birthday, and then Bob finished up the Mountain Village jobs. Bob's workers had gone back to Fairbanks earlier, and now Bob needed to go to Emonic to finish up where they left off. So once again we found ourselves packed up and traveling on the Yukon in our little boat.

In Emonic we rented a small old cabin by the river. While Bob worked the boys and I played airplane while we watched float planes land on and take off from the river. One day Stray ventured off into the village without his four bigger four legged champions. He was then attacked and severely injured by a dog or dogs. We brought him into the house and we were able to nurse him back to health. After that he stayed close to his friends and was never bothered again. Flint celebrated his third birthday and a very old, very fat, Eskimo lady came to visit and she sang happy birthday to him in her language.

During a pause in the Emonic jobs it was necessary for Bob to return to Alakanuk to finish the tail end of the buildings there. We bought a little tent and headed back, again in our boat. This time we camped on the beach by the river. It was fun camping and the village children found our camping spot and hung out there. Although it was now August, the Yukon River flooded again and we had to take refuge at the construction camp for a few days. I could look out the window and just see the little flag at the top of our tent above the water with our boat tied to and floating near it.

Bob finished the last of the Alakanuk jobs and now there was only the work in Emonic to complete. We moved back into the same little cabin but we had to wait until early September for the barge and insulation for beneath the floor of one of the buildings. When it arrived I hired a woman to watch the boys while I did the insulating and Bob finished the sheet rock. The cook at the construction camp sent over cup cakes for Timber's first birthday and after celebrating we were ready to move on. It had taken over six months but now the jobs were totally done and done well. Again with unexpected costs and several delays, Bob hadn't made nearly as much money as he had expected, but as always he could be proud of his work and we had no regrets.

Chapter 15
IT ALL HAPPENED IN 1976
1975—1976

Flint and Bob, Shageluk 1976

With the jobs complete we did not head for home, but instead Bob made arrangements for us to stay in what was once a store in the old village of Shageluk. With our boat tied behind we hitched a ride with Claud Demenitiff on his barge. For six beautiful exciting days we rode on the barge on the Yukon, Andresky, and Onoko Rivers. Bob helped Claude to steer the barge and I cooked. At first I was sick and dizzy enough to be afraid that I would pass out. When Bob was at the helm I worried that the boys might go overboard if I lost consciousness.

We stopped in Holy Cross and the nurse there found that I had an ear infection and she gave me antibiotics. I got better immediately and could really enjoy the rest of the trip. After that every minute on the barge, viewing the miles of lovely country with some of its inhabitants, was cherished never to be forgotten. For Bob it was like a boy hood dream coming true.

We got off of the barge in Shageluk on the Onoko River and made our way to the old village. It consisted of the store and several cabins. All but the two homes of our new neighbors, Ina and Riley and Dale and Martha, were vacated. We moved into the store where we had an abundance of shelves on which to arrange our clothes, food, and belongings, and we had lots of floor space where the boys could play. It made a nice roomy home.

We were barely moved in when Claud came to tell Bob that there was no one who wanted to be hired by the village to unload the barge. Bob went back to the new village, a few miles away, to do the unloading. Unfortunately with inadequate help Bob ended up with a double hernia. He went to the village health aid and she asked him what medicine he was taking for it. Realizing that she didn't know what a hernia was, he decided that he needed to seek help and advice elsewhere. We caught the next mail plane for Bethel and a doctor. We stayed in a hotel, shopped for groceries, and then we chartered a plane back to Shageluk. The choice of food that one could buy was much greater in Bethel that in any of the other villages that we had been in thus far. Bob had to catch the next mail plane back to Bethel, as the doctor had said that he needed surgery to prevent strangulation of and gangrene in the small intestines.

I received a message over the radio before Bob's surgery but none afterward. I was so worried that I walked to the new village where the health aid could call the Bethel Hospital to find out how he was doing. I was told that he would need to remain in the hospital for quite a while yet. I didn't meet the mail plane the next day, and I was surprised when Bob came struggling home from the air strip. He had to recover in bed but recover he did, and home was where he was determined to do so. Just as Bob was getting back on his feet Timber began to walk. We were enjoying our new home and delighting in spending our days with Bob, who was now free of the responsibility of so many big jobs.

In their fish nets and wheels people were getting an abundance of White Fish (much like the Halibut that I now love to catch, cook, and eat). The fish became a big part of the folk's diets, they dried fish for dog food, and they shared it with us. We often were invited to have dinner with our new neighbors in the old village and occasionally we had an invitation in the new village. Invariably the meal was fish soup with the fish (including head, eyes, tail, and fins) boiled in water with vegetables. When one family came to our house for dinner I filleted and fried some White Fish. I couldn't believe it when they asked me what I was serving. They had eaten White Fish all their lives but didn't recognize it cooked differently.

We spent many pleasant evenings with our new friends, went on lots of walks with the dogs, and had fun at home doing whatever we wanted to do. On the first of December I discovered that I was pregnant again. Because of this news and the fact that we were broke with no income, no work, and no means of getting to where Bob could find work; Bob did something that he had always before refused to do. He accepted a job at Hooper Bay, even though we could not go with him.

Bob was up early and drinking coffee on the morning that the company chartered his flight to Hooper Bay. Much to the pilot's annoyance he had to land for a toilet stop before they reached their destination. This was even more stressful for Bob who hated to fly, as he especially disliked landing and taking off. Years ago on my first flight in a small plane, I looked back at Bob and was startled to see a headless body. His head was zipped up inside his parka and he looked like he had been decapitated. This really surprised me as he had been a paratrooper in the army. He said that he had joined an air born unit because his family needed the extra money, and that he was less afraid when he wore a parachute. However this fear never prevented Bob from flying when he needed to do so.

Sissy was coming into season and on the day that Bob flew to Hooper Bay, (for the first time) the four male dogs got in a big fight. This was so dangerous with two small boys running around, and breaking it up was more than difficult.

Since this could not be allowed to happen again, I found outside shelter for Sambo, Stormy, and Stray, leaving just Stupe in with Sissy. It was out of sight out of mind for Stormy and Stray, but Sambo howled non stop day and night. After a couple of days I could look out and see Sambo still howling, but now there was no sound. Thank God he had temporarily howled his voice right out of existence. The silence was beautiful!

Ina and Riley had gone on a trip but Dale looked in on us while Bob was away. Bob had cut and split enough wood for me to use, but that didn't stop me from getting into a predicament. Bob always kept a good stack of wood in the house, but being the procrastinator that I am, I brought the wood in only as I needed it. The temperature dropped to -40 degrees and when I added two newly brought in frozen logs to the fire, it went capute! Try as I would I could not get it started again, and the building was getting colder by the minute. Dale noticed that I had no smoke, he came over, somehow restored our fire, brought in a bunch of wood, and left instructions for me to always keep wood warming in the house.

Dale also went out and chopped down a Spruce tree for us to decorate and use for Christmas, and on mail days he brought our mail from the new village. Bob sent us a few letters; they were the only ones he'd ever written to me since we had always been together. He also sent us messages over the radio, a kindness that Alaska stations offer people in the bush. Dale not only brought me the stack oven that I'd ordered, but he installed it in our stove pipe as well. Now I could not only bake things, but when not baking the open oven door allowed extra heat to come into the room. We didn't have electricity so we used a Coleman lamp and I cooked on top of our wood stove.

Bob flew home on Christmas Eve which made it one of the most delightful Christmases ever! In January I started teaching Flint, and although he was only three he quickly learned all the letters, numbers, and sounds. He began to write letters to his Grandmother with me spelling the words for him.

Nineteen seventy six turned out to be one very eventful year! In January, while Bob was in the new village getting our mail, I had a miscarriage. It was really early in the pregnancy and although it was sad it wasn't so bad physically. Even so in spite of my protests Bob made me go to and stay in bed for a few days. This had been the only pregnancy in which I hadn't gotten sick, and I had been able to continue cooking, eating, etc. When I was allowed to get up I was lighter but fine.

When some of the villagers found out that I love to work with numbers they brought their income taxes for me to figure. I had fun doing this but it turned out that it was no favor for some of them. Some of the refunds harvested a crop of black eyes and bruises. Some cheerful happy people became feisty and argumentative with extra cash and the liquid refreshment that it bought. I don't think that there were any lasting feuds, divorces, or deaths, at least I hope not.

Ina and Riley came back from Anchorage after visiting her children for Thanksgiving and Christmas. Ina was like a grandmother to the boys and they loved to visit her and her talking miner bird. Dale and Martha had pet chickens that during the winter months resided in a pen in their cabin. One evening when we were invited to their house for dinner, we were quite surprised to find that chicken was on the menu. While we were eating Henrietta, Martha told us about how she had had to chase her all over the place after she had been beheaded.

In February Sissy had six beautiful little puppies. They were like three sets of twins; each set was a male and a female. One pair was black, one dark grey and one light grey. They all were beautifully marked with white face masks and paws, and tails that were tipped in white. People came to claim the puppies even after they had all been given away. Stray took such a liking to one family and they to him, that we agreed to let them have him too.

I wasn't feeling too well on March 3rd and as the day wore on I only felt worse. Thinking that I must have an infection of some sort I took an antibiotic. At that time some doctors would prescribe antibiotics for people in the bush to use if necessary. We always had some whenever we were living out of town, and although we often disposed of them unused there were times when we were thankful that we had them. This time the antibiotic did not help.

In the late afternoon I went to bed and by evening I had no doubt but that I was in labor. Labor is quite a shock when one doesn't know that they are pregnant. After my miscarriage in January I had lost weight and I showed no signs of still being pregnant. The pains started with an ache in my lower back that became acute as they shot around to the front. I began to hemorrhage with each shooting pain. Bob was frightened and he went to the new village and came back with Claude Deminitiff's sister-in-law, Jean Deminitiff. Jean, a registered nurse, stayed with me all night. She had grave concerns about my prognosis and she said that if I come out of this, we should be happy with our two beautiful wonderful boys and not try for anymore children. Bob adamantly agreed!

The next morning the whole country was a huge pool of fog with a visibility that seemed to be in the minus. Bob arranged to have us flown into Bethel with an argument that was just short of gun point. When we landed in Bethel there was an ambulance waiting to take me to the hospital. There they put me to bed and they took my blood pressure. The nurse couldn't get any reading and thinking that the machine was broken, she got another one and tried to take it again. She still couldn't get a reading so she had another nurse take it. Failing again they started an I V and they left the cuff on my arm and took my blood pressure every ten minutes all night long.

The doctor came in and asked that I be wheeled into surgery so that he could do a D and C. I started to cry and asked if there was anything that they could do to save the baby. The doctor said that he saw no possible way, but he agreed to examine me before proceeding. Afterward he was glad that he had examined me, they had thought that I was about six weeks pregnant but he discovered upon examination that I was five months along. In January it must have been either an incomplete miscarriage or I had been pregnant with twins. I was too far along in the pregnancy to safely do a D and C so they put me back to bed. I lost the baby the next morning and he or she was very small and underdeveloped.

We went shopping when I got out of the hospital and arranged to have the food and supplies shipped to Shageluk. We flew home in the mail plane and while we waited for our shipment we packed. Bob had made arrangements for us to fly to a little cabin on the Iditarod River.

Chapter 16
OOPS!
1976

The first flight to the cabin on the Iditarod River carried Bob and I, the boys, the four dogs, and a small portion of our food, supplies, and possessions. Everything else was packed up and waiting for future trips. Unlike Bob I love to fly, but that morning for the first time I was nervous. I was worrying that the dogs might get in a fight or something, but as always while flying they sat totally still. Just as we were descending, in preparation for landing on the frozen river, the pilot exclaimed, "Oops!" Before I could wonder about what might be wrong; here came the trees, bombarding us and crashing their way into the plane! Before I could check to see if we were all still in one piece, the boys and I landed outside in a snow bank. Bob had thrown us out, wasting no time in case the plane blew up.

The plane didn't blow up and we were all unhurt, the only damage done was to the plane and to the pilot's pride and confidence. He had intended to land on a straight stretch of the river, but he over shot it and crashed into the bank where the river bends. He took pictures of his plane for the insurance company and radioed his friends who came in with enough parts to get his plane back into the air and home.

Bob and I struggled through the deep snow with the boys and our baggage, plowing our way to the cabin where we intended to stay. It sat close to the river with mountains behind it. It was an eight by eight foot cabin that was built of logs. It had a wood floor on the outer two feet of all four sides and a dirt hole in the middle. Two long wooden shelves on one wall made a bunk bed and there was a wood stove that doubled for heating and cooking.

When inside the boys played in the dirt in the middle of the cabin, but except for eating and sleeping we spent most of our time outside. We went for walks and explored and waited and waited for the arrival of our food and belongings. They didn't come! I guess the pilot didn't want to push his luck by making another attempt at landing there. Later ducks, geese, swans, and cranes began to fly over head. We needed food and Bob had a shot gun—but no shot gun shells. We saw new country and lots of animals and we had a camera—but the pilot had used up our film taking pictures of his plane. Bob had used so much foresight in planning this trip and in purchasing everything that he thought that we might need. He had used the money from the Hooper Bay job to pay for the flights and for all the purchases. The only thing that he didn't foresee was the crash landing and that there would be no future flights to bring our things. All the things that we couldn't bring this first time in, wasn't coming.

For a while we had a small amount of dog food, oat meal, sugar, flour, canned vegetables, macaroni and cheese, and bacon. We had brought food to last for a week or so but the bulk of our food was left in Shageluk. I made oat meal cookies for breakfasts and we ate sparingly at night. All too soon item by item we began to run out of food, until we were down to little more than rice and bullion, the only things of which we had plenty. Bob had a twenty-two rifle with shells and occasionally he could shoot a bird if it was flying low enough. I cooked rice for the dogs also and they supplemented their diet by occasionally catching a small animal.

Without books or toys we made up stories, games, and songs for the boys. We also amused ourselves by going on long walks making a trail both ways on the frozen river. One day while returning from a walk a cow moose and her young calf were using our trail. She would not move but stood her ground, worriedly eyeing us and the dogs. We weren't looking for a confrontation and we were afraid that she would become alarmed if we tried to walk around her. Communication with the moose was at a low level while we waited and struggled to keep the dogs under control. Finally she moved on and we could go home.

One day Bob found a stash of tobacco stuck in a tree. He had been out of cigarettes for quite a while so he was most anxious to make and smoke some. The tobacco smelled funny but we thought that it was stale from being stuck in the tree for so long. It wasn't until much later when we were visiting some people who were sharing their home grown, that we knew exactly what Bob had found and smoked. The smell was not mistakable! Other than enjoying a smoke, Bob had not noticed any other effect probably because the weed was so old.

When we realized that the delivery of our supplies was not likely to happen, Bob decided to walk out to make arrangements for our eventual departure.

He had ordered and received a detailed map of the area, which (of course) was with the rest of our things back in Shageluk.

Not knowing exactly where or how far he had to go, he decided to travel lightly, too lightly as he didn't wear his parka. He was fine and moving quickly during the day, but that night it got cold and he was too tired from making trail all day to sustain his fast pace. He started to feel light headed and when he paused for a rest he looked back and saw that his trail zig zagged from one side of the river to the other and back. He was getting no where in a hurry. Realizing that he probably was getting hypothermia Bob stopped and made a fire. He used the letters that he had planned to mail to get the fire started and the warmth from the fire, a hot cup of broth, and some rice cakes revived him.

Early the next morning Bob walked into our cabin and collapsed on the bed. His face was grey, he was discouraged and almost frozen, and he could barely walk with the huge blisters that he had on his feet. We stayed close to the cabin for a few days.

We were especially glad when the days started to get warmer because none of us had a change of clothes. When we bathed and washed our clothes we had to do without until they dried. This was especially difficult for Timber who while he had them had still been in diapers. Along with the warmer weather came a rise in the water table and the hole in the middle of the cabin filled with water. An eight by eight foot cabin is too small to have an in door swimming pool! As we walked along the wooden sides of the pool, we had to be careful not to fall in. It was even more difficult to keep the boys out of it and they were wet and muddy more often than not. Despite the inconvenience we were just thankful that we'd been able to keep them from drowning or from drinking the muddy water.

Bob had ordered new boots for all of us from an army surplus store. Although they had been unused I think that they must have been stored since World War II, or maybe even World War I. Bob's and Flint's boots were barely holding up with the help of gray tape and mine literally fell apart and were beyond repair. When I absolutely needed to wear something on my feet I could wear a pair of men's size 13 boots that we had found in the cabin. The only boots in good shape were Timber's and he was the only one who didn't have to walk much.

Although the Iditarod River is much smaller than the Yukon River I found its break up even more exciting than the Yukon's. The water began to rush wildly over the ice, sailing chunks of ice and snatching small trees and brush along the way. As we watched the noisy race from time to time we would hear a loud crack, see the water whirl making a funnel, then from out of the depth of the river, a giant chunk of ice would splash to the surface. We'd hold our breaths as it seemed like a monster emerging from the sea. Whenever we heard the warning crack we'd rush over to watch the show. It was kind of scary, yet we were fascinated.

As the water was rising and nearing the cabin Bob pitched a tent on the side of a mountain and put our sleeping bags and what was left of our food and things in it. Before night fall we had to climb up to our new residence. By morning we were surrounded by water with only the top part of the roof of the cabin showing above the river. There was no place to go and nothing to do other than to watch our fifth flood. While we talked and watched, a bear went into our tent, rummaged around, and drug off the little bit of food and things that interested him. It was poor pickings for him and we followed the trail of dropped things that he left behind him. Fortunately the bear did not come visiting again and apparently he did not want our rice and bullion. Now that was absolutely all that was left of our food.

The water eventually receded so we returned to the cabin and prepared to walk out, this time it would be all of us. It now was late May, two and a half months after the plane crash. Since no one in the area had a plane with floats it was a certainty that no one would be bringing our food or coming for us, at least not until freeze up next winter. The nearest town, Flat, is not on the Iditarod or on any other river. The only hope of finding it was to follow the river to the old town of Iditarod and then follow a trail leading to Flat. Without a map we had no idea of what we were getting into. So I roped the size 13 boots on to my legs and we started out. Bob led the way carrying a pack, Flint who was now three and a half years old walked, and one and a half year old Timber rode on my shoulders.

The trip began with us making our way in the dim dawn light, just before sun rise. I felt and heard a presence in the bushes beside me and just as I headed into the brush while calling to the dogs, I noticed that all four dogs were up ahead of Bob. There, almost in touching distance, was a cow moose looking at me. She was without calf and unworried and after one glance she resumed her munching.

As the crow flies Flat is much less than 100 miles from where we had stayed. However we needed to follow the river on its winding path which made it several times farther. It was also much tougher going than walking on the ice. As we wound around on the banks of the river we had to walk through mud and brush, wade through creeks and marshes, and go around lakes. When we came to a creek that was too deep and swift to wade, we would search and find a beaver dam on which to cross. In some places the mud was so deep that it sucked us in up to our knees or higher. Flint had to be carried through these parts and I fell every other step. Each time I fell Timber would laugh and cheerfully call out from his perch on my shoulders, "Get up and go!" I think that he thought that I was falling just as a lark to add to his amusement.

At mid day we paused long enough to heat water for cups of bullion. I asked Flint if he wanted beef or chicken bullion and he looked confused. Finally he answered that he'd have moose bullion, he had no idea what beef or chicken was. I was amazed at how much nourishment a cup of plain broth offers. I had always thought that even eating soup was like eating nothing, something that one had only when they're too sick to eat real food. I gained new respect for broth and I felt much stronger after having a cup.

Once when we couldn't find a beaver dam to use as a bridge, Bob chopped down a tree, pushing it so that it fell across the creek. After he took his pack across he carried first Flint and then Timber over. After that I slowly crawled over on my hands and knees, fearfully hugging the tree trunk all the way.

Sometimes we would watch beavers swimming and at work in the river. We were so quiet that we didn't get to see or hear them slap their tails on the water. We saw several moose and towards the end of the first day Stupe and Stormy took off after one. There was no way that we could find them but we hoped that they would find us again. Sadly they did not!

That evening the boys and I were sitting on a mountain side while Bob went down to the river for water. He saw a black bear heading up the mountain toward us. He didn't want to shoot the bear, being afraid that at that distance the twenty two shells would only wound him. Bob yelled and started running up the hill but the bear went on by us, continuing his climb.

We made a campfire and cooked bullion flavored rice for dinner. I had refused to eat rice when I was pregnant with Flint, but now it was a different story—rice or nothing. We all licked our cups clean of every morsel. We hadn't brought our sleeping bags or tent so I sat by the camp fire holding two sleeping boys in my arms, with my parka tucked around us. Bob fed the campfire all night dozing in-between trips after wood. We had hung our wet socks by the fire but they and our pant legs were still wet in the morning and every morning there after.

On the second morning after another cup of rice we were again on our way. As we walked along we sang a little made up song, *Walk a little. Rest a little. Soon we'll be at Iditarod!* Flat was really our destination but our first and hardest goal was to get to Iditarod. The town was populated by one family of five and it was back away from the river, out of sight. It was also on the other side of the river. If we passed Iditarod we would never get to Flat and the next town, if there are any, would be hundreds of miles away. Also there was the problem of getting across the river, a beaver dam or a fallen tree would not do it. We thought that we were probably going to need to build a raft to get across.

As Flint got more and more tired I tried to encourage him by promising him ice cream when we reached a place where it was sold. The second or third time that I made this promise Flint asked, "What the heck is ice cream anyway?" Later he assured me that, "Even nice people get tired."

That night Bob shot a low flying goose. It landed in the lake and we tried to get the dogs to swim after it. Bob would throw them in the water but each time they climbed back out with empty mouths. Eventually Bob was able to snare the floating goose with a fish hook that he tied onto some fishing line. (As you may have guessed our fishing poles were back in Shageluk.) My goodness how we relished that goose! The bones, when we finally turned them over to the dogs, were barer than Old Mother Hubbard's cupboards.

On the fourth day out seeing no trails, tracks, or signs of people; we were afraid that we had unknowingly passed Iditarod. What to do? Should we go back to the cabin and scrounge what we could to survive, or should we go on to who knows what? Bob flopped down on the banks of the river and took a nap, while I sat fretting and stewing as I watched the boys play. It was the classic example of one of my dad's favorite sayings, "If you cross your bridges before you come to them you'll have many more bridges to cross." The distant sound of a chain saw startled me and woke Bob. People were near!

Bob shot into the air and it wasn't too long before Jim Fleming came across the river in his boat. At first Jim's sons had thought that it was him shooting and he had thought that one of them had made the shots. After they learned that none of them had shot; Jim decided that he should investigate. We had never before been as glad to see anyone, as we were Jim when he pulled ashore on our side of the river! Bob's first words to him were, "Have you got a cigarette?" We rode across the river with Jim in his boat and Sambo swam behind. Sissy refused to attempt the crossing and we could see her pacing and hear her howling from across the river. Jim had been afraid that the dogs might tip over his boat, but when Jim saw how miserable Sissy was and realized that she wasn't going to follow, he decided to take a chance and go back for her. She rode half way across the river then jumped out and swam the rest of the way.

As we walked from the boat to Jim's house Flint hung back, dragging his feet. I thought that he was exhausted after four days of walking, but I found out that he was timid and reluctant to go around new people. Jim and his family (the entire population of Iditarod) soon put us all at easy with their wonderful hospitality. The hot nourishing meal and warm shelter for the night was unbelievably delightful. Jim and Katharine have two sons and a younger daughter. I don't remember the ages of the boys but I remember their birthdays. Jim, the older boy's birthday is on August 7th as is Flint's. His brother Shawn's birthday is on September 10th as is Timber's. I've often wondered about the date of their little sister's birthday wondering if it is June 27th like our daughter's. But of course at the time we did not have our little Shianne.

The next morning with renewed strength we headed out on the trail to Flat. At one point it rained so hard that we sought shelter under a tree, huddled together under our parkas until the rain subsided. Toward evening we reached Flat, picked up almost three month's mail, and Bob was able to radio phone out. Along with the mail Bob got the promise from the postmaster that he would sell us a house there, for $300. He said that sometimes people fly in, wanting to buy antiques and he won't sell anything. We were the first ones who had ever walked there, at least since the late thirties when he first came there to live.

The Flemings had graciously offered their house in Flat to us for the night, and Bob made arrangements for us to fly to Fairbanks the next morning. Our clothes by then were filthy rags and we were a mess! Our mail contained many frantic letters from my mother and others, wondering where and how we were after such a long silence. There was also a package from Hazel, a dear friend from my girlhood. The package contained new clothes for the boys, Easter candy, toys, and hot chocolate.

Chapter 17
LIFE IN A CHICKEN HOUSE
1976 and 1977

Flint, Timber, Booger, and I by a water pump.

Our flight from Flat to Fairbanks was both fascinating and scary. Although it was early in the day the sky was like a dark menacing dragon, with its turbulent wind, rumbling thunder, and shots of lightening striking all around us. We made it safely through the obstacle course to Fairbanks and were dropped off at an air strip just out side of town.

Bob and I, the boys, the dogs, and our few possessions were a sorry sight standing forlornly on the airstrip. I would say that once again we owned little more than the clothes on our backs, except that this time our torn and muddy clothes were really just rags and I was barefoot. As soon as we had reached Flat I untied the ropes and stepped out of those huge, heavy, clumsy boots. I never intended to tie them back on. All that I had left of those boots was their memory and the rope burns that criss-crossed up my legs.

We had no transportation having lost our truck over a year ago. We had traded the boat and motor we had in Shageluk for our flight into Fairbanks. The river boat and motor that we had in Fairbanks had floated away with new owners, and this time we hadn't been there to prevent it. Our food, supplies, and belongings that had been left in Shageluk had all walked away to new homes. We gave our tent, shot gun, sleeping bags, and all that we had left at the cabin on the Iditarod River to Jim Fleming, as he had promised to go back there by boat in search of Stupe and Stormy.

So what we owned such as it was, was what we had on and beside us. It's surprising that as scraggly and motley as we were, and looking as much like road kill as we did, that we ever managed to catch a ride anywhere. However a kind man took pity on us and drove us to Tommy's and Margaret's house, and being who they are they opened their door to us. They told us that the boys looked fine but that Bob and I looked like we didn't have long to live.

I took Flint into their bathroom to wash up and when I switched on the light, Flint twirled around in surprise. "How did you light the lamp so fast?" He was also flabbergasted when I turned on the water faucet.

It's amazing what a bath, clean clothes, good and abundant food, wonderful company and a good night's sleep will do to make one feel human again! A brisk walk of about 100 miles with little food is a real effective way of losing weight. I didn't have to be careful about how much I ate for quite some time. Now that we had safely made it through, we relished the memory of our experiences. We had always hoped that we could go on another even longer hike, but next time we wanted to have good walking boots, packs, sleeping bags, shells for our rifles, film for our camera, dehydrated food, etc.

Bob found work, we rented a big (compared to our cabin) house on Farmer's Loop, and we bought a used car. Once again we would sometimes go on the job with Bob, shop in town, eat out, and visit with friends. Now with more room than we usually had we could have our friends over to our house for a change. We had several parties and picnics at the house. When we did stay at home there was lots of room for the boys to play and a large yard with an abundance of blue berries, raspberries, and strawberries to pick.

Along with the regular jobs Bob sheet rocked a couple of houses for friends. The payment for sheet rocking one house was to be a steak and beer dinner. As it turned out the owner didn't have the money for steak but the hamburgers were just as good.

Just as Jim Fleming had promised he went by boat in search of Stupe and Stormy. He found them waiting at the cabin and in good shape, so he left them there with a supply of dried salmon strips. It was an all together different story later in the summer when Jim returned to the cabin. The dogs were skin and bones, their eyes were swollen shut from mosquito bites, and Jim could read from tracks in the mud that a bear had stolen the salmon strips. Jim was concerned about how the dogs would behave in the boat, but he decided that he had to risk capsizing the boat in order to get them home. Stupe climbed into the boat at his call but Jim had to trap Stormy and put him in.

On the trip both dogs sat still in the boat and then at his house he tied them next to his dog team.

As Flint's fourth birthday neared it was all that he could talk about. Timber, who was not yet two, seemed to be a little jealous of all the commotion that it was causing. Every time that Flint told someone that he was going to be four, Timber piped in with, "I'm six!" No one believed him. We had intended to go to Alaska Land on Flint's birthday but it was raining too hard. We gave him a construction set, visited friends, and then we went home to eat his blue berry birthday cake.

When Bob got a job at Fort Greely in Delta Junction we rented a little cabin at Clear Water. Mom and Barbara, a friend of ours, came up for a visit so we rented the cabin next to ours for them. Barbara was a tiny lady with beautiful silver hair who had taught a class of mentally challenged children along with Mom and me. She was a very intuitive lady and when Mom was living alone, when ever she wasn't feeling well or was worried, Barbara would telephone with, "Elinor, what's wrong?"

While Bob worked Mom, Barbara, the boys, and I chatted, played, and went or walks finding pretty rocks and things along the way. Sometimes we would go on Fort Greeley with Bob and let the boys play on the playground, and then we would have dinner in the Officer's Quarters. We also had some great dinners at the Trophy Lodge and occasionally we went into Fairbanks.

I would love to have taken a trip like Mom and Barbara had on their way home. We drove them to Fairbanks, they flew to Whitehorse, took a little train over the Chilkoot Mountains to Skagway, and then they took the Ferry down to Seattle.

In September, we celebrated Timber's second birthday in the car while we were driving down to Summit Lake. Here we spent the weekend while Bob sheet rocked the cabin of a friend. Right afterward Bob finished his job and we went back to Fairbanks. Here we shopped and prepared to charter back to Flat and to the little house that we had bought.

When we reached Flat the first thing that we needed to do was to walk to Iditarod to get Stupe and Stormy. Jim said that he knew that we were coming even before he saw us in the distance. Stupe and Stormy, who had been subdued and quiet the whole time there, were yowling and going crazy on their chains. Jim's dogs just stared at them in wonder. We spent the night and then the next day after we had walked almost the whole way back to Flat; Stupe took off after another animal. It was too late to go back then so Bob went after him the next day. Jim told him that he had heard a ruckus and had gone out with his rifle to investigate. He saw Stupe desperately running for his life barely ahead of a pack of wolves. He shot into the air, the wolves scattered, and he saved Stupe's life again.

Bob repaired the floor of our little house and we moved in. It had two rooms, a kitchen and living room that contained two single beds and a hutch filled with old dishes and medicine bottles. For my birthday in October Mom sent me two Indian blankets for the beds and curtains for the windows. The cabin was looking good and feeling like home.

There was an old wooden paddle hanging on the wall and I mentioned to Flint that it was just the thing to use on his back sides, if he didn't listen to his mom and dad. I don't believe that I would have ever used it in that capacity, but I didn't have the chance to do so even if I had wanted to. It disappeared, I found and replaced it, and then it went floating down the creek, never to be seen again. I'm sure that Flint was the perp.

The population of Flat was three before we moved there and boosted it to seven. There were several houses that were used while people were mining there but only two were occupied in the winter. There was a house belonging to the postmaster John and his wife Bertha and another for a trapper Ernie. John and Ernie had gotten into an argument and had not spoken to each other since World War II. Every week Ernie would pick up his mail in silence. Luckily we enjoyed talking with all three of them and occasionally with Jim and his boys when they dog sledded into town. On Halloween we used white sheets and took two little snowmen trick or treating at both houses. Right after that Sissy had another litter of puppies.

We had found a wood cook stove but as of November 10th, Bob had not yet installed it in the house. I was cooking breakfast on our little gas burning camp stove while Bob and Flint went looking for Sambo, who had wandered off. Suddenly the stove blew up, shooting streams of gas in several directions. Flame followed the gas and as I put out one fire more fires started up. When I saw that I wasn't making any progress, I grabbed Timber and took him out side to safety and then I went back in after the dogs. I had to drag Sissy out and she broke away and ran back in. After dragging her out again I was looking for a way to tie her up when I saw and heard that it was too late. Flame was everywhere and it sounded like a war with Bob's ammo going off. My mind was running on a single track that said, Timber first, our dogs next, and then the puppies. If I had been able to see past my nose and think at all, I would have known that all I had to do was to take the puppies out first and Mama would have been right with them. Better yet I should have tossed the camp stove out through the kitchen window before it burned the house down.

Back when we had first arrived in Flat I complained that some of our food (especially the cases of eggs) looked like they had been air dropped. I didn't know at the time that it wasn't going to make any difference anyway, that I was going to cook all our food at once on November 10th. That was the most food that I ever cooked at one time, but I cooked it too thoroughly and there wasn't any food left to eat.

Again we were down to nothing other than what we were wearing and again I wasn't fully dressed. I discovered after the fire that my shirt had mostly burned away. I didn't even feel the burns I had until later. We did salvage one thing from the fire; I still have an iron flat iron from Flat.

Back when people were mining in Flat one of the miner's wives had some chickens. From what I was told there was a big feud about who was going to get the chicken droppings to use for fertilizer. Now the miners, wives, and chickens were all gone but the chicken poop was still there, lots of it! We stayed in Fleming's town house for a time while we prepared to move into the chicken's house.

What a time that was cleaning the house. I started with a pick and shovel, graduated to a chisel, and it was a long time before I was able to use a broom and mop. The chickens were even worse house-keepers that I am! Our kind neighbors shared what they had with us and eventually we were able to get the house clean and move in. We found a wood stove with the bottom burned out so we put it in a big wash tub (also without a bottom), with rocks under and all around it. The rocks were really nice they kept the boys from getting too close and burned and they radiated heat, keeping the house nice and warm. Once we were settled in it made a nice home. We were saddened for a while as Sissy searched everywhere for the puppies, and there was nothing that we could do to help her. Finally she seemed to forget them and she became her old self again.

On Thanksgiving we rode to Iditarod on a sled behind Ernie on his snow machine. Along the way we sang, "Over the River and through the Woods to Fleming's House we'll go." We had stuffed moose roast for dinner and a jolly visit.

In early December we saw a huge airplane and as it approached Flat, everyone was skeptical about whether it was too large to safely land on the small runway. It did and it was full of food, clothes, house hold goods, books, toys, a rifle with ammo, bedding, everything that we would need, and more. Our wonderful friends, led by Tommy and Margaret, had gathered everything and had arranged the delivery! Bob took the rifle and shot the biggest moose with the biggest rack that we had ever seen. Now we had meat and were all set for the winter.

I found some old bottles and with the food coloring that came along with all the other treasures; I filled them with colored water and put them on the window sills. We got a tree and with the aluminimum foil that had also been sent to us, we made silver bells and stars for decoration. We didn't do any Christmas shopping, make any orders, or have a single penny to our name; but it was one of the loveliest Christmas' ever. Just before Christmas the mail plane came with more toys for the boys. Among them was a battery operated record player with the record of Peter Pan from Tommy and Margaret. Flint thought that it was magic and he was enthralled with Peter Pan. He wrote him a letter asking how he could get to "Never Never Land" to see him. I explained to him on each mail day as he waited for a reply that it takes a long time for a letter to get to and return from *Never Never Land*.

As 1976 drew to a close we were thankful that we'd made it through all in one piece. With the miscarriages, the plane crash, a flood, the long trek out, the multiple losses of our belongings, and the fire; it had been a very eventful year! We were all together, healthy, happy, and we had everything that we needed. We were blessed in so many ways.

Chapter 18
THREE FIGHTS IN THREE DAYS
1977

Timber, Bob, and Flint, Davis Creek 1977

That winter in Flat was somewhat difficult for Bob, but it was a pleasant time for the rest of us. Our warm cozy house was costly for Bob who had to walk through deep snow into the woods, saw or chop down and debranch the trees with a hand saw and axe, drag them back to the house on his back, cut them to size, and finally split them. It was a full time job and one that he had to do every day.

While Bob worked on the wood pile we went to the old school house and brought back two desks and a bunch of school books. We began working on Flint's early education where we had left off in Shageluk. Timber colored and joined in with activities as he wished. He was really good at making things with clay, they were even recognizable. I read the stories out of the primary school readers to the boys and I found the novel "Christy" which I also read aloud. Flint actually followed and responded to the story, but although Timber liked some of the stories "Christy" was a bit much to hold his interest.

That winter Ina and Riley sent a box containing the things that they had salvaged from the house in Shageluk. We opened the box to find our pictures, some out of print Alaskan books of Bob's, and my second manuscript. The first one had been sent in to a publishing company and they had sent it back with some suggestions for a few changes mostly explanations for some unfamiliar terms that I had used. This manuscript had disappeared along with the other things that we had left in the house. We were certainly thankful to get our pictures and the books, Ina and Riley knew exactly what we most wanted!

Bob never was interested in trapping animals for their fur but some how the trapping urge was strong in Flint. Perhaps his heavy interest was born of Ernie's influence, but what ever the source that winter our little four year old red head had snares set all over the house. All of us were always tripping over them or getting caught, in spite of all our efforts to watch where we were stepping.

Timber didn't echo Flint's desire to set snares out, but it was his habit to take his nap when ever and where ever he wanted. One day I found him asleep outside under a light blanket of new fallen snow. Another time I searched inside and outside and was getting desperate before I found him sleeping under the bed, hidden behind the four huskies.

We all slept in one full size bed and every night before the boys dropped off to sleep, I would tell stories and sing nursery rhymes to Timber. His favorite was "Hey Diddle Diddle, the Cat and the Fiddle. The Cow Jumped over the Moon." Before he dropped off to sleep Timber's hand would always creep up to find its place on my cheekbone.

It was a very warm winter and it even rained in January. We were afraid for a while that we would lose our moose meat, but because it was hanging whole in a shelter outside instead of having been cut up and packaged, it remained Okay. I would go out and cut off a chunk as needed. We found a little sled and Jim loaned us an extra dog harness so that Sambo could pull the boys in it when we went on walks.

One day while Bob was getting wood Sambo ran off and got caught in two traps and one of them had teeth. Fortunately Bob found and released him before he became a meal for the wolves, but he did have a very sore foot for a while. We were without our usual supply of emergency antibiotics so we were really lucky that his foot didn't get infected.

There were no dogs in Flat other than ours, but we often saw wolf tracks. When the dogs were tied outside one or two fox would often visit. The fox would communicate just out of reach of the dogs until we untied them to go for a walk, then the fox would vanish out of sight and smell.

The first and last cold snap of the year came in March when it got and stayed -40 degrees and colder. That year during the Iditarod Dog Sled Race a couple of the racers from "out side" (lower 48 states) got lost. Bob joined Ernie and Jim in the search and they were found before too much harm was done to men or dogs.

The unemployment insurance from Bob's work the summer before had not been turned in to the Department of Labor. When Bob received and turned in a W2 form with his income taxes, he received all of the Unemployment checks at once. Suddenly we had money again so we began to plan a trip out, not only to Fairbanks but also to California. Since it was too cold to be outside for long the boys and I arranged the desks, chairs, and bed into a line. This became a plane for a pretend flight to Anchorage, a train for a ride to Fairbanks, a car for a drive to Haines, a ferry for a voyage to Seattle, and a train again to take us to Grandma in San Luis Obispo. Our game was surprisingly exciting and it kept us amused for a long time. It was only surpassed by the actual trip which happened shortly afterward.

It was March and still very cold when a man chartered into Flat. We quickly grabbed the dogs and some of our things from the cabin and caught a ride on the return trip to Aniak. That way neither of us had to pay the full charge for the plane flying both ways. We had to temporarily board the dogs in Aniak and then catch a regular flight to Anchorage. We turned quite a few heads in Anchorage dropping and struggling with our fancy luggage which consisted of assorted pillow cases stuffed with our clothes and things and tied with shoe strings. At the security gate Bob had to unpack bunches of things from the six pockets of his outer pants, and then drop his draws so that he could remove everything from the pockets of his inner pants. Quite an audience gathered commenting and laughing about the conglomeration of things (snare wire, fish line and hooks, leatherman, matches, gauze, water purification tablets, etc. etc. etc.) that had come out of his pockets.

We spent the night in Anchorage and then took the train to Fairbanks. The train ride took all day and we saw beautiful scenery, McKinley and other mountains, moose, bear, and caribou. Our dogs were shipped down to us in Fairbanks and Bob hung some sheet rock. Soon we were ready to resume our trip, so we boarded the dogs with Terry and Joan, bought a Maverick from Tommy and Margaret, and headed out. The road between Haines Junction and Haines was so muddy and full of ruts that Bob could hardly keep the car moving and on the road. By the time we reached Haines the car was barely running and we were the last people to make it over the road.

The next morning we left the car at a service station for repair and storage and boarded the ferry. My excitement was mounting as the ferry neared and it was almost insurmountable by the time we walked on, still carrying our pillow case luggage. Because of the impassability of the road there were not many other passengers. It was our intention to sleep on the lounge chairs on deck as people often do but we immediately saw that that wouldn't work. While I was arranging things on and under the chairs, Timber decided that he would climb up on the rail! We saw that there could be no chatting, reading, sleeping, or anything, if our eyes were off of Timber for even a minute he might fall over board. Fortunately since the ferry was not at all crowded we were able to get a cabin. There we could lock the door and safely sleep, bathe, or read while the boys played.

That part of the trip was so luxurious and exciting. I thrilled to eating out in the dinner, walking along the deck, and being rocked to sleep in a bunk. All the while there was gorgeous scenery, all the new towns that I hadn't seen before, and sometimes a show put on by the dolphins which were playing in the wake of the ship. It was so much fun!

Our overnight ride on the train going from Seattle to San Luis Obispo was also very enjoyable. The challenge of going from car to car without landing on someone's lap, eating in the dining car, and watching the scenery clatter by while we were eating or playing added frosting to the joy. On the train in Alaska the boys had watched the moose, bear, caribou and other animals with interest. Now in Washington, Oregon, and California, the boys were ecstatic when they saw a horse, cow, or sheep. Other passengers smiled and shook their heads at their screams of delight.

Jim and Betty were visiting Mom when we arrived in San Luis Obispo. It was the day before Easter and they had brought eggs to color, candy, and toys. We enjoyed a ham dinner, Easter egg hunt, and a wonderful visit with Jim and Betty before they had to return to their home and jobs.

The days that followed were filled with trips to town, the beach, lots of visiting with family and friends, and some work for Bob. Then we caught a bus to Seattle and rode the ferry back up to Haines. We discovered that the car had needed no repair. Once the ton of mud on the underside of the car dried and fell off it was again in good mechanical condition. We picked up our dogs and drove back to Davis Creek. It had been a wonderful trip; but we were glad to be home again at last!

As was so often the case we were not able to stay home as long as we would have liked. It was necessary that we go back into Fairbanks for work, and once we were there Bob quickly found a job. The boys and I would go on the job with Bob in the mornings, he would take us to Alaska Land for the boys to play in the afternoons, and we would mostly visit with our friends in the evenings.

In July we (Bob, the boys, the dogs, and I) all flew to Kaltag, so that Bob could sheet rock another high school. We moved into the elementary school for the summer. It was on the out skirts of the village so it was peaceful and we had privacy. Again we slept on the floor and used a camp stove for cooking. In the evenings we often went for walks, fished, and cooked hot dogs and roasted marshmallows on the banks of the Yukon River. Occasionally they would show a movie and since they only showed films of good taste, we could take the boys to see them.

Sometimes the boys and I would walk to the General Store in the center of the village. This should have been a pleasant time, one to be looked forward to; except that I was becoming somewhat leery. Some of the village men were too pushy and they didn't seem to think that my being married should be a deterrent to their overly friendly behavior. With difficulty and embarrassment, I was able to avoid and discourage their advances but then there was the problem of convincing their wives that I had not been flirting with their husbands!

During the day children came to play in the school yard so the boys had lots of children to play with. The children played amiably every day except for one day when a boy was pushed off of the top of the slide, breaking his arm. I tied a magazine around his arm and took him to the health aid who then called in a plane to take him to the hospital. I was thankful that both of our boys were inside with me when the incident occurred. That way no one could point a finger at either of them.

The construction camp sent over cup cakes on Flint's fifth birthday and we had a little party with the village children. His grandmother sent him Miggs, a stuffed monkey that became his companion for years to come.

At the end of August when they had to get the school ready for fall, we had to move to a little cabin right behind the store. I had misgivings about living right in the middle of the village but we managed to avoid all mishaps. In the three days that we stayed there, there were three fights right in front of the cabin. On the first day the fight was between two young men, on the second day it was between two old men, and on the third day it was two women fighting. I brought the boys inside during the first two fights but they were playing with another boy outside when the third fight broke out. The other boy paid little attention while the women pulled hair, screamed, and kicked as they rolled around on the ground. Shortly after one of the women had run off, with the other woman right behind her; another child passed by asking, "Who won the fight, your mother or the other one?"

The boy nonchalantly answered, "My mom did."

On the day that Bob finished the job I was packing up in preparation for going back to Fairbanks, when a man stopped by the cabin. He asked me if Bob smoked and I told him that he did. It was a mistake I guess because when Bob was walking home the man wanted him to smoke a joint with him. When Bob said that he didn't use it the man called him a liar, saying that I had told him that he did. Bob managed to avoid having to fight the man, but he told me that in the future I need to be careful of what I say to people. I guess that smoking means different things to different people.

Chapter 19
A NEW LITTLE GAL
1977—1978

Flint and Shianne, San Luis Obispo, Calforrnia 1978

Once back in Fairbanks we celebrated Timber's third birthday with a big party; then as the kids (mostly teenagers) continued partying, we took our adult friends out to dinner at Club Tokyo. Bob started sheet rocking the new post office in Fairbanks and Flint started kindergarten at Wood River Elementary School.

The school offered a room with toys and books for mothers with preschool children. When the principal, Darrelyn dropped her daughter off in Flint's class on the first day of school the little girl was happy, but Darrelyn was in tears. It was the opposite with Flint, he was scared and cried and although we didn't cry and we were able to leave him in the class room, we didn't get any farther away than the parking lot that day.

After that first day of school Bob was able to go back to work, and I would take Flint to class and then Timber and I would hang out in the other room with other mothers and preschoolers. Timber considered that room his school and I enjoyed visiting with the other mothers. One of them was a free lance writer and after talking with her; she asked if she could write an article about our experiences on the Iditarod River. I agreed but I didn't know that she actually wrote the article until much later when friends began to tell us that they had read it in the *Alaska Sportsman*.

On Friday evenings Wood River School would show movies for children and the gym was available for the use of the parents. A bunch of our friends would come with us to play volley ball while the boys watched the movies. It was like old times playing volley ball again and Bob was in his element. He was still fast and could have been a one man team except for his consideration of the rest of us who wanted to play. I'm not so sure that he couldn't have played on both sides of the net if he had so chosen. After wards we'd all go out to eat just like we used to do in San Jose.

On my first parent-teacher conference the teacher informed me that Flint could now write an F on his papers, and that they were working on the other letters in his first name. She said that if I would help him learn things like the colors and a few numbers, he would then not need to answer all questions with, "I don't know." Since he'd been writing the alphabet and counting to 100 since the age of three, I was confused about what he was trying to pull off, or why. I told her what he could do but she didn't seem to believe me. Since we didn't stay in Fairbanks long enough for a second conference I don't know if she ever learned the truth.

After the conferences they had a little get together in the gym. I stepped away when someone wanted to show me something and the moment that I was out of Flint's sight, he panicked. When I came back to him he was in Principal Darrelyn's arms, as she assured him that she knows me and knows that I wouldn't have left him. Timber on the other hand would have loved to have run off to play if I had allowed him to escape.

Our friends two brothers had bought a lot of the property just out of town in the hills over looking the Chena River. Now that property is all houses and many of them were built by the brothers. They would build a house one at a time, sell it, and then they would build another. Bob sheet rocked a house for them and they asked us to pick a spot, buy building materials, and then they would build a house for us. It was agreed that we could pay for the property and labor on down the line as we could afford to do so. We went ahead with the plan and we joined them in working on the house evenings and weekends. It turned out to be a beautiful little A framed house and we moved into it in October, just before my birthday.

Bob finished sheet rocking the post office in November and there was no more work for him. At that time I started getting sick and found that I was pregnant again. After going through double miscarriages in Shageluk and since we were broke again after paying for all the building materials, Bob was not happy! In fact he was down right angry! Perhaps because of the way Bob felt I was even sicker than usual. On top of the usual inability to keep food down I was getting dizzy and I had to keep stopping what I was doing to sit with my head down by my knees to keep from passing out. It was not a happy time!

When Bob was laid off work they gave him a turkey for Thanksgiving. Bob was in such a bad mood that we turned down all invitations and we planned to keep to ourselves at home. Our wood stove went out the night before Thanksgiving, so our turkey was still frozen when it was time to bake it. We had a wood cooking stove too, but on that day I was having a difficult time getting the fire lit, and keeping it going once I got it started. Because of Bob's mood I was not about to ask him for help. Consequently our turkey was still mostly raw at dinner time. I had had to run in and out of the house all day (the plumbing wasn't yet complete in the house) and it didn't seem to matter if there was anything in my stomach to lose. I had also been up and down all day trying to stay conscious. It was not a pleasant day!

Bob retained his fear but his anger became subdued enough for us to celebrate Christmas, enjoy a camp fire and hot dog roast on New Years Eve, and to play volley ball at the school on our thirteenth wedding anniversary. However, things worsened again right afterward. The brothers who had built our house sent a son to Germany over Christmas vacation and they brought their mother over from Germany. These costly trips put them in a financial bind and they wanted the rest of the money that we owed them. We didn't have it and feelings were rough!

In Fairbanks it had cost $4,000 for Flint's cesarean birth and $6,000 for Timber's. We had finally been able to pay the hospital bills and now we were facing an $8,000 bill for the new baby, along with what was still owed on the new house. Since we were broke and out of work it seemed like everything was falling down on us. I was still sick and considering everything, we decided that the wisest thing to do would be to borrow enough money to go back to California. There the medical expenses would be less and Bob could probably find work. It would be difficult for friends to board our dogs in the winter so we took them to a kennel. Then, again in the Maverick, we drove to Haines and took the ferry outside. We stopped and visited with family as we drove down to San Luis Obispo and Grandma. The trip was fun especially since by then I was finally over being so sick.

We stayed with Mom throughout February while we looked for a house to rent. It was not easy hunting as we needed to find a place that allowed children and dogs. We needed to have the dogs sent down to us as it was expensive boarding them in Fairbanks and we wanted them with us. We looked at several small houses that we wanted to rent, but when they saw that we were a family of four with one on the way, they wouldn't rent to us. They said that we would be too crowded and would not stay. We told them that we were used to living in a one room cabin but they still refused.

Bob found work right away but because it had been raining so much he had to wait to start. I registered in a maternity program that cost $2,000 for the doctor, hospital, and all. The $6,000 difference from what it would have cost in Fairbanks paid for our trip out many times. To keep costs down they said that I would not need to see the doctor until the last month of the pregnancy.

In March we rented a four bed room house with a fenced in yard in Grover City. We were not used to all that room so we stored our things in the bed rooms, and we all slept on the floor in the living room. That was cozy and more like what we were used to. Bob's work was now ready to go and Flint started back in kindergarten. Timber and I would walk him to and from school with a wonderful view of the ocean along the way.

I caught a cold and called the clinic to see what medicine was safe for me to take. The doctor happened to answer my call and I told him that I was going to be his patient in a couple of months. He asked me questions and when I told him that I was forty, he said that he wanted me to start having weekly visits immediately. Each week I would go to Mom's, wash clothes, and leave the boys with her while I saw the doctor. Bob was working so much that he didn't get to meet my doctor until after delivery. This was probably just as well since he may not have liked the fact that he looked like Matthew McConaughey.

Friends in Alaska told us that the ex-friend (our partner in the new house) wanted to talk to Bob. Bob called him but he hung up as soon as he heard Bob's voice. So much for talking, instead he up and sold the house! I never did find out what happened to our belongings that we had left in it. Still another financial set back!

We had Sissy and Stormy sent down to us and we were anxious to be able to send for Stupe and Sambo. In the evenings and on weekends we would take them running on the beach or take them with us when we went fishing at Lake Lopez. Between these trips and doing things with Mom and friends, we were enjoying a busy happy spring.

School ended for the year and Bob's work began to slack off. We decided that since the baby's due date was nearing, that we would move back with Mom until afterward. We moved in with Mom on June 26th and I went to the hospital in the early morning on the 27th. On that day we were blessed with our beautiful little daughter, Shianne. I thought that the three children would be enough so I had agreed to have my tubes tied while I was still on the operating table. I had so much scar tissue, probably from the miscarriages, that the doctor had a difficult time finding the tubes at all. At first when Bob saw the umbilical cord he thought that we had another son. He suggested that they put him back; until he discovered that he was a she. Shianne was still very small when I began to wish that I could have more babies. I never did get over the urge and in my mid fifties; right after losing my Bobby I almost had myself convinced that I was expecting a child. I still sometimes dream that I am pregnant, and in my dreams the doctors shake their heads in dismay. None of them are very anxious to have a maternal patient in her seventies!

Mom brought the boys to see their little sister and as they looked through the nursery window, Shianne started to cry. Before anyone knew what he was doing Timber was out the door, down the hall, he had grabbed a nurse by the skirt, and demanded, "My baby is crying!" Nothing would do except for the nurse to go right in to tend to his baby. On my last night in the hospital they gave Bob and me a steak dinner with champagne. There was even a vase with a red rose on the tray.

For the next few weeks the kids and I stayed with Mom, and Bob went down to Concord and found work. There was a steady parade of friends who came to visit Shianne, bringing gifts. There were too many occasions to get out the ice cream and cookies to be good for our figures, but it was all fun. Shianne was such a delight and she rarely cried. I started feeding her chopped food from the table when she was a few days old and we gave her cotton candy at the State Fair when she wasn't much older. Putting her in dresses, bonnets, pinafores, and sandals was fun and so was buying girl type toys and books. She nursed hungrily but she refused to drink water or juice out of a bottle. After she had chucked enough bottles for me to get the picture, I started letting her drink from a glass with just a little help.

Bob bought an old truck to use for work, leaving me the maverick while he was away. In July I found another house in Oceano that had a fenced in back yard. Bob came home for the weekend and after we ate the cake that we had baked for his forty second birthday, we drove out to look at the house. We drove separately as Bob wanted to leave the Maverick parked there. It was dark and when I got to the end of the speed-up lane leading to the highway all I could see was lights coming toward me, lots of them. I couldn't judge how far away they were or how fast they were coming. All I knew was that there wasn't a gap anywhere near as big as I felt that I needed. One is not supposed to even slow down on the acceleration lane, but I was scared and I came to a full stop and stayed there. I sat there afraid to get on to the high way until finally Bob went around me, pulled onto the highway, and stopped, leaving an open lane for me to go in front of him. There were some bellowing horns and some angry drivers on the highway that night! I still shutter at the thought of the danger I had put Bob into!

We moved into the house and celebrated Flint's sixth birthday. Jim and Betty came to visit bringing Nancy, their youngest daughter, who would be living with Mom while she attended Junior College in San Luis Obispo. It was fun having Nancy to join us in our trips to the beach, down town, fishing, and on picnics. She loved playing with the boys and the dogs and she took rolls and rolls of pictures of Shianne. Then of course Bob had someone new to tease.

Flint was afraid that now that we had the truck we were going to sell the Maverick. To prevent this from happening he hammered nails into the tires. Luckily they did not blow up and hurt Flint, but there would be no driving the car until we could afford to get them fixed. Before we were able to get the car back on the road, it had another mishap. We had gone on a job with Bob in the truck and we returned home to a burned up Maverick. Tony, the seven years old boy who lived next door had taken papers out of the glove compartment, placed them on the front seat, and set fire to them. He must have been a really good fire starter, because all that was left was a charcoaled shell. It was one very frightened little boy whose mother made him wait in front of our house until we returned. It was fortunate that Flint had also taken and hidden the gas cap, if it had been in place the car would probably have become a bomb that blew up the house as well. If we had owned the house instead of renting it, it probably would have been gone with the car. We were really beginning to think that we just weren't meant to own and keep anything. However no matter how many times that we got knocked down materially, we always felt that we would still all be Okay and all together.

We celebrated Timber's fourth birthday and Flint started school in the first grade. Just as before we walked him to and from school, but now we had Shianne to bring along, pushing her in a stroller. After a while Flint began to complain that the children didn't like him because of his red hair. I thought that he must be imagining it until in the first teacher-parent conference the teacher said that the children were giving him a bad time for that reason. Almost all the children were dark skinned with black hair; maybe they thought that his red hair was freakish.

We sent for Stupe and Sambo and our delight in having them with us again was only surpassed by Sambo's determination to be near Bob. He greeted us all with his enthusiastic devotion, but while we were petting and hugging him he kept his eyes on Bob. A nod from Bob and he would be out of our arms and by his side. We had checked carefully to be sure that the fence was high and sturdy enough to keep the dogs in the back yard. We didn't have any problems with them breaking out; on the contrary when we wanted to take them for a run on the beach they kept running back in the yard.

The gate did get opened by someone a couple of times and Sissy was the only one who ever left the yard. One time she caught and brought a neighbor's hen over to the house. The chicken was a ruffled ball of angry feathers but she was unhurt. We returned her to her owner. The other time that Sissy got out we had returned from visiting Mom and Nancy to find her hurt in front of the house. She had been hit by a car and we thought that she might have broken her leg. Fortunately she soon began to put it on the ground and although she was limping, we knew it wasn't broken. One night while Bob was working and the dogs were resting in the house they suddenly jumped up and ran into the bed room. All I heard as I headed that way was the sound of the window being slammed closed. Someone hadn't bargained for four big dogs when he tried to break in. After that I kept them in the house whenever Bob was away.

Nancy helped the boys make costumes for Halloween and she took them trick or treating. Flint was a pizza, wearing a baker's tall hat. I don't remember what Timber was but I do remember that they were two very excited and happy boys! While Nancy was with friends we took Mom to share Thanksgiving with Bob's family. Mom and Nancy went to New Jersey to spend Christmas with Jim and Betty, who had just moved there. We had a quiet pleasant holiday at home. Mom and Nancy got back in time to celebrate the New Year, and then Bob had to find work out of town again.

Chapter 20
WHERE IS TIMBER?
1979—1980

Flint, Shianne, and Timber, Las Vegas 1979

In mid January Bob found work in Las Vegas and I packed up and cleaned the house. He came back early February in time to help us celebrate Mom's 74th birthday and then we moved to Las Vegas with him. We bought a cab over camper and moved it to a camp ground. It was too big for our truck and Bob needed the truck for work anyway, so we put it on the ground and hooked up to electricity and water. It was a little crowded with five in the camper but we were comfortable and happy there and dogs were allowed. Flint started in another first grade; and still using the stroller for Shianne, Timber and I walked him to and from school.

When we first arrived in Las Vegas it was unusually cold and there was a snow storm that left a few inches on the ground. Bob went to work like always but he found that no one else was there. It was surprising news to him that people can not work or go about their usual business in the snow. So being well acquainted with snow we went camping instead. Again we were reminded of the meaning of the term "four dog night;" and the heat that our four dogs provided in the camper shell was well worth the price of being a little squished.

The first time I walked to the grocery store I found that the prices were so high that I couldn't bring myself to buy anything. Poor Bob returned from work, tired and hungry, with no supper ready and no food to cook. Bob went shopping and brought home lots of food. After that I faced the prices with gritted teeth and determination, and forced myself to buy what we needed.

In the evenings we would often go out to dinner, driving, and target practicing in the desert. Every weekend we went exploring; camping at an old ghost town, at the Red Rock Park, or camping, fishing, and wading at Lake Mead. Contrary to the grocery stores the restaurants in Las Vegas were inexpensive. The town made its money from the gambling, drinking, etc. We didn't indulge in the drinking or etc. and Bob only gambled enough to win the cost of our dinners. He did this so often that finally his favorite dealer suggested that he ought to save the time and just give Bob enough money for our meal.

While we were there Timber could not resist playing in water and mud. I made a half hearted attempt to stop it at first, but soon I found that it was easier for all concerned to just let him play and it was even more fun to join him. Wet and muddy clothes were a small price to pay. We began to notice that Timber's speech was not as clear at four as it had been at three. Also when he was younger he had had a larger vocabulary, using surprisingly big words. Often we would ask him to do something and he would respond by doing something all together different. We took him to be tested and they found that he was very definitely hard of hearing. He should have had tubes put in his ears but at that time they used them much less frequently, only as a last resort. He was given medicine which decreased the fluid in his ears and improved his hearing for a short while. However the problem kept recurring for many years and his hearing suffered because of it.

We were outside most of the time and in the warm spring sun, Timber's and Shianne's hair turned almost snow white. It was a striking contrast to the dark brown tan that they acquired. Flint kept his red hair and he only freckled or burned in the sun. We were all enjoying the weekly trips and daily outings. The children could play with enough room in the camp park and they found other children to play with. One day a mother in the park stopped by the camper to talk to me about Flint.

"Your son threatened to beat up my son and I'm not having it! You've got to do something about it! "

"Isn't that your son with the dark hair; the one who rides by on his motor bike?"

"Yes. So?"

"He must be about thirteen, isn't he? Flint is only six. I don't see how ... he can't be afraid of him, can he? Um... well ...I'll talk to Flint about it."

"I hope so. I didn't know that he was so little, but still ... he shouldn't go around threatening people."

Flint said that he had told the boy that he would beat him up if he didn't stop chasing him with his motor bike. The next day as I was watching, I saw the boy attempt to run Flint down and I went out to talk to him. "You need to ride more carefully on your bike and get your amusement with kids your own age. Flint is only six years old."

"So what! Tell him to stay out of my way!"

I told Bob and he talked to the boy. I don't know what was said but he never came back on our side of the park, either on or off of his bike.

In May Bob finished his job, we sold the camper, and then we surprised Mom by showing up at her mobile home unexpectedly. We had a nice visit with her and were there to greet her with a special dinner and gifts on Mother's Day when she returned from her volunteer work at the hospital. Our time with her was followed by visits to all of Bob's family, in their homes or by joining them on fishing-camping trips.

In June with all our visiting done we were finally ready to head home to Alaska. Since the old truck had over two hundred thousand hard miles on it, we were keeping our fingers crossed that it would hold up for the trip home. While driving back up the highways, Bob looked for work. The first stop was in Idaho where we camped by a little creek and Bob searched the work scene with no success. The boys played happily in the creek but Shianne was teething and she had a very rare cranky spell.

Next we drove to Spokane, Washington and the children and I played in a park while Bob made some calls. While I was watching Shianne play in a sand box, checking to be sure that she didn't supplement her lunch with sand; Flint and Timber brought me almost two hundred dollars. Of course I asked them where they had gotten it and Flint pointed to the mother of some children with whom they had been playing. I took it back to her and she explained that she had the feeling that we might need it and that she wanted us to have it. Until then the lady and I had never even exchanged one word, only smiles. I couldn't accept the money but the fact that she was more than willing to give so much money to people who she didn't even know really impressed me! Over the years her intuitiveness, kindness, and generosity has been an inspiration that has meant so much!

Bob didn't find work here either so we drove on up to Vamp and Jasper, through the beautiful Canadian Rockies. Here we saw an abundance of moose, caribou, elk, antelope, mountain sheep, mountain goats, and bear; all intermixed with the breathtaking mountains themselves. I've always hoped that I could return and view the gorgeous spectacle again. If only I could do it with my Bobby!

The trip home was all pleasure, all the way past Dawson City almost to the Canadian-Alaska border; then the truck decided that it had done enough and it quit. We were towed up the side of the last mountain to the border and we were then able to coast the rest of the way down to the cabin. After a bit Bob was able to get the truck running again. It was so good to be home after over a year's absence! We celebrated Shianne's first birthday on June 27th and then went up to the lodge for a fish fry on the 4th of July.

While we had been "out side" in the lower states my brother Jim's and Betty's eldest daughter Patti, had moved up to Eielson Air Force Base near North Pole, Alaska; along with her husband Rob and their daughter Carolyn. Early in July we made a run into town for food and supplies, visited with our friends, and we stayed with Patti and Rob.

When we went to see Margaret and Tommy an unexpected visitor was waiting for us. She was the wife of the ex-friend who had sold our house. She was shaking in her boots before we arrived, and she was very relieved to see that I was with Bob. I don't know what she expected Bob to do or say, but she had known us long enough that she should have known that Bob would be nothing other than kind to her. She had a list with the prices of most of the building materials that we had bought and she wanted to pay us back herself. She was a carpenter-electrician and part of the building team along with her husband and brother-in-law. Over the next several years, little by little, she paid us back a lot of what we had spent without the help of her husband.

As I was shopping for groceries in the big Hub store that used to be in Fairbanks; Timber walked beside me encouraging me, giving me assistance, and applauding everything that I put into the cart. The assistance was in the form of grabbing everything that he thought that I should be buying. He put a big can of Crisco in my cart because he thought that it was cherry pie, like the pie pictured on the label of the can. So my shopping was a process of selecting what I wanted to buy and taking out what I didn't need. The real trouble started when I started loading the food on the counter in order to pay for it. Timber was aghast! (She's going to give all the food back? NO WAY!) Before I could convince him that we would get the food back as soon as I paid for it, he ran away. Bob had just gone out to the truck with a load of food and I thought that Timber had run after him. After I paid and pushed the groceries out to the truck, to my horror I discovered that Timber was not out with his dad! We hurried back into the store and searched and called but there was no Timber! The management and workers in the store all searched and called over the loud speaker, both in the store and in the back storage. Still no Timber!! The police were called and they searched the store, the parking lot, and the surrounding streets. It was put on the radio and T.V. that we were searching for a small blond boy. Hours passed with no sight or sound of our little boy and we were desperate! The police were just having their dogs smell Timber's sweater, when Timber crawled out from behind a stack of stored soda crates, where he had been soundly sleeping.

He walked up to a policeman proclaiming, "I want my mommy and daddy!"

The policeman was only too happy to bring him to us. We experienced about every imaginable feeling from joy to anger! After that day many people stopped us to say that they were glad to see that we had found our Timber.

Shianne took her first steps while we were in town. I think that the wavy rough floor in the cabin at home had her buffaloed. Apparently the smooth carpeted floors in Patti's house looked more inviting. Once on her feet she couldn't seem to get enough of walking and she toddled around with a proud grin on her face. Once at home she had to master the ocean like floor of the cabin and the rough mountainous terrain of our yard.

Later in July John and Katharine came up to Davis Creek with friends who were visiting in order to have a picnic and to do some hand mining on the creek. We joined them and the hand mining intrigued us so much, that we continued to hand mine for the rest of the summer. Just as John had done we set a small wooden sluice box containing ripples in the creek, set at an angle. Then we built a dam so that the creek water would run down through the sluice box. Bob and Flint would dig in the side of the hill and put in the dirt, shovel by shovel to wash down the sluice. I would sit beside the sluice, washing the dirt off of the bigger rocks and then throwing them aside. All the while Shianne played, ate, nursed, and took naps on the ground beside us.

Timber had his own little operation down stream from us, using a teaspoon and an egg carton. Just before his soggy sluice fell apart I panned his pay dirt and found quite a bit of gold. His spot looked more promising than ours did so we moved down by him. At the end of each day we would take out the riffles and I would pan the dirt. Before I was finished I would be soaking wet up to my arm pits. Then unless the day was really warm it would take hours for me to get warm again. We did this every day for the rest of the summer, and although it didn't make us materially wealthy we had some gold to go along with our real wealth.

Fall comes to the Forty Mile Country by early August and the fall colors are brighter than those in Fairbanks. We have more orange and red amidst the yellow. It's a wonderful time of year, it's so beautiful, the creeks are full of grayling, the hills are covered with blueberries, and the nights start to freeze, killing the mosquitoes. We celebrated Flint's seventh birthday and then some children from a neighboring mine came to visit for a few days. Patti and Rob also brought some of their friends up to stay with us, hand mine, and to pick blue berries. Flint dug into the side of the hill and carried bucket after bucket of dirt to their sluice box for them. At the cabin we called him our running water because he would go down to the creek and run up the hill carrying two 5 galllon buckets of water for us. We also called him our garbage disposal because his appetite matched his size and strength, and we never had any leftovers or scraps after dinner.

In September we made a trip into town to get our winter's provisions and we stayed with Patti and Rob again. Now Fairbanks was getting its fall colors so we got to experience my favorite season twice. While in town we celebrated Timber's fifth birthday along with their daughter Carolyn's second one. It was our intention to return to the cabin for the winter after we had shopped and visited with our friends; but Thelma, Margaret's mother; asked us to stay out at her homestead on the Parks Highway. Her husband, our dear friend Swede, had passed away while we were in California; and Thelma had moved into Fairbanks next to Tommy's and Margaret's house. With some reluctance we agreed and went home just to pack up instead of going home to stay.

At the homestead we stayed in a trailer with a small wanigan attached. There was no electricity or plumbing so our life style was similar to what it was at home. One difference was that now we hauled water whenever we went to town and only had to supplement it by melting snow. We went into town to shop, wash clothes at a Laundromat, and to see friends about once a month. Bob looked for work but that didn't happen, some winters just don't have much going on. Flint started riding the bus in to school in Fairbanks starting in the second grade, again in Wood River School. Thelma's home-stead is where Swede and Thelma lived near the Nenana Road School, where I taught their son and where *I* first met them and Tommy and Margaret. Now the school was gone, school aged children were bused into Fairbanks, and Nenana Road had become the Parks Highway.

I started teaching Timber kindergarten through a correspondence course that was mailed to us from Juneau. The activities were fun for both of us and Shianne could join in with some of them. We had our usual monthly trips to town and on weekends Patti and Rob would frequently come out to stay for a day or two. We had planned to go to their house to take the kids trick or treating on Halloween, but it warmed up enough to turn the roads to ice. Flint was very late coming home from school and driving fifty miles to Patti's and Rob's on slippery roads was not what we wanted to do in the dark. So instead we walked down the road to trick or treat the neighbors, but no one was home. Then we returned to the trailer to party on our own. With all his usual clowning Bob made it more fun anyway.

We did make it to Eielson for Thanksgiving, however. We picked Flint up from school the day before and went straight to their house. After nice hot baths in a tub, T.V., wonderful meals, and catching up on everything that was going on with everyone, we returned home, stopping for pie with Tommy and Margaret on the way.

We spent Christmas Eve with Tommy, Margaret, Thelma, and the kids (theirs and ours); and Patti, Rob, and Carolyn came out to spend Christmas day and night with us at the homestead. Then on New Year's night, Sissy had two puppies, both female. We named the biggest pup Sugar and called her Sugey and Shianne named the littlest pup Pupa. Sugey, who was probably Sambo's daughter, was mostly black and she grew up to be sleek and graceful. Pupa was also black but with a very pronounced white mask and markings. She stayed small, looking like a miniature husky. Now we had six dogs.

Chapter 21
GOLD, JOHN, GOLD!
1980

Timber and Shianne, Parks Highway 1980

It was a nice winter with many happy times, but by early spring we were more than ready to go home. After celebrating Easter with Patti and Rob we packed up and drove back to the cabin. When we stopped in Chicken to see John and Katharine, John said that he wanted to start mining with Bob on Davis Creek. The cabin sits on John's mining claims and several years earlier he and Katharine had spent a couple of months there exploring. During the week John worked on the highway and on weekends he came to Davis Creek to make plans and then to get ready for mining.

There was a lot of preparation before we could begin mining. John had a D6 dozer at his homestead in Chicken and he brought it up to the mine. After they decided where they wanted to start mining they built a big sluice box out of steal. The sluice consisted of an old truck bed for a dump box with a long open ended sluice box (about 18 ft by 4 ft) attached. A nugget box with holes in the top was placed where the two boxes were attached. Carpeting was put in the bottom of the sluice box and riffles were placed about six inches apart all the way down. A hill had to be made so that the sluice rested at the correct angle for its length. Then a ditch had to be dug that went from the creek, along the side of the hill to where it was piped into the top of the dump box. The cut that we were going to mine had to be stripped down to pay dirt. We were lucky we only had a few feet of overburden to strip; some places have to be stripped down hundreds of feet. A dirt ramp had to be built leading to the top of the dump box and several settling ponds had to be made to catch the mud so that it wouldn't wash down the creek.

When we were finally ready to mine, the creek was diverted so that it ran through the ditch and into the sluice. John used his dozer to push pay dirt up the ramp and into the top of the dump box. The water from the ditch washed the dirt and rocks over the nugget box, down the sluice, over the riffles, and out at the bottom. Large rocks would not wash down by themselves, so we had to keep them moving with shovels. When a rock was too large to push with the shovel we had to shut off the water and it had to be manually picked up and thrown out. Sometimes it would take both Bob and John to pry a big boulder out. When the rocks piled up at the bottom of the sluice, they had to be pushed away with the dozer into a tailing pile. As all this was going on the gold would drop down into the nugget box or down into the carpet beneath the riffles. We panned the dirt from the nugget box after each day of mining. When we were finished with a cut we would take the riffles out and wash all the squares of carpeting into a big tub and then pan all the dirt. This took all day and then the gold would still need to be blown to get fine pieces of sand out of it. This was done very carefully by mouth while one is shaking the plate that it is on. After that we would need to start all over again, setting up a new spot to mine and moving the sluice box.

On mining days we heard the greetings, "Gold, John, Gold!" or "Gold, Bob, Gold!" being called up and down the creek. John was the operator and Bob, Flint, and I worked the shovels, keeping the rocks moving. The original plan was for just John and Bob to mine, but I don't think that they made even one day before I was out there with them, shovel in hand. I loved it and I only left the sluice to fix us all some lunch and later to prepare a late dinner for after we were done. We had a big wall tent set up at the cut with a camp stove for cooking. At night John slept in the tent and we returned to the cabin.

It was fun herding the rocks with a shovel and my mentality is such that I can happily do the same thing hour after hour without getting bored. However this was not the case with Flint and he soon turned in his shovel to learn how to operate the dozer. He learned immediately, did a great job, and we were both happy. As I worked during the day I could look up and see trucks with campers driving over the mountains into Canada. They looked like a wagon train traveling across the country. At the end of the day it was exciting to see how much gold was in the nugget box.

While we mined Timber and Shianne played close by. I was fortunate that I could depend on them to stay close, out of the way of the dozer, and to stay out of mischief. However Shianne did become known as the Davis Creek Streaker because she kept removing her clothes and scattering them up and down the creek. Every wash day entailed walking the creek to gather up her clothes before I could start the wash. We all got our clothes so dirty that I had to scrub every inch of every item with a scrub brush in order to get them clean. We only got two small cuts mined that summer, since we were only mining two days a week and we weren't mining many yards an hour. In a dry spell the creek would get too low for us to mine at all and then we would need to wait for rain. I sure liked it when we could mine and I would look forward to rain. It seemed like it rained whenever I hung clothes out to dry so I began to wash our clothes accordingly. We got a lot of gold considering how little we did.

Katharine and the kids came up to the mine on the weekend in June to help us celebrate Shianne's second birthday; and they came again in August to join us when we celebrated Flint's eighth. On Bob's birthday in July we went up to the lodge and they gave him pie with a fire cracker stuck in it for a candle.

In between our mining days we did all the usual things. We'd go up to get our mail on Fridays and visit with the other miners and their families. Sometimes kids came down to stay at the cabin with the boys for a night or two. Then Bob embarrassed Flint by doing things like playing peek-a-boo, using a baby's voice as he peeked around the pole that stands in the middle of the cabin. The boys went fishing and Flint got a fish hook stuck in his head. Bob had to remove it with great difficulty and pain for both of them.

We had shrews in the cabin and they got braver and braver in spite of our six big dogs. The dogs all caught and ate little animals outside, but I guess they thought that an animal in the cabin must be a pet. They would lie on the floor and let the shrew run across the room right in front of their noses, and they'd just look up at us with silly grins on their faces. We kept throwing things at the mice but that didn't deter them, they were too fast for us to hit. Then Timber was given a little black and white kitten who he named Gunsmoke. The kitten was barely bigger than the shrews but his lack of size or their being in the cabin didn't make him hesitate to chase and catch them. Once the shrew was caught the battle began, and the sight and sound of it chased me right out of the house, regardless of what I had been doing. Cooking, eating, sleeping, it didn't matter what, when the fight began I was gone! I know that Kee Kee Watusee for the FBI (as Bob called Gunsmoke) always won in the end, as he would still be there contentedly licking his paws after the shrew had become his meal. I was glad when the mice were finally cleared out of the house and the war ended.

In September after the second and final clean-up, we again headed back to watch Thelma's homestead for the winter. When we stopped up at the lodge to buy drinks and snacks for the trip in to town, Timber suggested, "Let me go buy them. They'll give them to me for a dime." Apparently they had been giving him cokes and candy for what ever coins he had in his hand when asking, "Is this enough?" The little con man knew perfectly well what things cost, and we put an end to that little scam right then and there.

That night it had been a long drive in, and we stopped at Denny's in Fairbanks to get something to eat. When we came out we found that someone had opened the back of the camper shell and our Sissy was gone. We searched and called but we finally had to go out to the homestead without her. The next morning and on the day after, we drove the thirty some miles into town to search for her. Each evening we sadly returned home, slumping with discouragement. On the morning of the third day Bob was getting coffee at Denny's while I waited in the car. As I waited I got a glimpse of a light gray dog going by some distance away. I ran out to where I had seen her and to my delight, she was trotting down the road. I called and she stopped and warily watched me walk towards her. It wasn't until I got quite near to her that she recognized me and came a-running. I put her in the cab with us and she licked our necks, hands, and faces all the way home.

We celebrated Timber's 6th birthday by going out for pizza with Terry and Joan. Then both boys started school, Flint in the third grade and Timber in the first. While the boys were in school, riding the bus to and fro, we relaxed at home: walking, reading, and playing. I bought some panties and told Shianne that now that she was two years old, she should start using the toilet. Even though she had to go outside to an outhouse, in all kinds of weather, I never had to put another diaper on her. She had no accidents and she let me know when she had to go in plenty of time for me to get her there.

We continued to go into town about once a month to shop, wash clothes, and to go out and do things with our friends. Whenever we were eating in a restaurant if people at a neighboring table were talking about something of interest, I would pretend not to be listening. This was not so for Bob, he would not only openly listen; but he would join in the conversation. I would be embarrassed but the people never took offence or told Bob to mind his own business. Instead they would push their table over by ours and afterward they would join the ranks of our friends. There was something about Bob that allowed him not only to get away with saying and doing anything he wanted, but he drew people to him and once he did no one ever forgot him!

Thelma asked us to take care of one of her dogs who had been getting in trouble in town by nipping people. So we brought her dog Sassy out to the homestead. Although none of our dogs ever growled at her, she was too scared to eat or sleep around them. Our dogs were typical huskies and they talked, using a series of sounds and tones, instead of barking. Our Sissy was the biggest chatter box of all, always having long conversations with us. So now along with our sassy Sissy, we found ourselves with a sissy Sassy.

One day while going for a walk Bob bent his knee, and then try as he did he couldn't straighten it out again. With my shoulder to lean on he had to literally hop all the way home, and then after we drove into town he had to hop into the doctor's office. His knee cap was loose and it had moved into the joint, keeping his knee bent. The doctor correctly speculated, "Let me guess, I'll bet you were a paratrooper." Bob required surgery and the kids and I stayed with Patti and Rob while Bob was in the hospital. Every day we would ride the bus from their home at Eilson Air Force Base to the hospital to see him. At night I would cook dinner and then we would talk to Bob on the telephone. After a few days we all returned to the homestead for Bob to recover.

That year we made it to Patti's and Rob's for Halloween. On base there are lots of houses all close together making it really accessible for trick or treating. The kids had a blast and their pumpkin baskets were soon overflowing. At one house when a man answered the door in costume, Shianne turned around and ran. The man chased her across the yard with her treat in his hand. "Little girl, stop! I won't hurt you." After that she held back, staying real close to her Mommy. While at Eielson with her cousins Shianne watched *Friday the 13th*. Then when a trick or treater came to the door dressed as Freddy Kruger, she panicked! Now (in her thirties) she loves scary movies, but she still refuses to watch any of this series.

We spent Thanksgiving with Terry and Joan and we took a turkey across the highway to our neighbors' house on Christmas. They were a family with five children with whom the kids liked to play. The children were told not to take their Christmas presents over to their house, but Timber did anyway. He gave all of his gifts to his friends, but when we found out we told him that he could share his things but he had to keep some of them. Since the children were all older than Timber they were not surprised that they couldn't keep all the toys.

Chapter 22
DOG GONE!
1981

Flint with his first caribou, Boundary 1981

That winter, Sissy's back end gave out on her and she couldn't stand or walk alone. We took her to the vet but he said that there was nothing that could be done for her. When she needed to go outside I would walk her out using a cloth sling placed below her belly. She also was in pain and she wouldn't eat or drink much. We had made arrangements to take Patti and Rob out to dinner on our sixteenth wedding anniversary but Sissy died that morning. We didn't want to spend a gloomy night out so we postponed the celebration for a couple of weeks, going out with them on January 16th instead. As a gift they had a wooden sign made up for us reading: WOLFF'S DEN, which we hung over our door at the cabin.

Late January we made arrangements to buy five acres of land on the back corner of Thelma's homestead. After that we would walk back there to look at it from time to time. Doug, the oldest child in our neighbor's family didn't get along too well with his step-mother, so he started hanging out at our house on evenings and weekends. It was like having an older fourth child, as Doug was fifteen. Often when we walked or went to town Doug would go along with us.

In March the road opened earlier than usual and we made our plans to move back home. Doug came with us and Patti, Rob, and Carolyn also came hauling a truck load of supplies for us. A couple of days later on their way home, they slid off the icy road. No one was hurt but they had to walk to

John's and Katharine's house to get John to pull their truck back up on the road. Luckily there was not enough damage to prevent them from driving back to North Pole.

We began to get ready for mining again and I started doing school work with the boys, Doug included. There was still ice on the creek and while playing down there Shianne fell through the ice and into the frigid water. Luckily the boys were playing nearby and Flint managed to get her out before she was washed down stream. He rushed his wet, teeth chattering, shivering little sister up to the cabin and we quickly got her dry and worked toward getting her warmed up.

The experience was very traumatic for her and it was all that she wanted to talk about. "Yesterday I fell through the ice!"

I corrected her, "No Honey. That happened today."

The next morning Shianne informed me, "Today I fell through the ice!"

Once again her ornery mother corrected her, "No Sweetie that was yesterday."

It wasn't until many years later, that she overcame the fear of water that the experience had given her. She did however, with great determination; squash her dread and she learned to swim and dive. She is still somewhat leery and respectful of water.

That summer we mined with John on the dozer on weekends and with Bob or Flint on it during the week. Doug helped on the sluice box for a short while, but he found that it was hard work and he elected to go help an elderly couple with their hand mining instead. Although Flint at eight preferred to be on the dozer, he had no difficulty taking over working the sluice box after Doug had quit.

Now instead of the tent, we had a school bus with the seats taken out to use up at the camp. It had a propane cook stove, a table, and a couple of bunks and it made a comfortable shelter for us. One day when friends were coming to visit, I waited at our cabin so that I could show them the way up to the mine. As we walked up to the cut carrying a broom and dust pan, I answered their questions about mining. I also told them that one day we would have a bigger operation; we would be a two broom operation with a broom for the cabin and another one for the mining camp. However this was never achieved so I had to continue carrying it back and forth.

One evening while I was at the bus washing dishes after supper, Bob and Flint went up to the lodge. While they were gone a bear walked up near the bus. While the bear was deciding what he wanted to do, and while I was hoping that I wouldn't have to shoot him, Stormy and Pupa got in between him and the bus. The two dogs looked very much alike except that Stormy was at least twice as big as Pupa. They started singing a duet and the bear held his ground. There was Stormy's deep loud *whoof*, then Pupa's high pitched *yip*. The song, *whoof yip whoof yip* lasted until the bear turned around and lumbered off into the trees.

One day the new man working at the Canadian side of the border ran over to Roy, who worked on the U.S. side. "I just saw a wolf! He walked over and squirted on my truck tire."

Roy shrugged. "Naw, it couldn't have been Wolff. If he'd been here he would have stopped in for coffee."

Bob was called Wolff more often than he was called Bob. Now that two of my Wolffs are gone, I have two grandsons with the name Wolff as their middle or last name. I hope that one or both of them will someday want to use it as a first name, as did their grandfather. Both boys also inherited pronounced cleft chins from their grandfather, to bear along with his name.

Stupe was now sixteen years old and showing it. In the middle of an early July night he wanted to walk, but he didn't have the strength to do so. I woke up to hear him whimpering and struggling to get up. Like I had done with Sissy in January, I made a sling under his belly and we talked and paced the cabin floor together. Finally when he was ready, we lay down together and I petted him until he went to sleep. He never woke up. We buried him on the hillside across from the cabin and we visited there often. He was our very first dog and he filled the sixteen years that we had with him with joy.

We were mining on Flint's ninth birthday, and since it was Friday we paused long enough for Bob and Flint to go up to the lodge for mail. Flint was happy that he had gotten a package from his grandmother that contained a watch and a pair of tennis shoes. They did not see Sambo when he followed them up to the lodge. We had eaten dinner and were just going to have Flint's birthday cake, when someone came down to the mine telling us that Sambo had been shot. Danny, a miner from a near by creek had a poodle who was almost blind. The dog had been hit and killed in the lodge parking lot by a tourist's vehicle. Sambo being curious had gone up to him to investigate and a man saw Sambo by the dog and ran into the bar where Danny was drinking. "Danny, a big black dog just killed your poodle!" By now Sambo was on his way home but Danny jumped in his truck, chased Sambo down, and shot him.

When Danny found out the truth about what had really happened to his dog, he was frightened and went up to the border asking for protection. Bob didn't say or do anything to Danny, but we were all heartsick. The loss of three of our beloved dogs in one year was hard to take! Sambo was shot in the stomach and he had almost made it home before he died. It must have been so terrible for him, he was in great pain and he struggled desperately through the woods in his attempt to get home to us! We searched for hours before we found him and could bury him next to his father. The night before that, I had dreamed that Sambo was sick and dying. As I was petting Sambo the next morning, I told him how glad I was that it had been just a dream and that he was alright. My relief was short lived since he didn't live to see another night. It just wasn't the same without our black gentle giant, Bugger!

In September after the final clean-up at the end of the mining season, we stopped to visit with Patti and Rob before going back to the homestead. It was already cold with a couple of inches of snow on the ground. When Shianne came into the house after playing outside with Carolyn, I helped her take off her boots, snow pants, mittens, and parka. I had no sooner put her winter gear away when she wanted to go back out.

"Not now, Shianne. We just took your things off. Wait awhile and then you can go back out to play."

"But Mommy, I want to go out now. Please!"

"Shianne, I said later. Find something else to do for a while."

Shianne tried to wait and she looked at me so pleadingly that I was just about to give in and go get her winter clothes again. Before I could do so, low and behold; a puddle appeared on the kitchen floor. It hadn't occurred to me that Shianne had been using an outhouse ever since she had gotten out of diapers. She didn't know that there was such a thing as an in door potty, and now when I wouldn't let her go outside the poor child didn't know what she was supposed to do! I got her clean clothes and showed her where the bathroom was and how to use the toilet. She never had another accident.

We got settled out at the homestead again, celebrated Timber's seventh birthday, and the boys started riding the bus into Wood River School. Bob also found steady work and things were going well. That is they went well until the neighbor's dogs over at Doug's house were let off of their chains. They jumped and killed little Pupa! Sugey went wild and she chased all around looking for her sister. Two days later Sugey was hit and killed by an eighteen wheeled semi-truck driving on the highway. In less than one year we had lost five out of our six dogs. Now we only had Stormy left and we were afraid to even let him outside to take care of his business. The house was so quiet and sad and even Stormy was moping.

It wasn't long before we decided to get another puppy so we bought little Sissy III. She even looked like our other Sissy; so much so that I have to stop and think about which Sissy is in our pictures. She quickly became Flint's dog and she complained loudly each morning when Flint got on the school bus, she moped around the house waiting for his return, and then excitedly jumped all over him when he got home.

In November after doing quite a lot of work in town, Bob had to go to Delta to do another job at Fort Greely. I took the boys out of school and again we stayed in a cabin at Clear Water. Mom made another trip up to visit and we had a great time. She quickly learned that her shoes, purse, etc. had to be put up high, or Sissy would drag them off, and she would find them all chewed up. We had many pleasant days there and we had our Thanksgiving dinner near by at the Trophy Lodge. At the end of the month we went into Fairbanks, had brunch out, and bought Mom a new purse and suitcase for an early Christmas gift. She flew back to California the next day.

Bob finished up his job in time for us to move back to the homestead and to get ready for Christmas. While visiting a friend, I was taking a long longed for bath when Shianne, now three years old, kept rushing me and insisting that we needed to hurry so that we could go see Santa Claus. With regret I cut my bath short and we rushed down to the store to wait in line. When it was finally Shianne's turn she started to cry and would not go anywhere near him.

Patti, Rob, Carolyn, and their new little daughter, Becky had had to move way down South when Rob was transferred. We had Christmas dinner with Thelma and I figured four years of back taxes for her. It took a long time to sort through a garbage bag full of receipts and things, but she got a nice tax return. Luckily I find that sort of thing fun.

Chapter 23
BOUNDARY WOLFFS
1982 and 1983

Boundary Wolffs, 1982

That winter we didn't manage to stay at the homestead all the way until spring. In February we drove to Tok, taking all day on icy roads, and we flew up to Boundary on the next day. We arrived there to find the temperature in the minus 60s, so we spent a couple of days up at the lodge with Action Jackson and Big Jim. As soon as it warmed up alittle we hauled our supplies and things down to the cabin, got settled, cut and hauled wood, etc. I had brought the boys school work along so we were able to finish their year's work. It felt peaceful and so great to be home again! Margaret has always said that we need to go home frequently to get ourselves put back together again. She's right, everything gets out of prospective when we're away too long.

In March we heard that state land was open for staking so Bob and Flint staked our claims on Walker Fork. The staking was no easy task. They had to climb the mountain through waist deep snow, over and over again. They had to cut four stakes for each claim and carve the claim's names on each one. At first the names were long like, Two above Wolff Discovery, but they got shorter and shorter as we went along like, W 7. The stakes had to be placed in each corner of each claim, and they had to be placed in a north-south direction and at a particular distance apart. They had to be flagged and the brush had to be cut so that each one was plainly visible. One has to redo the flagging and brush cutting as necessary to keep the stakes visible. Papers are put in a jar that is nailed to stake number one of each claim, stating the name of the claim, the owner's name, the date that it was staked, etc.

When the road opened in April the miners began to come in to the country. When we got our first visitors to the cabin, I looked for Shianne as she had seemed to vanish. I finally found her curled up in the toe of her sleeping bag. I guess that she was a little timid. All the boys who came to the country congregated in our cabin, often spending the night. There were no other little girls in the area for Shianne, but there were several boys who wanted to play with the boys and to see what Bob would do or say next. From the time the children were little they wanted to be with their father, and to do what ever he was doing. It's wonderful that they were able to spend so much time with him, even going to work with him a lot of the time.

That spring we had to make another trip into town to get supplies and to record our mining claims. Since Patti and Rob were gone from the state we stayed in a motel. The kids got to watch T. V. a couple of times a year and the rest of the year they played games that they made up from the movies that they had watched. One year they played "Calendar Girls" for several months. The kids watched "Poltergeist," and Shianne found it especially scary. After watching a big toy clown grab and run off with a little blond girl who was just her size; Shianne went home to get rid of the big clown that she had received as a gift.

Much to my pleasure we got all ready and started mining with John again in June. June 27th was Action Jackson's birthday and they were having a big dinner celebration at the lodge in his honor. I'm not sure if we would have gone up for it, except that it was also Shianne's fourth birthday and they baked a special birthday cake for her. There were lots of people there, miners from the surrounding creeks, tourists, and people from Chicken, Eagle, and Dawson City. People showered Shianne with cokes, candy, and money. One woman tried to talk Shianne into trading her American dollars for prettier Canadian dollars. Flint prevented the trade since at that time Canadian money had about one half the value. The Sanders' family had come into the country to mine on Poker Creek with Poker Creek Bill. They are wonderful singers, especially Dale and Vickie, and they not only sang for us that night but also on all the following Friday nights. It was a recipe for lots of fun!

In July Bob started working for the Transportation Department on the highway. At the age of nine Flint was already stronger and more able to handle all the big rocks in the sluice than I was. So Bob began teaching me how to operate the new track loader that John had bought. It was our hope that the boys and I could mine on our own during the week. The loader had no steering wheel, it is run with just a stick shift and foot pedals.

Sitting there in the cab empty handed, made me feel like I had no control, so I clutched the handle on the door with both hands. Going up hill on a track vehicle is very different from one on wheels. The loader keeps climbing after it has reached the top of the hill until the front end is up in the air. Then it flops down on the other side of the hill and the rear end is sticking straight up. Each time this happened I felt like I was falling off of a cliff! Then giant sized eyes and my song of terror, "Ooooooohhhhhh........." was added to my fierce grip on the door! When Bob was giving me instructions I could never hear what he was saying over the engine. He did not teach me the hand signals that the guys used when talking to each other, so all I could do was shrug my shoulders in confusion. However, I did get the impression that I was not doing so well when I saw him take off his hat, throw it on the ground, and jump up and down on it. My career as a cat skinner was short lived, since to everyone's relief the guys soon took over.

The scenery along the Taylor Hwy is spectacular but it scares some people because it's narrow, has blind hairpin curves, and there are many cliffs that threaten a deadly plunge of many miles. During the years that Bob worked on the highway he had many close encounters with timid or careless drivers. Many people are afraid to drive on the cliff side of the road, choosing their lane down the middle instead. Sometimes people would try to force Bob off the road, and one time he pulled as far off as he could get and stopped. The motor home still side swiped his truck and broke the side mirror. When Bob talked to people about the danger that they were putting other people in, they would reply that they were scared. That summer Bob cut down trees and brush all along the 150 miles of highway to improve the visibility around the sharp curves. He used a chainsaw

before they had had to install anti vibration devices on them. Consequently when it started to get cool in the fall Bob's fingers began to turn white, and he had to struggle to keep adequate circulation.

With the mining, Bob's work on the highway, and Friday night music; it was a busy, pleasurable summer and early fall. After we had celebrated Bob's and the boys' birthdays, had the final clean-up at the mine, the boys had enrolled in Correspondence School, we had hunted and gotten our winter's meat, the other miners in the area had gone, and we had made trips to Fairbanks and Dawson City; the road closed for the year and Bob's job was over for the season. For a while the sudden change from a lodge and surrounding country that is bustling with people, to a quiet almost deserted landscape; has great impact. However, we got used to and enjoyed the exclusion quite quickly. This year the country had a greater population than usual. Action Jackson had Big Jim and a gal named Lorna staying at the lodge with him, and two tourists, Daryl and his girl Cindy, were passing through. They decided to stay and found an unoccupied cabin about ten miles away. We frequently got together with both couples.

With Flint's share of the summer's gold he bought a used snow machine. We hadn't had a snow machine since before the children had been born, so after the roads closed we had been walking everywhere. Flint was so tickled and he could hardly wait to ride it. That fall we didn't get snow until Halloween, the latest that I ever remember it coming. We built a sled to pull behind the snow machine and once it was ready it was so hard for Flint to have to wait to use it. On Halloween Bob turned out all the lights and chased the kids around in the dark. After they were worn out and had used all their screams and laughter, we looked out the window and saw the snow! The kids were up early in the morning, eager to go out and ride.

Now we were able to use the snow machine to get our mail, to visit our neighbors, to explore, and for pleasure. Also with the money from the gold we had been able to order things for Christmas. All through November we received packages from family, friends, and our orders. We had been making plans for a trip stateside in January, but after dinner on Thanksgiving night Bob suddenly popped up with the idea that we should go then and spend Christmas with Grandma. I drug my feet at first, being reluctant to leave after all the Christmas preparation that we had made. However my family's enthusiasm soon caught me and our new plans were finalized in one day. We arranged to leave Stormy and Sissy with Daryl and Cindy. We made numerous blanketed shelters and filled tubs of snow and dishes of dry food all around the cabin for Gunsmoke. Also, Big Jim and Lorna promised to come down to the cabin every couple of days to check on him. They wanted a place to go to get away from the lodge anyway. We let the children open their Christmas presents early and to choose one gift to take with them. Then we quickly packed and were ready to go the next morning.

We caught a ride to Tok with John, and stayed with friends there for a couple of days until we could catch a bus down to Seattle. I thought that riding a bus day and night for three days with three children might be hectic, but it was surprisingly easy. The children amused themselves during the day and slept well at night. We then had several shorter bus rides going from Seattle to San Luis Obispo, making stops to visit with friends and family along the way.

Our second Christmas celebration at Mom's mobile home was very nice. We had gotten and decorated a tree, shopped, wrapped presents, rode around to see the decorations, listened to Christmas hymns, watched special Christmas programs on T.V., and had made all the preparations all over again. When we were buying the food for our Christmas dinner Shianne asked, "Could we please go to a stuff store?" She got her wish and got to shop in several stuff stores. After Christmas there were dinners in restaurants and with friends, a trip to the quiet lovely Swedish town, Solvang, a picnic and fishing at Lopez Lake, and several trips to the beach.

While we stayed in Mom's mobile home Bob kept her in a perpetual state of fluster and confusion. To everyone's amusement he was skilled at making her say and do things up-side-down and backwards. Sometimes he only had to look at her in a special way to get her going, and other times he would go so far as to pretend to be sick down the back of her neck. It sounds gross, but like I said before he could get away with saying and doing things like no one else. One day when an acquaintance of Mom's stopped by the house Shianne informed her, "It's a good thing that my dad's not here or he would spit in your tea." The lady gasped in astonishment and placed her hand over the top of her cup.

We bought a Buick and made trips to visit friends and family again on the way home. While visiting Bob's sister Hazel, who is a registered nurse, she told him that if he didn't quit smoking he would eventually lose his fingers. Bob did quit and the next few days were traumatic for Bob and stressful for us all. Bob could neither sleep nor stay still and it took many miles of pacing before the worst was over.

We left the Buick in Washington with our friends Ski and Coleen, since they were planning to go up to mine on our claims during the summer. David our red headed teenaged nephew was planning to drive our car up to the mine when they came up.

We boarded the ferry for another grand trip back to Alaska and as always it lived up to our expectations. On the trip up we temporarily had a fourth child in our family, a little boy aged four like Shianne. He took a shine to Shianne and his parents could not keep him with them. They soon discovered that when he was missing all they had to do was find one of us. We could tell them where Shianne was and invariably that's where he would be. Allowing him to stay with Shianne was as good as having him on a leash, he wouldn't be going anywhere without her.

When we got off the ferry in Haines we caught a ride to Tok with some tourists who had been on the ferry and then we chartered a plane with Ron Warbelow back to Boundary. At the cabin Gunsmoke was just fine, but he was lonesome and awfully glad to see us. We picked up Stormy from Daryl's and Cindy's, but Sissy had been unwilling to leave Flint's snow machine. They had had to feed her there beside it while she waited for her Flint. When she saw Flint she howled and wet all over the snow!

We had our third Christmas celebration back at the cabin. Not only were the gifts that we had opened back in November before our trip unused and unplayed with, but more packages had arrived after we left. Pushing the time of our trip to December instead of January had worked out well; and the kids thought that celebrating Christmas three times was great.

Chapter 24
COME OUT OF THE CABIN
1983—1984

Flint and I mining, Davis Creek 1983

We had had a wonderful vacation but it was good to be home again. We still had half the winter to go and it was peaceful and pleasant. We used the snow machine and sled to ride up to the lodge for mail, to haul wood, to visit with the folks there, and Flint started a small trap line. Daryl and Cindy had used the machine while we were outside, and it wasn't long before it broke down. Flint took it apart, we ordered parts, and after a considerable amount of time, when the parts finally came in; Flint was able to fix it. Bob hated mechanics but although Flint had never had a class, read a book, or been taught anything about machines, he somehow knew how to repair them. He said that if he took something apart he would know how to put it back together again. We soon discovered that this instinctive knowledge also applied to chain saws, cars, trucks, furnaces, and even big equipment.

That winter Sissy and Stormy had two puppies, Smokey who we called Big Guy and Kisses who we called Kisses. As a puppy Smokey was all out of proportion and awkward looking. When he got bigger and grew into his feet, head, etc., he was big and beautiful, hence his nick name. He reminded me a lot of Sambo being as big, gentle, and as good natured. All of our neighbors, except for Action Jackson who never left the lodge, came down to the cabin to see and play with the puppies. It was good to have four dogs again, and they enlivened the winter. In the spring they were able to go on our walks with us.

I had started the boy's school through Correspondence back in the fall, continued it on our trip out side, and we finished it up during the winter and spring after we got back. Through out the years I read aloud to the children, reading a variety of books from classics like *My Friend Flicka* to adult novels like *Battle Cry* and *Mila 18*. When we neared the end of a suspenseful book like *The Unforgiven* we couldn't stop to go to bed, so we had to stay up most of the night to finish it. One winter when Bob was discouraged about something and in a bad mood, he listened while I was reading "The Long Hard Winter" by Laura Wilder. The difficulties that they were having knocked things back into perspective for Bob; and he was once again his teasing fun self. Since the children grew up seeing television only twice a year, they all acquired a love for books and reading.

The road opened and people poured in including Ski and Coleen, Hoss and Jan (their friends who came up to mine with them) and our nephew David with our Buick. The Sanders came back to mine on Poker Creek and once again that spelled Friday night music fests.

The population increased by long leaps with only a decrease of two. During an argument Daryl shot Cindy in the foot. He had to leave the area in a hurry, and without him there with her she left shortly afterward. Cindy said that being shot damages one's soul. Now that I have been shot, I can't agree. The only shot that damaged my soul was the one that killed my Flint.

Bob had used a guy named Ken to help on a couple of sheet rocking jobs, and that spring he came up to visit. His visit went on and on, through the spring, summer, and part of the fall; he just didn't leave. He wanted to try a little hand mining and that he did, for almost six months! With David and Ken, our little one room cabin now housed seven people, four dogs, and one cat. For the first time it seemed a little crowded until all of us except for Ken, moved up the creek to sleep in the school bus at camp.

Bob started working on the high way again and David helped us with the mining. On weekends we mined with Bob and John. On June 27th they had another big dinner and music, celebrating Action Jackson's and Shianne's birthdays. Right after that Flint and I walked all day up Davis Creek and staked two claims on the Canadian side. Foolishly we didn't carry a rifle (we're not supposed to take one across the border) and that day we saw three bear, two black and one grisly. Fortunately we were able to stay out of their sight and smell and they didn't attack us. The staking of the claims meant that we needed to make a trip to Dawson City to record them. This necessity is one of the nicest things about having Canadian claims; it requires that we repeat this pleasure every year.

One day Flint and David had to put the mining on pause in order to go hunting. Moe a miner from down the road had shot and wounded a bear. He had tracked him up near our mine and then had lost the trail. David and Flint found and shot the bear at the cost of one day's mining. Toward the end of August, Ken bought and moved into a camper and then we moved back down to the cabin. One day when we returned to the cabin after a days mining, we found Stormy had died in the yard. He'd gotten too old to want to follow us up there. We sadly buried him on the hill side across the creek next to Stupe and Sambo, his father and brother. Now all of the original four dogs that we had had and loved for so long were gone.

After finishing up the season's mining we made our fall trip to Fairbanks for supplies and put David on the plane going back home to California. We made two trips to town each year, in the spring and in the fall. Shortly after we got back Ken finally left, Bob completed his work on the highway, Bob and Flint shot a moose and a couple of caribou for our winter's meat, and the guys cut and hauled wood for our winter's warmth. Now we were all set with everything that we needed.

This year we got the school books and supplies in for all three children, as Shianne was starting in Kindergarten. Flint's snow machine broke down and this time the parts would come to more than Flint chose to spend. In November Flint set out a trap line which he walked on snow shoe. He walked a good many hard miles over the mountains without getting any fur. I thought that he'd give up and pull his traps, but not so. If Flint got discouraged he didn't show it and he persisted. After what seemed like forever when he finally did catch a martin, he was ecstatic and for a while he walked on the air about a foot above the ground.

That winter the tree that grew in the sod on our cabin roof, decided to join us inside the cabin. This caused quite a mess and too much fresh air! A warm cabin was not something that we could now maintain, so a new roof was in order. Bob managed to repair our home and later with new sod we again had grass, weeds, and wild flowers growing there, but we didn't choose to replace the tree.

I kept really busy with the children's school. On Thursday nights I would be up late gathering the children's school work and making sure that everything was done and ready to be mailed down to Correspondence School in Juneau. Timber had been doing well with his school work while he was printing his papers. He often printed his letters backwards but we weren't concerned and one could still read what he wrote. When he had to start writing in cursive, all hell broke loose! In the first place Timber is left handed, and I didn't know how to show him how to hold his pencil to write correctly. Then when he started writing in cursive he tried to go to the right across the paper, but instead he kept going to the left on to the table. I had no idea how to help him shift gears and to go in the right direction. I wrote to his correspondence teacher asking for help, but she replied that he was doing fine. It's true that he was managing to get his work done, but only after way too many painful hours, some tears, and a hefty load of frustration. After a short time with his death grip on the pencil, his hand would really hurt and he'd need to rest it.

Along with the school work I found that I had to bake bread almost every day, the fresh bread usually all disappeared while it was still warm from the oven. When I cut up our moose or caribou for dinner, Gunsmoke would sit beside me watching. I would give him little scraps of gristle as I trimmed our steaks. If my cutting got behind his eating he did more than watch, he would bat at my hand until I hurried and got him some more.

He ate a lot of scraps before leaving in satisfaction, much to the dogs' displeasure as there wasn't as much left for them as they would have liked.

That fall Crazy Larry came into the country with Joyce his new bride, and two brand new snow machines to use on their trap lines. The first part of Larry's nick name was well earned with the things that he did and said. I never heard anyone claim that the name didn't fit him, even Larry seemed to agree with it. A few years earlier, up at the lodge; he had bragged that he was going to whip everyone there, including "that boy" indicating Flint. Bob had something to say about that and he didn't lift a hand to anyone. Another time again in the bar, he got into an argument with Moe. Bob had to take his rifle away from him to prevent a shooting. When Larry and Joyce came to visit at the cabin, Bob made sure that he understood that he had to be sober and he had to leave all weapons outside on his snow machines.

In December Kisses had one puppy. We hadn't even known that she was expecting until a couple of days before she delivered. He was a cute puppy and we named him Scamper but called him Little Guy. He grew up to be a normal sized husky but he remained smaller than Big Guy. While Sissy remained Flint's dog, Kisses took to Timber and could always be seen at his side. Sissy definitely thought of herself as the boss of the dogs. She didn't throw her weight around with her son, Big Guy, who towered above her; but she had her way with Kisses, who would not challenge her about anything. I thought that Kisses was afraid or just hated fighting, until she chased off a large tourist's dog that she thought was threatening Timber. I guess that it was just Mama that she wouldn't fight. Both Big Guy and Kisses were gentler and better natured than their mother, who had always been rather feisty.

The winter was filled with all the quiet pleasures that meant so much, at least it was until mid January. Bob and Flint were up at the lodge getting mail, when Joyce rushed in. She had just shot Larry and had left him alive and wounded in the cabin. She thought that the only one that he might not shoot would be Flint, and she wanted him to use her snow machine to go up to the cabin to check on him. Bob said that that was not going to happen! Instead the pilot was asked to notify the state troopers when he took the mail. Joyce said that she had wanted to go home and Larry wouldn't let her, threatening to tie her up if she tried. She settled the dispute with his 22 rifle.

The troopers flew in, they snow machined back to Larry's cabin and found him dead, they asked all kinds of questions, and then took Larry and Joyce back with them. At Joyce's request Bob and Flint used their snow machines to run their trap lines and they kept all the fur for her to pick up later. They also hauled Joyce's personal things back to the cabin for safe keeping. Several days after Larry's and Joyce's departure, Bob and Flint found a candle burning in their cabin. It hadn't been there before and there was no one else there for miles around. It was creepy!

In February a helicopter flew in and hovered overhead. When a loud speaker demanded that we all vacate the cabin, we were alarmed and came out, almost with our hands in the air. We wondered if we were being arrested for something. Instead Bob and Flint were subpoenaed to go to Tok for Joyce's trial in March. Bob did not want to leave us alone at the cabin and he was angry when he couldn't get out of going. Since the road was still closed they sent an airplane up to get them for the trial, but still being angry they chose instead to ride Joyce's snow machines the 120 miles into town.

In court Bob and Flint had to relate again the little that they knew about the shooting. Bob was asked if he thought that Joyce had shot Larry in self defense, and still being angry he answered, "I DON'T KNOW, AND I DON'T CARE IF SHE DIGS HIM UP AND SHOOTS HIM AGAIN!"

They determined that Joyce had killed Larry in self defense and she was acquitted. She had said that she had shot him because he wouldn't let her go home, but once she was free to leave she still remained in Tok for many months. They had already chartered and paid for a plane to take Bob and Flint to and from Tok, so Bob bought groceries to fly back to Boundary and he and Flint rode the snow machines home.

Later in the spring after the road was open, Joyce drove up to get her fur and belongings. She was sitting with us in the cabin, having coffee when she looked at Bob. "We're going to have a baby."

Bob choked on his coffee and sputtered, "Uh …excuse me?"

"Larry and I, we're going to have a baby!"

We looked at her and wondered what she was going to tell her child about Larry and about what had happened to him. I'm not sure whether the child was born in Tok or not, I just know that she lived there for quite a while after she was free to go.

Chapter 25
OVER THREE BEARS
1984 and 1985

Timber, Shianne, and Flint with Sissy, Davis Creek August 1984

Bob started working on the highway again in the late spring and we started mining shortly afterward. The Sanders were back up mining and singing up at the lodge on Friday nights. Ken also came back up to hand mine, but this year he stayed in his camper only coming up to the cabin occasionally for a meal. We mined with John and Bob on weekends, and the boys and I mined during the week whenever the loader was working and we had enough water. When we couldn't mine we went to work with Bob and camped out. He did quite a lot of work in Eagle so we camped there, saving him the long rides to and from work each day.

When we heard that a veterinarian was coming to stay a few days at O'Brian Creek (on the road to Eagle), we decided to have Sissy and Kisses spade and give all the dogs their shots. We all went to work with Bob that morning and we stopped at the vets for the shots and left Sissy and Kisses there for the day. Later when we let Big Guy and Little Guy out of the truck, Little Guy was weaving around like he was drunk. We thought that he was having a reaction to his shots and we rushed him back to the vet.

The vet looked really sheepish as he admitted, "I was hoping that I wouldn't have to tell you this, but I mistakenly gave him the first anesthic shot before I noticed that he was a male. It *won't hurt him and it* will wear off in time."

We picked up Sissy and Kisses at the end of the day and carried them into the cabin. During the night Sissy pulled all of her stitches out so we took her back to the vet in the morning. He said that he couldn't really do anything to help her and that we would just have to keep her quiet and not let her jump or move around. That was easier said than done but she eventually healed up just fine.

One morning I knocked Bob's mini 14 rifle off of its hook and it fell to the floor. Bob was really annoyed and he decided that he needed to take it to work with him to be sure that it would still work Okay. Later that day when nature called, he thought that the gravel pit that he was stopping at would be a good place to test the rifle. Just as he was about to tend to his business he saw a big black bear on his right, coming towards him. Then he saw another big bear on his left, also heading his way. He didn't know if they were headed for each other or if they were both headed for him! He couldn't wait to see what their intentions were and he shot them both with his pants still around his ankles. If the first shot hadn't killed the first bear, he wouldn't have had time to shoot the other one. If I hadn't knocked his rifle off of the hook that morning, he wouldn't have even had a rifle with him. His rifle tested out just fine killing two bear with two shots, but when all was said and done he couldn't remember if he'd taken care of the call that had brought him there in the first place.

Whenever Bob worked in Eagle he would stop in the store and bring home treats. That afternoon Bob asked Flint to get a bag out of the back of his truck. With one hand on the tail gate, Flint was just swinging himself into the back when he saw the two bears propped up like they were ready for attack! He leaped straight up into the air and fell to the ground in fright. Earlier Bob had had to shoot a bear that he had found in an argumentive mood on the grader one morning when he went to work.

In August after a long dry spell that was preventing us from mining, we had a snow storm that left several inches on the ground and had the leafed trees bent over across the road. It was an unusual sight with the red, yellow, and orange of autumn showing through the white. It took a long time to get the trees along the road shook off and standing again so that trucks could drive by. Getting winter pictures in August gave me plenty of time to have Christmas cards made and the melting snow brought the creek up enough so that we could mine again.

In September we finished up the mining, Bob was laid off work on the highway, and we had trips to Dawson City and to Fairbanks. John was going on a trip to the lower 48, where his family had already gone, and we had agreed to stay in his big house near Chicken to watch Kathrine's three Great Pyrenees dogs. We were packing when we heard excited barking and looked outside to see Sissy circling and nipping at a good sized bull moose. Bob shot him which saved Sissy from his antlers and hoofs, and it provided us with our winter's meat. We hung him right by the cabin and other than from the grocery store it was the easiest meat that we had ever gotten.

John's house is big with two bedrooms up stairs and two more bedrooms in the full sized basement. It has a fireplace in the living room and a wood stove in the basement. We weren't used to having all that room, but like our cabin it doesn't have plumbing or electricity. However it's a lot fancier and easier than our cabin; and with all its cupboards, closets, and its pantry, I didn't need to have food, clothes, and belongings stored in boxes all around the cabin. In spite of or maybe because of how nice the house was, I couldn't relax and feel at home. My feelings must have spread to the children because when a neighbor occasionally left his two boys at the house while he went for mail, the kids followed them around trying to keep them from making messes and breaking things. I hadn't realized that I had impressed my uneasiness so strongly on the kids. I didn't mind the messes so much they could be cleaned up, but when things got damaged or broken I couldn't fix or replace them.

John's and Katharine's dogs had their own little fenced in house with hay inside. They were mother, son, and daughter. On the day after Thanksgiving the son died in his sleep. He had been lively, eating well, and had shown no signs of illness. We never knew what had caused his death. It was so difficult to have to write Katharine about her dog. Mama and daughter continued to be Okay, at least as Okay as Mama could be.

Some years ago she had been hit by a car and she was disoriented and had seizures. She would ask to go out the front door, walk around the house, and scratch to come in the back door. This continued most of the day and when she was inside even if a door was open; it wasn't uncommon to find her scratching and pushing against the wall beside the door way, whining for someone to open it for her. Once she was shown the way out and helped to go through, she often would turn around and try to go through the wall to get back into the room.

Besides taking care of ours and their dogs and doing the children's school with them, I was busy writing letters to send along with the picture Christmas cards that I had had made in September during our fall trip to town. For the first time ever thanks to our August snow storm, I was given the opportunity to have Christmas cards made in time.

Mail came to Chicken on Tuesdays and Fridays and we sometimes went for mail or sometimes our neighbor would get our mail when he picked up his. He did this on Christmas Eve, leaving his boys with us while he got the mail. The boys were handfuls, running all around getting into everything. When the neighbor and his girl friend came back with the mail, they agreed to stay for dinner. This would have been pleasant except that the girl friend had received an invitation elsewhere for a livelier party with more interesting beverages. Being unwilling to leave his sons with us all night the neighbor had refused the invitation, and his girl friend was angry. She sulked in silence for too short of a while, then her pouting turned very vocal in the form of every imaginable swear word. Her boy friend tried to quiet her but her rage turned to hitting, kicking, and throwing things. As he struggled with her in the house Sissy became alarmed with all the fighting and she bit him. He ignored Sissy and drug his girl outside dumping her in the snow, and then Kisses bit him. It would have been more appropriate if the dogs had bit her instead. I hope they weren't bad bites, he never said, and he took his family home and didn't come back. I was really surprised that the dogs would bite anyone, but huskies are very protective pets.

In January John came back up to Alaska, so we were able to move back to Davis creek. It took all day by one 4 wheel drive truck and a few snow machines, as the roads are not maintained in the winter and they were deep in snow and ice and treacherous. Then it took another day to haul our things down from the lodge. Our snow machine held up long enough to get everything down to the creek before it gave up. Then Flint harnessed the dogs to a sled, broke them in for the task, and set out a new trap line. He snow shoed many miles with the dogs pulling his supplies, but he got few furs. In spite of the luxury of John's big house I was really glad to be home again!

Action Jackson had a man nick named Grader staying at the lodge with him. I knew his name at one time, but as it was never used and I don't remember it now. He was quite a character and he considered himself a warlock. When someone crashed as they were landing on the run way by the lodge, he claimed that he had moved the run way and then had put it back after the crash. During the winter he was not willing to make coffee for himself so he ate dry instant coffee with a spoon. He wore several shirts at once, one on top of the other and when the top one was stiff and so torn that it was falling off, he just removed it and continued wearing the others. A few times a year he would bathe and put on enough shirts to last several months. All year long he wore a parka when outside.

When he lost a button on his suspenders rather than sew another one on, he got a block of wood and nailed it to his suspenders and his pants.

Grader sometimes came down to visit with us and to have a cooked supper, as cooking was something else that he didn't do. When he returned to the lodge after a visit in early February, he found Action Jackson outside of his trailer dead in the snow. Apparently he had had a heart attack and had gone looking for somebody.

Patti and Rob had finished another tour and were again stationed at Eielson Air Force Base. In April when we made our spring trip into town, we stayed there and celebrated Easter with them. Shianne was always anxious, all packed, and ready at least two weeks before our trips into town. She was never the procrastinator that I am; she always kept up with all her school work, answered letters immediately, and did everything promptly.

At the first of June we crossed the shallow creek and drove to Dawson City to see the dentist, shop, have lunch out, buy ice cream cones, etc. On the way home we were just crossing the creek again, when we were hit by a four foot wall of water that came around the bend. It went over the hood of the truck and in the windows, and the truck died right in the middle of the creek. The dogs and kids in back climbed on top of the camper shell until Bob was able to get them to shore behind the truck. We waited beside the creek for hours until Bob was able to cross the creek, get the loader, and come back for us. The truck was pulled to dry land and the dirt was cleaned out of the engine, carbonator, etc.; but it never again ran well enough to be trusted.

We started mining again and now Richard, the foreman of the road crew, was also mining with us. One night after a day's mining while we were all having dinner in the bus, Shianne passed gas.

"Shianne you should say excuse me."

She looked at me in total confusion. "But Mom, I did it on purpose!"

I didn't know what to say to that. At that time the radio frequently played a song about a tu tu (something about don't hurt my tu tu or be careful of my tu tu) and Shianne giggled every time she heard the song. It made us all laugh just because she found it so funny. She never did tell us just what amused her so much or explain what she thought the song was about.

On June 27th, Shianne's seventh birthday, they had a wake up at the lodge for Action Jackson. His son John Junior had come up to take over the lodge. Also on that day Flint bought a motor cycle and then Bob also bought one to use to ride to work since he was starting work on the high way again on July 1st. One day Flint and a friend were out riding the two motor cycles when they got in between a mother and baby bear. Mama sent her cub up a tree and she took off after the boys. While Flint was crossing the creek his motor cycle quit and he jumped on the back of the other bike. The bear was close behind them until they pulled into our driveway, then she turned and went back to her cub. I didn't notice whether Flint was shook up or not, as I was looking at the white face and huge eyes of his friend. Later Flint had to shoot a bear on Bob's 49th birthday.

Bob spent his work time that summer, building and repairing all the bridges along the road. Several times we went with him and camped beside the bridge that he was working on, cooking over a campfire. I am so thankful that the kids and I got to spend so much time with him and that he had such a wonderful impact on our lives. With the life style that we chose, since we weren't going our separate ways to school and work, our days and nights were spent together and we formed strong bonds that couldn't even be broken by death.

In June Patti and Rob came up to the mine with a bunch of friends and they came again in August bringing Grandma for a visit. Both times they hand mined with Flint doing the digging and hauling of the dirt for them. We took Grandma over to Dawson for the day. The ride over the Top of the World Highway with all the fall colors is spectacular, and Grandma loves to ride the ferry across the Yukon River. While we were having lunch at the Klondike Inn, Grandma mischievously kept untying the waitress's apron strings.

We leased a little bit of Walker Fork to Neal, a neighboring miner, and we were able to buy another used truck with our gold.

Chapter 26
DOUBLE WHAMMIE
1985 and 1986

Shianne and I camping near Eagle, 1985

When mining and work was done that September a hunch had us packing and moving into Fairbanks for a while. We didn't know what the hunch was about; we just felt that we should go. We headed out with Bob, Timber, and Shianne in the truck, and Flint and I followed in the Buick. There was snow and some ice on the road but we had no difficulty driving in, arriving at the homestead on the Parks Highway in the early morning hours. Later that morning we rented a little house from Thelma and moved in.

I had thought that our cabin at Davis Creek was rather dark, having one room with three small windows. The house we rented now was darker yet, it had three rooms and only one small window. The window was in the small kitchen and the two windowless rooms were a bedroom for the kids and one for Bob and I which doubled for a living room. If we wanted to see, we needed our oil lamp lit day and night. The house was off in the woods tucked quietly away from the highway and neighbors.

Bob looked unsuccessfully for work and the kids started in school. Flint was 13 and in the eighth grade in Ryan Middle School, and Timber and Shianne went to Pearl Creek Elementary School. Timber's fifth grade teacher looked very severe, but Shianne's second grade teacher was young and she looked nice. They had to get up early in the morning and ride the bus for a long time before school. This was difficult for Shianne as she has always hated to get up early. Timber's teacher turned out to be an exceptionally nice and understanding teacher and they formed a lasting friendship. The only difficulty that he was having in school was fighting. When someone said something rude or tormented his little sister; the fight was on. Also when kids picked on her classmates she turned to her big brother to take care of the situation. One day I met the principal of the school in a store. She told me that Timber had been awarded "King for the Day" because he hadn't been in a single fight for the whole day. He still frequently had problems with his hearing but when we had him tested and tried to have it corrected, they again just provided a temporary fix—medicine. We never knew whether Timber was hearing things just right or not. One day he asked me, "Why does everyone call me Toad head?"

Bob and I mostly stayed at home, occasionally going into town together. On one October day, we discovered what the hunch was that had brought us to town. I didn't go to town with Bob that day because I wanted to catch up on some things at home. I had the house all to myself and was having a nice hot bubble bath in our tin tub, when I discovered a lump in one breast. Back when I was in college I had had to have a lump removed and they had found the lump benign. I wanted to ignore this one but Bob insisted that I go in to see the doctor, have a mammogram, and eventually have it removed. Fortunately again it was not malignant.

One day in November Flint asked me, "Mom, how would you take it if I got kicked out of school?"

"I don't know. It would depend on what you did and your reasons for doing it."

"Well, you remember what the principal said about there being no fighting allowed at school? I've tried to do as he said but I just can't take it anymore. Some boys keep slamming my locker shut on me, spitting at me, calling me names, and things like that. I've had it with doing nothing and I can't keep from fighting any longer!"

"Well …un..since the principal can't seem to keep things like that from happening, he can't expect kids to observe that kind of a rule. I think that you're going to have to take care of it yourself, regardless of what the consequences might be. The boys think that you're not responding because you're afraid. Let them go on thinking that but the next time that they bother you, pick the biggest boy and let him have it!"

Flint followed my advice and WHAMM; he broke the kid's nose! He got suspended for three days but the boys didn't bother him again.

November was also the month for parent-teacher conferences. At Flint's conference a teacher told us that they knew what was going on with Flint and the boys, but they thought that any intervention from them would only magnify the problem. He said that if they had not suspended Flint along with the other boy; the kids would have considered it favoritism and it would have only made things worse.

At Timber's conference his teacher explained the effects of dyslexia and told us how remarkably well Timber was doing in overcoming his learning problems. It is true that Timber has made the term dyslexia nonapplicable because he learned to read and can comprehend everything that he wishes to. If he reads a word one way and it makes no sense, he turns it around and reads it the other way. There should be a different term for people with the problem who have learned to read. Although the term by definition doesn't fit him anymore, he still has difficulties while he is in the process of learning something new. Unlike Flint who learned everything so quickly and easily that it seemed like he was born with the knowledge, learning has always been difficult for Timber. It has affected almost everything: karate, shooting, mechanics, etc; he tries to do everything backwards at first. Difficult as it may be he still does accomplish everything that he sets out to do, and once he has learned something he doesn't forget it. The only thing that he hasn't been able to master yet is spelling, and in this day and age with computers and such, that shouldn't be a problem.

It only took a minute in Shianne's conference to determine that her sweet looking young teacher didn't like her at all. We had told her earlier that Shianne had never before been in a classroom, and that all of her schooling had been at home on a one on one basis. Unfortunately that information did not help her to understand that Shianne would need time to make an adjustment. Shianne committed the crime of calling her "teacher" instead of using her name! Also, although "teacher" had explained a lesson to the class, Shianne had asked a question about an instruction that had already been presented to the class. "Teacher's" distaste was so evident that without another word Bob got up and walked out. I sat silently through the rest of the conference with a stone face. When "teacher" finally stopped talking I made an astounding statement, "Oh." Then I too left the room, never to talk to her again. After that, Shianne began to bring home blank papers which she would quickly do without help as soon as she got home from school. She was unwilling to do any school work in class.

Rob had been sent away on a short tour so Patti, Carolyn, and Becky came to our house for Thanksgiving. While the turkey was baking, we went for a walk to see our property that was a couple of miles on down the trail. When we returned, the oven had gone out so I struck a match to relight it. "WHAMM!" The explosion singed my hair and eyebrows and burned off my eye lashes, but no one was really hurt and the house didn't burn down. It startled us all, especially me, but the turkey was fine, and we had a good dinner. My eyebrows and eyelashes eventually grew back.

We cut down and decorated a Christmas tree and were shopping, wrapping gifts, etc. when we all got the flu. We were all really sick and not wanting to eat anything other than a little soup; but by Christmas we were feeling well enough to bake and eat some turkey. I didn't have the energy to prepare a whole Christmas dinner and the turkey was all that we wanted to eat anyway. Then we were hit by the flu's aftermath, pneumonia and ear and sinus infections.

In January we sold the last of our gold to pay land taxes and we didn't have money left to buy anything. Being broke at home on Davis Creek is one thing but having no money in town is something else all together. At home with the roads closed and no stores anywhere near, the only financial crises that we had could be solved by something like an I O U note from the tooth fairy. In town there were always things that the kids wanted to do, a truck needing gas in order to move, and a lamp that would shed no light without oil. Also we had rent and doctor bills to pay. We borrowed just enough money to get by and we prepared to go back to Davis Creek.

We had to go part of the way home by snow machine, as the road had not been opened yet. Then after we made it there we found that we had had an unexpected visitor, a bear. What a mess! I don't know what kind of a concoction that he was trying to make, but he had dumped our corn meal, flour, soy sauce, syrup, ketchup, etc. over everything. That mixed with bear pee and poop was not very appetizing. We could see where the bear had gotten into a fight with our mirror too but there was no other damage to the cabin or our belongings. It took quite a while to clean up but it was not as bad as the chicken house in Flat had been. I had to start cleaning with a shovel, but at least I didn't have to use a pick and chisel this time. Before long we discovered that the bear had also gone into the bus up at camp as well, so there was a mess to clean up and some repair work to be done there too.

Once the cleaning was done and we got settled in, everything seemed easier. We had to cut and haul wood, melt snow for water, wash clothes by hand, and work on school, but it was a pressure free life style and one that we all wanted and enjoyed. It was good to be together and home!

The road opened, people started coming in, Bob started work on the high way, and we began to get ready for mining with John and Richard. It was good to have an income early on in the year so that we could pay what we owed. We had a fun productive summer's mining with the boys and I mining when we could during the week, and mining with the guys when they were off work on the weekends. When we weren't mining the kids and I would still go to work with Bob and camp in Eagle or along the road.

We had lots of visitors that summer. One group of friends would leave and another group would come. Patti and Rob came with the girls and they brought Patti's sister, Lou Ann and her family along with them. When the kids were growing up Lou Ann was the only one unfortunate enough to look like me. When I visited the house I used to tease her, pretending that I didn't remember her name. This would greatly disturb her since she seemed to think that I belonged to her. Lou Ann, her husband Frank, and their two boys Jerry and Dusty, were up from Roy, Washington where they had a goat farm. Jerry was almost exactly Carolyn's age and Dusty was Becky's age; their mothers, the two sisters had a lot in common. They brought what seemed like a truck load of materials for making tacos, insisting that I get busy cooking them. I make tacos one by one, there were fifteen of us at the mine, and I think they averaged five tacos each. I thought that they would never get done asking for more and that I would be cooking forever.

In September we finished with the mining, Bob was laid off work, we made our fall trip into town for supplies, and Bob and Flint got some caribou. Then our truck broke down and a mechanic who was staying in the area worked on it. When he was done with it, it never ran again. That meant that we had to haul our winter's wood in on foot but at least Bob was off work and we already had our winters food and meat.

In November Flint started trapping, extending his trap lines until they totaled about 100 miles. He ran his lines on snow shoe with the dogs pulling a sled with his supplies, traps, fur, bait, lure, etc. He would take provisions so that he could stay out over night in a deserted cabin or in an improvised shelter of some sort. It took several days every week for Flint to run all his trap lines, and then it took more time for him to skin, stretch, and to do any little touch up that the pelts needed. He had greatly improved in his ability to trap the animals and he handled the pelts well. He caught mostly martin but he occasionally got a wolf, lynx, or wolverine.

Flint was starting in high school and he enjoyed it and he had no trouble with any of the subjects. We did his school work after he had run his trap lines and had skinned the fur. We never had to live by the clock so we had no problem with doing his school whenever. However he did often have a problem of staying awake for his school. Like his mother, he would keep right on going with his school work after he'd fallen asleep. Sometimes when we were discussing a lesson, his answers would make no sense or he'd say that he'd never heard of something that he knew as well as his own face in the mirror. Then it was time to put the books away and try again another time. Sometimes when I was reading aloud or telling a story to the kids, I would fall asleep and go off in a direction that had nothing to do with the book or the story that I was telling. Then the kids would look at each other and at me in disgust and say, "Wake up, Mom; you've gone to sleep again!"

For Christmas we were able to buy a snow machine and John brought it up to us. After that getting wood, Flint's trapping, and going up for mail was much easier and less time consuming. In late February and early March the nights were -40 to -50 degrees but the days were all blue skies and sun shine and they were so much warmer. We enjoyed many long snow machine rides, going up to the high country where we could view the Ogilvie Mountains. There's not much that I wouldn't give to be able to go back there to that life style, if only I could have my whole family with me again!

Chapter 27
BUMPS, CUTS, BRUISES, AND PUNCTURE
1987—1988

In the spring when the road crew had gotten to the Y we walked most of the 12 miles to where the road crew was working and caught a ride into Tok. The next morning Rob drove to Tok to pick us up and he took us back to his house in North Pole. We rented a car and began to look for a new truck, since that mechanic had put our old one permanently to rest. On the way into town while we were waiting for the Richardson Highway to clear enough for us to cross, we were suddenly smacked hard in the side of the car. There were no vehicles in sight, only a plane flying overhead. I thought at first that the plane must have dropped something on us, but then we got out and saw that we had been hit by a run away tire. The tire had come from the highway off of a teen aged boy's car. The damage to the rental car entailed extra paper work but we got it done and were able to buy another pickup.

After we were back home Brian, a friend of Flint's from school came to stay with us. For the rest of the spring the boys hand mined and ran around with Bob. At the first of the summer Bob started back to work on the Hwy and Brian's family came up to manage the lodge. During the summer the boys and I mined during the week and we were joined by Bob, John, and Richard on the weekends. When we couldn't mine, we'd go to work with Bob and camp in Eagle or beside the road.

Shianne was given a bicycle and she was a mass of scrapes and cuts while she learned to ride it. She reminded me of myself when I started riding a bike. At first I didn't have a bike of my own and I learned to ride on my brother Jim's. The problem was that while I could reach the pedals when they were up, and push enough to make them go around, I could not push the pedals down to use the brakes. My only method of stopping was to lean far enough to the side to tip me over or to crash into a tree or something. One day I rode down a steep hill and the something that I used to make me stop was a moving semi truck that was crossing at the bottom. I don't know if the driver heard, saw, or felt me crash into his side but he stopped and got out of the truck. The poor man was cloud grey in color and he was shaking so badly that he could hardly help me up. I was afraid that he was going to fall and that I would have to help him up. Although I was hurting enough to be sick to my stomach I assured him, "I'm okay. I always stop this way." I suspect that he was praying that I would never choose him to bump into again!

Shianne continued to get cuts, scrapes, and bruises even after she had learned to ride her bike. She would come into the house all banged up but without tears or complaints. Timber attributes her toughness to him but I rather think that Flint had a hand in that as well. She tagged along behind her brothers doing what they did, and they made little concessions for her being younger. They were not trying to let her get hurt and they were sorry when she was hurt, but they were certainly willing to gamble with hers and their own safeties. There were rock fights, rides on bikes or snow machines through brush with jumps off of hills and banks, and rolls down the mountain side in barrels. If I had known all the things that they were doing, I would not have had to wait so long for my long sought after gray hair.

All that summer we mined, worked, and visited with Brian and his family up at the lodge and they visited us down at the cabin. In the fall Bob finished his last few days of work on the highway in Tok and we all went with him, staying in a motel, eating at Fast Eddy's, and watching TV. After our fall trip to town for supplies and getting wood and caribou, we settled down for another winter of school, trapping, snow machining, walking, and play.

In February we snow machined to where we had parked the truck and then we drove to Tok. Here Flint who was now fifteen got his learner's driving permit and he helped drive on the long ride out side to the lower 48. With all the merriment that went along with the scenery while driving and the stops in different restaurants and motels, I found the trip almost too thrilling to contain. Bob was always cheerful and full of fun, except in the mornings when he was in a hurry to get packed and off. One morning I stepped out of the shower to discover that Bob was packed and ready to go.

"Where are my clothes? I laid them right here on the bed?"

"Must be in the truck. It's all packed up, I can't find them now."

"Well I can't go like this. This towel doesn't even belong to me!"

Bob was reluctant but he did go and get me some clothes to wear. He even brought me my shoes. I wasn't sure that he would because once after he had packed them when we were leaving Patti's and Rob's house, I had had to go home barefoot.

We stopped for a few days at Lou Ann's and Frank's goat farm in Washington, and we were having so much fun that we were reluctant to leave when we felt that we should. We were afraid of overstaying our welcome but when we said that we were leaving, Lou Ann stated, "It's time now, Frank; go let the air out of their tires." After a couple more days visit, we drove on to California to visit with Jim and Betty, all of Bob's brothers and sisters, Grandma, and friends. After a wonderful visit with Grandma, we kidnapped her and took her with us while we visited with Bob's family again.

The highway was still unopened when we got back into the Forty Mile country so we had to snow machine and walk on the last stretch home. Once back we resumed our life just where we had left off except that Flint had already pulled his traps. When the road opened Flint went up to the lodge to watch it until the new family who were buying the lodge arrived. When they came in they hired Flint to stay on and work for them.

Timber was hand mining and one day when I waded in the creek to help him set up his sluice box, I stopped and pulled my foot out of the water and it had a board nailed to it, right through my big toe! "Timber, I need you to pull this out!" Blood was dripping down into the creek and a very pale Timber was reluctant to yank the board off of my foot. The nail was deeply imbedded and it was not easy to pull it out with me wobbling around, trying to stand with my foot up. I think it hurt him worse than it did me but he finally got it out. I had to stay off of my foot for quite a while and it was still sore more than a week later, after it was mostly healed. Then Bob had to open and doctor the wound again, as it was infected.

We didn't get started mining until late that summer, since Flint was working up at the lodge. He worked ten hours a day, seven days a week, until there was a forest fire on the Alcan Hwy that made all the traffic use the Klondike Loop through Dawson City and Boundary. Then with such a huge amount of traffic Flint had to work eighteen hours a day for several weeks until the fire was contained.

At the end of June there was an argument up at the lodge and the family who was buying it decided to leave. We made arrangements to buy the large trailer in which they were living, a freezer, and the food that they hadn't used. It was mid July and we finally got started mining since Flint came back down to the creek to mine with us. A family with eight children, all Shianne's age and older, came to mine on a near by creek. Through out the summer theirs and our kids got together for a picnic or just hanging out. Flint took a liking to Kaylee, their oldest daughter who like Flint was fifteen. They spent a lot of time together and one day they took off for Dawson City for the day. This really worried Bob since Flint only had a learners permit at the time and Bob was hurt and angry. Flint had been making his own decisions for some time and this was the first and only time that he went against our wishes. In August after his sixteenth birthday we went to Tok and Flint got his driver's license.

Action Jackson's son John Junior came up to take care of his inherited lodge, and he hired Flint to work up there again. When John Junior left in September we moved up to the lodge staying in the big trailer that we had just bought. There were still some tourists stopping by and the usual hunters coming up and Flint sold gas, food, and gifts, and provided meals for people who rented the cabins. When he was repairing a split rimmed tire for a trucker, the stem blew off of the tire and like a bullet it imbedded it's self in Flint's leg. By then the road was no longer being maintained and there was a considerable amount of snow and ice. Bob did not know if the road to Dawson City was passable or if he could still get across the Yukon River on the ferry. He had to try however, and although it was touch and go they made it and got Flint into the hospital.

When the last of the people stopped coming through and all was quiet, we settled down again to school, our usual chores, walks, and fun. Timber was now in high school along with Flint. The year before down at the cabin, Shianne had been given an assignment to write a memoir about breakfast of all things. She did the assignment and submitted it to her teacher along with the rest of her school work. We didn't know it at the time but Shianne's teacher entered it in a contest that McDonald House has every year for young writers. One winner is chosen for each state and their entrees are then put in a book, Rainbow House that is published each year. That year Shianne was Alaska's winner. This is her entree:

MEMOIR OF BREAKFAST AT THE CABIN

The cabin is still cold after a night with the wood stove banked down. Now the stove is sending out waves of comforting warmth and a coffee pot rests ready and hot on top. From the cooking stove comes the rich, meaty smell of moose steak sizzling. The potatoes are fast becoming brown and crisp, and the eggs are gently turned over and removed from the heat when the whites are solid and while the yolks are still a golden soft liquid.

My stomach growls as I take my fork in hand. My breakfast is neither fancy nor beautiful but it is solid, nourishing, and good. It brings the heat and energy to see me through the work and fun of a cold winter's day, and adds to the impression of the simple, pleasing life that is my girlhood in the cabin at Davis Creek.

———

Shianne received a copy of the book and a personal letter from Senator Ted Stevens congratulating her. He said that she made him feel like he was right there in the cabin with her, and he thanked her for inviting him. Unfortunately we no longer have the book or his letter. She loves to write, has written countless poems on just about every subject, and just now she has gotten her first novel published and has two more in the making. Her writing is easy reading with descriptions that put the reader right in the book with the characters. After she starts a novel the story takes a life of its own, captures the reader and goes in the direction that it chooses. Shianne isn't given the choice of what, when, or how things are going to happen; but the end result is a pleasurable journey for the reader.

Chapter 28
ON THE MOUNTAIN TOP
1989—1990

Flint with Big Guy, Sissy, and Kisses, Boundary 1987

The trailer that we bought was much bigger than the cabin and had closets, cupboards, furniture and such. There were two bed rooms, one for the boys, one for Shianne; and Bob and I slept on a cot in the living room. I don't know if Bob found the cot too crowded but I liked it. In case we got angry with each other there was not the option to sleep apart on the other side of the bed, there was no other side. We still did not have electricity or plumbing but since we were already at the lodge we didn't need to go up for mail. Often on Fridays we would need to pack down the run way so that the mail plane could land. Sometimes too, we would need to chase a herd of caribou away before the mail plane came. Since the lodge is at the top of a mountain we did not lose direct sun light for three months as we did down at the cabin. Although we were the only people there and in many ways it was convenient to be up there, I still missed living down in the cabin. Sadly we never returned to the cabin to live but it will always be my most cherished home and it will be my final resting place. Now I understand that it has become a national historical monument and can not ever be mined.

In November Flint set out his traps and ran them with the dogs and sled. Bob and or Timber would sometimes go on the trap line with him, but usually not on his longer lines when he had to stay out over night. He sometimes was not able to get home at the time that we expected him, and although we

189

were uneasy we knew that he knew how to handle what ever situation came up. Sometimes he started out the trapping season with a snow machine, but I don't think that any of the snow machines with held all the miles and the rough terrain of the mountains for the whole trapping season. He always had to run the trap lines on snowshoe for at least part of the year. Many times over the years he was stuck out over night at -40 degrees in what ever shelter that he could dig or make for himself. Through storm or cold he always eventually made it home with no more than sore feet, aching muscles, and a little frost bite.

At Christmas time a neighboring trapper in the area (30 miles away), left a beautiful husky puppy with us when he took the rest of his dog team home to spend Christmas with his family. The puppy was sweet and smart and we all became very fond of her. In mid January when her owner returned he took her with him but not for long. She did not grow as big as he had hoped; so he killed, skinned, and cooked her, feeding her to the other dogs. Flint found her hide when he stayed at Crazy Larry's cabin, which they both sometimes used when out on their trap lines. When Bob found out what the trapper had done he was furious, and he told him so very descriptively, up one side and down the other. Because he did not want his children to get attached to the dog, he left her with us for our children to grow to love.

That winter it got very cold and stayed that way for two weeks or so. The radio made a big fuss over the cold, and many people began to write asking us if we were all right. They need not have worried for Bob always prepared for anything that might come up. Anyway it was not as bad as or at least no worse than it used to get every year back in the 60s. Later Bob got a case of shingles and then first Flint and later Shianne came down with the measles. Unlike our usual winters we had some visitors stop by before the road opened. One set of visitors flew in and another set snow machined in for a few days.

One cold day while I was straightening up in the trailer, Shianne came in from out side. We started talking about this, that, and the other thing; until about forty minutes later, I began to hear something but I couldn't make out what it was.

"What is that noise? Is it an animal or someone calling?"

Shianne listened then replied, "Oh that's right! Flint's in the out house and he needs toilet paper. I was supposed to bring him some."

It was a very cold, disgruntled brother who finally made it into the house.

When the road did open we made our usual trip into town. With the money that Flint had made mining and up at the lodge; he bought a brand new Toyota truck. The car dealer said that when he was sixteen he was still using his allowance to buy games, he couldn't have even dreamed about buying a new truck. Flint was always in a hurry to learn and do everything. When we got back from town Flint sold gas, gifts, etc. until John Junior arrived on Memorial Day. After that John Junior hired Flint to manage the lodge and Timber and Shianne to help him.

Some years ago they had closed down the restaurant part of Boundary Lodge because they got their water from the creek. Times change I can remember when the health inspector found Carol Ann's toys in the barrel that Norma used for water, and all he did was ask that she find another place for Carol Ann to play. Also one year when a guy named Bill and his family was up at the lodge he had two out of season caribou hanging in plain sight. When a man from fish and game unexpectedly flew in, Bill and his wife were really nervous. After talking to them over coffee and pie, while they were walking out to his plane; the inspector commented, "Gosh darn, rabbits grow big out here!"

Bob started work on the high way on June first and he began to tend bar sometimes in the evenings and on weekends. Bob had given up drinking back when Shianne was a baby, but that didn't stop him from being a terrific bar tender. He kept the customers laughing and turned every night into a big party. People who were just passing through sometimes stayed several days, and people who had planned to return home taking the other route would change their plans and again take the Klondike Loop so that they could see Bob again. People always remembered Bob but he sometimes had to call many people something like "Sam" or "Easy Money" if he didn't remember their names.

Some friends of Patti's were telling her about their trip to the lower 48, and they told her that they had stopped at a lodge that was run by three kids.

Patti replied, "Yes, and I'll bet that their names are Flint, Timber, and Shianne."

"That's right, how did you know? Have you been there?"

"Yes, I have. They are my cousins."

In August they revoked the liquor license and so the bar needed to be closed. John Junior and Flint went into town to sell the liquor, and Flint came back with a big very fast motor cycle. I hated that motor cycle! Flint would ride it down the run way and he was just a blur as he passed the trailer window. He'd be going so fast that it looked like he was going to take off, flying over the mountains and trees. I was contemplating smashing it, but it broke down so I didn't have to do so.

In September when John Junior left the lodge, Flint also left driving out to California, Arizona, and Colorado. His main reasons for the trip were that he needed to finalize the deal that he had made with John Junior to buy the lodge, he wanted to drive his new truck, and he wanted to see Kay Lee, his girl from the summer before last.

It was really quiet and sad without Flint around and Bob took it especially hard. Timber shot the caribou that we needed, and on his fifteenth birthday we drove to Tok, shopped, washed clothes, and met Patti and Grandma for lunch at Fast Eddy's. We brought Grandma back home with us and Timber insisted that she was his birthday present. After another great visit we needed to return to Tok to meet Patti again so that Grandma could fly back home to California.

Flint came home just in time to set out his traps in November and he brought Kaylee's brother Grady with him. Grady has red hair and coloring like Flint's and he was eighteen, one year older than Flint. The three guys had good times on the trap lines and chasing all over the country. They would come home tired and prevail upon Shianne to fix them snacks and run errands for them. It was like having three big brothers to make demands and to tease her, and they only included a touch of pampering. The boys told Grady that to be an Alaskan he had to take a snow bath, and of course they chose a cold night to make him take it.

They all got along real well for the most part, except for one night when Flint and Grady got in an argument. Grady was smaller than Flint's six foot three inches, and so to keep from hitting him Flint stuck his fist through a window. Then he had to come into the trailer to wash and bandage his hand. That was Flint's way of keeping his temper in check, and to avoid doing something that he would regret. I always told him that there is nothing wrong with having a temper, but that if he didn't control it, it would control him. He didn't have red hair for nothing.

Along with spring and the opening of the road, came Bob's work on the highway and we were all working to get everything ready at the lodge. That summer the State had contracted work on the run way, so the contractor Glen Martin, his wife Jody, and their son's brought in a trailer in which to live. Now Boundary was inhabited by Wolffs and Martins. Also two guys, Norm and Lloyd had been mining in the area and they brought their trailers up to the lodge. Over the years with them living there in the summers, they came to be like family too. Earlier Norm had been mining with Danny, the miner who had shot our Sambo. One night before we knew Norm, he was accidently shot in the leg and he walked ten miles to our cabin at Davis creek. We had gone to bed but when Norm woke us, Bob took him to the hospital in Dawson City. Norm and Lloyd had come up together, they were working together; and everyone soon began to almost think of them as one. People said "Norm and Lloyd" so much that one day a man asked me if I knew where Norman Lloyd was. He said that he knew him, but I would think that if that were true he would have noticed that he is two men instead of one.

That was a crowded summer with tour buses, caravans, and tourists all over. Flint sold lots of gas and diesel, the gift shop was rocking, and they repaired tires and did some mechanical work as needed. Shianne did a lot of the tire repair and sometimes the boys from the local mines would stand in the gift shop talking to me in order to watch her out of the window. When I told her that the local boys like to watch her change tires, she said that it would be better if they came out and helped instead. In the gift shop Shianne made friends with the tourists, they remembered her, and she corresponded with many people from all over the world for several years. I met, enjoyed, and talked to lots of people too; but I never kept track of them afterward. Even my special people who I promised to write, think about often, and who I love dearly; rarely receive letters from me. The only one who I wrote to regularly was Grandma. I wrote to her every week, except for the months that we were on the Iditarod River.

We kept the lodge open from 7 a.m. to 9 p.m. seven days a week, and after we closed Shianne and I would usually prepare a late dinner for all of us, Wolffs, Martins, Grady, Norm, and Lloyd.

In July I had to go into town for eye surgery. I recovered immediately and we continued with our busy schedules in the lodge. Something happened involving a friend of Timber's and it had him so angry that he and Grady tore out in the Buick. Timber was taking the sharp mountainous curves all to fast and he drove off of a steep cliff. The car rolled over several times before it was stopped by a tree. We have the sturdiness of the Buick to thank for keeping both boys alive and unhurt. The accident only served to allow Timber to get control of his anger, but it thoroughly shook up Grady. He would have liked to have never had to get back into a car, and he had no intention of ever riding with Timber again. The Buick, what was left of it, retired from travel permanently.

Patti, Rob, and the girls came up in August to help us celebrate Flint's 18th birthday. They hand mined for a couple of days and when I finished panning out the gold that they had found, Flint and Glen (who had just finished work on the air strip) went down to the creek to do some mining. They leased Norm's equipment and after a couple of weeks mining, Flint and Glen had agreed to be partners in the mine and in the lodge, and to buy Norm's equipment.

As Glen and his family, Norm and Lloyd, all of the other miners, and most of the tourists pulled out of the country; Bob, Shianne, and I took care of the lodge so that the three boys could go fishing. They camped by a lake, borrowed a boat, caught several lake trout, and had a great time.

When the boys got back from fishing they stayed at the lodge while Bob, Shianne, and I had to go into town for Bob to have surgery on his hand. After driving and using the chain saw so much at work, cutting down brush and trees to improve the visibility on over one hundred miles of highway; his hands had curled up making it difficult for him to use them. The insurance company refused to pay for the surgery, so I went to the Workman's Compensation Office. There I was told that I would need to go to a lawyer and we did. Once back home the district attorney sent me a book of papers to fill out and one of the questions was to tell about the things that Bob did when he wasn't working. I wrote that he walks, reads, listens to the radio, etc.; but I was told that my answer was not good enough. So I answered in greater detail, describing how he uses a fork and knife while eating, that he pets his dogs, plays with his children, kisses his wife, walks out to the out house, wipes with toilet paper, etc. etc. etc. After about a page of listing everything that I could think of, I ended by saying that if it's really what he doesn't do that she wants to know—he doesn't drive a truck since the road is closed, he doesn't ride a snow machine since we don't have one, he doesn't use a chain saw since we're burning oil, etc. I don't know if she liked my answer, but we won the case and the insurance paid for his surgery.

After Bob's hand had healed we had to go back into town for him to have surgery on the other hand. The doctor had said that if he had them both done at once he wouldn't be able to dress or wipe himself, and that option didn't appeal to him. Again the boys stayed at Boundary while we were gone, and when we got back we discovered that Little Guy had gone on a run and had never returned. He probably had run into a pack of wolves and that was all she wrote. It made one less dog pulling the sled and one less personality to laugh at and enjoy, we missed him! Sissy was Flint's dog, Big Guy was Bob's and mine, Kisses was Timber's, and Little Guy had been Shianne's.

Chapter 29
FIRE, TOIL, AND VANDALISM
1991—1992

Bob at Christmas, Boundary 1991

It was a busy but quiet and pleasant winter with trapping, school, walking, dog sled rides, our weekly mail, the radio, playing games, and teasing and romping at home.

While it was still winter and cold, we decided to have another trip out side. We would be too busy with work, mining, and the lodge, to wait and go after the road opened. Flint and Grady were staying at the lodge to finish up the trapping. Bob and Timber flew in to Tok on the mail plane one Friday, and Flint was bringing Shianne and me in by snow machine. Flint likes to scare people who ride on the snow machine with him by jumping off of steep banks and such. He had really scared Shianne a time or two, but I had always refused to ride with him. Now he said that he had me where he wanted me, I had no choice but to ride with him. I told him that if he went too fast he might have a hysterical woman on his hands, but he only laughed. As we got ready to go, with Shianne behind Flint on the snow machine and me bringing up the rear on a sled, I gritted my teeth and prepared for the worst. What a shock! Flint stopped three times before we even got off of the run way asking me if he was going too fast and if I was Okay.

It was a fun but cold ride to South Fork where our truck was parked. The day was well below 0 degrees, and we had ice and snow blowing on us for hours. When we got off the machine, our clothes were frozen stiff, our limbs creaked and would barely move, and we weren't sure whether we were human or snow people. Since the truck had been parked there since October, it took Flint over an hour's work to get it started. All the while Shianne and I watched and shivered. Then when it did start the heater wasn't working so the truck was not only cold, but the windows had to be kept open so that Flint could see out. No relief it was a cold slow ride on in to Tok. Bob and Timber had gotten a motel room and after finally arriving there I could hardly wait to have a hot bath. No such luck, their heating system wasn't working; and not only was there no hot water, but the rooms were cold. Without undressing, I climbed in bed under the blankets and waited to thaw. It was the coldest day, from morning until well into the night, that I have ever had!

We had the usual great time both driving down and in California, and did too many fun things and saw too many loved people to mention. However we did find Grandma, who was then in her late eighties, quite changed. She hadn't learned to drive until her mid forties and she had always been a nervous driver. She and I learned to drive at the same time, but I was sixteen and it didn't bother me. I never understood why she was so nervous until I learned to run equipment for the first time in my mid forties. Somehow it just isn't the same as when one was a kid. As the years passed she did more and more crazy things behind the wheel; turning right from the left hand lane, driving all around town to avoid left turns, stopping and even parking in the middle of the road, going around blockades into road construction, etc. etc. It's a wonder that she was still alive! Then along with her nervousness and multiple driving mistakes, she no longer could remember where she was going. It spelled disaster! One day when we were following her to a friend's house for dinner, she abruptly stopped the car in the middle of the street and Timber walked back to our truck.

"Grandma doesn't remember where we're going."

"Tell her that we're going to the Woodworths."

He told her but he had to return to the truck. "She doesn't know the way from here. She says that she needs for you to show her the way home, and then she'll try again from there."

We didn't return home but by hit and miss (since it had been a long time)

I eventually managed to find the way to their house.

Grandma's bank account was another hurdle to jump. She had written books of checks without writing a single number on any of the stubs. (That was before the day of the wonderful duplicates.) No one, least of all her, had any idea of what she had spent; or of how much money she had left in the bank. She had been talked into buying a new vacuum cleaner and the sales-man had taken the good vacuum that she had been using. She had no idea what it was costing her, just that she paid some each month. We found that these payments went on forever, and that the vacuum was costing her thou-sands of dollars (a not so small of a fortune back then). We tried unsuccess-fully to talk her into coming home with us to live, but we had to worriedly return home without her.

By the time we got back to the Forty Mile the road was open, so we could drive all the way back to the lodge. Flint and Grady were there, getting things ready for opening the lodge; and one of Grady's brothers, Cedar, had joined them. Both Grady and Cedar joined the rest of their family shortly after we got back. Glen and his family came up and he and Flint got started mining down in the creek. Bob started work on the high way so that left Timber, Shianne, and I to run the lodge.

With everybody working long and heavy hours, it was difficult to keep everyone in clean clothes. Although the guys work pants needed lots of scrub-bing, I enjoyed washing the clothes by hand. What I didn't enjoy doing was wringing big heavy things out by hand, and I would always get sopping wet. Bob bought me a hand wringer that fastened on to the tin tub. How I loved to feed the clothes through it and to turn the handle. The clothes got a lot cleaner too, since the wringer did such a better job of getting the dirty wash water out. On wash days Big Guy, who was tied out in the yard near me, and I had a competition to see which one of us got our picture taken the most, him with his paw up begging for attention, or me using my tub, wash board, and hand wringer. I lost count, so I don't know who won.

Norm had been leasing ground to mine from Danny, but when he found too little gold he sold his equipment to Glen and Flint. Danny believed that the equipment should have been left to him, and he resented the fact that Norm and Lloyd lived in their trailers up at the lodge and hung out with us. We strongly suspected Danny of causing the only break down at the mine that summer. Someone sawed a part of the water pump in half. The guys had to stop mining long enough to go into town to get it fixed, but that was not an insurmountable delay. We all, Glen, Jodie, Norm, Lloyd, Bob, the kids, and I; used to make bets on the amount of gold that we would find in each clean up. Unfortunately it was usually won by the one whose bet was the most conservative. Flint always bet high and each time that he lost, he'd say that his turn would come. We were all happy and richer when he finally did win.

Patti, her friend Sam, and their daughters: Carolyn, Becky, Amy, and Carrie came up to visit and hand mine in August, and they were here to help Flint celebrate his nineteenth birthday. In September after we celebrated Timber's seventeenth birthday Glen, his family, Norm, and Lloyd all pulled out for the year. Both Glen and Flint were glum when their mining was nearing the end, but they were both looking forward to next year's mining, and to another season's work in the lodge. We continued working in the lodge, and then when the road closed; Bob, Shianne, and I went into Tok for Bob to work for a few days again. When Bob finished his work Flint came into Tok to drive us home, since Bob had driven a work truck in to Tok. The road, as is usual in October, had a considerable amount of snow and ice; and just as we were going around a sharp curve, we slid right off of a cliff! The truck and we would have been in sad shape if a tree hadn't stopped our descent. We got out unhurt, walked to South Fork, and then caught a ride back to Boundary. The truck had to stay where it was until spring when it was winched out, towed to Tok, and sold.

After another rollicking winter we began to look toward spring and to prepare for all that would need to be done. There were ups and downs, but mostly ups. Flint's trapping had been good in November, fair in December, poor in January, and terrible in February. That didn't deter him from making the long trek every week on snow machine, or the much longer slower ones on snow shoe, which ever circumstances required. School had gone well, we had everything that we needed, we had lots of time to do the things that we wanted, and we had each other. Our daily diet was mostly all ups.

That spring Grandma decided that she was going to make another trip up to see us. We were so relieved not only because of the concerns that we had discovered when we were with her, but because of letters that we had gotten from friends about how she was doing. For safety reasons my brother Jim had insisted that she sell her car. It was the plan for me to fly down to California to help her get ready and to fly back up with her. Rob had just tearfully left on a three year tour in North Dakota, and because they had bought their house and Patti had a full time teaching job, they decided that she and the girls would stay in North Pole.

After putting me on the plane Bob was pacing between Patti's living room and kitchen. "Patti, how do you stand it?"

"Give me a break! Rob's gone for three years, and you want sympathy because Margaret will be away for a few days?"

With or without sympathy he did survive and he had Shianne with him to assure him that everything would be all right. Patti and Rob also got through their three years. Rob flew up to North Pole every Christmas, and Patti and the girls spent summers with him in North Dakota.

Although I had been on lots of small bush planes, I was terribly excited to be flying on the big air line. I kept my face pressed against the window constantly in an attempt to see everything, and I was delighted when I was served breakfast, two lunches, and a snack on the plane. When the stewardess explained how to inflate the life jackets, in case we went down in the ocean; I thought, (that would be interesting, I haven't done that before.) When we were nearing San Francisco the plane started flying oh so slowly and so close to the ocean that it was almost touching. I thought that we were going down, and I quickly revised my earlier thoughts. (I didn't mean it! I don't feel like going into the ocean just now!) Suddenly land appeared and we were landing on the run way's pavement.

Jim met me in San Francisco and after we both reassured Bob on the telephone, we drove to San Luis Obispo. There we stayed with Mom in her trailer, took care of her business, visited with everyone, and helped her pack. It was so nice to see Jim and to have time to talk. It had been many years since we had been able to do so. Jim drove us to San Francisco and we took a plane to Seattle where his youngest daughter Nancy and her husband Roy met us. The next day Lou Ann and Frank came to visit and the following day we caught a plane for Fairbanks.

This part of our trip was eventful. Grandma had to use the bathroom and since she was wearing pants with an elastic waist and she was standing on her pant legs, they did not stand up when she did. It surprised me that standing there in her underwear did not bother her more than it did, but I had another surprise coming. Our plane didn't get very much farther before the cargo door came off and the plane began to jerk. The stewardess told us what had happened and that we would be returning to the air port. I was concerned for Mom because she has always been afraid of flying but I discovered that she was calm.

"Are you alright?"

"Oh yes, I'm fine. She said that there was nothing to worry about."

I agreed with her, but I wondered what she thought the stewardess would have said if she had been really concerned – ("Everyone panic, we're going to crash!")? We had to stay in our seats with our seat belts on, and we were instructed to hold our heads in our laps when we landed. However the landing was not too bad, and as far as I know no one was hurt. We did have to wait in the plane for a long time while they got it fixed, and everyone received a free flight. We gave ours to Patti and Rob as they fly several times a year.

Patti was glad that she only had Shianne with her, and that she didn't have Bob to contend with when meeting our late late plane. I was concerned that our luggage might have fallen out of the plane, but that didn't happen. However the relief that I felt when we picked up our luggage was short lived. Patti drove Shianne and me to Tok to meet Bob on the next day, but Grandma stayed to visit with her until Bob picked her up on Memorial Day.

One morning a couple of days after Bob had brought Grandma up with us, Shianne brought Grandma and I breakfast where we were sitting in the newly opened gift shop. The breakfast was good but Shianne had left the burner on under the frying pan in the trailer. There is no view of the trailer from the gift shop, so we didn't know that anything was wrong until the smoke got to the parking lot in front. By then the whole trailer was in flames and it was too late to save anything. There went Grandma's and my luggage that had survived its open plane ride. There went Bob's old Alaskan books and all our pictures that had been rescued from the vacant store in Shageluk but had not yet been sent to us when we had the fire in Flat. There went many of the gifts that Flint had bought which we hadn't yet put in the shop. There went over $20,000 cash which was to be the payment for Flint's first order of gas and diesel. When the fuel truck arrived all we had to offer him was ashes. He left the fuel anyway but it wasn't easy to get it all payed for after such a big set back. Yet again most of what we owned was knocked away causing the fumble that brought a halt to our forward progress.

As bad as that mishap was for us all, it wasn't the only one that we had that summer. Glen had bid and received the construction of the new gravel pit that was going in on the road to Eagle. He was leasing the dozer that they were buying from Norm, and his time driving it to the construction company. He had left his trailer at the lodge so that he and his family could live there again, but instead he came up and got the trailer because he had accepted another job else where. That left Flint with the lodge to run and pay for, the mining with the equipment to pay for, and the responsibility of the gravel pit to do alone. It was a lot to chew for a nineteen year old who had spent most of his life alone with his family. He probably wouldn't have bit off so much if he hadn't thought that he had an experienced partner to help him.

Patti and Rob had the truck and camper that Mom and Dad used to use. It had quit running for the most part, but after the fire Patti, Sam, and other friends gathered food, clothes, and necessary items and put them into the camper. Flint and Lloyd went into town and somehow they got the truck to run long enough to get to Boundary. It never ran very far again but now we had a place to sleep and everything that we needed to get by on. It was like Christmas, looking through all the things that they had so kindly sent up.

Flint hired two women to come up to help at the lodge. They both wanted to come up and work, but neither of them wanted to work for the whole summer. So for part of the time Anita came up, bringing her son and daughter; and the rest of the time Sam was with us with her daughters, Amy and Carrie. The girls are friends of Shianne's so it was especially nice for her to have them around. They were up there to help Shianne celebrate her fourteenth birthday. The lodge was busy all the time and we sold a lot of gas, deceil, food, and gifts. Flint was run ragged between his three jobs, and he used Timber both in the lodge and down at the mine, where ever he was most needed. When they had a clean up at the mine, I would pan the results out in a tub in front of the gift shop. The tourists would watch me pan and that seemed to stimulate them to go into the shop and buy gold. Whenever Flint was up at the lodge, I would snag him and take his picture with the people who bought some of his gold. Then his face would be as red as his hair. Flint designed and had special Top of the World Tee and sweat shirts made up and we sold lots of other gifts. However we sold more gold, both jewelry and raw gold, than everything else put together.

We got a bunch of slab wood from Tok and covered the gift shop, cabins, and out houses with it. It took quite a while to do it, but it was kind of fun and our reward was that now they looked like old log buildings like the two buildings that constituted the original lodge. When the job was finished it looked good.

One day a man and his son broke down on the Taylor Highway and they caught a ride up to the lodge. They had no money but were waiting for a friend who was bringing the necessary parts. I thought that they might be hungry and mentioned it to Flint.

His answer, "No one gets fed without paying for it." got my dander up.

(We'll just see about that!) So I asked them if they would like something to eat.

"Oh no thanks, we're full. That big red headed boy over there gave us all the food that we could eat."

One morning at about 6 a.m. on his way to work on the gravel pit, Flint met Danny going the other way. When Flint approached the dozer he saw that there were pieces of foot long wire all over the ground. The entire wiring system in the dozer had been cut and with enough cut out so that the wires could not be put back together. Of course we suspected Danny but we had no proof and Flint was the kind who would rather put his fist through a window or a wall than fight, unless it was necessary. Flint had to pay the mechanic on the job to rewire the dozer and the cost was huge. The bills that Flint was receiving all too regularly had me staggering as it was. Flint stood up under them but with all the set backs it seemed like he was having to dig his way out of a hole that only

kept getting deeper. Flint felt that he was losing money at the bid that Glen had made on the gravel pit so he pulled off. Between the lodge and the mine he had his hands and mind full anyway.

After the fire some people from a church in Tok sent us a box of food and in it was a cake mix. It was awfully kind of the people and we appreciated it greatly, but I'm not sure how old the cake mix was, maybe fifty years or so. I baked it in August for Flint's 20th birthday, and somehow it turned out to be a flat heavy chunk on the bottom of the pan. I didn't have any powdered sugar or a recipe for frosting made from regular sugar, but I tried to make some anyway, the chunk needed it. The frosting turned out to be both runny and grainy. After dinner I plopped the mess down on the table and then quickly ducked out the door, going for a walk. I don't know what they did with the mess nobody ever said anything about it. However in September on Timber's 18th birthday and on every birthday that followed for years to come, Flint bought the cakes. It turned out to be the last but best birthday cake that I ever baked.

Chapter 30
RUN AWAY
1992—1994

Bob and I and Flint and Gizila, Boundary 1994

That fall, after the work was all done, everyone had pulled out, and the road was closed; we moved from the camper into two one room cabins across the highway from the lodge. We put a propane cook stove and a table in the cabin that Bob and I stayed in, Grandma and Shianne stayed in the other cabin, and the boys stayed in the lodge. The boys trapped and chased around; Shianne did her school work, read, and wrote poems; and Grandma, Bob, and I walked, read, and took it easy.

After watching a super bowl foot ball game at Skinny Dick's on the Parks Highway when he was thirteen, Flint had became an avid foot ball fan. He especially liked the Cowboys and the Dolphins. One day he talked me into listening to a Dolphin game on the radio with him. As the end of the game was nearing, the Dolphin's kicker missed a field goal that would have won the game. Flint was disappointed after all the excitement and the hard work that the players had gone through to get them within field goal range. It seemed that the game was lost, but then somehow they got the ball back and managed to make a touch down with only seconds to go. Flint was yelling, doing push ups, swinging from the rafters, and making so much commotion in all his excitement, that he got me hooked on professional football. I liked football a lot when I was in high school and in college because I knew many of the players and really wanted our school to win. I had paid no attention to professional football, but now my indifference came to an abrupt hault. Flint started talking to me about different players and giving me articles to read from his sportsman magazines, the hook sunk in farther and football became a big part of my life. I have a *Football Mama* sweat shirt to prove it.

Bob listened to the talk shows on K G O regularly, he sometimes wrote to the hosts, and when ever we were in town he made calls to the shows. When he could he talked a good deal to the hosts, especially his favorites Bill somebody (it's been a long time) and Lee Rogers. In the summers we occasionally had other listeners stopping in to ask if this is the Boundary where Bob Wolff lives. Lee even invited Bob to stop by and have lunch with him the next time that he got to San Francisco.

Sometime after Christmas when the fur catch was slowing down, we decided to make another trip outside. Grandma had originally only come up for a visit, but we had been able to talk her into moving up with us for good. We needed to go get the rest of her things and to sell her mobile home. Flint had a big four wheel drive truck in which he was able to drive us to Tok, where Bob's truck had been stored. After one night in Tok we drove to Whitehorse. The next morning we were on our way again, on a brisk day with a temperature of -50 some degrees. Something froze and stuck making transmission fluid or oil or something leak out in both of our trucks and they both had to be towed back to Whitehorse. We got Flint's truck repaired at once, so we all headed out in it leaving Bob's truck for repair in Whitehorse.

The rest of the trip out had no further mishaps and we had a good time and accomplished what we needed to do. Being able to have lunch and a tour of the radio station with Lee Rogers was a big bonus for Bob and watching the football games on TV for a change was another high light of the trip. We watched a football game where the Buffalo Bills beat the Dolphins coming from way behind in the last minutes of the game. Flint and I were disappointed but Timber was awed. After that game he became an avid Buffalo Bill fan and has been ever since. After packing up Grandma's things we divided the treasures that she had saved: dishes, jewelry, new vacuum, etc. among her children, grand children, and friends. Then we sold her trailer and headed for home, stopping to pick up our repaired truck in Whitehorse.

We got back to Boundary in plenty of time to get resettled and to prepare for another season of work on the high way, at the lodge, and on the mine. Before the road opened Timber began to get some sharp pains. He ignored them and didn't say anything throughout the day, but the pains kept getting worse and worse. By dark the pain was so acute that he could barely move, but with no lighting on the run way we couldn't call in a plane. We sat with him through-out the night while he went in and out of consciousness. Often I had to feel his pulse and listen and watch for breathing to be sure that he was still alive. It was a long and dreadful night and with the morning light, when a plane finally arrived, I cried in relief and in exhaustion from all the worry. Timber flew to the hospital in Fairbanks where the doctors determined that he had a kidney stone lodged in a duct. They gave him morphine for the pain and he went to Rob's and Patti's house in the hopes that he could eventually pass the stone. After a week without success he went back to the hospital for the very painful surgery of running a tube and basket all the way up the urethra, through the bladder, and into the kidney to take out the stone. After the surgery he spent more time with Patti, still on morphine. When he finally got off the morphine and was al-lowed to come home, his digestive system was all messed up and he didn't have a bowel movement for weeks. He was in time finally able to use the out house, but the stomach pains and indigestion did not go away.

On most summer days Grandma sat in the gift shop, talking to the locals and the tourists. She called Lloyd who was from Arizona, the man by the stove and she called Norm the man in the corner. She was especially fond of Norm as he kept her amused and was very sweet to her. The tourists enjoyed talking to her also and they told her about their trips. One day someone came up to me inquiring just where they would have to be hooked up to a dozer to get through a bad stretch of the road. He was quite relieved when I explained that that had happened back in the sixties and that I was quite sure that it was no longer the case. In the evenings after the bunch of us had dinner Grandma would often play the piano for us. She didn't remember the names or the words to many of the songs and she would switch songs in the middle, but her fingers still knew how to make music. She was so gullible and said so many funny things that we all had a lot of fun with her. One day she told us that people no longer have large fannies. We knew that she meant families but it was more fun to confuse and fluster her by arguing that some people do indeed still have large fannies.

Finally she indignantly asked, "Why don't you pay attention to what I mean, instead of what I say?"

In pretended innocence, not wanting to admit that it was more fun not to oblige, we assured her that we were trying to do just that.

She expected a lot from people, not only unraveling her jumbled sentences to get their meanings, but when she stumbled she would demand of who ever caught her, "Why don't you watch where I'm going?"

One crispy August morning while Grandma, Bob, and I were enjoying our coffee, Grandma fell out of her chair and lay on the floor giggling. While I watched her, wondering just what had gotten into her; Bob gave her an aspirin and called for a plane. I flew with her in the plane to the hospital in Fairbanks, and she told the attendants that she was fine and that they could ask her mother (me) if they didn't believe her. She had had a stroke but was able to talk with some difficulty. She called Patti "Potty" for a while. Patti didn't complain and although we all knew who she meant, that didn't stop us from giving both Patti and Mom a bad time about it.

I returned to Boundary but Grandma stayed with Patti for a while after she was released from the hospital. She was able to walk with a walker, she had a special fork with a handle which decreased the mess while eating, and her speech improved. By the time that we brought her back to Boundary she was well on her way to recovering.

Flint went into town and bought a satalight dish and the receiver necessary for getting television at Boundary. His main reason was for foot ball but we all enjoyed seeing movies also. I watched all the football games with the boys, rooting for both the Cowboys and the Bills. Flint and Timber made bets with each other about whose team would have the best record. The competition between the boys was especially high with the Cowboys and the Bills playing against each other in two consecutive super bowl games. It was a win and lose situation for me since I was rooting for both teams.

Two guys came up from Oregon to hand mine and they visited up at the lodge. In the fall when everyone started pulling out of the country, one of the two left but Robert (whom we soon nick named Snuffy) stayed. He was staying in a cabin down in the canyon but he frequently came up to the lodge to get his mail, have a meal, and to watch foot ball and or some movies. All winter he arrived every Friday and sometimes it was two or three days before he went back down to his cabin. When he was at the lodge he was like Flint's shadow with his short legs taking about three steps for Flint's one, he was right behind Flint every where he went. We never saw one without the other, except occasionally we'd see Snuffy waiting for Flint beside the out house door. Although Snuffy was in his fifties and Flint just twenty-one, it soon became apparent that Flint had all but adopted him.

The winter passed peacefully and happily and then along came spring followed by summer. That year Bob quit working on the high way and withdrew his retirement in order to buy gifts for the lodge. The boys continued mining and we had Bob with us working at the lodge. Snuffy and Lloyd went down to the mine to work with Flint and Timber, and Norm was there as usual exploring in search of diamonds.

On one of Flint's trips to town the summer before, he had met a girl from Brazil named Gizila. I guess they had hit it off pretty good because this summer he brought her up to the lodge and unknown to us they were engaged. During the weeks that followed they were inseparable, with Flint showing her the country that he had loved so much his whole life through. She went down to the mine with him every day and he took her to Dawson City where he bought her a little Mackenzie River husky puppy. Tasha was black and white, beautiful, lively, and a little terror; but she grew up to be well behaved, gentle, and well over one hundred pounds. Later Gizila's parents arrived from Brazil with her small daughter Analua. Then Flint and Gizila showed everything to them. We had a big party at the Lodge at the end of the summer with her family, all the miners in the area, some tourists, Snuffy, Norm, and Lloyd, and people from Chicken and Dawson City, all there. Shortly after the party when the road closed Norm, Lloyd, and others left for their homes; Snuffy and Timber stayed at Boundary to hunt; Gizila's parents went back to Brazil; Flint, Gizila, and Analua rented a house on Chena Ridge, Fairbanks; and Bob, Shianne, Grandma, and I again rented a place at the homestead on the Parks Highway.

Shianne started attending West Valley High School. Contrary to her second grade teacher she found that her teachers liked her, the classes were easy but interesting, and the kids were very different from her and mostly weird. They kept to their groups, with each group dressing and acting alike. Shianne had no desire to join any of the groups or to wear low baggy pants almost around her thighs, shower caps, her hair half combed with a comb left hanging in it, etc. She was probably considered somewhat of a nerd. She made a few friends on the out skirts of the groups, but no close friends. Because she didn't fit in most of the kids were snotty to her. One boy asked her out for lunch and when she agreed and went with him, he didn't even talk to her. We bought her a really pretty dress and she went to one dance, but she was uncomfortable since she was the only one not wearing jeans. No one danced with partners; they just got out there and danced any way they wanted. She didn't care to dance to the rap music that they were playing, so she only danced a couple of times and then left. Three guys asked her to the prom. One was a senior and a jock, and he just told Shianne that she was going with him. He was quite surprised when she declined. She thought that one of the boys who invited her was nice, but she refused since she just didn't feel like going to another dance.

Bob didn't find much work so I began to do some substitute teaching, so that we could scrape by financially. I didn't teach every day and I never knew until morning if or where I would be subbing. I found this rather nerve racking, not knowing until mid morning what I was getting myself into or whether I would know how to do the job. I subbed for teachers, assistant teachers, and once I subbed for a speech therapist.

We had extremely heavy snow falls that fall, and Flint got a job clearing many of the parking lots around town. Gizila enrolled in the University and Analua started in the first grade. Analua loved school, made many friends, and she began dancing and piano lessons. She was pretty, talented, precocious, gregarious, and she loved to perform. Flint worked at night and when he got home in the mornings he would get Analua up, cook her breakfast, and get her ready for school. She adored Flint and did exactly as he asked, but her relationship with her mother was more up and down, more push and pull. On Halloween when Analua was trying to tell her mother about her day at school, Gizila distracted her with kisses all over her face and head.

A short time later when Analua asked, "Can we go trick or treating now?"

The answer that she received was, "I told you that we would go when I was ready and not before! Go to your room, I don't want to see or hear you again until we're ready to go."

Analua did as she was told without another word. When ever she angered her mother she was threatened with being sent back to Brazil. She lived in constant fear of that possibility.

One day when Flint and Analua were visiting us out on the Parks Highway Flint said, "We've got to go now, Analua. It's time to pick your mother up at the University."

"Not yet, Flint. Let's just leave her there."

"We can't, you know what she'd say if we did that."

Analua jumped in the truck. "Okay let's go."

One morning on their way to Analua's school, Gizila and Analua kissed Flint good by, and they never came back! Flint searched, called the hospital and the police, and called us to help look for her. Finally he discovered his truck in the parking lot at the air port. Unknown to Flint she had put some of her's and Anna Lua's clothes, toys, etc. in the car in preparation for going back to Brazil. She had saved enough money to buy the tickets after telling Flint that clothes, food, and other things had cost more than they actually did. I guess that she felt that she had to do it that way or Flint would try to talk her out of going. Flint was in total shock and so distressed that we came into town and stayed in the house with him. Snuffy and Timber also came into town so we all stayed there for a while. Gizila had run away from Analua's father, saying that he wanted to sell Analua. Flint felt somewhat better after he talked to another man who had brought Gizila up to Alaska. He said that she had run away from him too, so then Flint felt less like the monster who had done something terrible enough to chase her away. I often wonder how Analua is doing; she was so happy here, loved their home, school, her puppy Tasha, her life, and most of all Flint. Then the thing that she most dreaded happened! I hope that Gizila was able to make it up to her!

Flint's house on the ridge was built on a hill side and there were a few steps leading down from the kitchen to the living room. On Thanksgiving Day I was preparing our dinner while listening to the Cowboy football game and everyone else was in the living room watching the game. When I heard about something that I wanted to see, I dropped what I was doing to run toward the living room. I tripped at the top of the stairs and went flying through the air to land on my belly in front of the TV. Flint thought that I was trying to tackle somebody and yelled, "What the hell are you doing!" I was unhurt, but I didn't get to see the play that I wanted. Now my family knows that it's not safe for me to cook during a football game.

We moved back to the Parks Hwy before Christmas; and Flint, Timber, and Snuffy shared an apartment in town for a while. We were able to enjoy the holidays to some extent, in spite of the shadow of grief that had us all shook up. I can take whatever life brings to me but it is so hard to take it when one's children are hurting!

Chapter 31
NOT MY BOBBY!
1995

Bob's and my last picture together, May 21, 1995

Snuffy and the boys came out to the homestead with us to celebrate the New Year and two days later, Bob bought me ice cream and cherries for our 30th wedding anniversary. We frequently visited Snuffy and the boys in their apartment and we watched the football games with them. Timber got a job working in a grocery store and I continued subbing for a while, until I got a job working at Sophie's Loving Day Care. The pay per hour was much less than subbing but it was much less spotty, I knew where I was going every day, and I could plan what activities that I wanted to do in advance. I had fun with the children. Every day Bob drove Shianne to school, me to work, and then whenever Grandma wasn't visiting with Patti he hung out with her until he picked us up again.

Timber had continued to have severe stomach aches so he finally went to a doctor. The doctor put a picture taking scope all the way down his throat into his stomach. Afterward the doctor understood from where all the pain was coming, Timber had 12 ulcers. They couldn't cure them but they tried to control the pain with diet, medicine, and good advice. It helped to understand what was going on and Timber was able to decrease the discomfort, but from time to time he has been troubled by the ulcers ever since.

Our dear feisty Sissy lost control of her back legs and just like her predecessor fourteen years ago, she was unable to walk alone. She died soon after and we sadly buried her on a hill side on the Parks Highway.

Timber was accepted into Job Core and he left for Wolf Creek, Oregon. Here he was learning carpentry and he liked it. His leaving left a big gap in our lives and we sorely missed him. Now that he was grown, Timber no longer got into all the scraps that he had in school. However he was like his dad in that he was intimidated by no one and although he didn't look for fights he wouldn't take anything off of anyone. Timber isn't very tall and he is of slight build, but he was wiry as all get out and fast. Some bigger and stronger guys were quite disconcerted when regardless of what they had to dish out, it wasn't enough and he kept coming back for more. One night when Timber and I were having a late snack at Denny's, there were several guys at the table next to us. I wasn't paying any attention to them but apparently their tough talk annoyed Timber. When they started to leave one guy paused by our table to pick up something from the floor. Timber suggestion for him, "Anyone who wears his pants that low should wipe better." The guy glared at Timber and his friends returned. The look that Timber gave them was an invitation and I thought that a fight was on, but instead they shrugged and left.

We celebrated Grandma's 90th birthday, both at home and at Patti's house. Patty invited some of her friends and we started the tradition of celebrating her birthday together, a tradition that is still carried on. Grandma had names for Patti's friends: there is the woman in the hat, the pretty one, the nice one, Patti's man (not Rob but Patti's assistant teacher), etc. Sometimes we celebrate at Patti's house, sometimes in a restaurant, and other times at our place; but we haven't missed a single birthday in the last fifteen years.

Shianne went to work with me each day over spring break and not only was she a great help but the kids loved her. We went on several field trips and had fun. Timber got sick, was taken to the hospital, and he decided to come home from Wolf Creek. I wasn't used to having any of my Wolffs away from home and I was happy to have him back. Flint sold Boundary Lodge and after all the arrangements were made; he, Timber, and Snuffy went to Boundary to get ready for another season of mining. It was too quiet and lonely without the guys; so I put in my notice, we packed up, and we weren't too far behind them.

The guys stayed down in the canyon on Walker Fork where they were getting ready and starting to mine. Besides Timber and Snuffy, Flint had hired three other guys to work on the mine, Big Tony, Little Tony, and Brian. Grandma, Shianne, Bob, and I, temporarily moved into the same two cabins at the lodge that we'd lived in before. We often visited down at the mine and the guys frequently came up for dinner. Bob arranged to buy a big two bedroom trailer and we prepared a pretty little spot for it down by the creek near the mine.

We made arrangements with the new owner to run the gift shop for a percentage. The gift shop was to be in the old original log lodge. Bob started work strengthening the structure and repairing the roof of the building and I began to plan how we would have it set up. I gathered the old things that I had been collecting: my flat iron from Flat, an iron toy train car that the boys had found when digging a garden patch for me, several old oil and candle lamps, an old cabin shaped Log Cabin syrup can, old bottles, an old doll that we had found buried in the ground while mining, etc. I had planned to use these things along with the old gold scales that Bob and I had given Flint on his birthday in the décor of the shop. I also planned to use lots of pictures of the old and new miners in the area.

On May 22nd we visited down at the mine and Shianne stayed down there to cook some food for the guys and to wash their dishes. When Bob and I returned to the lodge Bob decided to go for a walk, and because it had begun to snow Grandma and I stayed at home in the cabin. While Bob was gone, Bob and Carol (Y), who mined just across the Canadian border, stopped by as they wanted to see my Bob. While they were waiting for him, they went across the highway to the lodge to get their mail. They left their eighteen wheeled semi truck parked and running by the cabin; but the brakes gave out, the truck began to roll, it was picking up speed, and it was headed right for the cabin! As Bob was returning from his walk he saw the truck and ran and jumped on its side. Somehow he was able to turn the truck away from the cabin, but then it went over a ditch, threw him off, and it ran over and killed my Bobby!

I had heard the noise and I went to the front door to see just what was happening. I saw the truck turn and roll past the cabin and on down the road. Bob (Y) came out of the lodge and started running after his truck, then someone called to him and he turned and started running the other way. As he passed the cabin I could hear him moaning, "OH NO! NO, NO!"

As I stood there in the door way, wondering just what was going on, Carol came over and told me, "Margaret, I'm so sorry! He's gone!"

I was totally confused, "Who's gone? What happened?"

Carol, who had assumed that I had seen it all, looked stunned. "I'm sorry, it's ...it's your Bob, he's ...d...dead."

"It can't be my Bobby! It can't happen. Let me out, I've got to go see him!"

"No, I wouldn't do that, there's nothing that you can do now." She saw my distress and she relented. "At least wait until I can cover him up."

Bob was lying a few feet away from where I had stood. I had to have seen him get thrown but I knew nothing about it and I still can only remember seeing the truck roll by. I don't expect to ever be able to remember what I saw and I probably don't really want to. Actually I'm a little afraid of how I would react if I did remember. I'm afraid that someone might find me crouched in a corner in the fetal position. I'm thankful that the children were all down at the mine at the time. Bob was covered up with a blanket but I had to peek, to be sure that he was dead. Bones were sticking out of his legs and the top part of his head was missing, so I knew that he could not be alive. I sat there beside the highway in the snow and held him in my arms. For six hours I sat there holding him while cars crept slowly by, staring at us. I wasn't cold or embarrassed, all I could feel was the most comforting warmth that vibrated from his soul, filling my body.

Until that day I had been sure that no matter what happened, regardless of how many times we were wiped out of all that we owned; we would be materially poor but still all Okay. I also had just assumed that we would always be together and would die at the same time; it didn't seem possible that he could go without me. He had been there for me; providing me with protection, shelter, laughter, love, amusement, our children, and everything that was wonderful about my life. He had given so much, why did he now have to give his life to save mine? How could I go on without him?

Some one went down to the mine to tell the kids and they came up. Another trucker had stopped there and when Flint saw him with his truck parked near us, he thought that it had been him that had hit and killed his dad. Flint punched him, knocking him on the ground before he found out what really had happened. The trucker understood and said that no apology was necessary.

Both boys reacted to their father's loss with anger and it hung around to trouble them for a long time. Years ago I had been so distraught when I learned that my ex-fiancé Ken had married someone else. The loss of Bob was a thousand times greater, and one would expect the pain to be excruciating. Instead, the pain was over powered by an over whelming feeling of gratitude for the thirty two blessed years that we had shared. I miss him terribly and I always will, but somehow he has prevented me from grieving. I feel like he is still with me, *death did not us part!*

When the troopers finally arrived Flint made me leave Bob so that they could put him in a body bag. I wanted him back in my arms and I asked to ride into Fairbanks with him. The troopers said that it was allowed for me to ride in with them, but that I would not be allowed to sit in back and hold Bob. So I rode into town with the kids and we arrived at Patti's house in the early morning hours.

I retained the feeling of holding him in my arms for weeks before it gradually began to slip away. It was that feeling along with the picture of Bob that I carried with me, that got me through those first several days. When I had to use both hands and put the picture down for a moment, I panicked until I could find and pick it up again. It wasn't too long before I looked down at the picture to discover that Bob's face had been rubbed away. Patti bought me a locket which I wore all the time, but over the years I had to keep replacing both the chain and the picture. Sometimes when someone asked to look at the locket they would give me the strangest looks, since Bob's picture had been rubbed off again. I'd tell them that the picture was of my husband, but sometimes they would see that there was no one there.

In town Flint looked for a good lawyer to help us take care of all the necessary business. He had to search for quite a while to find one who did not insist on taking Bob and Carol for all they had. It was only after several tries that he finally found one who left what we did up to us. Poor Bob already felt so badly and he certainly had not intended for that to happen. We had no desire to take what they had or to cause them any additional grief. Bob Y sold his truck, saying that he never wanted us to have to see that truck again.

Everywhere I went: in the stores, banks, restaurants; etc people kept asking me where Bob was. He had talked to and kidded with people all the time while I was content to quietly watch from the side. I was surprised that so many people thought so much of him and that they had even noticed me in the background. That was a sad time for a lot of people! Patti had a gathering in Bob's honor. All of our friends from the area came, it was very nicely done, and her house was full of laughter amongst the tears.

When we got back to Boundary Lodge we found that some gold jewelry that Flint had given to Shianne was missing from the cabin, and that my old things had been taken out of the gift shop. Flint and Timber went after my things and got them back for me, but they kept Flint's old gold scales and Shianne's jewelry. It took me eleven and one half years before I was able to find another set of gold scales to buy for him. A smaller but nice set was among Flint's presents on Christmas 2006, but he only got to enjoy it for two months. Flint went ahead with buying the trailer that Bob and I had intended to purchase, and he moved it down to camp for Grandma, Shianne, and I. Norm and Lloyd came back up, and they moved their little trailers down to camp also. Now we had quite a little community down in the valley.

Back when Flint first started buying the lodge, he thought that he was through with mining and he and his dad agreed that we should lease some of our Walker Fork claims. Flint made about two weeks without mining before he decided that he wasn't done after all. Flint had been mining on the lower claims and now he wanted to work one of the upper claims. The guy who we had leased to, I'll call him (M) for man, did not choose a particularly good spot to mine the summer before and he did not want to pay the minimum that was required on the lease. Flint said that he did not want to tie up so many claims if the minimum was not going to be paid, so (M) said that we could have all but two of the claims back. Unfortunately we did not get it in writing. When we went to town with Bob's body, Flint called (M) and told him where he intended to mine. (M) said that it would be alright since it was on the ground that he had given back to Flint. However when (M) came up to mine and found that Flint was finding gold, he changed his mind. He went to the Department of Natural Resources and told them that Flint was mining on claims that were leased to him and they shut us down. In order to be allowed to mine Flint had to agree to pay (M) a percentage of what he mined, and (M) continued to pay the same percentage of what he and his son (S) mined. The only problem was that Flint got a lot more gold than did (M) and (S), so he ended up paying them to mine our ground. They still felt that they had gotten a raw deal but when one is paid to lease something, instead of having to pay a lease; the deal doesn't look so raw to me. We wouldn't mind being paid to mine some one else's ground.

We had to make many trips into town and since Patti had now joined Rob in North Dakota for the summer, we just about supported the Klondike Inn. We received some money from Bob (Y's) insurance and we bought some equipment. We celebrated Shianne's 17th birthday in June, we had another gathering at the mine in honor of Bob on his birthday in July, and Flint brought Sherry (his new girl friend) out to the mine just after his 23rd birthday in August. One of Flint's hired men, Big Tony, became very interested in Shianne. Both Flint and Timber were very much against this budding relationship since he is almost thirteen years older than she and she was so young and inexperienced. Tempers flew, Flint and Tony got into an argument, and Tony and Brian left the mine.

Not long after Tony and Brian left, Flint tried to walk away from an argument he was having with Sherry. She followed him to Norm's trailer and stood outside, yelling and pounding on the door. Flint picked her up, dumped her in the creek, and it was a very wet, cold, angry girl who climbed out of the creek and asked Norm to drive her back to town.

Chapter 32
BURIED IN THE SNOW
1995—1997

Uncle Timber with Megan

We bought a house in North Pole and Shianne, Grandma, and I moved into it; while Flint and Timber were still out at the mine. The house is large, with six bed rooms and three bathrooms. Along with an oil boiler, it has a fire place up stairs and a wood stove downstairs. The yard is an acre and a half with hundreds of trees on it, and it is adjacent to an air strip with which we have access. It was the air strip that sold Flint on the house, as he wanted to get his pilot's license and an air plane.

On our first night in the new house there was a moderately severe earth quake. I was standing, keeping my balance with my hand on the wall when Grandma ordered, "Margaret, stop that, right now!" I guess that she thought that I was strong enough to shake the house, just to tease her.

Shianne saw Tony in town, and she started going places with him. I don't know what she thought was so bad about dating, but she kept insisting that when she went out to dinner or to a show with him that it was not a date.

Flint and Sherry had broken up, but unbeknownst to Shianne and me, Sherry moved in down stairs. By the time we discovered that she was there, she was all settled in. I couldn't ask her to leave, so she was still there later when the boys came in to town. Little by little she and Flint got back together.

When her brothers discovered that Shianne was going out with Tony, they were angry and tried to put an end to it. If anything their efforts and threats only made Shianne all the more determined to go out with him. She had never gone out with anyone else and I wanted her to date others as well, but that didn't happen. Much to her brothers' displeasure, Shianne went to be with Tony every day. We tried to enroll Shianne in the North Pole High School, but they said that it was too late in the year for her to start. Instead she studied a little and passed the tests to get her GED.

Now that Timber had turned 21, he sometimes liked to go to the refinery in the evenings to play pool and to have a beer or two. He usually won at pool and when they brought in a Robo Surf board and had contests on riding it, he became the champion and won some cool prices. One evening I had to reach Timber and I called the Refinery. The bar tender answered my request to speak to him with, "There's no way that I'm going to announce that there's a call for no timber wolf." After my assurance that it really was his name she finally suggested, "Well…, tell me what he looks like, and if I see someone like him I'll quietly ask him if that's his name." After my description she was able to find him and he came to the phone.

On my birthday that year I celebrated at Patti's and then again at home, where my family gave me a witch (I collect them) and a rocking chair. Finally we went to a movie and then out to dinner at the Turtle Club. It must have cost a lot because there were a bunch of us, including Little Tony and his family.

Flint and Sherry were in and out of Boundary all winter, with Flint trapping some. On one trip they brought Snuffy into town to have Thanksgiving and Christmas with us. After celebrating Thanksgiving at Patti's, Flint and Sherry left on a trip to Hawaii. While they were gone a guy who the boys knew came to the house in the middle of the night, needing money. Earlier he had asked for money, also in the middle of the night, and I had given him what I had. This time I didn't have any money, so I told him to go down stairs where Timber was sleeping to see if he had some. He went down stairs all right, but instead of waking Timber he took a gold watch and matching ring that we had given him in September for his 21st birthday. The next morning when Timber found out, he was angry and distressed. He found the guy and made him take him to the drug dealer to whom he had given his jewelry. He wasn't able to get them back and so Timber went to the police. The guy said,

"Timber I thought that you were my friend." Timber's answer was, "A friend wouldn't steal from me."

Flint and Sherry came back from Hawaii in time to share a pleasant Christmas with us, and they took Snuffy back to Boundary after his usual Christmas visit. Timber went out to the homestead with Tony and Shianne to trap there and I got a job working at Northern Lights Educare. It wasn't long before I became the evening supervisor, starting work at 3:30 pm and closing at 11:30 pm. That winter not only did I suffer culture shock, learning to live in town with electricity, plumbing, and running hot water, but I discovered that civilized living is not so easy. The temperature dropped down to -50 degrees, the furnace acted up and went out, the water pipes froze and broke, and when I tried to leave for work, the longest fan belt in the car broke, leaving me stranded in my driveway. Grandma went to hang out with Patti, and fortunately Flint returned from Boundary. He walked to an auto parts store, bought a new fan belt, just about froze while lying in the snow to repair my car, repaired and cleaned the furnace, and fixed the water pipes. After all that I'll bet he wished that he hadn't come back from Boundary at all. He didn't complain, but I know that at least I was longing for the peaceful life that we had had there. With the roads closed we never had to struggle to get cars started or repaired, and we had no furnace or water pipes to break in the cold.

Late one night Grandma fell on her way to the bathroom. When her head hit the floor it split open and started to bleed profusely. I was the only one to awaken and hear her, and I quickly held a cloth over the wound to stop the bleeding. This was easier said than done, because Grandma insisted on going back and forth between her bed and the bathroom. She absolutely refused to stay either in bed or on the toilet. I would just get the bleeding stopped, and off she would go again. Shianne who slept upstairs did not hear me calling to her, and Flint, Sherry, and Timber were asleep down stairs. When Grandma started to turn grey and go limp, I began to yell and thump on the floor. Then everyone woke up, we called 911, and she was taken to the hospital.

After ER had the wound cleaned and dressed, they said that she was good to go home. However before we could get her out of the door, she collapsed and they had to revive her with electric shocks to the heart. After the second or third shock she looked up and exclaimed, "Ouch! Why did you hit me? What did I do?" Then they decided that she wasn't so "good to go" after all and they kept her at the hospital for a couple of days.

On Valentines Day we went down to the court house for Flint and Sherry to get married. After the brief ceremony I was asked to go up front to sign papers as witness. I had gone to the rest room just before the ceremony and unknowingly had tucked my dress into my panty hose. I walked up to the front of the room and bent over to sign the papers. I heard a big gasp and then felt Sherry tugging on my dress. Flint was laughing too hard to move. He had been terribly serious and nervous up until then, but my mooning everyone put him at ease. I flatly refused to do repeat performances at all the future weddings.

Shortly after the wedding, Flint and Sherry went by snow machine on their honeymoon to the mine and to Dawson City. On the way back from Dawson City they rode over a lump and saw some cloth. They stopped to investigate and dug up a man. He had tried to drive on the Top of the World Highway after it was closed, and he had gotten his car stuck. He sat in his car for a couple of days and then had tried to walk to Dawson City. His car had only made it a few miles past the border, if he had gone back instead of forward he would have made it to Canadian and American Customs with shelter and food available. Dawson City was almost sixty miles away, and his decision to go in that direction had cost him his life.

They took his body to Boundary Lodge, and called to have him picked up. Then as Flint and Sherry were headed for home their snow machine broke down. Sherry started to cry and Flint asked, "What's the matter?"

Between her sobs she sputtered, "Next spring when the snow melts, somebody's going to find us buried in the snow!"

Flint was startled, such a thought had never even occurred to him. "Nonsense! We're not going to lie down and die! We're going to walk to the truck; it's not even thirty miles away."

Walk, or more like struggle and plow, is just what they did, with Flint helping Sherry when she got too tired or the going got too rough. Not counting heavy doses of cold and tired, and a smaller dose of frost bite, they made it home just fine. It was nothing that Flint hadn't had to do many times before.

Somehow Big Guy got out of the house without our knowing it. When we found that he was missing, we searched and called but we never found him. Gunsmoke (Kee Kee Watusi for the FBI) disappeared about that same time. Both animals were getting old, perhaps they just went off to die, or perhaps they ran into a car, predator, or a mean neighbor with a gun or poison. To counteract the quiet and grief caused by their loss, Thelma gave us a tiny all black kitten. She was part Siamese and part Manx and we named her Bobby because of her little bobbed tail. Over the years she had many kittens, some with long tails, some with no tails, and some were bobbed tailed like their mother.

That summer all the folks except for Grandma, Shianne, and I were out at the mine. It wasn't a good mining season, in fact it was a less than nothing season with no gold and lots of expenses. The year before Flint had leased some claims to a local miner, Neal. Neal didn't get the reclamation done that summer and then he died during the winter. Flint was not allowed to mine until Neal's reclamation was done, and while Flint was doing it, the transmission on the dozer went out. Flint didn't have $100,000 to fix it and so his mining was done before he even got started. Flint had hired two guys, Lee and Dale to work for him, but when he saw that he couldn't mine that summer he paid them and let them go. Dale went back to his old job, but he got into an argument with his boss and he asked Flint if he could hang out at the mine for the summer.

On the fourth of July, one week after Shianne's eighteenth birthday, she married Tony. Just before the wedding family and friends came in to town. The wedding was in our yard with the reception both in the house and outside. The counter was piled with all kinds of food, and the wedding cake was topped with Taz in a black top hat and Tweety wearing a white veil. Norm gave the bride away. Tony and Shianne went to a motel for their wedding night, and then they pulled a trailer out to our land on the Parks Highway I gave them the land as a wedding present.

Sometimes Shianne, Grandma, and I made trips out to the mine for the weekend, Tony and Shianne frequently visited at the house, and I visited them in their new little home on the Parks Highway. Watching them haul in snow for their water and light an oil lamp, made me nostalgic for the life that used to be mine. Even at the mine it is now very different from the way it used to be. Flint runs a generator for electricity, he pumps in water from the creek, he got a satellite for T.V., and he even put in a shower.

In August I got pneumonia for the first time and unlike all the other illnesses that I have had, it really laid me out. I managed to keep on working, but it was taking me so long to get the work done that I wasn't getting home until 1:00 am. Once home I collapsed and didn't get up again until I had to get ready for work. I had asked for time off work to go halibut fishing with Patti and Rob. Shianne was planning to go as well, but when she arrived and saw how sick I was, she called the trip off. She insisted that I go to the doctor and I was given an antibiotic and quickly got better.

Shortly after I had recovered from pneumonia, I jumped out of the bath and ran to answer the telephone. With wet feet on the slick cement floor, I slipped, fell, and broke my arm at the elbow. I couldn't get up and so I crawled to the phone. It was someone asking for Flint and when I told her that he wasn't there she replied, "He's never there; it would be easier to get in touch with Robert than it is with Flint!"

That statement caught me off guard, "Um…if you find a way to do that, let me know. I'd like to reach him too! I'll tell Flint that you called; but right now I'm wet, cold, and dirty from scooting on the floor, and my arm is broken and hurting. I need to scoot back to the bath tub so that I can get ready for work, good by!"

Luckily Shianne and Tony stopped by the house and she helped me get dressed for work, since I couldn't move my arm enough to dress myself. A week or so later the boys came into town and they made me go to the doctor. It was a good thing that it was one of my days off work, because I had to go to the hospital for them to break my arm again, put a pin in it, and put a cast on it. After that I had to argue with my coworkers, who kept trying to do my work for me. Over a month later, at the doctor's office, he asked me if I was ready to get the pin taken out. I said yes, and held out my arm but he just shook his head in wonder. "I'm afraid that it's not that easy. I'm not going to just pull it out! You have to go back to the hospital to get it taken out."

One night during a lightening and wind storm, a tall spruce tree fell across the yard smashing one end of our deck and stairs and putting a big dent in the top of my car. After that people were always asking me, "However did you get a dent in your car way up there?" Maybe they thought that I had had a collision with an airplane.

Kisses died quietly in her sleep and that left us with just Tasha and Bobby, until a short time later when Tasha had eleven puppies. Mackinsey River husky puppies are in great demand and we could have easily given away twenty five of them if we'd had them to give. We gave away ten puppies and Timber kept one and named her Little Girl. She stayed little for the blink of an eye and then she became a big little girl like her mother. She also resembled her mother in that she was sweet and gentle.

In December among the Christmas cards that we were receiving, was a letter from the court. Dale was suing Flint for wages for the entire summer. Flint had given him a trailer at the mine in which to live, and he had allowed him to help himself to the groceries he needed. Dale claimed that he had been the camp cook and dish washer. It's true that he did cook (for himself) and he did wash dishes (his own). I guess that because Flint gave him food to cook, and a stove to cook it on, he should be required to pay him to cook it as well. Dale had just hung out there, going fishing when ever he wanted, going to Dawson or into Fairbanks on whim, and just doing what ever he wished. Flint had thought that he was doing him a favor by giving him a place to live and allowing him to stay there. He didn't know that he was going to have to pay him to visit. I couldn't believe it when Flint had to settle with him, due to the original vocal hiring agreement that Flint had made before the dozer broke down. After that Flint never hired anyone, and he was careful about whom he allowed to come stay at the mine.

At the end of March Shianne and Tony were blessed with a daughter. They named her Margaret Sarah after both of her grandmothers, but she has always been called Megan. I stayed with Shianne over night at the hospital as Tony wanted to go home. After Megan was born Shianne and Tony moved into the house with us, since he was unemployed and they had no income. It was wonderful having a baby in the house again, almost as good as having one of my own. Both of Megan's uncles doted on her.

Chapter 33
SHOT!
1997—1999

Uncle Flint with Megan at the mine

Flint, Sherry, Timber, and Tony all went up to the mine in April and then I took Shianne and Megan up there in May. I was still working so Grandma and I stayed in town until July. After Shianne had gone, Grandma stayed with Patti or went to a center while I worked.

Mining went a lot better that summer, although we did have some break downs. There was a big rain storm which turned the creeks into rivers, and it would have washed away our mining camp if Flint had not used the dozer (he had managed to buy another used one) to prevent it. After the flood when Flint started up his generator so that he could get back to mining, he was severely burned by an electric shock. That stopped him from working for a few hours until he could withstand the pain.

Bobby gave birth to two little kittens. One was an all black bob tailed female (just like her mom) and the other was an all white, bob tailed, blue eyed male. Little by little the male began to get light patches of tan on his ears, nose, feet, etc. Then those patches got darker brown and other light patches appeared. By the time he was grown he was all tan, medium brown, and dark brown, with the markings and the voice of a Siamese cat. He kept his bright blue eyes. We kept him but gave his sister away after she grew up and continually wanted to fight her mother.

One August day Timber and Lloyd were out hunting, when Lloyd came rushing back with Timber. Timber had been shot right through the chest; he never would say exactly how this had happened. We rushed him up to the border to call for help. The regular customs officer was not there, and Flint was told that he would have to wait to be able to use the phone. Flint didn't agree with that at all, and he picked the man up, moved him to one side, and went inside to make his call. Timber was having trouble breathing and we all (including Timber) were afraid that he was going to die. A helicopter arrived and it flew him to the nearest hospital in Dawson City. On the way to the hospital the doctor ran a tube through the bullet hole into Timber's lung to drain the fluid. He was afraid to give him any medicine for pain, thinking that it might put him down. Flint, Sherry, Tony, Shianne, Megan, Grandma, and I drove to Tok and waited while Flint went to talk to the troopers. By then it was the middle of the night, and every minute seemed like an hour as we waited to hear if Timber was still alive. We were so afraid that Flint would return to tell us that Timber had died.

Timber lived and they flew him to the hospital in Anchorage. We drove down there to see him and after a couple of days everyone except for Timber and I went back to the mine. I stayed in the hospital with Timber for several days. The bullet had just missed his heart and his back bone by less than an inch. It split and went through one lung and broke his shoulder blade, going out through his back and under one arm. Eventually they pulled the drain tube out of his lung and he was released from the hospital. He'd been on morphine in the hospital and they gave him a prescription when he left; but not wanting to get addicted he didn't even open the bottle. When he visited a doctor in Fairbanks she said that she didn't see how he could manage with out the morphine, but if he could it wouldn't do him any harm to do without. I drove him back to the mine and on the way, when we got back to the house in North Pole; we discovered that we had been robbed. Someone had broken a window and had taken several rifles, pistols, pool sticks, and everything that they found of value. They also tore down some panels from the ceiling, dumped oil on clothes, and generally ruined what could be easily destroyed.

Timber and I returned to the mine but he had to really go easy for the rest of the season. When the mining was done it was back to the house for us all. I went back to work at Northern Lights, Timber started working at Taco Bell in North Pole, and Flint started working at Cost Savers, a furniture store. Both Flint and Timber quickly became managers, and they were told that they could go mine in the spring and have their jobs waiting in the fall when they came back.

Tasha had a litter of ten puppies and Bobby had five kittens. All of her kittens were either all black with yellow eyes (like her) or at first they were white and blue eyed like their father. There was only one exception and that was a gray blue eyed kitten. We gave all the puppies and kittens away with people calling for them long after they were all gone. Little Girl took off one day and although we searched, we were never able to find her. Timber got a little Pitt Bull puppy whose skin was five sizes too big. If one lifted her skin up she looked like a sail boat. He named her Sissy IV.

Flint and Sherry made a trip up to the mine and they brought Snuffy back to North Pole for the holidays. This was something that happened every year and before Flint closed down the mine for the year, he always got Snuffy his wood and groceries for the winter. He also took care of the paper work on Snuffy's claims when he did his own. It was a fun Christmas with a baby in the house, and at nine months Megan was old enough to enjoy the lights, gifts, and special food. Because I was always rubbing Bob's pictures off of my lockets, Shianne bought me a gold heart with Bob's picture printed right inside the metal. His picture does not come off of there and I wear it all the time, in the bath, swimming, in bed, and at work. The children in the center looked at his picture every day and called him by name. He came to be part of their lives, just as he is part of mine. When the chain broke I put the necklace away for a while. On the following Christmas Shianne bought me a gold chain. When I opened it I ran to get the heart, and I made Shianne immediately stop what she was doing to put it on me. I couldn't be another moment without it. After Christmas Sherry started working at Northern Lights Educare along with me, and often we could ride to and from work together.

One cold January night Megan got an ear infection and she had a fever so high that she had to be taken to ER. In February at the age of ten months she started to walk, so on her first birthday in late March we were able to take a movie of her excitedly toddling all around the room. She was such a darling baby; so smiley, lively, and affectionate. It was good for Grandma too to be able to watch and hold a baby again. It was good too that Megan was not yet talking much and was not yet at the age to be ornery or talk back. Contrary to earlier years Grandma was now inclined to argue with kids as they got older and behaved like children.

Right after Megan's birthday, Flint, Sherry, Timber, and Tony went to Boundary to get ready for mining; and Shianne and Meg joined them in April. I was still working so Grandma stayed in a center during my working hours until late May when we were able to join the rest of the family at the mine. Once up there I began to help mine, feeding the sluice with the backhoe. When

Flint took over the mining on Walker Fork, he designed and built a shaker and separate sluices to replace the dump box and sluice that we had used on Davis Creek. With the shaker washing and separating the rocks into different sizes, we retained a much greater percentage of the gold. This meant that my shovel and I were no longer needed to aid the rocks on their decent, so it was good that I could still help on the backhoe. Because the backhoe stays in one spot, it is not as dangerous or as scary to operate as is a loader or dozer.

When I wasn't working Megan and I loved to play in the sand and throw rocks into the creek. She also liked to ride on the equipment and in their old van as it bounced and jumped all over the rough roads. It was never long before she was bounced and jerked to sleep. When ever she got the chance she would toddle off to visit with Norm in his trailer. We had to have our eyes on her every second for fear that she would go into the creek or wander off.

Bobby had another litter of kittens and she kept them on my bed in the trailer where I was staying. As the kittens began to get a little older, she did the opposite of Gunsmoke who had rid us of the problem of shrews in the cabin. Bobby brought mice and birds into the trailer and onto my bed in an effort to teach her kittens how to kill for their meals. Many nights I had to vacate my bed in favor of a chair in Flint's and Sherry's cabin.

The gold was slow in coming and we had several breakdowns to hamper our mining. The worst breakdown was the boom on the backhoe; we didn't have the means to fix it so it was sold to someone who could. Fortunately we had a smaller John Deer backhoe that we could use for sluicing. We finally did get into a really good spot where we found a great deal of gold. That put us back on our feet, but unfortunately the price of gold was low and we had to give a good share of the gold to (M) and (S). Flint dug up a mastodon tusk that was longer than the bed of the truck. We searched but never found the bones or the other tusk.

We had some visitors at the mine. First Tony's mother and step father came up, then his father, step mother, and half sister. Finally Patti and Rob and the girls came and like all of our earlier visitors they did some hand mining and made a trip to Dawson City.

Grandma and I went back to town in mid September, several weeks before the rest of the family. I was sent to help out at another center, University West, and I liked it so much that I stayed there. Lynda was the director there and she made me feel really welcome. She was always saying that she needed more than one of me to open and close and to work with all age groups: the infants, toddlers, preschoolers, and the school aged children. I was unable to stretch that much, so she finally opted for me to be the supervisor of the toddlers and to open. Lynda and her husband Bob became my dear friends, my strength in troubled times, my advisors, and a huge source of happiness. They became family.

After the rest of the family got back to town they all went back to their jobs. Shianne got a job working at Value Village so Tony started watching Megan. She worked different hours than did the rest of us so she usually drove in and out of town alone. One day she broke down in the car and called a tow truck. It turned out that she was only out of gas, and so that turned out to be an expensive tank of gas. Late one night on the way home from work she again ran out of gas. This time she didn't call a tow truck, but she had no money with her and no way to call for help. Luckily, being a pretty young twenty year old, some guys stopped, went home and got a gas can, filled it, and brought it back to her. They wouldn't accept payment but she saw where they lived and dropped payment off at their house the next day.

We had good times at work and at home, made new friends, and sometimes we went out for dinner, to a movie, or swimming in an indoor pool. I wanted Timber to be Santa Claus for me at the center and he agreed to do it only if Phillip his friend from Taco Bell would help. Phillip is small and red headed and he made a perfect elf. With their help we had a terrific party for the children. Shianne came with us to Sherry's and my work party and I went with her to hers. With all the parties and all the preparation and celebrating at home it was a festive season. It was sad not to hang Bob's stocking on the fire place along with the rest of ours, but I still felt the comfort of his closeness. It's been over fourteen years now and I still feel that he is sharing our lives. I'm constantly turning to him, especially in times of trouble and joy.

With the boys working that winter they didn't make as many snow machine trips to the mine as they had in the past. They were always able to make a few trips up anyway, to pick up Snuffy, take him back, and check things out in the early spring. The trips started out by truck and ended up by snow machine. Sometimes they doubled their rides on the snow machines by going another sixty miles each way to Dawson City.

We took Grandma to the dentist to get some of her teeth filled and some pulled. She didn't get dentures or any bridges because she had had a bridge for several years and she refused to wear it. She didn't like to eat with it and she said that it made her talk funny and drool. We watched to be sure that she was still eating well, but as she was approaching her ninety fourth birthday she was becoming very picky about her food. Even before her teeth were pulled she had started picking things out of her food and throwing them on the floor, even things that she used to love. She would say that she was hungry, we'd give her food, she would take one bite, refuse to eat any more, and then in two minutes she was hungry again. Because of her eating habits and the decrease in her enjoyment of food, we started taking her to restaurants less often. It also soon became an embarrassment for Patti to take her to church. She had to sit in the front to be able to see and hear, but that did not prevent her from saying in a loud clear voice things like, "Isn't it about time for him to wind down?" or "I don't like him as well as the regular minister, he's too windy." One day she used the skirt of her dress to blow her nose, not caring that her undergarments were exposed.

Jim and Betty flew up to North Pole and stayed with Patti. It was great that we all got to visit with them, as they were meeting some of the family members for the first time. During their stay, Grandma spent her days over there and the time spent with them was especially good since this turned out to be their last time together.

Again Flint, Sherry, Timber, Tony, Shianne, and Megan went to the mine earlier than did Grandma and I. After I finished up my work we were able to join the family. It was a hot dry summer with the smoke and occasionally ashes from surrounding forest fires diming the luster of the country. One day while the guys were mining, we gals: Grandma, Sherry, Shianne, Megan, and I, drove into Tok to shop and wash clothes. On the way home our car stopped and wouldn't start again. We waited beside the road for quite a while until Sherry caught a ride back to Boundary to tell the guys. Tony and Flint came down to meet us and Flint was able to get the car started. A rock had bounced up and hit a protection device which shut off the fuel so that the car wouldn't explode in a collision. They had looked at the engine but could not find anything wrong. Then Flint looked in the trunk, hit the reset button, and the car started up. The rest of us had never heard of such a thing.

On another day we drove over to Eagle for the day. Eagle is a lovely town on the Yukon River with a beautiful drive over to it. After lunch as we were headed back to the car a guy stopped us asking, "Aren't you Flint's mother?"

I answered, "Yes."

Then he asked, "Are one of you Flint's wife?"

Sherry indicated that she was and he called to some other guys across the street, "Hey, come over here. Here's Flint's wife and mother."

They stood around us asking questions and making us feel like we weren't people in our own right, but like we were just Flint's possessions. I felt like saying, "And here is Flint's sister, Flint's grandmother, and Flint's niece. We drove over from Flint's mine, in Flint's car, with Flint's money, to buy some things for Flint's camp."

That evening Flint thought that we were all nuts when we kept saying things like, "Do you want one of Flint's cookies? Please turn on Flint's TV, or I'm going out to Flint's outhouse."

Along with the mining the guys were hauling over logs which we peeled and which Timber used for building a small cabin. It's only one room but it's sturdy and complete with wood and cook stoves, and a bunk bed. It reminds me of the cabin on the Iditarod except that it has a wood instead of a dirt floor and it doesn't have a big water hole in the middle.

Flint, Snuffy, and I made a trip into Fairbanks in August. Shopping trips are always fun but this one was especially so. While Flint was rounding up the parts he needed for the mine, I went to Valdez with Patti and Rob to fish for halibut. Tony and Shianne also drove down from the mine and joined us. After we got back to Fairbanks with our fish we went to the fair. Flint picked up a bunch of steaks and when we got back to the mine we invited the neighboring miners over for dinner. This started another tradition and we have supplied dinner and a campfire for our neighbors on Flint's birthday ever since.

Chapter 34

FATAL FALL

1999—2001

Grandma near Boundary

Again, Grandma and I returned to North Pole earlier than the rest of the family. Before this year her health had improved greatly after each summer at the mine. This year she just had not been able to take the walks as she used to, and I didn't see the usual improvement in her health. Once back and settled I went back to work and Grandma back to the center. She gave me a bad time in the mornings taking her there, saying that I didn't want to be with her etc. However once she was there she had a good time visiting, playing bingo, watching movies, etc. When I picked her up in the afternoons she had to kiss everyone good bye before leaving.

A few weeks later when the rest of the family got home, Grandma stayed at home with them. As she approached her ninety fifth birthday she was getting more and more feeble. With every bath it was more difficult to get her in and out of the tub. It was also getting harder for her to get in and out of the truck. For years she had pestered whoever she was with by asking over and over when I would get home. Until now I would be greeted with, "Oh Margaret! Good, you're home! Are you staying?" Now when I got home, before I could even take my coat off, she would ask, "Have I eaten yet?" She didn't know that I had been gone and I'm not sure that she even knew who I was anymore.

In December Flint took Sherry to Oregon to see her family. Timber was closing every night at Taco Bell and not getting home until around 1:00 am.

Since Flint and Sherry were away and I left the house at 5:30 am, Timber started sleeping upstairs in case Grandma needed something. Just after I left for work on December 21st, Grandma got up to go to the bath room and Timber did not wake to hear her. She got confused and opened the door to the stairs by mistake and walked in! Shianne woke to the sound of Grandma's walker clattering down the stairs. A dreadful thumping followed and Shianne jumped out of bed and ran to her grandmother at the foot of the stairs. Her eyes were open but she made no sound and she did not stir. An ambulance was called and they took her to the hospital.

I was alone at work with only a couple of children when I got the call. I called Lynda at home and told her that I had to leave, and then I rushed to the hospital as quickly as I could. I was too late; they had not been able to revive her. Patti took off from work to help make all the arrangements and Lynda would not let me return to work until after Christmas. Flint and Sherry returned from Oregon and we all had a quiet sad Christmas without her. The annual trip over to Patti's to make cookies and fudge was the last time that Grandma left the house and she cried out that it hurt when I lifted her legs into the car. We left the stocking with Grandma's name knitted on it along with Bob's in with the unused Christmas items, and we put Grandma's gifts away. We still had a big dinner but it was a quiet sad Christmas without her.

We had a memorial service for Grandma at the New Hope Methodist Church in January. It was a nice service and many of us spoke about what she had meant in our lives. I missed the dear old lady who I had been caring for so much, that at a party I was tempted to kidnap someone else's mother who reminded me of mine. I did not realize until later that I was not newly grieving for the loss of my mother. I had already been grieving for the last couple of years, as little by little I lost the woman who she had been. It explained something that had been confusing me, why I would get impatient when she did things like come out of the bathroom without pulling up her pants. I had worked in geriatrics at a hospital while I was in college and was never disturbed regardless of what ever any of the patients did or said. My impatience with my mother had been born of grief. I hope that if it comes up that either my son and or daughter get angry or impatient with me, that they will understand the reason for it. I did not cry much when Grandma died but later in a church service, when the organist began to play the songs that she used to play, tears poured down my face. Since then I've been shy of church and I keep my guard up when I hear the church music that I so love.

Tony found a job and then Megan started coming to University West Educare. She was in the toddler room with me until after her third birthday when she moved in with the preschoolers. Shianne also quit working at Value Village and she started working at the center also. She started working with different age groups but she ended up working with me in the toddler room.

Wayne was a friend of Flint's from Cost Savers. He went along on Flint's spring snow machine trip up to the mine and to Dawson City. In the middle of one night after they returned, Wayne called Flint. He had gotten beaten up by another worker from Cost Savers, and he was extremely upset and depressed. Although Sherry was against it, Flint told Wayne that he would be right over and then he went as fast as he could go. He was too late! Wayne shot himself moments before Flint's arrival. He was already dead but an ambulance and the police were called anyway. Flint was shook up and he desperately wished that he had gotten there sooner. I don't believe that Wayne really intended to shoot himself, or he wouldn't have called wanting to talk to Flint. Maybe he got a loaded gun for effect and in his distress as he paced it went off. Or perhaps he didn't intend for the shot to be fatal and he wanted Flint to find and help him. As much as he and Flint thought of each other, I just can't believe that he would deliberately set Flint up for such a traumatic shock.

Shianne and I both continued to stay in town to work during the following summer. The guys and Sherry would come into town occasionally when they needed parts, and Shianne, Megan, and I made trips to the mine once a month: on Memorial Day, Independence Day, in August, and on Labor Day. I always looked forward to these trips and on the night before each trip the thought of seeing the beloved country and my boys had me too excited to sleep. Flint was mining with Dennis and then Dennis's son, Ken joined them. After the summer Dennis left the mine but Ken continued to mine with Flint on many of the following years.

Flint has always been very upbeat and optimistic and I had never known him to get discouraged, even if they weren't finding much gold or had a serious break down. This summer was not difficult mining wise, but things were not going well between Flint and Sherry. Sherry was using drugs when Flint first met her and he had helped her to quit, now I think that she was back on them. Each time that Flint called me he sounded down, like I had never heard him before. On his birthday after working in cold, rain, and mud all day; he came home to a cold dark cabin. There was no wife, no fire, no light, no food; only a note saying that Sherry was up at the lodge. She didn't even wish him a happy birthday. That was the way that most of that summer went.

I talked Bob and Lynda into coming up to the mine, and they enjoyed it so much that they came back each year on Labor Day weekend. This year there had been a lot of rain and the creek was a raging river. They drove up to the edge of the water and stopped. Lynda was august, "Oh dear! Now what do we do?"

I suggested, "Just wait here. I'll take the side of the mountain to camp and get Flint to move the water."

After I had gone Lynda looked at Bob in bewilderment. "Flint can't really move the river can he? Should we wait, as she said?"

Bob shrugged his shoulders. "Let's wait for a while and see what happens."

With the dozer Flint changed the direction of the stream, amazing Bob and Lynda as they watched the water disappear. With new appreciation of Flint and the dozer, they drove across to spend the weekend with us. Bob always brings his guitar and he and Lynda sing our favorite songs, along with some that Bob wrote. Bob also tells some pretty spookem ghost stories.

On the Tuesday after Labor Day the day that we all returned to work, I had a strong feeling that I needed to go right back up to the mine. So on Wednesday with Lynda's permission, I headed back. I really surprised them and when Timber saw me he jumped off of the dozer and came running up to see what was wrong. Flint and Sherry were getting ready to drive to Dawson City so I went with them. Flint took care of his business, we went out for dinner, and then went to Diamond Tooth Gerty's to do a little gambling. Afterward when we went to our motel room, Sherry was hungry so Flint went to get some food. While Flint was gone Sherry told me that she was having an affair with (S). She was feeling very glamorous because she had been with several men and they all wanted her. Flint returned with the food and Sherry threw it across the room. "I told you that I didn't want Chinese food!"

Flint was both exasperated and puzzled. "Mom, why is she doing this to me?"

I looked at him sadly, "I think that you had better ask Sherry that question."

Sherry told Flint what was going on and when he cried I thought that my heart would break! When I saw how pleased and proud that Sherry looked I was bursting with anger. Flint didn't want me to say anything and Timber told me that I would only make matters worse if I did. I kept my mouth shut until on the way home. Alone in the car I drove over sixty miles per hour on the Taylor Highway and over eighty on the Richardson. As I raced along I waved my arms and ranted, but I finally got it all out even if there was no one to hear me! I made it home in less than four hours; it usually takes close to six hours.

Deep down Flint had really known what was happening for some time but he wouldn't admit it to himself. Sherry moved over to (M)'s and (S)'s camp, she and Flint got a disillusionment, and she went to California with them. That didn't last for long and she soon was on her own again. Over the years she has kept in touch with us, Flint too.

Later in the fall Flint went to Florida for part of the winter. Norm, who lives in Ontario, Canada; goes down to Florida every winter and he asked Flint to go along with him. A change of scenery and being with Norm was good for Flint, and he was able to have a good time. He came back eager to get back to his real home at the mine and to his business—mining.

Tony's and Shianne's marriage was never what they had hoped that it would be. Shianne thought that another baby might bring them together and she didn't want Megan to be an only child. Tony did not want another baby but Shianne was finally able to get him to agree. We were excited and happy when later she found out that she was pregnant.

On an errand during her lunch break one day, Shianne was going through an intersection with a green light when someone turned left right in front of her. The roads were icy and Shianne could not stop. After the crash the man in the other car told Shianne that he would meet her in the parking lot of his insurance company. Shianne drove over there and waited but he never came. Since the man had ducked out, the accident went under uninsured motorists and we had to pay the deductible. Shianne called work to tell them that she would be late as she had to go to the doctor. Neither she nor the pregnancy seemed to have been hurt, but she had been told to get checked after any kind of an accident.

We celebrated Megan's fourth birthday in March and her little sister Morgan was born in May. Instead of Shianne and me making our usual trip out to the mine over Memorial Day, the boys came in to town to see their new niece. After that we stayed in town to work, but we took the girls out to the mine several times over the summer.

While at work one day someone broke a back window in my car. After a picnic at Pioneer Park with the girls, before I had even been able to get the window fixed; I was stopped on the road waiting for it to clear so that I could turn right. A big motor home pulled up to my left, blocking my view. I planned to turn when the motor home went straight, but instead before I could even move, I saw that the motor home was turning right. We sat still in our tracks while the rear end of the motor home smashed the front end of the car. The driver hadn't noticed that we were there and when he saw the broken window and the girls, he was frightened. "Did I do that? Oh the babies! ..... Is any one hurt?"

"No, the window was already broken. We're all okay"

His insurance company took care of the damage with no questions asked.

Chapter 35
TRAUMATISED
2001—2002

Megan and Morgan

The boys mined into October before they closed up and came back into town. Timber went back to work as manager at the North Pole Taco Bell, and Flint got ready for another trip out to Florida with Norm. There he worked as a bouncer in a bar. One night he was bit while strongly encouraging a man to leave. Another time two guys who were after Flint's gold watch and nugget, jumped him as he headed for home. They managed to get a couple of punches in before the repercussions helped them decide to split without the gold.

Shianne took a class to become a certified nurse's assistant which entailed a couple of weeks work in the hospital. What Shianne learned from the class and training was invaluable for all of us, but she never did become employed as a CNA as she had intended. Instead she opted to continue working at the center with Lynda, the girls, and I. Much to our regret Lynda left the center to teach in Head Start. As our director she had been a shield for all of us, protecting us from any problems that came up and she made our work a pleasure.

At about one o'clock one winter morning, as Timber was cleaning and doing the closing work at Taco Bell, the furnace quit working. He called the number of the company that takes care of those kinds of things and he was told how to relight it. When he did as he was instructed, the furnace blew up burning his face and worse than that—his eyes. He had to walk home in great pain as driving without vision isn't such a good idea. We took him to the hospital and then to an optometrist. He had never needed glasses before and now he not only had to get some, but also he found that he had to replace them with stronger lens every time that he was tested. Finally his eyes stabilized but they were totally dry until they reconstructed his tear ducts, and they were so dilated that for many months they were black instead of blue. He was supposed to stay in his room without any light, TV, or reading for quite a while, however on the day after the accident and from time to time during the following week, he had to go to Taco Bell anyway. He couldn't see to use the computer, work the cash register (couldn't tell one bill from another), or to make up the orders; but for a while there was no one there who knew what to do, and they needed an advisor even if he was virtually blind. Once they got someone in to manage the store, Timber could stop working off the clock and in pain. At Flint's suggestion he decided to join Flint and Norm in Florida while he recuperated.

One morning I got a call from the troopers saying that they had found my Ford Taurus. Believing that it was parked in my drive way, I went to look and sure enough it was gone. I had left my keys in it the night before. The troopers told me where to find it and I did. It was a good thing that I took an extra key because the keys were missing. The next morning at about 1:00 am, on a hunch I looked out my window and the car was gone again. The car had just been taken, and when I called the troopers they found that the car still in the area. While chasing it they put a strip of nails down to stop the car, but the thief drove over them and kept going. All four tires were flat and the boy drove it until the undercarriage was ripped off. Then he got out and ran until a police dog caught him. My car was totaled out and it looked so forlorn and pathetic when I went to get my things out of it. The poor thing had had a tree fall on its roof, a window broken by vandals, and its side smashed in by a motor home. Now it was squatting on the ground with ripped up tires and undercarriage. The insurance paid the car dealer, I had to pay the deductible, and I had no car. It had been such a nice car and it drove so well even on ice. Later Flint bought a used car for Shianne and I to use.

In March we celebrated Megan's fifth birthday with a party at McDonalds. Timber came back from Florida and we celebrated his return by going out to Pagoda for dinner. Flint came back from Florida with Daphne—the small, red headed, feisty girl who he had met on this trip. We refinanced the house and Flint put down new tile and carpeting throughout the upstairs. After Flint, Daphne, Timber, and his friend Charley went to the mine, Shianne and

I finished up the last of the grouting. It took us all of Mothers Day weekend because we put way too much grout down and it was slow and difficult getting all the extra grout off.

Tony came up from downstairs, where he lived with his computer; and seeing us, exhausted and dirty, and still struggling with all the excess grout he commented, "I could have told you that you were doing it wrong."

"Then why in the hell didn't you?" Shianne retorted. It was late and there was no dinner cooked, so Tony made up for his lack of help by taking us out to Pagoda for a Mother's Day dinner.

Morgan was a plump happy baby. She was standing and walking while holding on to furniture and we were having fun playing with her. Then she got ill and we took her to the doctor. The doctor said that she had an ear infection and she prescribed an antibiotic for her. Morgan got worse instead of better and Shianne took her back to the doctor several times. Nothing seemed to help and Morgan stopped eating, playing, laughing, standing, and trying to walk. She couldn't even sit up any more; she toppled over when we sat her down. All she wanted to do was be in her mother's arms, nursing. When we got her out of her crib, she would wrap her arms around our necks in a desperate grip. We didn't know it at the time, but her world was spinning. We didn't celebrate Morgan's first birthday as she was too sick to enjoy anything.

Morgan started vomiting the day after her birthday and Shianne took her back to the doctor again. This time Shianne told the doctor that she was not leaving until they found out what was wrong and got her on her way to getting well. The doctor ordered a cat scan. I kept Morgan with me on the day that it was scheduled, as she wasn't allowed to nurse and she screamed when she was with her mother. An MRI followed the CAT scan and afterward the doctor looked very grave. Morgan had a brain tumor! They took her up to a hospital room and shortly afterward Shianne and Morgan were flown to the Children's Hospital in Seattle. They told Shianne that she needed to be prepared to come home alone!

Dr. Ellenbogen, the chief brain surgeon for the country got out of bed to see Morgan when she arrived at the hospital. The Fairbanks hospital had forgotten to send her CAT scan and MRI with her on the plane, and when they discovered their mistake they mailed it instead of faxing it. So the doctor had to order new ones. He said that it was amazing that Morgan was still conscious and that another two days delay would have been fatal. By holding and nursing Morgan almost nonstop Shianne had given her the strength to stay conscious and alive.

When Dr. Ellenbogen came to get Morgan for surgery, Shianne was so frightened that she didn't think that she could let her go. Contrary to what she had been told in Fairbanks, the doctor assured Shianne that Morgan would be all right. They gave her a cell phone to use and the doctor reassured her several times during the surgery and right afterward. The tumor was benign and since she was so young her prognosis for recovery was good. It is uncommon for babies to have brain tumors and usually when they do; they die before the tumor is discovered. When a baby is lucky enough to have surgery in time, their recovery is much faster and more complete than that of an older child or of an adult.

They told Shianne what to expect when she saw Morgan, but she still wasn't prepared for what she saw. Morgan had tubes coming out of her nose, arms, legs, and head. Her eyes were jerky and unfocused, she was having convulsions, she was pale yet blotchy, and she didn't know her mother. She wasn't able to suck in order to nurse or to drink from a bottle, so she was fed with an eye dropper and with an I V. Her mental development was less than that of a new born baby, but she quickly regained much of the knowledge that she had lost.

Morgan was attached to all kinds of things and she had to be tied down on a table at all times. After Morgan relearned how to suck, Shianne would crawl onto the table with her in order to breast feed her. The rest of the time she sat be side her trying to keep her amused and comfortable. After a few days when they were able to remove the shunt that was draining her head, Morgan was released from the hospital and they flew home. By now Morgan was more like her cheerful self but she still had many things to relearn. She didn't walk until she was nearing two years old, and for several years a loud noise like a plane flying overhead sent her running in sheer terror. Now at eight years of age, she still becomes anxious and covers her ears when she hears something loud. We are so thankful that Morgan made it through so well! Although Shianne was overwhelmingly relieved over Morgan's recovery, the trauma of being alone in Seattle with the fear of losing her daughter caused her to be more ill than she has ever been before or since. She started having severe allergy problems for the first time and she would just get over one illness to come down with something else. One day she was hurting so badly that it had her in tears. She went to see the doctor and she was told that she had pneumonia. She may have had pneumonia but that did not account for the severe pain she was having in her lower back. We took her to E R and found out that she was passing a kidney stone. Occasionally she still gets stones that hurt until they have passed, but so far she has been able to pass them all. Little by little both Shianne and Morgan got better.

Flint and Daphne came into town for a couple of days in June on Shianne's twenty fourth birthday. They stopped by the center and took Shianne and me out for lunch, then we celebrated at the center with cake, frozen yogurt, and flowers, and then Flint took us out to dinner that night at Elves' Den. It was a lot of celebrating and a lot of yummy calories all in one day. One week later on Independence Day, the center had a picnic at Chena Lakes. It was a fun day in spite of it being cold, windy, and rainy.

Later in July Patti's youngest sister Nancy and her son Torrance came up for a visit. I took a week off from work and went up to the mine with Patti, Nancy, Torrance, and Sam. We had a real good time visiting and they did some hand mining and took a trip to Dawson City. I didn't go with them as I was happy to spend the time at the mine and with my boys.

Shianne was interviewed for a job teaching at Early Head Start. She got the job but after her trip to Seattle she turned it down because she didn't feel that she could be away from Morgan all day. They really wanted her to work there so they pulled the necessary strings to get Morgan enrolled in the program. That is a really nice place to work and it's a great place for one's children as well. They practically adopt the whole family of the children who attend there.

When Shianne put in her notice at the center the management was angered. After Shianne was gone they not only didn't replace her, but they enrolled new children in my room. I had thirteen toddlers enrolled with eleven or twelve attending every day, with no help. By myself I couldn't leave the room to take a child to the bathroom and there wasn't room to take twelve toddlers in with me. Their toilet training took a huge step backwards, since I had to let them mess their pants and just change them. The activities that were planned for the children's development also slowed way down, as I was unable to do much more than keep them all safe.

I complained to the management that without help I was unable to give the children the care that they needed. I had twice as many toddlers as one teacher is supposed to have. Right after this the new director, Shianne, and I all received letters. They told the director that they didn't like the way she was directing, they informed Shianne that they were kicking Megan and Morgan out of the program, and they said that they were demoting me since they thought that I was no longer able to supervise my class. This was after seven years of being a supervisor. If they thought that I was incapable of taking care of the children, they shouldn't have entrusted me with thirteen toddlers all by myself. I put in my notice and they replaced me with two people.

I applied for work at Head Start with Lynda and at Early Head Start with Shianne, and I was offered a position in both centers. I accepted the position at Early Head Start and taught a class of children from the ages of six weeks to three years. Each class has two team teachers and I was lucky enough to have Tamara as my team teacher. There are no teachers or women more wonderful than Tamara. I loved the work but it took me a while to build up my self confidence after the letter that I had received on my last job. Tamara and I taught the half day class and I started substituting in all the other classes in the afternoons. I felt like I was queen of the center since I got to have my own class and still work with all the other children and teachers. I loved it!

The children and teachers all sat at tables and had breakfast and lunch family style. Even our little one year olds would sit at the table, serve themselves, pass food, eat with a spoon or fork, drink from a glass, and pour their own milk from a little pitcher. While eating they were learning table manners, new words, and how to socialize. At the end of the meal they would toddle over to the cart with their dishes, clean up after themselves, and wash their hands and face. Sometimes parents were invited to the classroom for a meal and they were always amazed at what their children had learned to do and at how well they did it.

Besides all the activities that we did with the children we had weekly meetings where we discussed every child and their family. We talked about the progress that the children had made, about their needs (and those of their family) and we developed a plan to meet those needs. There were no children at the center on Fridays so we teachers could have meetings and trainings and work in our rooms and on the children's records. Fridays gave us valuable time to prepare for the week to come. We also made home visits with all of our families and when the children transitioned to Head Start or attended Pre School, we would go with them to help them adjust. Shianne even went to the doctor and to the hospital with one of her children and her mother, in order to make sure that the child was getting good care. As a result she progressed from near death to become a much healthier little girl. While there I worked with so many wonderful people, took classes at the University, attended conventions, and enjoyed picnics, parties, and other activities.

Flint came into town and he bought a used excavator. It was a beauty but when it was being hauled up to the mine, the truck and trailer went off of the highway and down a cliff. It took a day to get it back on the road and the cab of the excavator was smashed up. That night Flint drank more than he had since he first came of age. However the excavator still ran and we are still using it today.

Morgan kept Dr. Ellenbogen as her doctor and in August (three months after her surgery) Morgan needed to go back to Seattle to see him. I had just received a bonus at work for various trainings that I had received, so I was able to take some time off work and buy an airplane ticket to go with them. My niece Lou Ann's husband Frank picked us up at the airport and drove us down to their farm and here we had a wonderful time visiting with them. Lou Ann drove us to Children's Hospital early on the morning of Morgan's appointment. She had another M R I, was examined by the doctor, and he was really pleased with her progress. We ate both lunch and dinner in the hospital and then took a taxi to the air port that night. Over the years Morgan has had to have regular M R Is which is sent down for her doctor to examine. He always calls and or writes to Shianne after he has seen them.

In the fall the folks came back from the mine and Daphne's brother Timmy came up from North Carolina. He had had some trouble down there, and he arrived with the clothes that he was wearing and with no glasses. Fortunately he was the same size as Timber, and Timber was willing to share his room, clothes, etc. It took a while but Timmy was able to get some glasses and once he was able to see again, he got a job working at Taco Bell along with Timber, Charley, and Phillip.

Megan started in Kindergarten. She had developed the habit of carrying a spoon around with her all the time and waving it in front of her face. When they took the spoon away from her at school, she threw a fit. The principal was called and he dragged her to the office with her screaming and kicking all the way. They didn't take her spoon away after that and she was able to stay in class most of the time. However her days at school were somewhat rocky and Shianne was too frequently called at work to come get her. She managed better at home but occasionally we would have difficulty reaching her and in helping her to understand the society in which she lives.

Chapter 36
LONG TREK
2003—2004

Tracie and Timber on their wedding day

After the mining season, Flint, Daphne, Timber, Ken, Timmy, and Charley came into town, and along with Tony, Shianne, Megan, Morgan, and I; it made eleven of us going out to dinner at the Turtle Club. The prime rib there is amazing in quantity and quality. It's so good that one wants to eat it all but there's so much that one can't. With all of us there we must have eaten at least one whole steer.

One afternoon after work the car wouldn't start. We had the girls with us, as Morgan was in Early Head Start and Megan was dropped off at the center after school each day. After many unsuccessful tries at starting the car, we tried repeatedly to call home. Somehow the phone was off the hook upstairs, and we couldn't get through to the down stairs phone because Tony was always using it while he played games on his computer. We were at the center for many hours before they put the phone back on the hook. Since Flint had already gone to bed, he told Timber to ask Tony to drive into Fairbanks to pick us up. Tony was still on his computer and he didn't volunteer, so Timber drove in to get us. Considering that he was still blind when hit by lights at night and he was only supposed to drive during daylight, we were lucky that he didn't have an accident. He was able to get our car started so we drove it home, but it was late and we were four hungry and tired gals.

Flint studied, passed the test to get his commercial drivers license, and he went to work for Laidlaw driving a school bus. They usually have an experienced driver go along on a driver's first day, but on Flint's they somehow didn't send one. They had shown him the route and the stops, but he didn't know any of the children. He had to rely on the children to tell him who was who and where they got off. Luckily they didn't take advantage of the situation and mix him up with wrong information. He never needed a bus attendant as the kids never gave him a bad time. He loved driving the children and he made lasting friendships with them and with the other bus drivers.

He hadn't worked there long before he asked, "Mom, what can I get for my kids? We're not allowed to give them candy or things to eat."

"How many kids do you have?"

"Seventy two."

"That might take some doing! I hope you have lots of money."

Together we managed to find some special pencils, stickers, small toys, and odds and ends, but it wasn't easy and it was expensive. Soon he started giving them things like certificates for ice cream cones at the Knotty Shop and buying them individual gifts on their birthdays. He talked to the kids about the things that he loved: hunting, trapping, mining, etc., and he brought some of them up to the mine for a couple of weeks during the summers. He really worried and felt badly when any of them were unhappy or in trouble.

Timber got a job working for Laidlaw as a bus attendant, but even with glasses his eye sight wasn't good enough for him to want to become a driver. While he was working for them he started going out with Tracie, another bus attendant. Occasionally he would bring Tracie and her children (Bruce and Tasha) over to the house.

On one of their trips out to the mine Flint and Daphne found a black, blue eyed, husky mix. She was a pretty dog, she was far from where anyone was living, and Daphne wanted to keep her. So Sugar (as they named her) came to our house to live. She was originally Daphne's dog but she soon made it obvious that she was devoted to Flint. Over the next couple of years she had two litters of puppies. Tasha had a tumor that was making it difficult for her to breath. She was taken to the vet and had some surgery but it only made her more miserable and she died. She was a wonderful dog – huge, sweet, and gentle; and we all missed her. Then Daphne got mad at Sugar and gave her away. Flint was saddened even more and Daphne wished that she could get Sugar back, but it was too late.

As a birthday gift Patti got Rob to take line dancing lessons with her. He was really reluctant and dreaded it at first, but much to his surprise he started to enjoy it. Patti took lessons on Tuesday nights and they both went to couples dancing on Thursday nights. They learned all the dances, bought special boots, hats, and shirts for it, and they became friends with their instructors. Soon they were going to parties, to each other's houses, out to dinner, and fishing with them. That turned out to be a very special birthday gift! That winter Patti talked me into going to the Tuesday night classes with her. It's always fun to go places and to do things with Patti, the dance instructors were understanding and very nice, and I learned to do some of the dances. It was a fun way to get some exercise, but I had one difficulty that I couldn't seem to over come. Whenever a dance required one to turn in one or more circles, I always ended up facing in the opposite direction from everyone else. After a few months of embarrassment I stopped going.

When school got out and the bus driving was over for the year, Timber and Tracie broke up and the guys went back out to the mine. Shianne and I enjoyed our usual trips out there and we would bring them their mail, all kinds of groceries and supplies, and any parts that they needed. It saved them many trips into town. On one of our trips out, we discovered that while Flint was working under his big fuel truck, Timmy had accidently knocked the jack loose and the truck fell on him damaging his back. When he was taken to the doctor in Dawson City he was told that he absolutely could not work and that he had to limit his movement to necessities only. The doctor said that the excellent condition that Flint was in and the strength of his back muscles, was the reason that he was able to move at all. Timber smashed his hand while working but he kept that knowledge from Flint, being afraid that if Flint knew he would insist on doing the work himself. Flint took it easy only as long as the pain was great, after that he was back doing all the things he was told not to do. Charley had stayed in town to work that summer, and after our trip he called to ask how things were going. When I told him about Flint's and Timber's accidents he took a leave from work and went out to the mine to help.

One night Morgan woke up screaming and we took her into E R. While she was with the doctor she briefly stopped breathing. They kept her in the hospital for a couple of days, but they didn't find out what had caused all the trouble. It gave us another huge scare and when I left the hospital to go to work, they sent me right back to stay with Shianne and Morgan. Many of the teachers and the director from work visited Morgan and brought her gifts.

Megan (who was now six) started in the first grade. This did not go over well at all! She was having so much trouble adjusting that they put her back into Kindergarten. This may have helped but not enough, and one day Shianne was called at work. They wanted Shianne to come to help get her down from the top of the flag pole. That was when they realized that her problems would not be solved by placing her in another class. She was diagnosed with Autism, was put in Special Education, and she received some counseling. She's had some wonderful teachers and has come an amazingly long ways. She's very smart, imaginative, beautiful, and sweet; and she's well on her way to becoming an awesome woman, like her mother.

For the whole year that Shianne and I had been working at Early Head Start, we had been working on becoming Child Development Associates. We had to study, just about write a book on child development, get a good many credits from trainings and classes, and pass oral and written exams. After we received our CDA certificates, the director took us out to lunch at Pike's Landing. Also after a year's work everyone gets an evaluation and if it's good enough, they get a raise. Shianne and I each got our regular raises and we also got merit raises which allowed us to skip one step on the pay scale.

One day the animal shelter in Fairbanks called us to say that they had our dog Sissy. I told them that that couldn't be, that she was three hundred and sixty miles away. We were very skeptical when we went to look, but sure enough it was her! She was thin and she looked beat, with all 360 miles showing; but there was no mistaking that it was our Sissy. She and one of Sugar's puppies had taken off while Flint and Timber were getting wood. After days of unsuccessfully looking for them when they didn't come back, they were sure that the dogs were gone for good. After I pet Sissy through the bars of her cage, they told me to go into another room and wait for her. When I left the room Sissy howled until they brought her to me. I wish that I had a picture of how surprised and delighted Timber looked when he came home from the mine and saw his long lost dog. We don't know what happened to Sugar's puppy, but we hope that she found a good home.

In October Tony, Shianne, and the girls took a trip down to Mississippi to see Tony's mother and step father and to Florida to see his father and step mother. They had a good time. In November Patti's and Rob's house burned down and it took many months for them to rebuild it, and to replace what they could of what they had lost.

That fall Timber got back together with Tracie and after that we saw very little of him. They got engaged in December and Tracie, Bruce, and Tasha spent Christmas Eve, Christmas, New Years Eve, and New Years Day with us. Tracie is a small dark pretty woman who had managed to do what she needed to do to get by and take care of her children. She is very generous and creative, she can fix just about anything, and shopping for her family and friends is a huge passion of her's. Bruce is a good looking, interesting young man with great potential and Tasha is a quiet beautiful girl and a darling. When they were together she was such a good influence on Megan and she helped her on the way to becoming the wonderful young girl she is today. They call Timber Daddy and he loves them dearly.

Flint and Daphne went to Boundary right after Christmas and they returned in time for Flint to go back to work after winter break. He worked more hours than did many of the drivers as he often had charters at night, and he often fueled all the buses and helped with their repair and maintenance in between his morning and afternoon runs. Flint won a certificate and a Laidlaw parka at a Laidlaw rodeo in a contest for backing up and parking buses.

Flint and Daphne went out often and sometimes I went with them. Sometimes it was just the three of us, and other times we were meeting with many of the other bus drivers. It was fun meeting the bus drivers and some of them became friends. After dinner one night they talked about going to a bar. As Flint walked out the door to start the truck he called, "Daphne and I will meet you there after we take Mom home."

A guy sitting nearby replied, "I'll take Mom home."

Daphne jumped out of her seat and got in his face. "You're not taking my mom anywhere!"

One of the other bus drivers chipped in with, "I'm a mom. I'll go with you."

I guess that Daphne scared him off, as he didn't leave with anyone.

Later in the winter Flint took leave from driving the bus, as he had promised to take Daphne back to Florida and to North Carolina to see her family. Tracie had already quit being an assistant on the bus and was working in a day care, and now Timber quit and started working at Alaska Steel. After he had worked there a while he was alone at the yard when there was a big order of steel that needed loading. It was heavier than one man is allowed to lift, but it needed to be done and since there was no one to help him he tried anyway. It would have been okay if the ground had not been so icy. Timber slipped and fell with the steel on top of him and it crushed three vertebrae. He went to a doctor, he had to have physical therapy, he has had to take strong doses of pain killers for over five years, he's had to have some nerves burned several times, periodically he has to replace the spinal fluid that leaks out, and he needs corrective back surgery. Unfortunately the workers compensation insurance company refuses to pay for the surgery, and now they are refusing to pay for the medicine and other treatments that he requires. When the spinal fluid gets too low he can barely stand and the injections to replace it are very expensive.

Early Head Start was open during spring break but since school was out Tracie's children, Bruce and Tasha came to the center to help with the little ones. They also came as guests to the Alaska Sports Club where Shianne and

I were members. Sometimes they hung out at the house or went places with us on weekends.

Spring always arrives with a magical delight that comes from following six months of snow and cold. The gifts of going outside without the struggle of putting on parkas, snow pants, boots, hats, and mittens; of the warm caress of the sun on one's skin; and of the splendor of new born green is almost overwhelming. I love the winters up here but I also relish their departure. At work, the outside play, picnics, stroller rides, and spring activity gave our classes new life and energy.

At home spring is the time for birthdays and festivities. In March we celebrated Tracie's birthday with dinner at the house, Megan had her seventh birthday party at Pizza Hut, there was Bruce's fourteenth birthday, Flint and Daphne came back in time to celebrate Easter with us, and finally Shianne the girls and I were the only ones attending Morgan's third birthday party in a park in the pouring rain. We followed up this pleasant but very wet party with a dry one at home with the rest of the family.

In April Shianne and I made a trip to Anchorage with two other EHS teachers, Joyce and Joanie. We gals drove down there, stayed in a hotel, did a bunch of shopping, and ate out in several good restaurants. We had a great but expensive time.

After our usual trip up to the mine on Memorial Day, we began to get ready for Timber's and Tracie's wedding. Shortly before the big day we helped them clean their apartment and move to a bigger house with a nice big yard. Here the four of them had room to breath; their apartment had been the size of a hall way with just room to walk single file from one end to the other. Everyone from the mine came into town, and as he had done with Timmy, Flint had Daphne's sister Heidi flown up to Alaska. She arrived on the day of the wedding. Timber and Tracie had asked me to perform the ceremony and being the procrastinator that I am, I didn't plan what I was going to say until I was bathing and getting dressed. The services were performed in a little church in Pioneer Park with the reception being in a near by park building.

Unlike Bob's and my wedding there were lots of flowers, decorations, food, music, gifts, pictures, and lots of people attended. It was a lovely wedding.

With his family to support and rent to pay, Timber could no longer spend his summers working up at the mine. With the damage to his back he was not supposed to lift more than thirty five pounds. Alaska Steel Company could no longer use him in his present condition so he found work else where, however it's necessary for him to do much heavier work than they recommend in order to keep food on the table. Megan and Morgan started staying with Tracie during the days while Shianne and I were at work. Both girls have always been crazy about their aunt and about both of their uncles.

Chapter 37
NO CAR AND $10,000 OWED!
2004—2005

Jason and Shianne

The summer of 2004 was very dry with many forest fires all over the state. We had to keep the children inside behind closed doors and windows on too many of the days at work. Sometimes planned outings and field trips had to be canceled because of the air quality. When our little ones couldn't go out they would not eat or nap as well, and for their well being and our sanity we had to provide lots of physical activities indoors.

The kids came in from the mine one weekend and they were delayed from driving back as the fire was across the road. At that time EHS had a picnic at Chena Lakes and not only did Shianne, the girls, and I attend; but also Flint, Daphne, Heidi, Snuffy, Timber, Tracie, Bruce, and Tasha. Our clan made up a good portion of the attendance. When Shianne and I made our weekend trips up to the mine we had to drive through smoke with blackened trees and flame being in view on both sides of the road. There was a scary stretch of time when the fire was threatening at the mine's doorway. At another mine across the border Ken's father, Dennis, was trapped with fire surrounding him. People came in by helicopter to rescue the other miners but there was not room for Dennis and he was left behind. They said that the fire was so bad that they couldn't go back for him; but Ken was determined to get him out one way or another. Luckily a pilot friend disobeyed instructions and followed the creek to the mining camp. The camp had burned but Dennis and the equipment had found safety in the stream.

It took most of the summer for Flint and the rest of the crew up at the mine to build a three room log cabin. The biggest room is a combination kitchen and living room with a counter separating the two. The other rooms are a bed room and a bathroom-laundry. It has a hardwood floor, big windows, running hot and cold water, a toilet, a washing machine, and a Jacuzzi tub. It's comfortable, beautiful, and very different from the old cabin in which the children grew up. Our mining camp is right where Davis Creek runs into Walker Fork, and the new cabin is just across the creek from the old one. The old cabin is no longer totally standing, but it has become an historical monument and that spot can not be mined.

In spite of all efforts to mend the marriage between Tony and Shianne they just grew farther and farther apart. Neither of them was happy and the girls, especially Megan, were well aware of the problems. In July they filed the papers and soon after that they got a disillusionment with both of them sharing custody of the girls. Tony moved out of the house and as soon as he got resettled the girls started spending weekends with him. The separation was not what Tony wanted, but without Shianne there to provide all the care for the girls; he built a much stronger, closer relationship with them.

Tony had bought a brand new jeep that he used for four wheeling off the roads and in the mud. With the new living circumstances, Tony could no longer keep up the payments so he wanted Shianne to take them over. It was too small for our needs (we needed family transportation rather than a toy) so we traded it in for a used station wagon. This car was just the size that we needed and it drove easily, even on ice. However since the jeep was so new, it had a negative equity which increased the station wagon's price by almost two thousand dollars.

In the summers Patti and Rob park their motor home and boat in Valdez, where they drive down to fish on the weekends. I always try to go with them once a year and that summer Bruce went along too. We went down on a Thursday night, fished on Friday and Saturday, and then came back on Sunday. We caught a lot of halibut (no huge fish), but it was a good catch and we got our limits. We always go out to dinner while there and have a good time.

At work about once a month, the teachers, supervisors, etc. would get together doing different activities for team building. That summer we had the best team building ever, we all drove down to Denali Park (it used to be called McKinley Park) where we went white water rafting. I was scared at first when they told us that we'd tip over if we didn't follow directions correctly and immediately. I was afraid that I would mess up and be responsible for someone drowning. However they let us practice in calm water and by the time we got to the rough places we were ready. It was fabulously exhilarating and I would love to do it again!

With Tony living away from the house Shianne bought a puppy as a comfort for Megan while she adjusted to the change. She bought a very small Chihuahua-Pomeranian mix, and Megan named her Tiki. Flint and Daphne were in town and so on the next day they bought Tiki's sister. Daphne named her Midget but she is almost twice the size of Tiki. She looks more like a Pomeranian while Tiki looks like the Taco Bell dog.

In September Shianne once again had to take Morgan down to Children's Hospital in Seattle to be tested. The doctor was pleased with her progress and it turned out to be the last time (so far) that she's had to go down there. Since then she has had all her MRI's here in Fairbanks, and they are sent down to Seattle for evaluation.

One day Megan had a doctor's appointment and after dropping Shianne off at work, I took her out to breakfast. After we ate and I asked for the bill the waitress replied, "I don't have one. The policeman, you know… the one who was sitting at table next to you? He already paid your bill. He said that he was impressed with the way you two seemed to be enjoying each other."

After a social function at work, Hilda (an EHS home visitor) said that her husband's cousin had seen Shianne and he wanted to meet her. They met and started going out, often with Hilda and her husband John. One night while she was out with Jeremy, Shianne met another of John's cousins, Jason. Shianne came home lamenting, "Why did I have to be going with someone else, when I met him?" That night Jason went home saying, "Shianne is the girl for me, and somehow I' m going to get her away from him."

Once again getting out of the bath with wet feet, I fell and broke my arm. Last time it was my right elbow, this time it was my left wrist. Unlike the last broken arm there was no mistaking that it was broken, my hand was at a right angle with my arm. Also this time since I was not alone, I was not allowed to ignore it for ten days. That night Flint and Daphne took me to ER to get it bandaged and two days later I went to a doctor where it was put in a pretty blue cast. We had planned to celebrate my birthday at Chena Hot Springs the day after I fell, and since I had no intention of letting a broken arm stop me, we went anyway. I went in the pools but I managed to keep my arm dry enough so that the bandaging didn't swell and cut off circulation, as they had told me that it might if gotten wet.

On Halloween I went out with Flint and Daphne. Flint was the Grinch who stole Christmas and he wore a Santa Claus suit and a green face, Daphne was a devil dressed in red chiffon and feathers, and I was a clown with a huge bottom (an even bigger bottom than normal). After going to the rest room I didn't get my bottom strapped on right and then as I walked it was bouncing off the back of my legs. Just call me saggy butt! On the following night we took the girls trick or treating as usual.

The rest of the year whizzed by with foot ball games, Shianne hit a moose with the car, and there was Thanksgiving, all the shopping and other Christmas preparation, parties, and Christmas. On New Years Eve Shianne got into an argument and broke up with the man she was dating. She was not unhappy about it and a few hours later on New Years Day, she went out with John and Hilda. Low and behold Jason just happened to be with them. That became one of their anniversaries as they were together from that day on.

The New Year brought some very cold weather and many people were having difficulty with their plumbing, heating, and water pipes. Jason is a heating technician-plumber and he had to work day and night. He stopped in to see Shianne in between jobs whenever he could. At that time Flint was also working nights to help friends with their trucks, furnaces, and water pipes. When the cold snap ended and things eased up, they were two very tired worn out fellows!

Jason helped Shianne move into a new apartment and as they were dating, he and his daughter Stephanie visited every evening right up until they moved in. The apartment was just down the road from the house, so Shianne and I continued to ride to and from work together and we visited back and forth. Stephanie is less than two weeks younger than Megan, they are the same height and size, and they get along famously. Stephanie was quiet and shy at first but she soon warmed to us all and became very affectionate. She is such a joy and we all love her dearly. There was an immediate closeness between Jason and Shianne and it was obvious from the start that they belonged together. Jason kept her well stocked in roses, often bringing her a dozen while she still had the last bouquet. It was a busy winter with all of us making lots of trips sledding, skating, swimming, going out to dinner, shopping, and going to movies.

One morning there was a puddle of fluid under the station wagon. Shianne checked the oil and misreading the stick, she added some oil. We took it to Seekens Ford where we had bought it, and we were told that since we had an extended warranty on the car they would fix it and pay for a rental while it was being repaired. Ford decided to sub lease its repair to the shop of the dealer. Since Ford was out of rental cars, we rented one from the dealer and it was originally to be paid for by Ford. The mechanic who worked on it found that the car had too much oil and that the differential had no fluid what so ever. Because of that they concluded that when Jiffy Lube had changed the oil they had drained the differential by mistake and had added new oil to the old, over filling it. They came to this conclusion in spite of the fact that Shianne had told them that she had added oil herself, and that on the day before there had been the puddle under the car. We were told that the differential had to be replaced as it was burned beyond repair and the seals had melted. We were told that Jiffy Lube had made that same mistake before and that they would pay for the repair as they had done in the past. However upon investigation Jiffy Lube did not agree. They had changed the oil two months and 2,987 miles ago, and they argued that they could not possibly have caused the problem at this late date. The dealer put in a new differential and at Jiffy Lube's request Shianne picked up the old one from the shop. She got there just as they were about to throw it away.

The car was still under its original warranty with the dealer so the extended warranty with Ford had not kicked in yet. The dealer would not honor the warrantee, claiming that Jiffy Lube had caused the damage; and Jiffy Lube refused to pay it, claiming that the car would not run that long and that far without differential fluid. It was at a stand still and since we didn't have the thousands of dollars to pay the bill, we continued driving the rental until it could be settled. We were told not to worry, that one or the other company would pay for the repair and the rental.

In early March Shianne was told to return the rented car to the dealer. When she did the manager demanded payment in full. Shianne told him that she didn't have the money and that she had been assured that either they or Jiffy Lube would be paying. He was enraged and he ripped her up one side and down the other. He as much as called Shianne a liar and a cheat and said that now his mechanics would not be able to feed their families. Shianne asked if we could make payments and use the car, but he said that she couldn't have it as long as one penny was still owed. He said that he was keeping it until the cows came home. If I had had the money I would have borrowed a cow to take into his office with me when I paid. I was waiting in the car with the girls, and when Shianne didn't come out in about an hour, I went in to see what was going on. He ended his tirade as I stepped in the door and we rented a car from another place.

Shianne was visibly shook up and raw, and she was stopped for speeding on the way home but the trooper let her go with just a warning.

The case was not getting settled and Shianne and I were having a hard time with car rentals on top of car payments. We filled out court paper naming both the dealer and Jiffy Lube in a suit for the payment of the repair. The court refused to accept the papers saying that we had to choose one or the other. Not knowing any better and having listened too much to the dealer, we chose Jiffy Lube. Just before the hearing I called the dealers mechanic asking if he could give me any advice to help in court. He said that he could not, and I now know why he had no suggestions, they had taken out a perfectly good differential.

The hearing was an embarrassment. Jiffy Lube had our differential, they had pictures of differentials that had been driven without fluid, and they had statements from different mechanics who said that it was impossible to have happened the way the dealer claimed that it had. They had even asked Flint to look at the differential to see if he thought that it could have been driven for nearly three thousand miles without fluid. Although Flint knew that we were going to court against them, he had to admit that he didn't think that it was possible. Jiffy Lube's mechanic admitted that once before they had made that mistake. That time the car had broken down the same day and Jiffy Lube had paid for the repair without hesitation.

We had no evidence what so ever and Shianne told the judge that since she didn't know what had happened, she had tried but had not been allowed to bring the suit against both Jiffy Lube and the dealer. The judge said that that was ridiculous, that they do it all the time. During the course of the hearing, Shianne and I had been totally convinced that Jiffy Lube had not caused the damage. We had had no trouble with the car during the two months that we had driven it, and there was a puddle of fluid under car the day before we took it in. We expected and wanted the judge to rule against us. However the judge said that he was no mechanic and that he needed to consult with one before making a decision. I don't know who he consulted with, but after several weeks he decided that Jiffy Lube was at fault and Jiffy Lube called for an appeal. In the mean time we were having a hard time maintaining transportation on top of the payments on a car that we weren't allowed to use. Finally Shianne was forced to give up the car. After they auctioned off the car at a fraction of its value and paid the dealers bill; Shianne still owed $10,000 on it. Over the years she has managed to pay off most of it, but it hasn't been easy. With interest the bill has amounted to a great deal more than the $10,000.

When I talked to the dealer after the courts decision, they totally changed their story. They no longer claimed that the differential had burned and melted the seals, now they said that it had the original seals. It made us wonder about their present reasons for replacing it. Believing that Jiffy Lube had not caused the car's problem we didn't think that it was right for them to have to go to all the trouble and expense of appealing the case, so we dropped the suit.

There are several factors that contributed to the almost overwhelming financial jam in which we found ourselves. If only one of these factors had been different, we would still have the car and be in a lot better shape financially. If the dealer had simply repaired the newly formed leak—instead of replacing the whole differential, or if they had honored the warrantee—instead of accusing Jiffy Lube, if the original warrantee had expired so that we could have used Ford's extended warrantee, if the court had allowed us to bring both parties into the suit, or if the judge had ruled in favor of Jiffy Lube; we would still have our car instead of damaged credit and money owed. All these factors combined to spell debt and empty pockets!

Chapter 38
A LAP FULL OF MOOSE
2005—2006

Flint on the backhoe

On Memorial Day Shianne and I took advantage of the long weekend to make our first trip of the season up to the mine. As usual we all had a good time visiting with everyone there. Heidi found a baby raven in a nest and she brought it back to camp. The bird was too young to be able to fly yet and I was amazed that it was so big, it wasn't much smaller than a full grown raven. On the first night there Heidi was able to calm him enough to feed and water him. On the next day when Heidi thought that he could use some fresh air and carried him outside, his parents found and called to him. Then he became desperately agitated and he began to flap his wings and peck at her. She brought him inside again, but now he would not let anyone near him. When he didn't relent and she could no longer feed or give him water, she decided that she had to let him go. He started walking across the creek and into the mountains. Even after he was out of sight we could witness his progress since we could see his parents hovering just above him. I hope that they were able to keep him and themselves safe until he learned to fly.

Shianne's father's day gift to Jason was a white water rafting trip at Denali Park. The girls and I rode down with them so that we could all camp over night. It's beautiful down there and the girls and I had fun exploring with Tiki while Jason and Shianne were rafting. A little later I camped out with more of my grandchildren at Chena Lakes. We took Tiki there too and she enjoyed the wading and playing along with the kids and me. Bruce set up the tent, built the campfire, and cooked our dinner and breakfast. He's handy to have on a camping trip.

By now Shianne and Jason were engaged and as their wedding neared, some of Jason's cousins gave her a bachelorette party. We had dinner at Brewster's first and then went to a house for some rather risqué games. This was followed up by a trip to Kodiak Jack's bar. Here Shianne was made to do several things – dance on a table, climb a rope net up to the ceiling, etc. At one point they gave a guy a spray can of whip cream and sicked him on to Shianne. The guy was drunk and confused and he came after me. I told him that I wasn't the bride to be and to go away, but he kept coming. By the time he realized that he was after the wrong person the whipped cream was gone, but I didn't let him get near enough to get any of it back.

Now Jason and Stephanie came with us on all of our trips up to the mine and they too love it up there. On our August trip Daphne chased Midget off of the bed where the girls were sleeping and she broke her leg. We brought her back to town with us, I took her to the vet, and Tracie kept her while she recovered. She's an awesome dog and is totally well, but it was awfully expensive to get her that way.

On Labor Day weekend after Jason, Shianne, and the girls left for Boundary, I followed later with Bob and Lynda. Bob's guitar and their things were behind Bob on the driver's side and I sat behind Lynda on the passenger side. We had gone about one hundred miles when Bob's legs began to cramp, and he asked if I would mind switching sides so that his seat could be moved back. We stopped, made the switch, and were back on the road for about five minutes; when a moose ran out right in front of us. We collided and the moose smashed through the back door on the passenger side. There was hair, blood, and glass all over their things. He would have been on the remains of my lap if we had not just made the switch! It was late and dark so we plucked the glass from our bodies sent a message to the kids, did what could be done for the moose and the car, and camped there for the night.

Back in town Timber and Tracie bought a house and moved, Shianne and Jason moved to a new apartment, and there was a wedding to prepare for. The wedding and the reception took place at the New Hope Methodist Church. The girls and their cousin Joanie were the four flower girls, their cousin Jamie was the ring carrier, Jason's cousin John was the best man, Jason was the groom, Shianne the bride, and Flint gave the bride away. Shianne could feel Flint shaking as they walked down the isle. She had intended to have both of her brothers give her away, but Timber had had some nerves in his back burned earlier that day and he could barely sit through the ceremony. It was a beautiful wedding and a happy occasion. Jason is a wonderful addition to our family and he is loved by us all!

Later in September Jason went hunting out at the mine. Back at camp after a days cruising in search of game they were surprised by a SWAT team with rifles. They searched everyone there and then searched the camp. (S) had gone to the troupers in Tok with an outrageous story about Flint running drugs into Canada and hiring a man named David to kill him. When we read the story later we could hardly believe that anyone could have made any sense out of the story, much less actually believe it. The story was a strange long drawn out one full of the ritual that was supposed to happen. It seems that (S) was going to watch a movie about bears, find a nugget, and then he was to watch out because David would be in the trees waiting to shoot him in the back. (S) watched a bear movie, found a nugget, and then he said he heard shots. He well might have heard some shots it was hunting season, but Flint and Jason had been hunting miles away in the opposite direction. Since they hadn't seen any game neither Jason nor Flint had fired a shot and David wasn't even in the country. I think the whole story came from something that (S) had been smoking, snuffing, drinking, or injecting.

When Jason returned to North Pole there was news that he and Shianne were going to be parents together. We all went through the holidays with excited expectations of what the spring would bring.

Earlier Tracie had had surgery to undo a tubal ligation and she and Timber were anxiously hoping to be blessed as well. They had gone to a lot of expense and worry, and Tracie had gone through a great deal of pain. They didn't know if the surgery would be successful and they were so afraid that it might not be. In January she got pregnant and both of the parents-to-be were walking on air in their delight. Their happiness didn't last for long as Tracie had a miscarriage in January and then another one in February. They both took the miscarriages so hard that we were all really worried about them. It was difficult for them to share Jason's and Shianne's happiness as they looked forward to the birth of their son.

Along with enjoying the children on his school bus, Flint was taking flying lessons. He completed the ground school and had some flying time. On his first flight he got really sick and upchucked into his Dallas Cowboy hat. Then he bought some special ear phones that balanced the pressure in his ears and after that he did all right. With the air strip right next to our house, it would have been really convenient for us all to fly to and from the mine, if Flint's plans for getting his pilot's license and an air plane had happened.

In February I flew down to Anchorage to attend a special education conference with Patti and Angela, the director at Early Head Start. I was filled with regret when Anne Marie, our very respected and dear director switched over to Head Start. It was a relief and a pleasant surprise when Angela became our director. She not only is well qualified and does her job well, but she is a pleasure to work with. The three of us stayed at the hotel where the conference was held and our breakfasts, lunches, morning and afternoon snacks, and a daily cocktail hour with orderves were provided. In the evenings Angela, Patti, and I went out for dinner and shopping. It was so exciting and fun! On the flight home my ears ruptured and bled. I went to the doctor and while there I found that I had high blood pressure and ever since I've had to take medicine for it.

March brought us much fun. We all: Flint, Daphne, Heidi, Timmy, Timber, Tracie, Bruce, Tasha, Jason, Shianne, Stephanie, Megan, Morgan, and I, spent a day swimming at Chena Hot Springs. This was followed by a baby shower for Shianne and Hilda with Hilda's week old daughter, Janna. Then we celebrated Tracie's birthday at home, Megan's 9th birthday at Pizza Hut, and on Stephanie's 9th birthday we had a laser gun war at Zip Zaps.

These good times were followed by trouble in the house of a family we knew. The father and mother got in an argument and the mother and children left at gun point in the middle of the night. The mother was dressed but the four children had been in bed and they fled, bare foot and in their underwear. Flint had planned a trip to Anchorage before he heard about the trouble, so he bought the kids shoes and clothes and picked them and their mother up on their way to Anchorage. They stayed in the hotel with Flint and Daphne and he bought what they needed in Anchorage. Then he brought them home and they stayed with us for a month or so. Flint has always taken Bruce, Tasha, Stephanie, Megan, and Morgan horse back riding, swimming, out for treats, and to movies. Now there were four more children for him to take places and to buy things for. Flint loved children and they all loved him, if he had to give up doing or buying some things that he wanted for himself he never complained.

On April 21st Shianne's water broke and she was taken to the hospital. Labor was induced and on the evening of April 22nd little Dustin Wolff Minekime was born. He was one month premature and he had to be kept in an incubator for one week. Shianne stayed at the hospital during that week and the rest of us went there as often as we could. Jason took off work the first week that they were home, and I took the second week off work to spend my days with Mama and baby.

During the night of May 22, on Dustin's due date (although he was one month old) he got very sick. Shianne took him to ER and after they treated him they sent him home telling Shianne to take him to his doctor in the morning. Shianne sat in a chair with Dustin in her arms for the rest of the night, and then took him in to the doctor as soon as Megan was off to school. The doctor said that he had RSV which is often fatal for anyone under six months of age or for anyone who has any kind of lung problem. Since Dustin was born prematurely, only one month ago, and he'd had difficulty breathing, the doctor called an ambulance to take him to the hospital. He stopped breathing on the way there but he was revived. Shianne followed the ambulance to the hospital and they had to stay there for another week. If Shianne had put him in his crib on the night before when they returned from ER, he would not likely have still been alive in the morning. After the week of treatment when he was released from the hospital, he was given an inhaler and Shianne was told to watch him closely. She does and except for giving us a couple of scares he's been fine.

When school let out and Flint went up to the mine, he took his adopted family with him. Whenever we were also up there (with all eight kids) the country was really rocking with children all over the place. Flint needed to haul food up there by the truck load, and it seemed that there was always someone hungry and asking for food. Cooking was an unending job from morning until night.

In June Tracie got pregnant again. We were all glad but we were afraid to allow our happiness to grow in fear that she would lose this baby too. Every time that I was away from Timber and Tracie for a day or two, I was afraid to call, fearing that I would hear that she had had another miscarriage.

Jason's mother and brother came up from Pennsylvania to visit in July. They went up to the mine with us for a while and they spent some time with Linda's sister in Fairbanks. Their stay here was all too short and we're looking forward to the time that they will come back, or that we can visit with them in Pennsylvania.

Shortly after Linda and Nathan left I flew down to Portland Oregon to another convention. Since this one was in July instead of February it was much warmer, but it was not hot enough to prevent the other teachers and I from having a lot of fun.

When our car was repossessed, the dealer had been paid the total amount of the bill for its repair. In August they sued Shianne for the rental car and we claimed that they owed her for failing to honor the warrantee which had forced her to lose her car. Shianne did not receive notification about the date of the trial. They knew that she hadn't been notified because the notice had been returned to them unopened with the wrong address on it. When of course she failed to show up, they ruled in favor of the dealer. Shianne asked for a repeat trial and the dealer agreed to it. Jiffy Lube gave her the differential and all the pictures and testimonies that they had. I showed the differential to four other mechanics and got their statements that this differential could not have been driven more than a few miles without fluid, certainly not almost 3000 miles. That totaled six different mechanics who said it could not have happened. We wrote a statement that we had driven the car for two months after the oil change with no trouble, and that the fluid had leaked out the day before we took it to the shop.

The regular magistrate was out of town and a girl just out of law school was chosen to substitute. The first thing that she did was to admonish Shianne for failing to show up for the other trail and Shianne was not given a chance to give the reason. Then she praised the dealer for allowing us to have a retrial. The only one that the dealer sent to the court was a lady regarding the rented car, and there was no dispute about whether we had or had not rented one. Although they had not telephoned Shianne at the first trial, they did call the dealer to talk to a mechanic there. The mechanic was new, so all he could do was read the original statement saying that Jiffy Lube had emptied the fluid from the differential and had poured new oil on top of the old, over filling the oil pan. He said that it was owner abuse to drive the car without differential fluid, and therefore they did not have to honor the warrantee. The magistrate asked him to repeat the statement and I saw her write it down.

Shianne was allowed to question the mechanic and his answer to each question was, "I don't know, I wasn't here." When he finished the magistrate thanked him and said that his testimony was creditable. Creditable? Yes, I guess that it was believable that he had not been there and that he didn't know anything about it. I didn't hear anything else in his testimony that would make it so creditable.

Then it was Shianne's turn to state her case. The magistrate didn't give any indication of whether or not she was listening and she only afforded a glance at the evidence that Shianne presented to her. Without a single question or comment, the magistrate immediately read the note that she had written before Shianne had presented her case, "Due to owner abuse, the dealer does not have to honor the warrantee. I rule in favor of the dealer." Then she looked at Shianne and said, "I'm sorry, but you never should have dropped your case against Jiffy Lube."

This probably isn't the place to write all this, and you readers may have gotten awfully tired of reading about it. I'm sorry but I just can't help myself. Even after three years I am enraged at the treatment that we received from the dealer, at the lack of justice from the court, and at the audacity of a court official telling Shianne that she should have continued with her suit against Jiffy Lube, even after she had learned that they hadn't made a mistake! Jiffy Lube had once made a mistake and they paid for it. It is not fair that they should be accused of and charged for mechanical difficulties that have nothing to do with them. If the dealer had admitted to their own mistake when they discovered that they had made one, it would have cost them only a small fraction of what it ended up costing Shianne.

After living with Flint and Daphne for almost five months, the mother of the troubled family decided to go back to the father. This was not what the children wanted and they came back to the mine and hid when their parents came looking for them. However they were found and taken home. At about that time Jason's cousin John, Hilda, and their three children moved into the house with me in North Pole until they could find a warm place to rent for the winter. They found a place and moved out just as Flint, Daphne, Timmy, and Heidi came back from the mine.

Sometime after Morgan started school in the fall, they discovered that she had a receptive language delay. Since she started talking early and clearly, we were not aware of the problem. She talked so well that when she didn't respond to what we told her, we thought that she was either paying no attention or was being defiant. Upon closer observation we saw that while sometimes she may ignore us, often she simply cannot process what she hears. Probably her difficulty is caused by her brain surgery or from scar tissue resulting from the surgery. In either case it may not be correctable and she may just have to learn how to function in spite of it. This has made it very difficult for her in school and it affects her socially as well. Like Megan, Morgan was put in special education and it helps but she is still struggling.

When Jason came into our family he got more than he bargained for. Stephanie is such an easy going sweet girl and although Megan and Morgan are darlings and we all love them, they are a handful to bring up. With Megan's autism and Morgan's brain injury it takes a very special man to understand and love them. Jason is just the right man to take on this difficult task and he does it so well. He is a well loved blessing to our family! Right after Jason bought a new truck (his pride and joy); Morgan used a pointed rock to scribble on one side of the truck, from the head light to the tail gait. Jason was horrified when he came home and discovered the damage. When he confronted Morgan she replied, "I'll help you clean it off." Morgan did not get punished since she hadn't understood that she was scratching the truck and that it wouldn't come off.

With the high cost of living Shianne felt that she needed to get a job on evenings and weekends, to tide them over in-between Jason's jobs. She found work as a waitress at Dalman's Family Restaurant, here in North Pole. She enjoyed the work and made new friends, but she missed being with Jason and the children. Jason now had to limit his activities since he had to take care of the children while Shianne was at work.

Tracie did not have another miscarriage and in December when we could all breath normally again, we had a baby shower for her. When school let out for Christmas vacation Flint reluctantly quit driving a school bus and got a job with Evert's Air Fuel. He really missed all the children and the other bus drivers, but he needed to make more money in order to save up for starting up the mine in the spring. He liked his work there and they treated him well. They told him that his job would be waiting in the fall after his summer's mining. They also said that for very little cost, he could get the flying time necessary for his pilot's license in their cargo planes. They paid for him to get several endorsements on his commercial driver's license and he was hoping to work for them for a long time.

Chapter 39
PLEASE HANG ON!
2007

Megan, Morgan, Stephanie, and Dustin

John Davis was a neighboring miner who Flint considered his friend. He had been mining in the forty mile when the boys were small, but they had very little contact with him. Several years ago John called Flint just after he had gotten out of prison and was struggling to keep his mine. Flint sold him a dozer that was to be paid for if and when he could, he and Timber spent a couple of days getting and keeping it in running condition, and they gave him some diesel. Timber complained, "Isn't it enough to give him the dozer; without working on it and supplying the fuel as well?" As usual Flint ignored his grumbles. During the next few years Flint helped John out when he could.

Just before Christmas, John was arrested on a charge of viewing child pornography. Flint and Daphne drove down to Delta to see if there was anything that they could do for John's family and to bring any of them who wanted to come back to the house for Christmas. John's wife, mother, and sons wanted to stay in Delta, but his girl friend and his daughter came back with them. I quickly knitted their names on Christmas stockings and scrounged up and bought them gifts. With all of us we had nineteen stockings hanging over our fire place that year.

John told Flint that there were several people in and out of his house who could have watched the porn. Flint believed him, was really worried about him and his family, and was outraged over the treatment that he said that he was receiving. He talked to him on the telephone every day, trying to keep his spirits up. Shortly after Christmas Flint rented a large van so that he could drive John's family down to Anchorage to see him. It was New Year's Day when they all got back from the visit. They had found John in low spirits and thin, and he said that they weren't giving him the medicine that he needed. Flint talked to John's doctor and the pharmacist and arranged for him to get his medicine. All during January Flint wrote to John and talked to him on the phone. He wrote a letter to the court on his behalf and got others of us to do the same.

That eventful but tragic February was a whirlwind of events, coming so fast that it seemed like it was all happening at once. The month started with Flint renting another van to take John's family down to Kenai, where they were keeping John at the time. They found John in even worse condition and he had to be force fed. Flint was afraid that John would die in prison! While there Flint talked to the prison psychologist and to the court to get John out of jail under his custody. John did not want to leave at the time, saying that it would be all the harder when he had to return.

The folks no sooner got back to North Pole when a bunch of us went out to the Pagoda to celebrate Grandma's 102nd birthday. That meal was followed by more people joining us to watch the super bowl. Two days later Dustin fell off of the couch and Shianne took him to the doctor. On the way home she stopped at the Great Alaskan Pizza Company to pick up pizza for dinner. She forgot to put her truck into park, so while she was inside getting the pizza the truck decided to join her, crashing right through the front window! The noise and the sight of the incoming truck startled and alarmed the clerk and customers! However it didn't surprise Dustin he was still asleep in his car seat inside the truck.

Shianne called Jason, "How much do you love me?"

"More than you know. What did you do to my truck?"

"I guess I forgot to put it in park and it kind of crashed through the front of the pizza place!"

Jason forgave her and when Shianne told Flint about it later, he laughed hard enough to make it all worth while. Because of all the trouble that was headed his way, it was the last time that I remember him laughing.

The next day February 7th, Tracie went into the hospital and little Victor Wolff was born. After work Flint took me over to see my newest grandson and then he dropped me off at their house to stay with Bruce and Tasha. Timber stayed in the hospital with his wife and son. During the latter part of the pregnancy, Tracie had had a difficult time because of an undiscovered RH factor. Little Victor also had a rough time with his blood combating that of his mother. They thought for a while that he might have to have his blood exchanged. At his young age that would be dangerous and it was a frightening thought for all of us!

Little Victor was only one day old and still in the hospital when Flint had to rent a van yet again, to take John's family down to Anchorage to pick him up. He had been transferred back to Anchorage and he called Flint saying that he had changed his mind about getting out. While John was in jail his girl friend Kathy had been telling us and writing to John about how much she loved and missed him. She said that she hated it in Delta without him and that terms between her and his wife were not good. She asked if she could live with us while he was away.

After talking to the psychologist in Anchorage and getting John out on bail, Flint drove them back to North Pole. As John and his family walked in the door, Flint's freedom and peace of mind walked out, never to return. On the first night that they were back Kathy dropped a bomb. She didn't want to have anything to do with John and she ran out crying when he asked her why. Then she went to Daphne saying that she was sorry but she couldn't help the way she felt, she was in love with Flint. Flint was flabbergasted and sick to his stomach. I heard him telling Kathy that he didn't feel that way and that even if he did, he would never do anything to hurt John and Daphne.

Flint, John, and Daphne were all distraught and literally wrecks. The next day Flint had to take John to ER three times, as he kept thinking that he was having heart attacks. Each time they couldn't find anything wrong and they sent him home again. On the same day Jason had been out snow machining and he crashed and broke his leg. He had to be off work for a while and it took a long time to pay off all the doctor bills.

Timber took a week off work to stay with Tracie and the baby; and just like I did with Dustin, I took the second week off of work to be there with them. I spent my days with Tracie and Victor and my evenings and weekends watching Shianne's and Jason's four children, while she was working at Dalman's.

We had open house for John's family to come and go as they wished, and Flint had to have a family member stay with John while he was at work. John's daughter Sam stayed in North Pole the whole time, neither of his sons wanted to stay with him at all, Kathy was sent back to Delta, and John's wife Dee came to stay with him.

John didn't want to be alone in his room at all and unless he was sleeping, Dee stayed with him keeping him calm. Flint spent his evenings and weekends talking to him and taking him for rides. John insisted on a McDonald's fish sandwich, fries, and lots of ice cream for dinner every night. Because he wouldn't eat the meat and vegetables that I cooked, Flint bought a case of INSURE for him to drink, wanting to supply the vitamins and nutrients that were lacking in his diet.

It was comparatively peaceful at the house until John's mother got sick and Dee needed to go stay with her. Since John's sons still wouldn't come to stay with him, Flint had to bring Kathy back to North Pole. This was fine with Kathy but not with Daphne! War broke out and there was no peace or sleep for any of us. I had never known Flint to give up on anything, regardless of how rough the going got. Now the explosive days and nights had him right on the edge of a break down. Flint called Ken in Hawaii and Vickie and Steve, his friends in North Pole, asking them to adopt him. Ken didn't get his message, but Vickie and Steve were alarmed by the desperation in Flint's voice and they arrived at the house ten minutes later. John was scheduled to go to court in Kenai within the week, and Flint was counting the minutes until he could make the trip. He had discovered in all of his long conversations with John that he was indeed guilty, and he had no intention of bringing him back under his custody.

Daphne's and Heidi's grandmother became ill and was taken to the hospital, so they needed to fly down to North Carolina to be with her. Daphne was jittery about leaving and she called Flint for reassurance many times during the next couple of days and nights. When Daphne said good by to Kathy she added, "Pack your shit up and go back to Delta." Kathy promised that she would, but she didn't follow through with the request.

It was quiet (the lull before the storm) on Sunday morning just two days after Daphne and Heidi left and three days before Flint was to take John to trial in Kenai. Kathy and Sam were asleep on the couches in the living room, John had been sleeping on the floor beside Kathy, I was down stairs studying for a university class that I was taking, and Flint was talking to Daphne on the telephone as he got ready to go out. He was going out to breakfast with some long neglected friends while Kathy, Sam, and I watched John.

I came upstairs just in time to hear Flint say to Daphne on the telephone, "John just went into my bedroom. I better go see what he's after."

From the bedroom I heard Flint exclaim, "John! What are you doing?"

I didn't hear John's reply but then I heard Flint tell Daphne as he walked down the hall, "Right now I have a mini fourteen in my back! Yes, that might be a good idea."

Then Flint came into sight with John and the rifle right behind him!

Kathy and Sam woke up and John held us at gun point while he addressed us all. "You people turned Kathy against me. She wouldn't even talk to me last night."

"John, I was tired last night. I'll talk to you now."

"It's too late now. You're all against me and I'm gonna kill you. All of you!"

He was talking to us all but he kept his eyes glued on Flint.

Flint spoke up, "You don't really want to kill us, John. We love you!"

"No you don't, I listen and I hear things. You're all against me and now you've got Kathy against me too!"

Flint pleaded, "You don't want to kill Sam. She's your daughter!"

"I don't care."

Flint reasoned, "If you put the rifle down before anyone gets hurt, I'll tell them that you were only threatening to kill yourself."

I was more annoyed than frightened as I didn't think that John really meant to kill us. Kathy went up to John and tried to put her arms around him but he pushed her away. Flint may have made a move toward John. There was a shot and I saw Flint almost fly past me. Then I was angrier than I have ever been, and I went for John with every intention of beating him with the rifle. Another shot and I felt a sting in my upper arm, but it didn't deter me from my mission.

We struggled over the rifle until I glanced toward Flint. I guess I expected to see Flint holding his wound, but instead he lay face down by the fire place in a pool of blood. John, the rifle, Kathy, and Sam no longer existed. There was my baby, my beloved, red headed, mischievous, kind hearted son, lying hurt on the floor! With my back to all others, I turned him over and held him in my arms, putting my hand between his head and the sharp edge of the hearth. He had been shot through and neck and the bullet had blown away one cheek. I attempted to stop the gulps of the blood gurgling out, but I was also afraid that I might be blocking his air supply. As I held him I begged him to hang on, we needed and loved him!

While Kathy struggled with John, Sam ran out of the house and to the neighbors crying, "He's going to kill them all!" Kathy knocked the clip out of the rifle and kicked it away. John grabbed a pistol that he had stashed between the cushions of the couch and they fought over it. In the process John was shot and he cried out in wonder. "You shot me!"

Kathy replied, "Yes I shot you, look what you did to Flint!"

Even with his wound John was too strong for Kathy and he threw her off of him. Kathy called out, "MARGARET LOOK OUT!" I was too involved with Flint to respond or care.

Daphne had called Timber and he rushed over to the house, without even pausing to get fully dressed. Without a moment's hesitation, he burst through the door and saw John standing with the pistol pointing at my back. He tackled John, took the pistol away from him, and threw him against the wall. By now the police and ambulance were in the yard and Timber sent Kathy out to tell them that it was safe for them to come in. They would not come inside so Timber had to watch John while he argued with them over the telephone.

By now I was aware of what was going on and I added to Timber's difficulties by yelling over and over, "Flint needs an ambulance and I want it now!" I was hysterical in my desperation!

They wouldn't come in until Timber went out, and he couldn't leave John and me alone. I wouldn't budge without Flint so Timber knocked John out before leaving. The troopers and medics came in and I left Flint in their care. They took me to an ambulance but could not or would not tell me about Flint. On the way into town the medics were alarmed to find that my blood pressure was at about 250 / 100 and something, and they kept taking it while giving me an IV in the other arm. I groped for the necklace with Bob's face, but one of the attendants prevented me from moving my arm. Then the other attendant arranged things so that I could reach up to hold it.

When we got to the hospital I begged for knowledge about Flint and was told that only John and I had been admitted. Jason and Shianne came in and I asked Shianne where they could have taken Flint. She said that she didn't know. Jason offered me his hand and I clung desperately to it, like it was my only link to this planet. Then a policeman stepped in and sadly told us that Flint was dead!

They took care of my wound, I moved, talked, dressed, and left the hospital; but I remember nothing past that torturing sentence.

Chapter 40
131 YEARS WITH NO PAROLE
2007— 2008

Jim and Margaret Lawrence about 1940, Arizona

It was about twelve hours later that my memory returned. I found myself at Timber's and Tracie's house, with the house full of family and friends. The table and counters were stacked with food that people had brought. It's all very hazy and I don't remember any conversations or if I ate or slept. My arm had been sewn up, bandaged, put in a sling, and I was wearing clothes from the hospital and shoes that I'm told that Vickie had bought for me to wear home. The troopers took and kept my clothes and winter boots, but I guess they were a bloody mess anyway. People brought food on other less hazy nights too. One night Bob and Lynda brought a stack of pizza, and on another night Tamara came to the house with a box of food. Daphne and Heidi flew back from North Carolina, and Ken flew in from Hawaii.

On the day after the shooting Shianne took me to a walk in clinic to get my dressing changed. The nurse there didn't seem to know how to dress wounds; she rolled up the gauze and crammed it into the wound before covering it with a bandage. It hurt badly enough when she did it, but when it came time for Timber to change it, it put me on the floor. We had soaked it in water but even so, the pain had me nauseated and dizzy. Timber bandaged my arm every day for over a month, but that was the only time that the bandaging hurt.

I stayed with Timber and Tracie in their house for over three month and Timber built a bedroom for me down stairs.

On March 2nd we had a memorial service for Flint in the New Hope Methodist Church. I was amazed at the attendance, there were about two hundred people there: the school bus drivers and other personnel from Laidlaw, the children and their families from his bus routes, people from Everett's Air Fuel, and all the family and friends. Sam decorated the church using rocks and toy dozers amongst his pictures and the flowers. Other people brought the food and made all the preparations. The service was lovely.

Daphne found a new boy friend and moved back to North Carolina to get married, but Heidi and Timmy stayed in the state. They lived near by and they visited frequently. Heidi was going with John's son A J, but after they broke up she started going with Kasey.

My arm didn't give me much pain or trouble, but I was not allowed to go back to work until April. At the house Timber insisted on walking me up and down stairs and guarding me against any kind of action, scolding me whenever I did anything at all. The first few nights Timber and Tracie tucked me into bed and they left a baby monitor in my room in case I cried out. I certainly didn't require all the TLC that I received from family and friends; but their concern, support, and love is cherished. How fortunate can a person be, to have a husband and a son who risked their lives in saving mine, and a family and friends who put no limits on what they are willing to do for my protection and happiness?

We didn't know exactly what we were going to do with the house. Timber and Tracie were buying their own house, and although Jason and Shianne were renting, Shianne didn't think that she could bear to live there. Finally she decided that she could manage by getting rid of all the blood stained furniture and carpets and redecorating. Jason put in a hard wood floor throughout the upstairs; we painted the walls, bought new furniture, and put down new area rugs. In May when it was finished they moved in, and I waited until early June. Megan, Stephanie, and I each have bed rooms down stairs, and Jason and Shianne, Dustin, and Morgan have bed rooms upstairs. Timber did not want me to move out of his house, but although they had room for me, they didn't have room for all of my things. To say that I am a pack rat and don't throw anything away is an understatement. Since Tracie is the same way it would take a huge place to house all of our things.

Before I had moved back into the house, Flint's ex-wife, Sherry, called wanting to talk to him. When Shianne told her what had happened, she was terribly distraught and asked Shianne to have me call her. I did try and would have liked to have talked to her, but she saw that it was my call and she was crying so hard that she couldn't answer the phone. Then her number was accidently tossed out so I couldn't try again. Maybe she'll call again some day.

Little Victor was only two and a half weeks old when we lost our Flint. Like Flint he has red hair, he's big, and he looks and acts a lot like him. Since he was so young it just seemed natural to name him after the uncle who we all loved and respected, and who he would never grow up to know. Timber and Tracie took all the necessary legal steps and we went to court for the name change. Now he is Flint Victor Travis Wolff. He is very smart, stubborn, mischievous, busy, and loving.

In June Jason and Shianne went fishing with Patti and Rob and I stayed with the children. Jason caught the two biggest fish with each one being well over one hundred pounds. On the second day out an unexpected storm came up with five foot waves. On the way into shore they stopped to unload their shrimp traps, and Patti accidently ran over the line, it got caught in the motor, and it tied them to the spot. Jason hung out of the back of the boat trying to cut them free, while Rob held him by his legs. Seconds seemed like hours as the waves crashed over them, filling the boat with water. As the boat sunk lower and lower Patti and Shianne watched in terror! Just as they were sure that the next wave was going to put them under, Jason got them free and they struggled to the shore of an island. They were all wet, cold, and miserable, and Jason was more ice berg than man. As they changed into semi dry clothes and got the water out of the boat, Patti spotted a bear. No one else was looking and fortunately (since they had no rifle) she couldn't prove that she had seen correctly. There was no confrontation with a bear over their fish or themselves. They were stranded there with low tide for several hours and when they did finally leave, early the next morning, they were showered with relief and thanks that the motor actually ran and the boat got them safely to land.

Over the long 4th of July weekend Jason, Shianne, and family went up to Boundary; and I went to Anchorage with Timber, Tracie, Tasha, and little Flint. We had a good time down there visiting the zoo, shopping, and eating out. Instead of driving home we met Jason and Shianne at the mine and scattered Flint's ashes where his father's and grandmother's had been scattered. In August Jason and family, Timmy, Bruce, and I went up to the mine for three weeks. Jason had promised Flint that he would mine with him during the summer and Flint had been enthusiastic about the prospect. He said that it would be perfect if Timber could also make it up there with them. Jason intended to mine during his three weeks there, but upon arrival we discovered that someone or some ones had stolen 1800 gallons of diesel and 700 gallons of gasoline. It was a loss of many thousands of dollars, and it put a severe crimp in our mining plans. Jason managed to buy just enough fuel to do a little mining.

The husband of Shianne's friend, Devon got into trouble and was put in jail. Deven was forced to leave their apartment, so she and her four children came out to the mine, shortly after we got there. They stayed with us while we were there, and then for a while they stayed with us back at the house in North Pole.

For their third anniversary Shianne bought Jason a long wanted Rottweiler puppy. Sheba isn't very large for her breed; but she's lively, beautiful, and sweet. She towers above Tiki but she seems to think that Tiki is her mother and she lets her get away with everything.

After the shooting, my brother Jim invited me to come to visit them in Prescott, Arizona, with him paying for my flight. I was totally thrilled and as I planned to retire in October, we chose that time for the trip. Come October I wasn't ready to retire but I took time off from work for the trip anyway. I was high on excitement long before, during, and after the trip. When my plane came down to land in Phoenix, there was another plane sitting on our lane. It was no big deal we didn't crash or blow up; we just pulled back up and circled until the landing was clear. I wouldn't mention it now, or have told anyone about it, except that on the shuttle that I took to Prescott, the driver asked if any of us had been on that plane. When I said that I had, I was bombarded with questions from the other passengers. "Was it a near miss?" "Was I scared?" "What was I thinking?" "Did people panic?" etc. The lady next to me exclaimed, "Now you'll have something to talk about for the rest of your life!" (Yeah, sure lady.)

While there I visited with my nieces Lou Ann and Nancy and their families, we shopped, took their dog Jesse for walks, ate out, took trips to some lovely places, and went to a play. Best of all was the time spent with Jim and Betty in their beautiful home. During the most recent past I hadn't gotten to spend much time with them, and they have always been such a big part of my life.

As a little girl I believed that my big brother had stood thirty feet tall, and that there was nothing that he couldn't do. He was the smartest most imaginative person alive, and he filled my childhood with excitement. He used to tell me stories about Timothy Mouse and read wonderful books to me. We would ride on his bike to the library with me on the handle bars, singing "Bumpity Bump" to the tune of "From the Halls of Montezuma, to the

Shores of Tripoli." We made dug outs—digging big holes and covering them with boards and dirt. We put a rabbit hutch that I was using for a play house over one secret dug out with the sliding door facing down. We fastened a rug over the door so that when I was playing house with my friends, upon a signal from Jim; I could slip down through the door, slide it closed (rug and all), disappear into the dug out, go through the secret underground tunnel, and out into the woods unseen. Other things we did were booby trap our bed rooms so that clothes or water fell on Mom when she came in, and sneak out of the window at night, running around in the dark and diving into the bushes whenever a car went by. Whether we were spies, cowboys, Indians, criminals, policemen, or soldiers; it was all very exciting and real to me!

Betty was Jim's first girl friend and occasionally he took me along on their dates. They were both valedictorian at their high school graduation, and afterward they went to Berkley to go to college. They couldn't see enough of each other so they got married and shortly afterward they quit school to start their family. While their children were growing up I spent a lot of time with them going camping and doing all kinds of other things. Betty was a pretty girl and she is one of the few women who grow even lovelier as they grow older.

At Christmas instead of putting Flint's stocking away along with his dad's and grandmother's, we gave it to little Flint along with his name. The holidays didn't have the worry and concern about John and his family, as they had the year before; but they were filled with a longing for the loved ones who could only be with us in our thoughts and hearts.

During Christmas vacation Jason put in new cupboards and counters in our kitchen. It was more expensive that we would have liked but it's beautiful! We had Grandma's 103rd birthday lunch at our house to show it off. There are spoon, fork, and knife handles on the cupboard doors and drawers, and I like to hand guests a screw driver and ask them to get their own silver wear.

I put in my notice at the center and all of us from work went out to lunch where they gave me a plaque and gifts. My last day at work was on February 29th, but I did continue to go back as a volunteer when ever I could. Shianne started subbing for teacher assistants in the schools, so I needed to stay home and watch Dustin. Both Dustin and little Flint were in Early Head Start Home Base, so Debbie (their home visitor) came to our houses once a week and both families attended social functions. It's great to still be a part of the program, and every time I go there I get more than a dozen hugs from the wonderful people who I worked with. Debbie is such a dear person that she enriches the lives of all who know her.

In April Heidi and Kasey got married in our house, with Jason performing the services. It was fun to decorate the house, prepare all the food, dress up, and visit with all the people who came. They continued to live close by and to visit often.

We went to two hearings in January when John changed his plea from not guilty to no contest, and we went to his sentencing in May. A fellow school bus driver had put pictures of Flint set to music on a CD, and we took it to the sentencing. When it was shown in court the whole court room, including the judge and the public defender, were in tears. John was sentenced to one hundred and thirty one years with no parole. John was asked if he had anything to say and he replied, "Flint was the best friend that I ever had and I miss him!" In the news account that night they showed some of Flint's pictures on the television.

In June Jason, Shianne, Stephanie, Dustin, and Bruce went up to the mine and Megan and Morgan went to spend some time with their father. A few years back he had moved away from the Fairbanks area, so the girls could no longer be with him on weekends. I stayed at home for the first few weeks to take care of Deven's two daughters, Ashlyn and Whitney, while she was at work. Devon had separated from her husband and was now with her present husband, Chris. On one of these weekends I went fishing in Valdez with Patti and Rob. I joined the others at the mine just in time to celebrate Jason's and Shianne's birthdays at the end of the month.

Ken also came to mine separately on Walker Fork, and he and his men stayed at our camp and ate dinners with us. Mining for us that summer wasn't all that good, as we were hampered by frozen ground and problems with the backhoe. However we did find some gold, three of Jason's cousins and their families came to visit, and we had campfires, fished, picked blueberries, walked, played games, watched movies, and had a good time. Megan and Morgan joined us later in the summer, and I kept busy baking bread, playing with the kids, and I started this story.

In September Shianne, the kids, Bruce, and I came back into town for school and Shianne's substitute teaching. Jason stayed on at the mine for a while to help Ken. Kasey was shipped to Iraq for a year and Heidi moved in with us.

Later in the month both Jason and Timber were working and things were going well, until October when Timber started having trouble with kidney stones. He continued to work for a while but he had to stop what ever he was doing while he passed them. Then one large stone would not pass and he had to be taken into ER. They gave him pain medicine and sent him home seven times before they finally realized that they needed to take it out. Each time that the stone moved it had him doubled up on the floor and he could do nothing. As it moved it was ripping the urethra and he was bleeding and vomiting. We were taking him in and out of the hospital day and night and seeing him in all that pain was terrible. Finally he had the surgery, but he still had problems and later he had to go back for reconstructive surgery on the torn urethra.

Shianne got the news that her first novel, *Dreaming of Jeanie* was being published, and we all have been just too proud and excited since then. Sharing the whole experience with her has been so much fun and it has made me all the more anxious to finish this story and see what I can do with it. Even if nothing comes of it I can at least make copies to leave behind for my family. Just writing it has been more than worth while for me, it's been like living my life all over again. I think about something that I want to write about and suddenly I'm back at that time, remembering things that I hadn't thought about in years. I've always been part calendar and could tell anyone what day their birthday would fall on, but while I was writing I wouldn't know what day, month, or even what year it was. I was sometimes twenty or more years off.

There also seems to be a connection between my writing and people from the past. The phone rang while I was writing about the party back in 1970 that had been busted up with a room full of mace. The call was from one of the tapers who had attended the party. I hadn't talked to him in thirty nine years. Then last November I was writing when I got a call about my dear friend, Margaret. She had become dangerously ill and had to be flown down to the hospital in Anchorage. After talking to her daughter Kathleen, I returned to my typing to find that the last three words that I had written were, Tommy and Margaret. Now Margaret is back at home, not well, but much improved. She has dialysis three times a week and she will need to have a kidney transplant. I'm hoping that my kidneys will test out all right so that I can give it to her if she needs it.

Later in November I slipped on ice and broke my hip in three places. I was with Tracie and little Flint and since I couldn't get up, Tracie had to get a man to put me back in the car. She took me to ER and later I was allowed to go home with a walker. Jason carried me from the car to a chair in the living room, and my first trip to the bathroom with the walker took me about an hour with several stops due to nausea. Shianne had to stop subbing for a while since I wasn't getting around well enough to watch Dustin. Patti's and my annual shopping trip on the day after Thanksgiving took about three times as long as it usually does. Shianne was able to go back to work in December after Snuffy came to spend Christmas with us, since he would be there to help if needed. By Christmas I found myself carrying my walker when I wanted to go someplace so I quit using it in the house. I was completely recovered and able to cancel the January and February appointments that the doctor had believed that I would require.

Chapter 41
THAT BRINGS US TO NOW
2009

Flint's namesake, Flint Victor Travis Wolff

From mid December through most of January the temperature neared -60 degrees, never getting above -45 degrees. This would have been totally normal back in the sixties, but it was unusually cold and long for present times. One day Timber's truck froze up as he was headed for work; and when Jason went to help him, his truck quit on him too. They both spent most of the day working on their trucks, out in the cold. By the end of January the weather warmed up nearly fifty degrees and people rushed out to enjoy the balmy -10 degree temperatures.

I had been passing gall stones for several years, but the attacks had always been short and never too awfully severe. I could sit quietly and hold my midriff for a while and then I would be Okay again. One cold January night I had a severe attack that lasted for hours and it sent me to the bathroom to wretch out my insides three times. I went to the doctor and tests showed that I had gall stones and that they were affecting my liver. They did not want me to have another severe attack like that (I wasn't too keen on the idea either), so they scheduled me for surgery very quickly. After fasting for twelve hours, I was scheduled to have my gall bladder removed mid morning. I waited and waited in the hospital but they weren't able to take me until eight pm. I got out of surgery and was taken to my room at eleven pm. I was allowed to go home the next afternoon.

Two days later I was well enough to attend a family appreciation dinner at Early Head Start and in another two days we had twenty four people join us to party and watch the Super bowl. Jason and I were rooting for the Steelers and when some of the guys were giving Jason a bad time about his favorite players, I had to hold Sheeba to keep her from jumping them. She was beside herself, wanting to get to anyone bothering her Jason. It turned out Okay, Sheeba didn't bite anyone and the Steelers won! The Super bowl was followed closely by Grandma's 104th birthday and little Flint's 2nd. Both of these parties were held in our house also.

While we were up at the mine Tasha had acquired herself a boy friend. They got serious in a hurry and Ben moved into the house with them. They wanted to get married but Tasha was only seventeen and they couldn't get an answer from her father, giving them his permission. In February they got married in Los Vegas where her mother's permission would suffice, and they had a Halloween wedding reception here at the Pioneer Park in March. Sometime afterward they moved to Texas where they have their own apartment and are both working.

We got word that Snuffy had died of a heart attack in April, and shortly afterward we drove to Tok where they had a memorial service for him. His son and daughter came up from Oregon and we met them for the first time. Last summer Snuffy had sold most of his things at the mine, and Jason had hauled the things that he kept down to Tok where he was renting a little cabin. I am so glad that Snuffy spent the month of December with us and I know that we'll all miss him this year. He was invited to come up to the mine with us in the summer, and he said that that was what he wanted to do. He and Jason were also talking about going fishing and hunting together. We're sorry that he couldn't carry out those plans, but we're glad that he had them to look forward to.

Through out the year Stephanie has been in her school violin orchestra and they gave several concerts. She had never played or even held a violin before, but she picked it up immediately and learned to play well. Her grandfather is known as the Yukon Fiddler and when he learned of her interest, he bought her a seven hundred dollar violin of her own. In May just before school let out, on their last concert, Stephanie was given a special award for making the most progress during the year.

In June Jason and his cousin Andrew went up to the mine and Megan and Morgan went to visit their father. Shianne, Stephanie, Dustin, Heidi, and I waited in town until after my fishing trip with Patti, Rob, and their daughter Carolyn, who had just returned from Iraq. After the trip we joined the guys at the mine. Ken again was mining on a separate place on Walker Fork. Ken had several guys working for him and they were mining around the clock most of the time. Because of frozen ground and trouble with the equipment, we didn't get started sluicing until August 21st and then we didn't get to mine for long or to finish the cut. However, we did well on the days that we got to mine.

While we were waiting to get started sluicing we went into town for Jason and Shianne to go fishing with Patti and Rob. They didn't get many halibut, but they went dip netting for salmon afterward and got their limit of forty five fish. Megan and Morgan went up to the mine with us after that trip.

Because of health reasons Timber and Tracie felt that they would have to leave Alaska. With regrets on all of our parts, they packed up their things and put their house up for sale. Timber got a job offer in Eugene, Oregon and after swallowing big losses on their house and possessions they headed south. When they got down there the job wasn't waiting for them after all so Timber frantically looked for work.

In the spring, Devin and Chris had moved to Anchorage, but things did not work well for them, so they moved back up here, staying at our house while they looked for a place to live. When we came back to town in September, there were fourteen of us, with eight of them being children. Jason had ordered a little pug puppy for Shianne's birthday in June and since she had to fly up all the way from Virginia, it hadn't been cool enough to send her until September. After picking her up at the airport, Jason and Shianne returned to finish up at the mine and the girls and I stayed in town so that they could go to school. The only mishap while Jason and Shianne were away was that Morgan fell through the deck and could not get her leg out. I called for help and then held her on my lap while Megan crawled under the deck to scratch her itching foot. Morgan was scared, hurting, and itching; but Rob came with a saw and he got her out safely.

Now Devin and Chris have just moved out to a new apartment, so the residents here are down to eight people, four dogs, one guinea pig, several fish, and three snakes. Jason is doing some jobs and working on enlarging our garage. Shianne is home with the swine flu, the girls are in school, and Dustin, Heidi, the animals, and I hang out at home. Kasey just got back from Iraq, and since his and Heidi's plans are unsettled, Heidi is still with us. Timber did not find work in Oregon so he and his little family moved to Millersburg, Ohio, where he was offered a job. The whole family, including Heidi took a trip to Anchorage to watch Jason's cousin Lee Jones play foot ball in the state high school play offs. Lee is the North Pole Patriots' quarter back, he also plays defense, and he runs with the ball about as often as he throws passes. While we were there we went to the zoo and the water park. The cost of the trip was more than we could really afford, but everyone had such a terrific time that it made it all worth while. That brings us to now, a few days before my seventy-second birthday. What will the future hold? Your guess is as good as mine.

We've all shouldered the loss of our loved ones and gone on with our lives, just as we know they would want us to do. They play an active part in our thoughts and conversations, and it feels like they are sharing in our lives. Although a sudden burst of memory can sometimes bring the tears, without these memories my life would be empty. There is something about Robin Williams that reminds me of Bob. They don't look at all alike, but they both are comics, both do voices, and there is an intensity under Robin's comedy that brings Bob sharply to mind. I enjoy his movies and the humor, but I may be the only one in the theater who is crying through her laughter. During his last years, Flint frequently said the things that his father used to say, saying them in the same way and with the same voice. I relish everything that brings them both to mind. I am so proud of all of my loved ones, those who have passed and those still with me. I only hope that I have been able to express some of the wonder of these awesome people.

54299603R00159

Made in the USA
Columbia, SC
28 March 2019